HALLEY'S

Halley's Comet returns every seventy-six years. Its last appearance was in 1910. In early 1986, it will again reach perihelion, its closest approach to the sun. The comet will be closest to the earth, however, in December of 1985.

The San Francisco Star
March 16, 1985

Three people discovered the frightening truth about Halley's Comet:

Simon, frail and old, still on a quest that began a half a century ago in Egypt. . .

Ted, a young teacher whose vision of the future terrified him. . .

Jill, his bride, beautiful and full of life, whom fate had singled out. . .

When the wind was spent, they had started streaming into hospitals by the hundreds. Many babbled on and on, pouring out their terror. Some said that just before the wind came, they had seen a face in the sky, a face with gleaming eyes and a hideous, evil smile. . .

SATAN'S CHANCE

ALAN ROSS SHRADER

ace books
A Division of Charter Communications Inc.
A GROSSET & DUNLAP COMPANY
51 Madison Avenue
New York, New York 10010

SATAN'S CHANCE

An ACE Original

First Ace printing: March 1982

Published simultaneously in Canada

2 4 6 8 0 9 7 5 3 1
Manufactured in the United States of America

SATAN'S
CHANCE

PROLOGUE

December 16, 1985

They found him high on the windswept hillside just before dawn. The powerful flashlight beam of a rescue worker picked out his face in the darkness. He was staggering in a zig-zag path down the slanted face of a giant slab of rock. The beefy rescue worker followed him with his flashlight and shook his head in wonder that the stumbling man did not fall.

Kicking his boot into the ground to steady himself, he called down to his partner twenty feet below. "I found another one!"

Further away, pencil-thin beams of light from other rescuers crisscrossed and darted over the massive headlands of Marin County. And on the narrow fire trail cut into the rock below, nearly a dozen ambulances and police vans waited high over the dark presence of the Golden Gate Bridge. The rescue workers were dead tired, having scoured the cold hills for most of the night. All told, they had found nearly a hundred dazed and suffering people, some lying motionless on the hard ground, others wandering aimlessly like the stunned survivors of a plane crash—and they had found in addition over two dozen lifeless bodies scattered about like windblown trash. The dead were men and women ranging from young to middle-aged. All were naked when they

1

were found. All had strange marks around their eyes as if the delicate skin there had been scorched by fire.

There had been no plane crash. And it seemed there was no survivor who could talk coherently enough to tell the rescuers what had happened.

The beefy man and his taller partner had little trouble reaching the staggering man and guiding him down to an ambulance on the narrow fire trail. He was not naked, as even some of the living victims were, but he was still suffering from exposure from the hours he had spent bearing the full force of the bone-chilling wind that was sweeping in off the Pacific. The beefy rescue worker pulled a drab green blanket from the ambulance and wrapped it around the man, who was standing mute before him, his mouth slack and gaping, his body shaking in uncontrollable spasms. The rescuer suspected that the dazed man was suffering from something more than simple exposure—he seemed to be hovering on the brink of insanity because of what he had seen this night.

"Look at his eyes!" his partner hissed urgently.

The first man aimed his flashlight at the victim's face. The man's eyes were full of tremendous pain. No, it wasn't pain. It was absolute horror—a horror so pure and intense it seemed to leap out at the rescuer and send his heart racing. He turned away quickly and wondered for at least the hundredth time what had happened. It was all crazy—the naked bodies, the incredible wind, the things in the sky, as if nature herself had gone on a mad rampage. He had been trying to piece it together all night, but couldn't see his way clear to any sensible explanation.

He turned to his partner. "Get the stretcher."

When the stretcher was set up, the two men grabbed the other by the arms and eased him firmly down onto it. The man struggled wordlessly against them, clawing with feeble hands against their restraining arms.

"It's okay! Take it easy now," the tall rescuer soothed. "Just lie down. We'll take care of you."

The man's eyes bulged out again with remembered terror. His trembling lips tried to form a word.

The beefy one bent over and put his ear next to the man's face. "What is it?" he asked gently.

The man whispered a name. "Jill."

"Jill," the other repeated, straightening up. "I guess she's his wife or girl friend. Or maybe his mother."

They bent down and lifted the stretcher, grunting under its weight, then slid it into the back of the ambulance.

"Come on. Let's get going," the heavy one said impatiently as he jumped into the back of the ambulance to stay with the man on the stretcher. His partner got in front to drive. He started the ambulance moving bumpily down the rutted fire trail, then got on the radio for directions.

"We're going to have to take him to San Francisco," he yelled after a moment. "All the hospitals on this side of the bridge are swamped now."

"Jesus," the other murmured.

The ride was lurching and bumpy until they got off the fire trail onto the main road. The man lay quietly on the stretcher, his eyes wide open and glassy, his mouth forming the name over and over again.

Jill . . . Jill . . . Jill . . .

Where was she? His swirling mind brought her face to him out of the darkness. She was dressed all in white and smiling radiantly. Her dark eyes were gazing at him lovingly. It was their wedding day. She turned to him, her lips parting slowly for a kiss. He loved her so much. He reached out to her. He wanted to hold her tight against himself and never let go. But she started drifting away from him and faded into the darkness.

He bolted upright, screaming in desperation, "Jill! Jill!"

The beefy man pushed him gently down. "It's all right now. It's all right."

The dazed man fixed his terrified eyes on the rescuer and in that brief moment the rescuer knew it was *not* all right for the man. Maybe it would never be all right for him.

He was taken to San Francisco, to St. Francis Hospital, whose emergency room was a crammed madhouse of frantic activity. Under rows of bright fluorescent lights white-suited doctors and nurses in surgical green raced in all directions, pushing people on litters before them. Litters with bloody and screaming victims were pushed two and three deep against the walls. Litters with people who lay moaning softly to themselves were shoved into adjacent corridors and even pushed outside beyond the swinging doors of the ER entrance to block the narrow sidewalk. And the injured who had no litters lay on blankets on the floor or found a tiny space to huddle and stare out blankly, waiting for someone to notice them.

The hospitals in Marin County may have been swamped, as the ambulance driver had been told, but the hospitals in San Francisco were no less inundated. The people now being brought down from the high cliffs of the headlands were adding to a flood of casualties that had come in hours earlier, after hell had broken loose all over the Bay area—when the wind had come up from nowhere, snapping power lines, uprooting trees, pushing the cars caught out in it off the road, and shattering literally thousands of windows in a circle of disaster thirty miles across. People's houses had shaken so violently that some thought it was an earthquake, but it wasn't that. It was wind—wind that came suddenly from nowhere and everywhere, wind with the force of a tornado. But it wasn't a tornado, either. It was more like a hurricane without the rain. No one really knew what it was. It had stopped as suddenly as it had come, leaving in its wake people crushed under fallen trees and in smashed cars, people streaming with blood from thousands of pieces of broken glass, people stunned at how the laws of nature could be overturned with such ferocious violence.

And when the wind was spent, they had started streaming into hospitals by the hundreds. Many babbled on and on, pouring out their terror in words. Some said that just before the wind came they had seen a face in the sky, a face with gleaming eyes and a hideous, evil smile. And there were those who said there was nothing in the sky, but up north, over Marin, they had seen a huge column of fire. But most people talked of the vicious hurricane wind. Those who had been hurt in car crashes or blinded by slivers of flying glass didn't talk at all, but lay on their litters and moaned or screamed or just cried quietly to themselves.

The man brought in from the hills lay on his stretcher outside the swinging metal doors of the emergency room, where he had been left by the rescue workers. He was left unattended while dawn broke in the east and the morning sun climbed higher and higher in the sky. It was nearly ten o'clock when a bone-tired young nurse came to take a look at him. She bent over him and looked at his eyes. They seemed blank, glassy, a sign of shock. Shock could easily be fatal, she knew.

She yelled, "Doctor!" as loudly as she could.

The man moaned, trying to lift his head up. He couldn't. "Jill . . . I've got to find her . . ."

A blood spattered doctor appeared at the nurse's side. "What is it?" she asked quickly.

"Shock, I think."

The doctor looked into the man's eyes, then ripped his shirt open and placed her stethoscope over his heart. The beat was faint and irregular.

"We'd better get him inside."

They wheeled the man in through the swinging doors and found a clear space near a wall to work. The doctor shoved a bunch of pillows under the man's legs, while the nurse's practiced hands raced over the man, stripping him of his clothes.

The doctor slipped an oxygen mask over the man's face. "He looks like he's sinking fast!"

The man screamed under the oxygen mask. Chaotic memories swirled and dissolved in his mind—seas of fire, the gyrating bodies of naked men and women, shouts of hysterical terror. *He had to find Jill!* An image of her came floating like a Greek goddess through the dancing flames. Wrapped in a golden halo, she was smiling a beautiful smile meant just for him. *Jill!* The halo swelled brighter, obscuring her face, then all at once became a monstrous column of seething flame.

"He's going under, doctor!" the nurse shouted.

"Dammit! I know he is!"

The man's brain needed more oxygen, but wasn't getting it even with the mask over his face. His vital functions were severely depressed. His breathing was shallow and irregular. His heart was pumping only feebly and his blood pressure was plummeting. The whole world was spinning madly in a swirl of inky darkness. *He had tried to save her! He had tried to save them all!*

The thought echoed back and forth, turned senseless, and flickered away into the drowning black nothingness.

HALLEY'S COMET RETURNING

Halley's Comet returns every seventy-six years.

Its last appearance was in 1910. In early 1986, it will again reach perihelion, its closest approach to the sun. The comet will be closest to the earth, however, in December of 1985.

—The San Francisco Star
March 16, 1985

CHAPTER 1

November 15, 1985

Jill Banner parked the small van and jumped out into the cold air. She went around to the back of the van, pulled its rear door open, grabbed the boxy ultrasound machine and with both hands pulled it out. They called it a portable, but it was heavy as hell. Its weighty momentum as it came sliding out swung her around and nearly toppled her over. But she managed to right herself and backed into the van's door to push it closed. The hard edge of the machine pressed painfully against the new wedding ring on her finger—placed there just three days before—and she had to shift her grip before taking another step. It always depressed her to come here, one of San Francisco's poorer neighborhoods, and it always depressed her to lug the heavy machine down to the old cracked concrete driveway past the clapboard house to the squalid cottage in the overgrown back yard. It wasn't even a cottage really, just an old garage that someone had decided many years ago would be more profitable as a rental. The driveway ran right into it.

Jill was a small, vivacious woman in her late twenties. She had long dark hair with a hint of red and a very pretty face with clear skin and a small mouth that broke

easily into a smile. She would have been absolutely
beautiful if only her nose had stopped growing when the
rest of her had—at least, that's what her sister Elaine
always told her.

Jill worked as a physical therapist for Hamilton Hospital, and lugging the ultrasound machine around was
part of her job. She had been coming to the converted
garage for two months now under the hospital's Home
Therapy Plan.

It looked as if today would be the last time she would
come here, though. She dreaded having to break the
news to Larry. He should have left the program several
weeks ago, but feeling sorry for him, she had kept him
on, even though he was perfectly able to get to the hospital on his own. She hoped he would understand that this
had to be the last time—no ifs, ands, or buts. The thing
was, he had so much hostility and bitterness inside him,
and he could be so irrational, that she didn't know how
he would react.

Larry met her at the door, his large body bent over
sideways as he leaned heavily on his single crutch.

"You're late," he said grumpily.

"Am I? I'm sorry." Jill knew her apology didn't
sound sincere. She didn't mean it to. Larry was too de-
manding, too possessive of her and her time, and she
didn't want to encourage him.

She went in and knelt down, depositing the ultrasound machine on the concrete floor with a thud. The
room was small, messy, and dim, its single little window
too dirty to admit much light even though it was sunny
outside. She started to sit down on the dilapidated
couch, then thought better of it when she remembered
how its springs always stuck in her backside.

Larry shut the door and came over to her. He was
limping badly.

"You can do better than that," Jill said, looking at his

leg. "It's not good to let yourself get into bad habits."

"Oh, fuck it!" Larry spat the obscenity out. He lifted his leg. Even under his jeans, you could tell it was withered and twisted badly and far too short compared to his good one. "That's the way it is. That's the way it'll always be. Larry the crip—that's what they'll call me. Larry the crip!"

Jill began to tell him to can the self-pity, but stopped short. Things were going to be difficult enough without starting off with an argument. She merely shrugged her shoulders and looked at him frankly, as if to say, 'I'm not going to play this game with you.'

"I mean," he continued, "with this face, what does it matter about my leg?"

He took a jerky step toward her and thrust out his jaw. His face was twisted, with his mouth just off center and one cheek pulled tighter than the other. One eye was perpetually squinting. He smiled at her, but the smile was a hideous grimace.

"Pretty, isn't it?" he asked bitterly.

Jill kept her eyes steadily on him. She knew he wanted her to turn away from the sight of his disfigured face. If she turned away or showed any discomfort, in Larry's mind it would be proof that there was no point in working on his leg. Just one more excuse for him to give up and wallow in self-pity.

"Go on," Jill said softly, "change into your trunks so we can start the therapy."

Larry didn't move. He was so close to her she could feel his breath against her face. She waited a moment, then burst out, "Larry! I haven't got all day! You're not my only patient, you know."

Something flickered in his eyes. She wasn't sure what it was. Anger? Hate? His eyes held hers a moment longer and then turned away.

"Yeah, okay," he muttered. He hobbled into the next

room, the only other room there was, to change into his trunks.

Jill absent-mindedly sat down on the old couch, got a nasty pinch on her rear, and quickly stood up again. Her eyes swept over the messy room. There were a pile of dirty clothes on the floor and beer bottles scattered everywhere. A Playboy magazine was on the floor in one corner with its centerfold pulled out, showing a voluptuous woman lying on her back with her legs spread wide. Well, so what? Jill thought. It was better for him to masturbate looking at that than to molest little girls or do something even worse. Something about the foldout caught her eye, though, and she went over to it to look at it more closely. There were a lot of little holes in it, right between the spread legs. It looked as if Larry had been stabbing the picture with a pencil or something. The idea made her shiver involuntarily. She reached out her foot and flipped the magazine over so she wouldn't have to look at it.

She remembered what Penny had told her about Larry. Penny was also a physical therapist at Hamilton and a good friend of hers. Penny had worked with Larry twice and then had gotten herself off his case. She thought Jill was being foolish in agreeing to take over for her. Even though his leg was withered, almost useless, he was a big man and his arms were powerful.

"Alone with him in his little shack," she told Jill, "there's no telling what he might do!"

"Somebody has to help him," Jill replied. "I can take care of myself."

"Your trouble is that you're just too nice," Penny said.

But it wasn't a matter of being nice, Jill thought. It was her job. You can't decide not to help someone just because you don't like him. And besides, in a strange way, she did like Larry. Maybe she was deluding herself, but she thought she could keep him under control. The main thing was sex, and female physical therapists were *always* having to deal with predatory males.

Her eyes wandered back to the magazine. She could see the little holes coming up through the jokes on the other side of the centerfold. Well, she thought, she had been right so far at least—she hadn't had any real trouble with him, and this was the last time she would be coming out to his little garage. She thought she would wait until the very end of the session before telling him she had to drop him from the program. In a way, she thought she understood how he felt about it. She meant more to him than just a therapist. Her coming out to his place made Larry feel that somebody cared.

The rhythmic thunk of Larry's crutch sounded against the floor as he came back into the room. "Okay," he said. "I'm ready."

He had on a yellowing T-shirt and blue trunks that revealed his bent and withered right leg. His left leg bulged with muscles, but his right, hung at an odd angle from the hip, was grotesquely thin. It had been so badly damaged in the accident, and his recovery had taken so long, that the muscles had completely atrophied. He was very bitter about the whole thing. But the accident had been his own fault, Jill knew. He had been speeding—something close to ninety miles an hour, the records said. And he was the *lucky* one. A passenger in Larry's car and the driver of the other car had both been killed instantly in the head-on collision.

Jill cleared a space on the floor and unrolled a small mat for him to lie on. "Let's get to work," she said.

Larry grunted and strained to get to his knees, the crutch vibrating from the tension. Then he dropped the crutch and fell forward, catching himself with his hands. Muscles rippled in his arms as he let himself down.

"Jesus Christ!" he exclaimed. "Just to lie down is a

whole production."

"At least you can do it yourself now." Jill knelt down beside him and plugged in the ultrasound machine. "When we first started, I had to help you."

"Oh goody, goody," he said sarcastically. "I'm practically good as new."

Flipping on the machine, Jill unhooked the metallic wave generator from its side and started rubbing it slowly over the back of Larry's leg. The ultra-high vibrations would help to relax his scarred muscles and make his exercises easier.

"You're not as good as new yet," Jill said softly. "But you *can* get a lot better if you keep working hard and don't give up."

"Hey, lady!" Larry shouted. "Open your eyes and look at that leg! Ain't no way it's ever going to be good again. Why can't you be up front for once in your life? Why can't you admit the sight of my body disgusts you?"

"I've seen a lot worse, Larry."

Larry scrunched his head around on the mat to look at her. "Oh yeah? What's that supposed to mean?"

"It means there are a lot of people worse off than you are," she said evenly.

"So what difference does that make? Babies are starving in India too. But that doesn't make *me* better off."

He waited for Jill to reply, but she just kept moving the ultrasound generator up and down his leg.

After a while, he said, "Hey, that feels good."

"That's what it's for."

"You know, I have another place that could use some massaging. It would do a lot more good there, I can tell you. I'll roll over and show you!"

Jill felt her muscles tense. The image of the punctured foldout flashed in her mind.

"Hey, Jill, how about it?"

"No!"

"The place I'm thinking of—"

"I know what you're thinking of," Jill cut in, her voice hard and edgy. "If you want we can just stop right now and I'll leave!" She meant it. In her mind, she drew an imaginary line. If he stepped over it by so much as an inch, she was leaving.

Larry lifted his head up. "Jesus," he said, his voice full of heavy exasperation, "I was just joking!"

"It wasn't funny!"

"Shit!" Larry dropped his head back on the mat, turning away from Jill. "Who needs you, anyway?" he said, petulantly.

Feeling the danger had passed, Jill relaxed. She sat back on her heels and turned the machine off. "All right. Time for your exercises. You know what to do by now, I hope."

"Yeah." Still on his stomach, Larry tensed his buttock and lifted his leg off the floor.

Jill stayed kneeling beside him, watching closely. If the exercises weren't done exactly right, the wrong muscles would be used and the leg would get no better.

For a while, there were no sounds in the room but occasional grunts from Larry. Then he started talking. "Know what I saw yesterday? I was out in the yard and I saw this cat, a stray I guess, and it was stalking a bird through the high grass. It crept up on the bird slowly, taking its time, moving forward inch by inch. The bird was twitching around the way birds do, real nervous looking, but I guess it didn't see the cat, because suddenly the cat pounced and caught it. It played with the bird awhile, just toying with it, and then it killed it. Something, huh?"

"Oh," Jill said, her voice as dead as the bird.

"I figured that's what life is all about really," Larry went on with a grunt, lifting his leg in the air, "kill or be killed. Most people try to pretend that's not the way it is. I don't pretend. There are your winners and there are your losers. And I know I'm one of the losers."

"Come on, Larry!" Jill said. "You know that's not true. If you don't give up, if you don't lose faith, if you keep on trying as hard as you can, you'll get a lot better."

Larry sneered. "The power of positive thinking, right?"

"I guess you could call it that."

"It's a crock of bull! That bird out there could have thought as positively as it wanted and it still would have ended up in the cat's mouth."

"But Larry—"

"I don't want to talk about it anymore," he said, perversely. He turned over on his back and began lifting his leg up in front of himself.

He was quiet a moment.

"How was your wedding?" he asked, changing the subject again.

"What?" Jill asked, taken aback. She hadn't told him about it. "How did you know?"

"The wedding ring. You never had it before. Was it a nice wedding?"

"Yes, it was—very nice." She and Ted had gotten married in Stern Grove, under the spruce and fir trees, just a small gathering with a few close relatives and friends, nothing at all fancy. But it had been a nice ceremony. She and Ted had made up their own vows. It had been only last Sunday, and on Monday she had gone right back to work. Ted was teaching at San Francisco State and couldn't get away from his classes for a honeymoon.

"So how's married life?" Larry asked. "Is Ted—that's his name, isn't it?"

"Uh-huh."

"Is Ted treating you well?"

"Perfectly." Jill smiled.

"Well, if he doesn't satisfy you, you know where to find me. My face ain't pretty, and my leg's a lost cause, but the thing that counts is in good working order." Larry leered at her.

"Larry! Enough!"

Finishing his last exercise, Larry sat up. "Torture time is over now. You can make your escape and get away from the sight of me."

Jill didn't bother answering. She handed him his crutch and helped him stand up. Nervously, she thought it was time to tell him he was being dropped from the program.

"Larry. . ."

"What?"

He had that look in his eyes again, and she hadn't even said anything. It was anger or hate or *something* inside him just waiting to explode. Maybe, she thought, she should just phone him later and tell him. She knew there was going to be a big scene. And she just didn't feel like going through it. But then she got mad at herself. She wasn't going to take the coward's way out!

She said, "I told you before that as soon as you were able to, you'd have to come into the hospital for your therapy."

He took a step toward her, his crutch hitting the floor hard. He looked mean. The eye that was always squinting started to twitch. "Yeah? So?"

Jill knelt down to pack up the ultrasound machine. "I tried to postpone it for as long as I could, but I'm getting more cases now and my boss at the hospital is giving me a hard time." Unplugging the machine, she coiled the cord in her hands. "So this will have to be the last time I come out." She braced herself for the explosion she was sure would come.

But Larry's voice was soft, reasonable. "I don't get it. Why can't you still come out here anyway? What's your boss got to do with it?"

"He's my boss!" Jill stood up again. "You know—he tells me what to do and I do it. But I can still treat you at the hospital."

"You fuckers are all alike," Larry muttered, turning away.

"Come on! You're not being fair! The hospital has rules and they're sensible rules. They can't afford to send me out to people who can get to the hospital on their own."

He swung around to face her. His face was red with anger. "That's right! Hide behind the rules. You're just following orders, like some Nazi. That's what I liked about that cat out there. It didn't tell the bird it was sorry. It just went and killed the bird because it wanted to. Right up front, it said, 'I'm going to kill you, you fucking bird, just because I want to!' "

Jill stared at him in shock.

"Why can't you be up front!" he shouted. "Why can't you just say that you're sick and tired of looking at my twisted face and ugly body!"

Jill was fed up now. "All right!" she snapped. "If that's what you want to believe, I can't stop you. But you've got to continue your therapy at the hospital or you *will* be a cripple for the rest of your life! You've got to stop your self-pity! You've—"

"If you really wanted to help me, you could keep coming out here anyway! No one says you can't come out here on your own!"

"You mean you want me to come out on my own time?"

"That's what I mean!"

Jill was amazed at his gall. "Larry, I can't do that!"

Larry's face bent itself into a horrible grimace.

Reflexively, Jill took a step back from him. "Fuck it!" he shouted. "I don't need you, if that's the way you feel! You can just walk away on your two good legs, twitching your ass the way you do, and leave me here. I guess you're tired of slumming, huh?"

He suddenly lifted his crutch in the air. Jill was afraid he was going to hit her with it, but he pivoted away from her on his good leg. The crutch swung around and knocked a dirty glass off the crowded coffee table. It smashed on the hard concrete floor.

Jill stared at him in silence a moment. His upper body was heaving up and down. She said quietly. "Sometimes you really demand a lot, Larry. You know, I've got my own life to live."

"Then go and live it and stop screwing up mine!"

He turned around now to face her again, and suddenly he just looked pathetic. He was still breathing hard and his face was still red, but Jill could see that his eyes were pleading with her desperately. More than anything, he needed someone to show him he was wanted and cared for, she realized. If she just walked out now and never came back, she knew he would never show up at the hospital for his therapy. He would stay in his squalid shack, full of self-pity, getting worse and worse. All her work with him would be wasted. Would it really be so much to see him maybe once a week on her own time? No. She could do it. But another part of her was telling her to get out. *Get out now, while you still have a chance. He is a dangerous person, violent and hostile and paranoid. You're not safe with him alone.*

She didn't know what to do.

"Go on!" he yelled at her. "Get out!"

Yes, she should get while she still had a chance. He wasn't her responsibility. She couldn't lead his life for him! He needed more than a physical therapist—he needed a psychiatrist.

But she didn't leave. She could picture him staying in his little shack, sinking deeper and deeper into depression while his leg got worse and worse. She couldn't let that happen to him. It was his *whole life* against only a *few hours* of her time.

"All right, Larry. I'll make you a deal."

"What?"

"If you promise to go into the hospital for your therapy twice a week on schedule, I'll come visit you once a week on the weekends. That's all I can do."

A look of victory came into Larry's face. "It's a bargain!"

She picked up the ultrasound machine and he followed her out to the van and waited while she loaded it in the back.

A hideous smile seemed to be pasted on his face like a paper cut-out. "You'll come by this weekend, right?"

"Oh, I can't come *this* weekend," she said quickly. "I'm sorry."

"Why not?" The paper smile on Larry's face tore apart.

"Ted and I are moving into our new place. I just won't have time. But I'll come next weekend for sure."

Larry examined her frankly a moment. Then he said sullenly, "All right. Next weekend. Is that a promise?"

"It's a promise." Jill got in the van, gave Larry a wave, and drove off feeling uneasy. Larry had looked too self-satisfied when she had given in. She thought of the story he had told her and hoped she wouldn't turn out to be the canary to Larry's cat.

But her misgivings about Larry were soon driven from her mind by thoughts of Ted. Being married still seemed unreal. It had all happened so fast! Only two months from their first meeting to their marriage last

Sunday. It was amazing, especially considering that the way she had met Ted certainly hadn't put her in the best light. She had fallen flat on her behind.

CHAPTER 2

Larry felt very proud of himself. Women were always suckers for sympathy, he thought. He watched the van until it disappeared around a corner, then pivoted around on his good leg to go back inside. There was a big blue '79 Buick parked next to the curb, and he caught his reflection in its windshield. The satisfied smile on his lips evaporated as he jerked his head around. He didn't need to be reminded of how ugly he looked.

Goddamn world, he thought. It wasn't fair. Only twenty-five years old and he was an ugly, disfigured cripple. It just wasn't fair! The idea that he was responsible for his own condition was totally beyond him. So what if he had been stoned out of his mind on angel dust and doing ninety? He had done it before and nothing had ever happened. It was just fucking bad luck. Just fucking bad luck.

No, it was Josie's fault, he thought. Goddamn Josie!

She had been too flaked out even to pop a can of beer for him, for chrissakes! It was late at night and though she was sitting beside him on the front seat, he couldn't see her. She was just a presence beside him in the speeding car.

"Goddammit, Josie! Where's the beer?" It was the

23

second time he had asked her. What was she doing over there? Playing with herself? The side of the road was rushing by at incredible speed.

"Can'd oben id." Josie's words were so slurred with drugs he couldn't understand her.

"What?" he shouted.

"I can't oben id, dammit!"

"Shit! You are one lame lady, you know that? Gimme it and I'll open it!"

"No. I can do id," she said, petulantly.

That made him mad. "Give it to me, I said!" He lunged across the seat at her and the car went wild. That was the last thing he could remember.

Josie had been killed.

Served her right, he thought. He started to turn up the driveway to his converted garage, but something in the gutter caught his eye. He hobbled over to it and looked down. It was just behind the blue Buick, a cheap plastic doll with no clothes, one leg stuck up in the air at an absurd angle. Its glass eyes were wide open and seemed to stare back at him. It looked like it was waiting for a little fuck, he mused, the way it had its plastic leg up like that.

He straightened up and looked around furtively. He couldn't see anyone. Straining to hold onto his crutch, he bent down and, grunting, grabbed the doll by the foot with his free hand. It was an effort to straighten up again. He looked around guiltily, but no one had seen him. A strange, almost ghoulish cackle escaped his lips.

He could barely maintain his self-control until he got back inside. He slammed the door behind him and leaned back against it, letting out a loud series of laughs that sounded more like screams. He held the doll upside down by its foot in front of his face.

"Bitch!" he screamed at it. "Goddamn bitch!"

He brought it closer to his face and stared at it intently for a second, his eyes crossed, and then broke out in hysterical laughter again. He tossed the doll up into the air and caught it around the waist. His hand was big enough for his thumb and fingers to meet in the middle. He squeezed the doll into a grotesque shape and brought it up to his face again.

"Fucking bitch!" he hissed at it. "I'm going to fuck you, you nurse physical therapist bitch! Fuck you till you bleed!" Specks of froth flew out of his mouth at the plastic doll. "You understand? Till you bleed!"

The doll's eyes stared at him unblinking.

He stopped suddenly and looked wildly around the squalid room. He was breathing heavily, panting.

Still clutching the doll, he hobbled over to the couch, his crutch thudding heavily on the floor. "Gonna get you, girl. Gonna get you good," he muttered. He let the crutch fall to the floor and flopped down on the couch. Leaning over, he looked through the junk on the end table. Old magazines. Beer cans. Underwear. Then he found it. It was beautiful. He loved it. He pushed the hidden catch and cackled with glee when the shiny blade shot out. He held the doll up and stuck the point of the knife under its chin.

"You understand what I'm going to do to you? I'm going to *get* you! I'm going to *rape* you!"

He shook the doll in the air and then threw it down on the floor between his feet.

"Fucking bitch!" he screamed and lunging over, stabbed it with the knife.

"And after I rape you, I'm going to kill you!"

The knife flew down again, cutting deep into the doll's plastic face.

"I'm going to kill you!"

He stabbed it again and again and again.

CHAPTER 3

Yawning sleepily, Ted Witherspoon opened the door to his apartment and blinked his eyes at the mess inside. It was early Saturday morning, moving day, and he had spent the night at Jill's, getting up before dawn to return to his old place to do the last minute packing. He thought of Jill still asleep in her warm bed and felt a stab of envy. But he knew it was his own fault—he had put off tackling all his books and papers until the last possible moment.

He went into his study and wondered how he had accumulated so much, especially when his office at the university was also overflowing with books, papers, and xeroxes of journal articles. The three tall bookcases crammed with books would go first, and then he would have to empty his old wooden file cabinet and clean out his desk.

He grabbed a stack of paperbacks he hadn't looked at in years. A letter slipped from among the books and fluttered to the floor at his feet. Dropping the books into a cardboard box, he picked up the letter and frowned. It was addressed to him at Hillsdale, San Mateo, California. It was over ten years old.

"Hillsdale," he muttered to himself. "Why did I save this? What earthly reason?" Hillsdale was not something

27

he wanted to remember. In fact, he had been trying to forget it ever since he left the place at seventeen. He started to crumple the letter into a ball, but curiosity made him smooth it out again. He opened the envelope and pulled out the pale blue paper.

June 15, 1971

Dear Ted,

I hope you can read my bad handwriting. My arthritis is acting up again, though I took some aspirin a while ago so I could write this letter. Otherwise, I am fine. Uncle Bert is having trouble with his prostate again and we are just praying that he doesn't have to go into the hospital for an operation.

Dr. Nathanson called us the other day. He is such a nice man, I think. He told us that you were improving, which we were *very glad* to hear. He said you still don't trust him, though, and that disappointed us. Remember, Dr. Nathanson only wants to help you, dear.

Your uncle and I still haven't received *one* letter from you! I know you feel hurt and resentful, but dear, we did what we had to do. We had *no* choice! I hope someday you'll be able to understand it was all for your own good. We did *not* want to send you away. You know that!

We would still like to come visit you, if you will let us. Please think about it. We still love you as much as ever. And please, dear, write to us.

love,
Aunt Mazie

Ted balled the letter up and tossed it into the waste basket. He hadn't saved it for any reason, but he was glad he had found it. He hated to think what might have happened if Jill had come across it. He felt he could trust her about everything else, but not Hillsdale. She would never understand he had had no business being in a mental hospital.

He thought of Aunt Mazie again, dead now for several years. He could almost hear her thin voice telling him, "We have to do it, dear! We have no choice!"

But they did have a choice. They could have believed him!

He was still cleaning out his desk when Jill arrived promptly at eight-thirty. He let her in, folded her in his arms, and kissed her hard. They came up for air a minute later and Jill pushed him away playfully.

"Down, boy!" she laughed. "Are you ready?"

"Not yet."

He led her down the short hall to the study. The bookshelves were barren, the posters down from the walls, and boxes were piled everywhere. His desk was covered with papers.

"Can I help?" Jill asked.

"I just have to clear out the desk and then I'm finished. Pull up a box and make yourself at home." He knelt down by the desk and started pulling things out and tossing them into boxes.

"You sure waited until the last minute," Jill commented.

"It's your fault."

"*My* fault? How?"

Ted smiled. "You made me fall in love with you so hard I was hanging around you like a love-sick teenager when I should have been here packing up."

It threatened to rain all that day, but never did. The two men Ted had hired to help them move showed up with their truck and they all set to work emptying Ted's and Jill's old apartments and filling up the new place.

It was a large apartment, the top floor of an old converted house set on a crowded hill at the edge of San Francisco's Sunset district—so high up and with so much privacy, it felt like a whole house rather than an apartment. It had lots of windows and magnificent views. The kitchen faced west to the blue line of the ocean far in the distance and south all the way to Mount Davidson. The living room looked west and north across Golden Gate Park and the Presidio to the two red towers of the Golden Gate Bridge and the massive headlands of Marin. The living room had a small balcony and Jill pictured romantic evenings ahead, going out there with Ted to watch the sunsets.

Getting the furniture up the two flights of wooden steps that ran up the outside of the house was a lot of hard work. It took all four of them to haul the beds and the sofas, Jill pitching in to do her part with the men. By early evening they were finished. The two hired men went away in their truck, leaving Ted and Jill collapsed gratefully on Ted's overstuffed sofa.

Ted surveyed the room. "Well, what do you think?" he asked, and kissed Jill lightly on the cheek.

"I think I like your kisses."

"I mean the furniture," Ted laughed.

Jill looked around the room, her lips pursed together. She shook her head. "It doesn't work, obviously."

"There's too much of it."

"And it doesn't go together."

The problem was their two sets of furniture. The things from Jill's apartment were aggressively modern—lots of glass and chrome and sharp angles. Ted's furniture, though of good quality, was decidedly old and overstuffed. The two styles jarred.

"We'll figure something out," Ted said. "Maybe we can sell off the modern junk."

Jill turned on him. "The modern junk!" she exclaimed, her voice high with indignation. "That's good stuff! It's your things that make this place look like a garage sale—" She broke off abruptly. There was a twinkle in Ted's eye.

"Why you!" She lunged across the sofa at him, her hands out to tickle his ribs.

"Hey!"

"I'll teach you! The modern junk indeed!" Jill darted her hands under his elbows and started wiggling them like crazy. Ted giggled helplessly, then took the offensive. He rolled over on top of her and pinned her arms between them. Jill was very ticklish, much more so than he, and as his hands attacked her ribs she shrieked with laughter.

Struggling wildly, shouting and laughing, they rolled off the couch to land with a thud on the floor. Ted redoubled his efforts.

"Help!" Jill cried. Tears were streaming down her cheeks. "Stop!"

"You started it, you little devil!"

"Oh please!" she gurgled. "No! I give up! Uncle!"

Ted stopped the tickling. "Give me a kiss then!" he demanded, still on top of her.

"Never!"

"All right." He twitched a hand against her ribs.

"No!" she shrieked. "Stop! I'll give you a kiss!"

"That's better."

They kissed tenderly.

"I love the way you kiss," Ted murmured after a while. Rolling sideways a little, he started unbuttoning her blouse with one hand. Neither spoke as he worked down from button to button, his fingers working slowly, carefully, as if engaged in a delicate operation requiring infinite patience. All the while, he gazed lovingly into her eyes.

He pulled the blouse from her jeans and parted it. She pulled his head down to her breasts and felt his warm breath on her skin.

They made love slowly, controlling their passion, feeding their hunger for each other while increasing it at the same time. Savoring the intensity of each moment, they held it until it slipped from their grasp. Their bodies melted together. The room dissolved. Time became eternity.

The atmosphere in the room seemed hot and swampy when they finally pulled apart, lying side by side on the floor.

"I love you so much," Ted whispered breathlessly.

Jill snuggled closer, her head on his chest. "How much is that?"

"I don't know. I haven't found the end of it yet."

"More than life itself?" she teased.

But Ted took the question seriously. "I think so. Before I found you, I felt so *lost,* as if I wasn't really part of the world, of life—as if I were only a spectator, looking on. If you ever left me, I think I'd go crazy—"

"Hush!" Jill put her finger to his lips. "I'm never going to leave you, darling. Never."

They showered and put on clean clothes, then went out to find a restaurant. They discovered a little Italian place two blocks from their new house and stuffed themselves with really excellent lasagna, polishing off a bottle of red wine in the process. They wandered back slowly, exploring their new neighborhood. There were Chinese, Mexican, and Japanese restaurants, a small bookstore, a grocery, a bakery, a shoe repair shop, and a delicatessen. It really looked as if they had found a nice area, they told each other happily. Even though it was dark, there were people out walking and, wonder of wonders, quite a few of them even smiled and said hello. It felt like a small town right in the middle of the city.

In bed that night, Jill fell asleep in Ted's arms almost instantly. He held her close, listening to her soft breathing and feeling the warmth of her body. He couldn't remember ever feeling so happy, so content. Jill had made his life whole again after years of emptiness. It was strange, he thought, finding Aunt Mazie's letter again, just as he was managing to put it all behind him. Thinking back on those horrible years, it almost seemed as though they had happened to someone else.

And they *had,* he told himself. He was a different person now.

Eager to show off their new place, Jill and Ted had a small dinner party the following Tuesday for Jill's sister and brother-in-law, their son, and Ted's only real friend in the History department, Frank Goldberg.

Frank was the first to arrive. Like Ted, he was a tall man. He was heavy set, his hair was graying, and his eyes had big bags under them. He gave Ted a firm handshake, pecked Jill on the cheek, then turned to survey the apartment.

"Rather bizarre, isn't it?" he asked, looking at the jumble of furniture in the big living room.

"It is," Ted agreed, "but we're getting rid of Jill's modern junk—"

Jill jabbed him in the ribs. "We're going to have a garage sale, Frank, and sell off *Ted's* old junk."

Frank laughed. "I can see a nice argument brewing here."

"Can I get you a drink?" Ted asked. "Whiskey?"

"And a little water, thanks."

Ted fixed Frank's drink and was handing it to him when Jill's sister Elaine arrived with her husband Roger and their son Randy. There were hugs and kisses and handshakes all around.

Roger had red hair and a florid face that made him

look older than he was. "Show Uncle Ted your new shirt, Randy," he said to his ten-year-old.

The boy came up to Ted and proudly stuck out his chest. "See?"

The T-shirt was yellow and across the bottom it said in big red letters, "HALLEY'S COMET—1986." Above the words a fiercely drawn comet blazed with a tail of fire.

Ted knelt down. "That's nice," he said blandly, unable to muster much enthusiasm.

Elaine turned to Jill. "Roger has a thing about this comet." The expression on her carefully made-up face implied that she couldn't see anything to get excited about. Though she was younger than her sister, the heavy way Elaine applied her make-up gave her a hard appearance that made her look older.

"Oh, I think it's pretty interesting, too," Jill replied. "After all, it only comes once every seventy–six years."

"That's right!" Roger put in. "I've been reading everything I can get my hands on."

Randy was being ignored. No one noticed him cock his head and stomp away to flounce down on a chair off in a corner.

"Why don't you fix drinks, Ted?" Jill said. "I've got to see about dinner."

"I'll help." Elaine said, and followed Jill into the kitchen.

The two sisters engaged in a slow sparring match in the kitchen. Though she had said she would help, Elaine didn't lift a finger. Instead, she sniffed around, murmuring how 'small and cozy' the kitchen was and comparing it to her own much larger kitchen. She looked askance at the small dinette set and told Jill of the new inlaid oak set she and Roger had just bought. Following Jill to the old gas stove, she said how much she loved her Jenn-Air grill. When she finished her little tour, she leaned against the counter and watched Jill get things ready.

Jill tried not to let Elaine's comments get under her skin. But she did resent the way her sister—her little sister!—patronized her. Elaine had always known exactly what she wanted—to be an integral part of the American middle class with a successful husband, a child or two, and a nice house in a good suburb. She had gotten it all, marrying Roger right out of high school. Jill, on the other hand, hadn't known at all what she wanted for the longest time. She had left high school to spend a year traveling around the world on the cheap, taking odd jobs wherever she could find them. When she got back to the states, she had tried college and had done well, but hadn't really enjoyed it. She had dropped out to train as a physical therapist. She had never liked the way Elaine assumed they were in competition, racing for the great American dream. And she'd never liked Elaine's calm assurance that she had won and Jill had lost.

Elaine was talking about the wedding. "Remember when Ted forgot his lines? His face turned so red! He just looked hysterical! It was all I could do to stop myself from bursting out laughing!"

Jill looked up from the lettuce she was washing at the sink. "Why don't you like Ted?"

Elaine blinked at her, surprised. "Huh? I like Ted."

"Sometimes it doesn't seem like it." Generally, Jill could let her sister's comments roll off her back, but not when it came to Ted.

"I just thought it was funny when he forgot his lines, that's all." Elaine frowned.

"It just seems," Jill said, "that you're always trying to sow doubts in my mind about him." When Jill had told her she and Ted were getting married, Elaine had asked darkly if she was sure she was doing the right thing.

"Like what, for instance?" Elaine demanded.

"Like saying I don't really know anything about him."

"But it's true he never talks about himself, isn't it? You said yourself he's never told you about his family or anything."

"He's an orphan—you know that! It's probably very painful for him to talk about it."

"But it's more than that, isn't it?" Elaine responded. "He never talks about himself at all. Sometimes when I'm around him I feel something dark in him. Yes, a darkness—"

"God, Elaine!" Jill exploded. "Sometimes . . ."

"Don't you feel he has a hidden past?" Elaine persisted.

In spite of her anger, Jill had to laugh. It was too absurd. "Elaine, I think you *like* to stir up trouble. Even when we were kids you always had to be stirring things up. And you're so melodramatic! A hidden past. A darkness! You watch way too many soap operas!"

Elaine turned away. "Perhaps it's best if I don't say anything at all . . ."

Jill stared at Elaine's back, tempted to throw a soggy piece of lettuce at her. She wouldn't admit it to herself, but deep inside she realized there was some truth in what Elaine had said.

Out on the balcony Frank was saying, "Looks like you and Jill found a nice place. The view is wonderful."

Ted nodded. "The view is what decided us on this place. We were really lucky to find it."

"Look," Roger said, pointing up at the sky. "You can see the comet."

Ted looked up at the pale smudge of light, hardly bigger than his thumbnail.

"Of course, it's going to get a lot bigger in the next

few weeks," Roger continued. "I sure hope nothing happens."

"What do you mean?" Frank asked.

"It's pretty well known that comets are omens of doom." Roger jabbed his finger in the air for emphasis. "Omens of doom."

"Oh, come on—" Frank started.

"It's true!" Roger interrupted. "Every time that comet comes around, something horrible happens—wars, plagues, disasters, you name it!"

"That's a load of bull, and you know it!" Frank asserted.

That started a big argument. Ted didn't pay much attention. He felt a headache coming on. A strange throbbing pressure seemed to be building up. He looked down at his drink. It was his first and he had hardly touched it, so the reason wasn't that he had been drinking too much.

Trying to will the headache away, he looked up again and fixed his attention on Roger, who had a drop of spittle at the corner of his mouth.

"Another comet appeared in 1665 during the Great Plague in England," he was saying. "People were dying like flies."

"But you always have coincidences," Frank said. "All that still doesn't prove anything."

"You can only have so many coincidences before you start to wonder. Anyway, the Great Plague was terrible. . ."

Ted could hardly hear what Roger was saying now, the throbbing was so strong. *It has to be just a headache!* he told himself. *Just an ordinary headache!* But the outlines of Roger's face seemed to be blurring into mists.

"You had bodies everywhere. All piled up and swollen black. They were carting them away in wheelbarrows and burning them. Hundreds every day. And if you think it's coincidence, listen to this. The very next year, another comet came. And the very next year brought the Great Fire of London, destroying damn near the whole city. Two comets in a row and two incredible disasters in a row."

"Sure," Frank said sarcastically. "But what about the times the comet comes and nothing happens. Like that last time Halley's comet came. What happened then?"

"Well, that was in 1910, not too long before World War I! You can only blame coincidence so many times, and then you have to realize something is going on that doesn't meet the eye."

"Let's go back in," Ted put in, his voice sounding strange in his ears. He felt that he had to sit down. "It's getting cold out here."

It has to be just a headache! he thought. *It has to be!*

He hardly said a word all through dinner.

CHAPTER 4

Ted waited until Jill's breathing descended to the deep and regular monotony of sleep and then quietly slipped out of bed. He didn't want to be with her when it came.

He went silently into the living room, slid open the balcony door, and stepped out. He sensed the cold night air, but the sensation seemed somehow unconnected to himself, only an illusion.

Before it had always come in waves, the first one hazy and chaotic, a kind of foreshock to the second, when he saw things all too clearly. The first wave had already swept over him. It hadn't been just a headache, he now knew.

He resisted an impulse to run back to the bedroom, grab Jill, and hold her tight in his arms. He had to wait. The second wave was coming.

He took a step forward and leaned against the balcony railing, his body suddenly too heavy for him. He looked down to the steep road below. It was a fifty-foot drop.

By morning, another wave would sweep over him, showing him a vision. What would it be?

Something horrible. It always was something horrible. And death. He always saw death.

His voice was harsh, fierce. "No! Not again!"

What would he see? Whatever it was, he knew with cold certainty his vision would come true.

"Not again!" he hissed urgently, his hands gripping the rail so tightly that its hard edge cut painfully into his palms. "Not after so many years!!"

At twelve, Ted had seemed a normal boy in every respect, dirt under his fingernails, scrapes on his knees, and an unruly cowlick that his mother Dorothy said made him look like Dennis the Menace. But one night a few days after his birthday he was lying in bed, unable to sleep, half listening to Hawaii Five-O playing on the television downstairs, when a feeling of shivering dread came over him. A strange hiss began in his ears and grew explosively to a thunderous roar. He tried to cry out, but couldn't get his mouth to work. It seemed that his head would split open. Just when he thought he could stand it no longer and would surely die, it had stopped.

He felt as though he was floating up from the bed. There was a moment of pure nothingness.

Then, somehow, he saw his mom and dad as clearly as if they were right in front of him. He could pick out every hair of his father's thick black mustache. His mother was wearing a purple flower pinned to her blouse. They were sitting very close together in narrow orange seats next to a strange rounded window. They were laughing happily.

Suddenly Dorothy's face turned absolutely white, drained of blood. He heard hysterical screams from people he could not see. His dad, Peter, opened his mouth wide, as if trying to scream, but not a sound came out.

His parents clutched at each other in terror, then Dorothy broke away. Screaming in high-pitched wails of terror like nothing he had ever heard, she started crawling backwards up into her seat. Peter grasped at her, trying to pull her back down. Then flames exploded in front of them, followed by thick billows of black smoke. There arose a horrible, rushing howl. And then there was nothing.

Ted hid under the covers, shaking in fear. After a while, he ran downstairs and into his mother's arms. Crying, he told her what had happened.

"It was just a nightmare, honey. That's all." She tried to soothe him.

"No! It was real!"

"Now, you're old enough to know better. You were dreaming."

"Are you sure?" he asked, wide-eyed.

"Of course, honey."

She held him a little while, then took him back up to his room and tucked him in.

He was still frightened, and not at all sure that it had been a dream. But after a few days he forgot about it.

A week later, though, his mother told him she and his dad would be flying to Hawaii for a vacation. Ted and his little sister Sally would stay with their aunt and uncle while they were gone. It would only be for ten days.

Ted suddenly knew what he had seen. "Please!" he cried. "Don't go! Please! PLEASE!"

Dorothy was shocked. "Now, now. Calm down. What's the matter, honey?"

"You're going to crash! You're going to die!!"

"What on earth? Teddy!"

"I saw it! I saw it! Remember? I told you it wasn't a dream! Please don't go! PLEASE! Oh Mommy! You'll be killed!"

She tried to reason with him, but it was no use. She was baffled. Ted had never been like this before. What could have gotten into him?

His father came home from work and tried to talk some sense into him. When Ted still wouldn't listen, he got angry.

"I don't know what you're trying to pull," he said sternly, "but it won't work! You are too old to be carrying on like this!"

"Please, Daddy! Please don't go!"

"Maybe we should put it off," Dorothy said.

"No!" Peter answered. "We deserve this vacation! Now I don't want to hear another word about it."

Three days later they drove him and Sally to their Aunt Mazie and Uncle Bert's place, then flew off to Hawaii

The phone call came in the middle of the night. Ted hadn't been able to sleep and he heard his uncle answer it.

"Oh dear God! No!" he heard Bert say. "It's Dorothy and Peter! Their plane crashed. They've been killed!"

A little piece of Ted died that night too.

Since the plane had gone down in the middle of the Pacific and the bodies couldn't be recovered, there was a small memorial service instead of a funeral. Listening to the sad, ponderous organ, Ted took Sally's small hand in his and determined that he would watch over her and protect her and never ever let anything bad happen to her. She was three years younger than he, with an angelic face ringed by golden curls, and she meant the whole world to him now.

"It's all right, Sally," he whispered through his tears. "I'll take care of you. I promise."

He and Sally stayed on to live with their aunt and uncle. Bert and Mazie were not affectionate people, but in their own way they were kind. Ted devoted himself to his sister, giving her all the love he could no longer give his parents. Gradually his pain lessened and the horrible memories of his vision faded.

In 1970, when he was sixteen and his life was back to normal, he had another vision. It came in three waves. The first two were nothing but jumbles of images with no rhyme or reason. When the third wave came, he was walking home from school, cutting through a vacant lot. His head began throbbing. Before he could react, the throbbing exploded into thunder so loud his legs gave way under him and he fell to the ground. After what seemed an eternity, the skull-shattering thunder disappeared. He floated in nothingness a while, then, as if someone had suddenly turned on the lights, he saw Sally riding on a bike.

He saw her very clearly, up close, as if he were standing next to her and miraculously moving along with her in the air. A mammoth old Chevrolet was coming down the road. It was battered and consumed by rust, and seemed to be falling apart, but it was going fast, very fast. He tried to yell at Sally to warn her, but of course she couldn't hear him. She was talking to a boy on the sidewalk and wasn't looking where she was going. She was coasting, going very slowly to keep pace with the boy, talking and laughing and flirting with him. The bike wobbled precariously at her slow pace, its front wheel turning first left and then right as she balanced to stay upright.

The Chevrolet came up the road behind her.

She started to lose her balance and automatically jerked the handlebars left, making the bike turn into the road. What Ted saw was the first look of surprise on her face, the look of complete and utter disbelief at what was happening. Then the look turned to horror as the bike crumpled, she and the bike twisting together in a tangle of flesh and metal. And then he could only see an arm and a leg. She was under the wheels of the huge old wreck being dragged along the pavement. A long red swath of blood was left on the road.

Ted dragged himself home after the vision ended and found Sally in her room. Wild-eyed, he told her what he had seen. "You've got to promise me you'll never ride your bike again! Never!"

She stared at him in silence a moment, frightened by his strange story.

"Please!" Ted begged. "You've got to promise!"

Sally shook her head. "You're being weird!"

"But, Sally, listen—"

"No! I don't want to listen. You're being weird!"

"Please!" Ted pleaded urgently. "If you ride your bike ever again, you'll be killed for sure! I saw it!"

"Stop it!" Sally covered her ears. "I'll tell Aunt Mazie on you!"

"I'll tell her myself!" he shouted. Surely she and Bert would understand and make Sally stop riding her bike.

They told him the same thing his parents had four years before. It was just a dream, they said, nothing more.

But it wasn't a dream and he knew it! It would all come true unless he made sure to stop it. He took Sally's bike and hid it in weeds and brambles down an old gully. He started following her around, trying to watch over her every move. Nothing else mattered, not his school work, his baseball practice, his friends, nothing. But it was an impossible task. Sally began to loathe him for his constant spying. His aunt and uncle began to suspect he was losing his mind. After several weeks they could take no more, and made an appointment with a psychologist. They had to drag him forcibly off to it. While they were at the psychologist's Sally borrowed a friend's bike and was run over by an ancient Chevrolet. Horribly mangled, her face unrecognizable, she had clung to life for another six days.

On the day she died, Ted went nearly insane with grief. It seemed to him that he was the plaything of some dark force that showed him the future only to make sure he was helpless to affect it. He withdrew to his room, refusing to come out, refusing to talk or eat.

"You've got to stop this, Teddy," Mazie told him after several days. She had come into his room and sat down next to him on his bed. "What's going to happen to you? It hurts Bert and I more than we can bear to see you like this."

She put her arm around his shoulder. "Sally is gone, but you're not. You have to go on with life!"

He pressed himself against her ample bosom. "I tried to stop it!" he wailed piteously, speaking for the first time since Sally's death. "I tried, but it happened just the way I said!"

"What are you talking about?"

"Y-you know! I saw it—"

"No, you did not!" Mazie pushed him away. "Don't say that! It's wicked!"

He stared at her uncomprehending. "But—"

"Not another word! You did not see anything! You hear me? You did not see anything!" She jumped up and stalked out of the room.

That night, Ted slit his wrists. Bert found him unconscious in a pool of blood on the bathroom floor. He was rushed off to the same hospital in which Sally had died.

Years later, he would grow to understand why Mazie and Bert did what they did and perhaps even to forgive them for it. He would realize that it was too frightening for them to admit he was a freak who could see the future. And there was probably guilt involved too—if they had listened to him, maybe Sally would not have been killed. But though he would grow to understand the reasons for what they did, at the time all he felt was a devastating sense of betrayal that pushed him even closer to the edge.

What they did, after he returned from the hospital, was to send him off to Hillsdale. It was a classy place— his parents' insurance money let Bert and Mazie send

him to the best—but in Ted's mind it was still a funny
farm. And it forced him still deeper into the walls of
silence he had built up around himself. He quickly developed an uncontrollable shaking, as if his body was an
alien thing. Dr. Nathanson, with his trendy medallion
and aviator glasses, would have him brought to his office daily. He would sit there mute and trembling while
the psychiatrist told him, "People just don't have visions, Ted. They aren't real. You feel guilty, that's all. If
you ever want to get better, you will have to admit the
truth to yourself."

Eventually, Ted began to believe he was crazy—it was
easy to believe, living as he was in a hothouse of insanity. But then he rebelled. He wasn't crazy! And because
he wasn't crazy, he realized he would have to give in and
go along with the game if he was ever going to escape
from the funny farm. So he pretended his visions had
never happened. He pretended so well that Dr.
Nathanson thought he had cured him and released him.

But he had spent two years of his life in Hillsdale, and
he had left it nearly broken. They had done everything
to convince him his visions were not real, and nothing
for his real emotional needs. At times he still shook so
uncontrollably that he couldn't even stand up. The shaking grew better with time. What time did not seem to
heal was his fear of life. He was terrified of loving and
needing people.

He had finished high school by correspondence
courses, and so was able to go directly from Hillsdale to
college. He went to Berkeley, one of 25,000 students,
resolved to avoid human contact as much as possible.
He lived alone in a small studio apartment. He ate
alone. He went to classes with others, but even then he
felt alone.

He spent all his time reading history. History was
where he made his friends—with men and women hun-

dreds of years dead. In pre-revolutionary France or in feudal Italy, he could get away from the frightening uncertainty of the present, where you never knew what the next moment would bring. With history, he thought, you could go back to the safety of the past, where everything was over and done with and time could not jump out at you and go "BOO!"

Gradually loneliness came to seem the natural state of affairs. By the time he had graduated, with a nearly perfect record, the possibility of an alternative to his solitary way of life was inconceivable to him. The only safety, he felt, was in his invincible isolation.

He went east to graduate school at Princeton. The students and faculty wondered about the strange recluse who appeared in their midst and they made many attempts during his first year to draw him out. Their invitations and coaxings only made him withdraw deeper into his shell. Eventually, he was left alone, an object of rumor and mystery. He finished his Ph.D. in a remarkably short time and got a job teaching history at San Francisco State.

Outwardly, he was doing well. At a time when teaching jobs were almost non-existent, he had snared one of the best. His courses were popular. His colleagues thought he was brilliant. But his life was empty. It held no meaning for him and he came to realize he was just going through the motions. He found himself thinking more and more of Sally and his parents. Often he would stare up into the night sky and ponder the infinite solitude of death.

Sunk in one of his blackest moods, he was wandering aimlessly in Golden Gate Park one day when he saw a beautiful woman running along a dirt trail. He probably never would have seen her again if her right foot had not gone into a hole. Her leg had caved in under her as if it was made of rubber and she had sprawled in the dirt. He ran up to her and hesitantly asked if she was all right.

She looked up at him, just managing to smile through the pain. Small trickles of blood oozed from her knee and elbow. Her white shorts were covered with dirt.

"They don't come much clumsier than me," she said. "And I *would* have to have a witness!"

She tried hopping on her good foot, but it was no use. Ted had to carry her back to his car and drive her home.

He didn't know how it happened. Perhaps Jill was not as intimidated as others were by the walls he threw up around himself. Or maybe the years of loneliness had become too much for him. Whatever it was, he was falling in love with her before he could stop himself—before he could warn himself how truly dangerous love was. He fell for her hard, with all the passion and joy and wonderment and awkwardness of a first love—for that was what Jill was, his first love. All the love he had denied himself since Sally had been killed just came exploding out of him. He felt like he was coming out of a lonely valley, working his way up into the sunlight after years of wandering in the shadows.

For her part, Jill was attracted by his brooding silences, his wise, melancholy eyes. He had depths that made the other men she had known seem childish and shallow. He was gentler and more truly caring than any of them. But most of all, she loved him because he so obviously needed her and she knew she could make him happy.

The weeks rushed by so fast he was almost surprised to find himself standing next to her in Stern Grove, getting married and feeling that his life was only beginning.

And now, it seemed, it was ending.

He pressed his palms hard against the sharp edge of the balcony railing, welcoming the pain.

He began to cry like a baby. He couldn't help it,

didn't even try to stop it. He crumpled to the cold balcony floor and cried in great choking sobs. After all these years he had given in and let himself love someone. And now . . . and now . . .

"Not again!" he cried. "Not Jill! Dear God, not Jill!"

He put his hand to his mouth and bit down hard but still the choking sobs came.

A while later, drained of tears, he stood up again and gripped the rail. The strange, pulsating throbs he had felt earlier came again. By degrees they grew stronger until they were so painful he balled his hands into fists and pressed them hard against his temples. His head exploded in agony. He tried to scream, but only a desperate rasping came out.

He lurched dizzily back inside, groping his way blindly. His legs smacked into something hard and he fell to the floor. He willed the pain to stop. It had to stop!

But it grew ever stronger. He forced himself up on his hands and knees and crawled frantically across the floor, wildly looking for a place to hide.

He ran into the couch. He had no idea what he was doing now. Overwhelming panic coursed through him. He reached out wildly for something, anything, to hold onto and pulled a seat cushion from the couch. He hugged it to his chest and curled into a fetal position on the floor.

It was the only safety he could find.

The throbbing and roar merged together, swelling louder and louder, filling his whole being until there was no room for anything else, until it seemed the whole universe was one pulsating roar of doom. It was unbearable. It could not possibly get worse. But it did.

And then, without warning, it stopped. There was nothingness. He floated in the infinite void of space. His senses had been stripped.

Then came swirling muddy colors and a feeling of ut-

ter coldness. There was the smell of . . . what? The
ocean? There was a sound like the sound of wind. Colored shapes flickered through empty blackness. Now a
face appeared suddenly, floating in space, surrounded
by darkness. It was a man's face, very old, with vastly
sympathetic eyes and fine parchment skin crisscrossed
with wrinkles. Ted felt that the old man was looking at
him with concern, wanting to help. He called out, or
thought he called out. *"Help me! Help me! Make it
stop!"*

The old man did not seem to hear him.

"Please! Help me!" But the old man disappeared
abruptly. He could not help. No one could help.

Ted lay on the floor curled up like a baby, clutching
the cushion to his chest. But his mind was not in the
room. It was somewhere else. Floating.

And now he saw Jill—saw her far away in the
darkness, the outlines of her face blurred as if by an
intervening mist. *(NO! NO! NOT JILL! NO!!)* She was
surrounded by the blackest night, except for a line of red
light arcing over her head. He could see nothing but her
face and the upper half of her body and the strange line
of light. Somewhere deep inside his mind, as if a part of
him were standing back watching dispassionately, he
heard a voice saying slowly and distinctly, *She is in danger.*

She seemed to move closer now, and the arc of light
grew thicker. It was shaped like a rainbow, but its color
was the color of fresh bright blood.

Then she moved suddenly and the arc of light was no
longer visible. She was turning around, as if looking for
someone or something. Again the dispassionate voice
came to him: *"She is in danger."*

And now she started screaming, her mouth stretched
wide, screaming her lungs out! He couldn't hear the
sound, but he could feel it. It felt like terror.

His body jerked spasmodically on the floor. The cushion flew from his hands. He was trying to run to her. He had to help her! He had to save her!

The harder he tried to run, the farther away she moved. He could barely see her. The darkness seemed like black ink in the air between them. She was screaming murder.

(Jill! Jill! JILL!!)

Abruptly, her screams were choked off and she stood motionless in the surrounding darkness. She floated closer, to hover it seemed just a few inches away so that he could see her perfectly. Her eyes were wide and staring ahead, unseeing.

The black of her pupils receded to tiny points and then disappeared entirely so that he was looking *through* her eyes as if they were only round windows. He could see through them for miles, it seemed, and in the distance beyond, torturing fires appeared—dancing, flickering, blazing red and yellow. The fantastical light spilled out of her window eyes to illumine her face.

It was an evil mask of pure hatred.

The eyes were dominating in their fiery intensity. They seemed to swell until he could see nothing but their burning flames.

And then she moved away rapidly into the black distance and disappeared.

CHAPTER 5

Ted went to the university the next morning, blindly following his daily routine. It seemed the only way to keep from pulling his hair out and screaming in horror. Feeling like a walking zombie, he sat down at his desk and tried to prepare his lecture for his two o'clock class on European history. But he could only stare blankly at the shafts of morning sunlight coming in through the venetian blinds. His mind kept calling up the horrible things he had seen in his vision.

Jill, her eyes glowing, her face twisted . . .

He pounded his fist down on his desk with a bang that echoed loudly in the small office. None of it made any sense! Something was going to happen to Jill, but what? Where would it happen? Outside? There was the smell of the ocean, he remembered. And the strange beam of red light. He had seen Jill clearly, had seen the complete terror on her face too clearly. And the part at the end, when her eyes turned into fiery cauldrons! What did any of it mean? Questions came at him out of the dark corners of his mind, and there weren't any answers!

He jumped up from his chair and began pacing back and forth in front of his desk. It was just crazy. Just plain crazy! He stopped his pacing, seizing on the idea that had just occured to him. It *was* crazy! Maybe *he* was crazy! Maybe it wasn't a real vision at all. If it wasn't a real vision, if he was going crazy, then *Jill wouldn't be in danger! She would be safe!* Yes! He was just going crazy! That was it! He was . . .

He let out a gruesome laugh. It started softly and grew louder and still louder and almost imperceptibly turned into great, choking sobs.

He felt his mind exploding. He had to talk to someone before he really did go crazy! He grabbed his jacket from the back of the door and went quickly down the hall to Frank Goldbaum's office. He knocked and didn't wait for an answer before pushing the door open.

Frank was at his desk, talking to a girl with long blonde hair. They both turned to look up at him and the girl's jaw fell open in shocked surprise.

Frank jumped up from his chair. "Ted!"

"I've got to talk to you, Frank!" Ted said desperately.

"Sure, Ted. Of course!" Frank looked at the student.

"Oh, don't mind me," she said, getting up. She gathered her books quickly, grabbed her purse, and swept by Ted out of the office.

"Ted, what is it? Come in!" Frank indicated the chair where the girl had been sitting.

Ted stayed by the door. "Not here, Frank. Can we go somewhere?"

"I guess so. Sure. Jesus, you look like you've seen a ghost!"

The bar was a strange anomaly. With white stucco walls and red tiles on the roof, it looked like an old Spanish mission. It sat all by itself on the edge of Golden Gate Park facing the ocean across the Great Highway. On the outside wall next to the front door was a small plaque that read "Veterans of Foreign Wars Post No. 46." Inside, the walls were covered with murals from the thirties showing scenes of old San Francisco—the harbor, Fisherman's wharf, Coit Tower, the beach, and the cable cars. Going in there was like walking into another era, and except for a few tourists and college kids, its patrons seemed to belong to another era as well. The place was pretty full for a week day, but Ted and Frank found a table near the front. Frank went to the bar and brought back a pitcher of beer.

He poured a glass of beer, set it in front of Ted, then poured another for himself. "Okay, Ted. Talk. I want to help you if I can."

Ted gulped half his beer before nervously asking, "Do you believe in ESP, Frank?"

"What?"

"ESP—you know, extrasensory perception. Precognition, clairvoyance, things like that."

"I don't know," Frank said slowly. "Is that what's bothering you? Do you think you've had some sort of experience?"

"I know I have."

"Do you want to tell me about it?"

Ted drained his glass and poured himself another. "First you've got to promise not to tell anyone, especially Jill."

"But why—"

"Just promise!" Ted barked.

"All right. I promise. Now tell me what this is all about."

Ted told Frank as much as he could remember of his vision. It was all so confused in his mind he was sure there were parts he was leaving out. Still, he went over it as carefully as he could.

He had to grope for words to describe the way Jill looked at the end. "Her eyes were glowing—no, that's wrong. It was as if I could look through them. And I saw flames. And the light came out of her eyes! It was horrible! Horrible!"

He broke off, unable to continue. Frank waited patiently.

"And that was it," he went on after a moment. "It ended. I have no idea what it means. I can't do anything until I find out what it means!"

"You really think it means something?" Frank asked. "Eyes can't burn with fire. It's impossible!"

"I know that! But it has to mean something! Jill is in danger!"

Frank drummed his fingers on the table. "It sounds like a nightmare to me, Ted."

Ted grabbed the pitcher and poured himself another beer. "It wasn't a nightmare!"

There was a blast of cold ocean air as the front door opened. A muscular man came in, pulling a girl behind him. The man dragged her to a table across from Ted and Frank's and sat her down roughly in a chair.

Frank asked, "Why are you so sure it wasn't a dream?"

"Because I wasn't asleep! I was wide awake!"

"But when did it happen? In the middle of the night, you said. You could have fallen asleep without knowing it."

Ted leaned over the table toward Frank, as if getting closer would make him understand. "I *know* it wasn't a dream!" he said fiercely.

"You sound like you *want* it to be a real vision."

"Listen, Frank! It's happened to me before!"

"What?"

Ted recounted his first two visions, telling Frank how he had lost his parents and then his little sister.

"Those were *not* dreams! I saw *exactly* what was going to happen and I couldn't do a thing to stop it either time!"

"You never told me any of that before," Frank said

quietly. He was looking at Ted as if he were only now seeing him for the first time. He was studying him, appraising him like a specimen under a magnifying glass. Ted had seen the same expression on the faces of his psychiatrists at Hillsdale.

"I never told anybody about it before. Not even Jill," he said. "It's not the sort of thing you tell people."

"The human mind is a very complicated thing," Frank told him earnestly. "People's minds sometimes play funny tricks on them. Sometimes . . ." Frank stopped.

"Go on! Finish it!" Ted shouted. "Sometimes people see things that aren't there! People just don't have visions! Sane ones don't, anyway. Only crazies have visions!"

"That wasn't what I meant."

"Then what did you mean? Didn't you listen to me? This has happened to me before!"

"Let's try to be reasonable about this—"

"I am being reasonable!" Ted shouted, pounding his fist on the table. He knew people were looking at him. But it didn't matter.

"Let me finish!" Frank said firmly. "You were pretty young when you had those first visions, as you call them. How old?"

"The first was when I was twelve," Ted answered sullenly, despairing of ever getting Frank to understand. "The second happened when I was sixteen."

"You were in adolescence. Adolescence is a pretty hard time, you know. You're under new pressures, and sometimes other pressures get added which sort of overload your system . . ."

It was hopeless, Ted felt. Frank was never going to understand. He let his friend go on with his amateur psychology and simply tuned out.

He looked over at the table across from him. The man and girl who had come in earlier were arguing, snarling at each other.

The man suddenly reached out and grabbed the girl's wrist, his fingers digging into her flesh. She winced with pain, but didn't cry out.

"You're hurting me!" she hissed between clenched teeth.

"Shut up, Becky!" A nasty smile of enjoyment appeared on the man's face. He was about thirty, and very big. He looked like a football player. He was well dressed, very clean cut, with a neat and well-scrubbed look. Incongruously, he had a gold ring in his left ear. Becky looked to be about eighteen or nineteen.

She tried to stand up. He jerked her back down hard.

"Just behave yourself!" he barked at her.

The people in the bar were watching with a distant interest, as if it were all a T.V. show. Ted wondered why no one was doing anything to help the young woman. The muscles in his legs were knotting and unknotting as he tried to decide what to do. He wasn't any better than the rest of them, he decided. He wasn't doing anything, either.

"Let go!" Becky shouted, no longer trying to keep quiet. "Johnny!"

Johnny twisted her wrist cruelly. "Promise to behave?"

Becky shook her head obstinately. A tear rolled down her cheek. Johnny dug his fingers still deeper into her wrist and she gasped in sudden pain. Ted's muscles tensed as he got ready to jump up.

She suddenly cried out, "I promise!" and Johnny let go.

Ted slumped back in his chair feeling nothing but hate for himself. He should have done something! He often imagined that other people had a solid core of selfhood inside themselves to which they could turn for strength. But when he looked inside himself there was a hollowness, a starry, black, fathomless void.

And he felt that nothingness now and knew he would never be able to protect Jill from the unknown danger that faced her.

"Doesn't that make sense?" Frank asked him suddenly.

Ted looked at him blankly. "What?"

Frank threw his hands in the air. "Weren't you listening? I said the whole thing probably comes from insecurity. You lost your parents and your sister. And now you are subconsciously afraid that you will lose Jill too. So it's your subconscious that created what you call your vision. Doesn't that make sense?"

"Yeah," Ted said wearily. "I'd probably agree with you if you were talking about someone else. But you're talking about me! I know what happened!"

"Well, I don't know what else to say. I wish I could help you feel better."

"I don't want to feel better! I want to understand what it all *means!* Jill is in danger! But I don't know how! I don't even know where to start in trying to figure it out! And you aren't helping by telling me I'm crazy!"

"Calm down!" Frank ordered. "People are looking!"

The people around them had their necks craned looking at the two men. Even the girl called Becky was looking at them, her eyes red and puffy. Ted thought he saw reproach there. He could have done something to help her, but he hadn't. He had failed her. Just as he was going to fail Jill.

His hands started to shake spasmodically. He put them out of sight in his lap.

Frank looked at his watch. "I've got a class soon. Let's go back."

"You go. I'll stay here."

"It's one-thirty. Don't you have a class?"

"Yeah, at two. I'm not going."

"But Ted!"

"Do you think I give a damn about a class! And even if I did do you think I could give a lecture in the state I'm in?"

Frank stared at his friend a moment. "No," he said finally, "I guess not."

Frank stood up and turned to leave, but then turned around again and put his hand on Ted's shoulder. "Try to get control of yourself. You're coming up for tenure soon, you know. You're going to ruin your chances if you're not careful."

"Just go, Frank!"

Frank shrugged. "Okay," he said, and left.

Ted hunched over the table. He started to pour himself some more beer, but his hand shook so badly he nearly dropped the heavy pitcher. He put it down with a thunk and looked up to see if anyone had been watching.

He met the young woman's eyes. They were still red and streaked with mascara. She had been shredding a paper napkin and little pieces of it littered the floor and table.

Johnny, the gold ring glistening in his ear, leaned over and grabbed her chin, making her lips pucker out stupidly.

"Look at me!" he barked, twisting her head around. "You *are* going to do it! Get that into your thick skull right now!"

Ted felt like snakes were writhing in his stomach. He wanted to smash Johnny—wanted to wipe the ugly sneer off his face and make him realize he couldn't treat people like that. But he didn't move.

Viciously, Johnny pushed Becky back in her chair,

leaving white finger marks on her cheeks. Ted jumped up at last. Johnny shot a menacing look at him and he felt like he was going to throw up. His whole body started shaking and his legs gave way. He fell back in his chair.

Johnny said loudly, "Asshole."

Ted dropped his eyes and stared at the empty beer glass. He felt his face going red. A feeling of self-hate swept over him. How was he ever going to save Jill? He couldn't even muster the courage to face a common bully. He *was* an asshole. A weak, spineless, asshole!

Johnny got up from his chair. "I gotta take a piss," he told Becky. "You just stay where you are."

Ted watched him swagger down the length of the big room and disappear around a corner into the men's room. He turned to the girl.

"Why don't you leave?" he asked.

She didn't seem to have heard him. She had a finger in her mouth, chewing on a nail. Ted looked toward the men's room quickly and then got up and went over to her. He had to help her. For *Jill's* sake, he had to help her.

"Why don't you leave?" he repeated in a loud whisper.

The girl jerked her head up to look at him and he realized for the first time how young she was. She had a lot of make-up on, but it had been inexpertly applied even before her tears had streaked it. God! She couldn't have been more than fourteen or fifteen! What the hell was she doing with somebody like Johnny? The utter fear in her eyes was pathetic. In a way, she reminded him of Sally.

She stared at him a moment and then said so softly Ted could barely hear it, "I can't."

"Sure you can. Just get up and leave."

She shook her head. "I'm afraid."

Ted squatted down next to her. "What's the matter?" he asked tenderly.

"He—he wants me to work for him," she said, ripping a napkin to shreds.

"What do you mean?"

"He wants me to *work* for him. You know . . . prostitute. He wants to be my pimp!"

Ted stared at her in shock. She was only a kid! "You've got to get away from him!" he said at last, his voice urgent.

"I don't have anywhere to go."

"Do you need money?" Ted stood up and pulled out his wallet. He had thirty–five dollars. He held it all out to her.

"Come on! Take it!" he urged. "You can get a room tonight and call your parents."

Becky made no move to take it. Her eyes weren't on Ted. She was looking beyond him fearfully.

"Take it!" Too late, Ted realized what she was looking at. He swirled around to see Johnny a foot behind him, a nasty smile on his face.

Johnny stood with his arms folded across his chest, utterly confident in himself. Ted was a tall man, but the other had a good three inches on him and looked about fifty pounds heavier. He had a jagged scar running down his right cheek that Ted hadn't seen before.

He looked at Ted as if he were a worm he could squash under his boot. "Trying to score off my chick, man?" he sneered.

"She told me you want her to prostitute for you."

"Well, Becky here is a liar!" Johnny let his arms fall to his side and clenched his fists. "I'll deal with her later. Right now, why don't you just stick your tail between your legs and walk out of here like a good little doggy."

"I-I d-don't think she's lying." Ted stuttered.

"Who cares what you think, asshole? You want to step outside so we can settle this?" Johnny took a step forward.

Out of the corner of his eye Ted could see the people in the bar staring at him. Some of the men had stood up for a better view. A woman shouted, "Show him! Show the bully!" A few others seemed to feel like her, wanting to see Ted mop the floor with Johnny. But most just wanted to see a fight.

"We can go outside if you want," Ted said, his voice sounding strangely distant. "But first I want Becky to leave."

He took a quick step back away from Johnny so he wouldn't have to turn his back on him and stuffed the thirty-five dollars into Becky's hand. "Take this and get out!"

The bar was hushed.

Becky wasn't moving.

"She ain't going anywhere without me, asshole!" Johnny growled. He put a beefy hand in the middle of Ted's chest and pushed him back hard. Ted staggered but quickly caught his balance.

An eager "Ah!" arose from the crowd and then there was a deeper, expectant silence. Ted could feel every eye in the room on him, waiting to see what he would do. Why didn't he turn tail and run? It wasn't his fight! He wasn't going to help the girl by getting beaten to a bloody pulp! But he couldn't run away. For Jill's sake, he couldn't run away.

Ignoring Johnny, he turned to Becky. "What do you want? You can leave if you want to!"

"She wants you to get the fuck out of here!" Johnny shouted.

"I'm asking her!" Ted shot back. Now he purposely turned his back on Johnny to kneel down beside the girl. *Let him try hitting me while my back is turned,* he thought. *He won't do it because he'll lose face.*

"I'll keep this ox here till you can get away," he told her. "Go on! *Leave,* damn it!"

Biting her lower lip, Becky stood up slowly.

"Don't you leave, chick!" Johnny shouted. "I'm warning you!"

Ted kept himself between Johnny and Becky. He *had* to do this. Somehow, he had to do it for Jill. "Go on! Get out!" he yelled.

Without a word, the girl turned and ran out the door.

Ted whirled around expecting to find a big fist flying through the air at him. But Johnny was just standing there staring at him, working the muscles in his jaw. His face was red with anger. The crowd was silent, waiting expectantly. Hoping for blood, Ted thought.

"Okay," Ted said, swallowing hard. "We can have that fight now." Would Johnny wait to go outside or leap on him here, he wondered. He waited tensely, but Johnny didn't move.

"Well?" Ted asked.

"Fuck you!" Johnny spat.

Ted stared at him warily. Johnny stared back, his eyes flooded with rage. Then he looked away. It took a minute for Ted to realize there wasn't going to be a fight.

Others were reaching that same conclusion. The crowd ended its self-imposed silence. Ted could tell they were disappointed. He wondered how he would have made out if there really had been a fight. Not too well, he thought.

Maybe there was hope. He had stood up to the bully. He no longer hated himself so much.

The tension draining out of him quickly, he felt himself start to tremble. He didn't want Johnny to see it, so he turned on his heel and walked out the front door into the bright afternoon sun and the refreshing ocean breeze.

He hadn't taken five steps away from the door when he heard it crash open behind him. He started to turn around, but he wasn't quick enough. It was like a pile-driver smashing into him. The first blow hit him over his left kidney. He started to fall. Another blow slammed into his right kidney.

The pain was excruciating. He fell to the gravel pavement and just before he passed out, a thought came to him. *He had failed.*

When he came to a few minutes later, he rolled over on his back and saw the people from the bar clustered around him. Johnny wasn't among them.

"Where is he?" he demanded.

"He left," a heavy, middle-aged woman answered.

A young man agreed. "He's gone."

Wincing from the pain in his sides, Ted got to his feet, pushed his way through the people, and staggered back inside the bar to the men's room. Johnny had probably caught up with Becky, he thought. He should have stayed out of it. He had only made matters worse. He didn't want to think about how Johnny would be punishing her now.

He splashed cold water over his face, then examined himself in the mirror. His clothes were dirty, but nothing else showed.

He got a bus back to the university to collect his car and drove home. Then he showered and changed into clean clothes so that when Jill got home from work she wouldn't see anything wrong.

She didn't have a chance to take off her coat before he took her in his arms and squeezed her tight.

"Well!" Jill exclaimed. "You're certainly affectionate tonight!"

"I love you Jill! I love you so much!"

She pulled away. "You're trembling, darling! What's the matter?"

"Just a chill, I guess. That's all." He pulled her close again and held her tight. He had decided to tell her nothing of his vision. Something horrible awaited her, but what could he tell her? He wished he could freeze time, keeping her forever as safe and happy as she was at this moment.

"Let me take my coat off," she whispered, extricating herself from his arms. She looked at him with concern. "Are you sure there's nothing wrong? You look worried."

"I'm just tired, that's all."

"Are you sure? You can tell me—"

"Really Jill! There's nothing wrong!" He forced a laugh. "You don't have to cluck over me like a mother hen!"

Jill smiled. "I'm sorry honey. I guess I'm just feeling a bit on edge myself."

"Why?" Ted asked with alarm. "What happened?"

"Oh, nothing serious. I just had a difficult patient for my last appointment." It had been an hour of sheer tension, she thought. Larry had been impossible, fairly bursting with hostility and paranoia. She wanted to kick herself for ever promising to go see him this weekend. She should have bitten her tongue! But she had promised. And she supposed she would have to go through with it.

After dinner, she left for her dance class. Relieved at no longer having to keep up a normal facade, Ted collected the dishes and stacked them in the dishwasher. The ordinariness of the action helped him to keep control of the thoughts screaming out loud in his head.

He worked quickly and efficiently until a sudden realization sent a wave of fear racing through him. Jill was out alone in the night! It had been nighttime in his vision! He threw down the pot he was holding and ran out of the kitchen. He had to go get her! He flew through the front door and raced frantically down the front steps, coming to an abrupt halt at the bottom.

"Dear God!" he moaned.

He couldn't go get her. He had no idea where her dance class was held.

The next two hours were torture. He paced the living room like a caged animal, sweating from fear and tension. Every time a car climbed the hill, he ran out to the balcony, hoping to see her home early. But she didn't come home early.

Finally, he did see her small Toyota laboring up the hill. Tears of relief streamed down his cheeks. He ran inside, turned on the television, and sat down in front of it. If he pretended to be absorbed in a show, maybe she wouldn't notice what a nervous wreck he was.

She came in, still hot and tingling from a strenuous dance class. "Hi!" she called. "I'm back."

"How was your class?" He glanced at her, then quickly looked back to the television.

Jill's heart skipped a beat. The glimpse of his face had been so brief she couldn't be sure it wasn't her imagination—but for a moment there he had looked like a very frightened little boy.

"I had a good time," she said uneasily, sitting down beside him. She put her arm around him. He felt stiff and tense. It was only a deodorant commercial, but he was staring at the T.V. as if it was the most interesting thing in the world.

"Are you okay?" she asked.

"Of course!" he answered, not moving.

She took her arm away and leaned back. She was frustrated, but she didn't want to make something out of nothing. She was more puzzled than anything by his behavior. But, she told herself, he had always been reticent and awkward with his own emotions. He didn't talk about himself easily. Perhaps he was just tired. Or maybe he was worried about something at the university. He was coming up for tenure soon, she knew. Maybe he was preoccupied with that.

She gave him a kiss and stood up. "I need a shower badly," she said, adding coyly, "Want to come in with me?"

Ted glanced at her furtively. "No, Jill, not now."

"Okay." She shrugged.

He watched her walk down the hall and sighed deeply. He wondered how much time he had left with her. A month? A week? A day? Or maybe it wasn't a real vision at all. Maybe Frank was right and it was all just his subconscious. It was true that this time none of it made any sense—it was nothing like his first visions. Maybe he was cracking up! That was his only hope!

Then something from the television broke through his tangled thoughts. He jumped up.

The local news was on. A man bathed in the harsh glare of television lights was standing in front of a North Beach restaurant. A microphone was thrust in front of him. He was talking very rapidly about a woman whose eyes burned with fire.

CHAPTER 6

Emilio's was a small restaurant set on the corner of a block in San Francisco's North Beach area. Broad windows faced out on both cross streets and white tablecloths covered a dozen tables. It felt like a man's place, smelled like a man's place, and there usually wasn't a woman to be seen in it. When Ted arrived in the early morning there were just a small knot of men there, clustered around the bar.

Ted soon recognized the man he had seen on the news. Joe Frantini was the center of attention for the men around him—the bartender, his fellow waiters, one or two regular patrons, and people who had just walked in off the street.

Joe was holding his hands up in a gesture of defiance, even the one that was in a fresh white cast and restrained by a sling.

"I tell you she threw me!" he said. "She picked me up and threw me through the air!"

He held up the cast in front of his face, shaking it. "And this is my proof!"

Joe Frantini was a third-generation San Franciscan. He was an older man with a big cannonball of a head, bald and shiny and set on a short bull neck. He talked fiercely, and when he talked he liked to gesture with his hands. A scratchy, low-fidelity record of the great tenor Caruso was playing in a back room and Joe's hands seemed to follow the golden voice in the air, rising and falling as Caruso went up and down the scale, even trembling in response to the singer's vibrato. When Joe spoke he expected people to listen and take him seriously. He watched his audience like a hawk, his low, bushy gray-black eyebrows over eyes ready to glare away the slightest sign of skepticism.

A waiter called Tony, young and pink-cheeked, stood out from the other men, who were mostly Joe's age. Tony stuck his elbow into the man next to him, a well-dressed man in a vested suit of banker's grey called Max. "She threw him. Sounds to me more like a bottle of booze threw him."

Joe's hands came to an abrupt halt in the air. He turned fiercely to Tony. "Bah!" he spat. "What do you know? Your momma still has to put you in diapers."

Joe appreciated the laughter his audience directed at Tony for a moment, then continued, "I tell you it happened! You don't believe me? It happened!"

In Joe's world there was only black and white, right and wrong. There was no room for shades of grey, no use for subtlety. Because of this he missed things that others saw, but he also saw clearly things other people passed by. While others would deliberate, weigh and balance all sides of an issue, Joe stuck to the plain facts. And the plain fact of it was that a naked young woman, hardly more than a girl really, had thrown him through the air and broken his wrist. And the plain fact of it was that she was filled with evil.

Ted stood on the outer fringes of the small crowd watching Joe's fierce countenance scan his audience. He could tell that the waiter was enjoying all the attention the television story had brought him. The only thing he couldn't tell yet was whether Joe was telling the truth, or whether, as Tony had said, it was just a bottle that threw him.

Joe called out to the man in the gray suit. "Hey Max! You're dressed so fine, you must be smart. What do you think?"

Max smiled, shrugged. "I don't know, Joe."

"Hey," Joe said. "You can speak your mind with us. You come here so much we consider you an honorary Italian!"

Max joined in the laughter of the other men and then responded, "An honorary Italian? I always considered you guys honorary Jews!"

This produced gales of laughter.

"The thing is," Max said, "I don't know the story."

"I'd tell it again," Joe said. "But I don't know if the diaper boy here will let me."

Tony's face turned red for the second time that morning. "Jesus, Joe! Give me a break!"

Max got a bill out of his wallet and handed it to the bartender. "Pete, give Joe some wine. Not the stuff you give me. The good stuff."

Joe looked at Max appreciatively. "But who cares what Tony thinks?"

Ted looked at the wine Pete set down on the bar. He badly wanted a drink himself, but he had to keep his head clear.

Joe took a sip of the wine. "It was late at night," he began, "sometime after midnight, not last night, the night before, and I was here with some of the boys. Pete was here that night, weren't you, Pete?" Joe looked at the bartender.

"Yeah."

"Anyways, I'm walking home along Chestnut and it's pretty late at night. I've had a few to drink, but I'm not drunk. You guys know I can hold my drink, no matter what diaper boy says. So I'm walking along Chestnut and I pass that little alley that's about two blocks from here, and I hear this noise coming out of it, a very strange noise. I look down the alley and it's pretty dark. The light from the street lamp only reaches in a few feet. I say to myself, 'Joe, you don't want to go down there, could be some punk there with a knife or a gun,' and I turn around to keep on going home. But then this sound comes again, and I say to myself, 'Maybe somebody is in trouble. You just can't walk away from somebody in trouble.' So I turn around again and look into the alley. I don't run in right away. I'm not stupid. I take a few steps in slowly, trying to figure out what's going on, you know? I don't want to run my stomach into a knife. That won't help anybody. I look into the darkness and don't see anything at first. And then I see some kind of movement and I ask who's there. But nobody answers."

Joe stopped a moment and looked around at his audience, satisfying himself that they were paying the proper attention. He took a drink of his wine.

"So what'd you see?" Max asked.

"I'm coming to that. Like I said, I see some kind of movement and call out, but nobody answers. I start to walk into the alley, when all of a sudden, this girl comes staggering backwards into the light from the street lamp. I knew right away that she's in trouble. She's small, hardly five feet, I guess, and she has long dark hair down to her waist. And she doesn't have no clothes on!"

"Huzzah, huzzah!" someone said.

Joe shot Tony a dirty look.

"It wasn't me, Joe!" Tony exclaimed. "Honest!"

"Anyway, there wasn't anything sexy about her. I see her there and sex is the furthest thing from my mind, even though she's young and from what I can see she's got a good figure. Like I said, I know she's in trouble! She kind of staggers halfway into the light and stops there, her back still to me. She's moving funny. And she's making strange gurgling sounds, like pouring wine out of a gallon jug. I think, right away, drugs. With kids these days it's got to be drugs. I take a step toward her and I'm kind of worried. I'm not worried about handling her. I know I can handle her. But she's naked as the day she was born and what would happen if somebody comes and sees me with her in this dark alley at night? They might think I'm some sex maniac trying to rape this girl. And if she's hopped up on drugs she might think the same thing and start screaming. So you see my problem? I want to help, but I don't want to find myself in a big mess with the cops and my wife crying and all my friends thinking I'm a sex maniac."

Joe paused for another sip of wine. Ted kept his eyes on him nervously.

"So I approach her real careful, not knowing what to expect, not wanting to get in trouble. I get within reaching distance almost and all of a sudden she starts thrashing around like she's being eaten alive by ants or something and starts screaming bloody murder! 'Oh God!' she screams. 'Oh God! NO! NO!' Well, that gets me moving. I forget about whether she's going to think I'm a rapist and I reach out and grab her. The way she's thrashing around and screaming, I'm afraid she's going to fall and smash her head open on the concrete. But I can hardly keep hold of her! I try to hold her still, but it's no use. She's got the strength of a man and that's no shit. I try to yell at her to calm down, try to tell her everything is going to be all right. But she doesn't even seem to realize I'm there."

Joe looked away distantly. He wasn't seeing the men around him or the restaurant. He was seeing what had happened that dark night. No one in the place was making a sound. Even those who had heard the story before were waiting expectantly for Joe to continue.

When he started again, his voice was hushed and

somber. "Now here comes the first thing you might not believe. It's up to you. But I know what I saw. I'm holding her by her arms, using all my strength to try and hold her still, and she's in front of me, facing away from me. And while I'm there holding her like that, trying to get her to calm down, her head starts turning. It starts turning and doesn't stop! It turns all the way around to face me! Understand what I'm saying? She's got her back to me and her head turns all the way around backwards to face me! I am so spooked I don't even notice her eyes yet and I let go of her so quick I almost fall over backwards. And then I see her eyes. Her eyes . . . I don't know how to describe them. They were red. They were red like smoldering fires. They were glowing!"

He paused, his eyes still distant, unseeing, his face taking on the shock and fear he must have felt. No one looking at him could think he did not believe every single word of what he was telling them.

Ted felt as if Joe were recounting his own vision. Following Joe's story, he didn't picture some nameless, faceless girl. He saw Jill. He saw Jill terrified, fighting something he couldn't see, her body thrashing violently. He saw Jill as her face suddenly constricted into a mass of evil hate. He saw Jill's eyes blazing with fire.

"Well . . ." Joe sighed. "Her eyes are on me and they're horrible. She keeps her face toward me, not moving it, and turns her body around so finally everything is lined up in the right direction. And her eyes are still on me and I feel like I'm going to die. Honest to God, I feel like I'm dying the way her eyes are on me. I start a Hail Mary—I can't remember it very well, but I try—and her evil eyes, glowing like bright red torches, just keep boring into me deeper and deeper and I feel like I'm dead already. I feel like I'm dead and in hell. And the next thing I know, I'm flying through the air. The girl—or whatever it was—just picked me up and threw me like I was made of paper."

Joe shook his head slowly, looking suddenly very old and frail. He picked up his wine glass and emptied it. Looking at him, Ted realized he was telling the truth. It was impossible for eyes to burn with fire—and yet it had happened! It had happened to that girl and it would happen to Jill! Breaking the silence, he asked nervously, "What happened to the girl?"

Joe shrugged. "I didn't see. I was on the ground holding my broken wrist. She ran off somewhere, I guess."

"But you must have seen something!" Ted insisted. He *had* to know what had happened to her!

"I tell you I don't know!" Joe said angrily. "I was lying on the ground!"

What could have made the girl's eyes glow? Ted asked himself. What on earth could do something like that? Nothing! It was impossible!"

He remembered something from his vision. "Was there a strange light?" he asked. "A beam of red light over her head?"

Joe fixed a wary gaze on Ted. "No, there wasn't any red light," he said slowly. "Weren't you listening? I said her eyes glowed red. That's all."

"No offense, Joe," the bartender said. "But eyes can't glow. It just ain't possible!"

"I don't know about possible," Joe replied. "I just know what I saw."

A white-haired man, looking very frail and ancient, moved out from the others closer to Joe. Ted hadn't noticed him before, but he looked vaguely familiar. He studied the old man intently. He was poorly dressed, but his face looked kind and his voice was surprisingly strong.

"We should not be too certain of what is possible and

what is not," he said. "Perhaps it *is* possible for eyes to glow."

Joe looked dumbfounded at this unexpected support.

The old man continued. "What do you think she was?"

Joe moved his hand up in the air. He didn't reply right away. "What was she?" he wondered out loud after a moment. "Something not human. Or something that was human once, but not anymore."

"Yes, I see." The frail old man nodded as if he understood exactly what Joe meant.

But Ted didn't understand, didn't understand it at all. "What do you mean, not human any more?" he interrupted, knowing his voice sounded wild and desperate.

Joe shot a wary look at him again. "She was a young girl, yes. I suppose about 19 or 20. But she didn't *look* like a young girl. She just didn't look human! I can't explain it."

The old man said, "That's not surprising," and started to say something more when the restaurant's front door banged open and a young man called out:

"Hey Joe! Looks like Bob Santini found your girl in the lot behind his place. He's just called the cops. If you hurry you can still get a look at her."

Questions became impossible as the men around the bar broke away and ran to the door. In the rush, the white-haired old man was thrown back against Ted. Ted caught him and held him upright. The room emptied quickly, leaving the two of them behind.

"Thank you," the old man said.

A paper bag the man had been carrying was on the floor by Ted's feet. He picked it up and handed it to him.

"What did he mean?" Ted asked. "Why did he call the cops? Is the girl dead? She can't be dead!"

The old man looked at him kindly. "I'm afraid she

could very well be dead," he said sadly.

"She can't be!" Ted exclaimed, and ran out of the restaurant.

He caught up with the others at the entrance to the alley where Joe had encountered the girl. Crowding in with them through a small door at the end of the alley, he followed them through a dark, cluttered storage room to another door and outside into a cement-covered square filled with smelly garbage cans and surrounded by high fences. It was a clear day and the bright, late-morning sun reflected blindingly off the white concrete. A putrid smell was coming from the garbage cans. Flies swarmed everywhere.

The men had run out of Emilio's but now they were moving cautiously. Ted kept his distance behind them, dreading what he was going to see but knowing that no matter what he would have to look with the others.

They stopped their uncertain milling when the man who had come to the restaurant with the news pointed to a corner. "She's there, behind the cans."

Ted felt his heart sink as hope drifted away.

The young waiter called Tony was standing in front of the cans. He turned around and peered behind them and then quickly straightened up. His face was pale, drained of blood. No one moved as the young man pushed by them and out of the stench-filled lot.

There was a moment of hesitation and then Pete the bartender stepped up to the cans.

"We might as well all get a look," he said.

Joe spoke up. "Just pull the cans out of the way, Pete."

Pete did so, scraping the bottoms of the cans across the rough concrete gratingly and sending up a swarm of buzzing flies. The harsh sound sent shivers up Ted's spine. He saw a bare leg. Then the other men moved forward, blocking his view.

There was a murmur and then an eerie silence.

The rotting smell from the garbage cans was overpowering.

Trying to breathe as little as possible, Ted moved up and looked over Max's shoulder. The sunlight was directly on her. She was sprawled on her back—naked, as Joe had said—one arm twisted back and under her at an unnatural angle. There were flies all over her.

"Look at her face!" someone whispered.

Ted felt sure he would vomit. He looked at the dead girl's face, her long dark hair spread around it like a fan. Her face was frozen in pure terror. The area around her eyes looked black, as if scorched by fire.

"She must have seen something—something horrible," Pete said.

"I ain't never seen a look of fear like that on a stiff's face, and I've seen plenty," someone else put in.

"Well, she saw Joe, didn't she?" came another voice.

There was a nervous giggle that died quickly.

"Have some respect for the dead!" Joe hissed fiercely.

Ted stared down at the horrible gray face frozen in death. The world started spinning dizzily and for a shattering moment, Jill's face replaced the young girl's. He saw *Jill* lying there, her face frozen, the area around her eyes scorched as if by fire.

Then Max was large in front of him, looking concerned. "You okay?"

Ted backed away a step. "Yeah, sure."

He swallowed hard to keep his stomach down. The smell of the garbage seemed to be entering every pore of his body. Then he realized it wasn't just garbage he was smelling and his stomach heaved.

The frail, white-haired old man he had left back at the restaurant came into the small lot and walked to the front of the crowd to look down at the dead girl.

"She won't be the last one, I'm afraid," he said sadly.

"The cops wouldn't believe me before," Joe whispered. "Now maybe they'll listen. It happened exactly the way I said."

Ted backed away from the others. It was getting harder and harder to keep his stomach down. The old man's words echoed through his mind. *She won't be the last one. She won't be the last one.* He backed into an overflowing garbage can and knocked it over. Rotted black pieces of meat coated with maggots spilled out with swarming clouds of flies. In his blinding panic to get away, his foot went down into the middle of it all. He found the door finally, stumbled through the dark storage room and out into the alley.

And then his stomach exploded. He propped himself up against a brick wall, let his head hang down, and his belly heaved and heaved until it was empty.

He left the alley on unsteady legs to see half a dozen cops piling out of two police cars that were blocking the street. They ignored him and hurried down the alley. He wandered down the block a short way and sat down on the broad steps of an apartment house. There was a slight breeze and it felt good. He breathed it in deeply, trying to get rid of the stench from the hot enclosed lot. The old man's words still ran through his mind like a broken record. *She won't be the last one, I'm afraid. She won't be the last one.* The old man knew something! And he was familiar. Ted was sure he had seen him before.

An ambulance pulled up behind the police cars. Ted watched the attendants get out and unload a wheeled litter. They disappeared into the alley, leaving behind them the sound of their radio randomly spewing out squawks and voices.

Ted took a deep breath and let it out slowly. He tried to think of where he had seen the old man before. He seemed to remember it was at night, outside somewhere. But where?

In his vision!

He had seen an old man's face at the very beginning and had called out to him for help! It was him!

He jumped up from the steps and raced back to the alley. Hurrying out of the dark store room into the bright lot, the stench hit him immediately. His stomach wanted to start heaving again, but he swallowed hard and willed it to be quiet. He looked around trying to spot the old man. A guy in plain-clothes was over near the far corner, straddling the dead girl's body, clicking off picture after picture on his camera. The ambulance attendants stood a few feet away, waiting, a plastic body bag at their feet. They looked bored. Another two men, guns under their sport coats, notebooks in their hands, had cornered Joe. Joe was red-faced, yelling at them angrily that they didn't have to read him his rights, he knew his rights and he had just tried to help the poor girl, that's all. Didn't they remember he had gone to them yesterday to tell them about it? Didn't they remember that they hadn't paid any attention? Max stood by nervously, shifting his weight from one foot to the other, back and forth. Pete the bartender looked sick.

Ted took them all in and didn't see the old man. Where the hell was he? he asked himself in a panic. He moved over to Max and grabbed his arm. "Where's the old man?"

Max looked a little ill. "Who?" he asked weakly.

"He was here just a minute ago. With all the white hair! I've got to talk to him!"

"Oh, him." Max looked around the lot. "I don't see him. I guess he must have left."

Ted asked him if he knew the old man, but Max had never seen him before. Ted turned away abruptly and cornered Pete. But Pete didn't even know who he was talking about.

He turned around to see the ambulance attendants trying to stuff the girl's unwieldy body into the plastic body bag. Her arms and legs flopped around grotesquely as the men struggled with her and he looked away quickly. That was what would happen to Jill! He *had* to find the old man!

He ran back through the store room, up the alley, and onto Chestnut Street, hoping the old guy hadn't gotten far. He searched up and down the street frantically and couldn't find him. Then he thought he might have gone back to Emilio's and raced back there.

No one was there but Tony, fiddling absent-mindedly with the place settings at one of the tables. No, he said, he had never seen the old man before.

"I've got to find him!" Ted shouted, running out again.

When he got back to the alley, the ambulance and one of the police cars were gone. Joe Frantini was with a couple of cops next to the other police car, still protesting his innocence and calling the cops stupid bums.

Ted ran up to one of the cops. "I'm looking for an old man who was here a while ago. He had white hair and—"

"Save your breath," the cop interrupted. "I'm just a dumb cop, not allowed to say boo without permission. You'll have to talk to Lieutenant Bates." He jerked his thumb at the other cop, who was wearing civilian clothes.

Ted went up to the lieutenant, who was yelling at a red-faced Joe Frantini to shut up and get in the car, and tried to ask his question.

Bates snarled at him. "Can't you see I'm busy, mister?" He turned to the other cop. "Come on, Finch! Stop playing with yourself and help me get this turkey in the car!"

"But I'm telling you the truth!" Joe Frantini yelled.

"I don't think he's involved in this," Ted said. "There was an old man here—"

"Get out of the way!" Bates shouted. "And shut up!"

Ted reluctantly moved aside as the two cops grabbed the protesting waiter and maneuvered him into the back seat of their car and slammed the door, then he moved up and grabbed Bates's elbow.

Bates whirled around and yanked his arm away. "Beat it!" he yelled.

"I'm looking for an old man," Ted persisted. "He was in that lot a while ago. Did you get his name?"

Bates thrust his fist up next to Ted's face. "If you want to talk to me, come down to my office at Central Station. Now, beat it!" He opened the front door and got in the car.

Ted grabbed the handle. "But I just want his name! He knows something!"

"Tough shit!" Bates pulled the door away from Ted and slammed it. Ted clenched his fists in anger as the car pulled away, its tires squealing. There was nothing for it but to play the cop's game and go to his office. He had to find the old man!

All that afternoon, Ted paced up and down the yellowed corridor outside Bates's office on the third floor of Central Station. By five o'clock the building started to empty. The sounds of people's conversations, of steps going down the stairs, of doors opening and slamming, swelled loud for a few minutes and then died away leaving behind lonely silence. It was dark out. Ted's nerves were shot and he wanted to get home to Jill, to make sure she was safe. As long as it was light out, she was safe, he had decided. But now it was dark.

He couldn't wait for Bates any longer. He went to the elevator and pushed the button, then turned away indecisively. He had to find the old man, and to do that he had to talk to Bates! The elevator door swept open and he didn't get in.

Half an hour later, he decided to phone Jill.

She answered on the third ring.

"Jill? I'm glad you're home!"

"Ted? Where are you?"

"I'm busy," he replied, trying to keep the nervousness out of his voice. "I'm not sure when I'll be home and I want you to promise me something."

"What's the matter?"

"Oh . . . uh, something came up. I'll get home as soon as I can, but I don't know when that will be. Meanwhile I want you to promise me you won't go out. Stay inside."

"Ted, I don't understand—"

"Please, Jill! I can't explain. Just promise you won't go out for any reason. No matter what, understand?"

"I wasn't planning to go out, anyway, Ted. But I don't—"

"Good! Stay home and I'll be there in a little while! Okay?"

There was no answer.

"Please, Jill! It's important!"

"All right," Jill answered finally, her voice showing her uneasiness.

"I love you, Jill."

Ted hung up the pay phone, heard some mechanism inside it gobble up his coin, and ran a nervous hand through his hair. Then he climbed the stairs wearily to the third floor.

Bates was just unlocking his office door.

"Lieutenant Bates!" he shouted, and ran down the hall to the cop.

Bates looked up at him questioningly, then broke into a leering smile. "Oh, it's you," he said, opening his door. "Come on in." Ted followed him inside.

Bates was impeccably dressed in a dark blue suit, cut so that only the slightest bulge showed from the revolver in his shoulder holster, and the way he carried himself showed years of police discipline. Everything about him was rigid and controlled—everything except his face. The features of the lieutenant's face seemed to operate independently of each other and he seemed to be in a constant battle against anarchy, pulling down an unruly eyebrow here, replacing a curled lip there, and generally having to crack the whip to keep all his features in formation. He was looking at Ted quizzically now, his left eyebrow jerking up and down erratically.

"I just have one question," Ted said, "the same one I asked earlier. There was an old man in that lot with the dead girl. He was shabbily dressed, had white hair and a thin face with wrinkled skin. Do you know who he is?"

Not answering, Bates simply stared at Ted. The way he was examining him reminded Ted of Brad Hawswer in the fifth grade and the way Brad would come up to him in the playground and stare at him, gauging his size and strength and whether he could be pushed around.

"Do you know who he is?" Ted demanded again.

"So, you're interested in that dead girl," Bates said. "Why?"

"I'm interested in the old man," Ted countered.

"Why?"

Ted shrugged. "It's kind of complicated. I've got my reasons. I'm a concerned citizen."

The lieutenant's eyes opened wide. "Oh! A concerned citizen! Fine!" He slapped his hands together and went behind his desk. "And I've got some work to do, and it's late, so if you'll excuse me . . ."

"Wait!" Ted shouted, rushing forward. "I think I can help."

"That's better." Bates smiled unpleasantly. "Tell me what you know, Mr. Concerned Citizen."

"I don't know anything, that's the point! But I think that old man I told you about does!"

"But you don't know anything yourself, is that it?"

"Right," Ted lied. There was no way he would tell Bates about his vision.

"Well, if you don't know anything, I don't need to talk to you. The door's right behind you, Mr. Concerned Citizen."

"Give me a chance!" Ted exploded. "I've been waiting all afternoon to see you!" And before Bates could make another comment, he told him some of the things the old man had said. "And the last thing I heard was, 'She won't be the last one, I'm afraid.' So he *must* know something!"

"That's very interesting." Bates walked around to the front of his desk and sat on its edge. His lips did a little dance. "There *was* a strange old man there, muttering to himself. I know who you're talking about now."

Ted's heart leaped. "Did you talk to him? Did you get his name?"

Bates indicated a wooden chair in front of the desk and asked Ted to sit. "To tell the truth," the cop said, "I didn't talk to the old guy."

Ted moaned. He had waited all afternoon for nothing.

"We were concentrating on that waiter, Frantini," Bates continued. "But we couldn't shake his story an inch. We had to let him go." Bates paused a moment, then asked, "So you think this old guy knows something?"

"I'm sure of it," Ted said, realizing all hope was not lost. Bates would want to find the old man, and with the resources of the police, he *could* find him.

"You think he knew Billie Martin?" Bates asked.

"Who?"

"The deceased. We got a positive ID on her from her

roommate, her former roommate I should say, Cindy Schultz. We took her down to the morgue this afternoon. Made her turn kind of green, but she made the ID. She was positive."

Ted could picture the scene and felt sorry for the girl. "I don't know if the old man knew her. I doubt it. But he knows something about what happened to her. I'm sure of it."

"The roommate told us a lot of garbage the night Billie disappeared. It was the night before Joe Frantini found her. Boy, did she tell us garbage! We had to take her down to the psych ward at General Hospital."

"Did she know anything about what made Billie's eyes glow?"

Bates jerked his head back. "Eyes glow? You're not telling me you believe that shit!"

"I—I, well. . . ." Ted fumbled. "Anyway, Joe Frantini seemed awfully positive about it."

"And a lot of people are positive they're Napoleon too," Bates countered. "Anyway, you may have something in the old man. But you don't know who he is, so there's not much we can do. We'll keep an eye out for him though, in case he shows up again."

"That's it?" Ted asked, stunned by the other's easy attitude. He stood up. "That's all? You're just going to keep an eye out for him? You've got to find him! He knows something. There's a dead girl and—"

"There's a dead male too, about 20, whom we haven't identified yet," Bates said, relishing Ted's surprise.

"What?" Ted blurted. "When was this?"

"Three days ago. We found him at Billie Martin's place the night she disappeared." Bates stood up and moved behind his desk. "So we have two bodies."

"Then you *must* find the old man!" Ted exclaimed. "It's vital!"

Bates shook his head. "Not at all."

"But—"

"I don't have a case, Mister. I've got two dead bodies. I've got a bunch of crazy stories. And I've got a big fat question mark. I'll tell you what I don't have."

"What's that?"

"I don't have a crime! There's no evidence of foul play, no evidence of sexual molestation, no evidence of anything illegal! And besides, the M.E.—"

"The what?"

"The M.E., the Medical Examiner. He says they both died of massive heart failure—somehow their systems overloaded."

"They were both just kids!"

Bates shrugged. "That's the way it goes."

"But something is going on! Something horrible! You've got to do something!"

"I tell you I don't have a crime!" Bates shouted. "It is the business of the police to investigate crime! It is not police business to get tangled up in strange puzzles and stories about glowing eyes!"

Waiting for a response, Bates stared at Ted. But Ted didn't have anything to say. Sighing, he turned away to look out the small dirty window into the night. Something monstrous was going on out there. But what? What could make a young woman's eyes burn with fire and then burst her heart? It sounded like the occult. But there had to be a rational explanation! And if anyone had that explanation, it was the old man. It might take him weeks to find him, but the police could do it in a day or two. Bates had to realize how important it was!

He turned back to the lieutenant. "You've admitted you don't know what's going on. It could be anything! And it's your duty to find out what! You can't wait until more and more people start turning up dead on you! You've got to help me find that old man!"

"It's been a long day," Bates said wearily. "And I'm

going home now. But don't misunderstand. I appreciate your telling me my duty. I really do."

"You're not going to look for the old man."

"Nope. I'm going home." Bates went to the door and flicked out the light. "Coming?"

"No!" Ted ran to the wall and turned the lights back on.

"Hey!" Bates barked.

"Wait! Just one minute!" Ted went to the desk, ripped a sheet of paper from a pad lying there, and scrawled his name and phone number. He thrust the paper out at Bates.

"If you find anything—anything at all—let me know."

Bates looked at the paper in Ted's trembling hand a moment, then took it and stuffed it in his pocket. "Don't hold your breath," he said.

CHAPTER 7

His breathing strained, the frail old man paused at the top of the first flight of dimly lit stairs and leaned his stooped frame on the banister. It sagged under his weight, light though he was. He wished the elevator could at least manage to work half the time. The old apartment house in the Tenderloin was a run-down fire-trap, but he could not afford better. When his heart had slowed and his breathing came easier, Simon Agoropoulos continued up the second flight, paused again, and then walked down the dirty hallway to his apartment.

It was small and dingy, with the yellowed look of old newspapers. It had a bed-sitting room, a tiny kitchen, and a bathroom with a tin stand-up shower. In the front room, there was a neatly made bed, an easy chair, and a trestle table with a straight-back chair. They were all so close together it was hard to walk between them. Without taking off his coat, the old man sat and rested in the easy chair a minute, waiting for his heart to slow. Then he got up, took off his coat, and hung it up on the back of the door over the faded 'In Case of Fire' sign. In this building there was only one thing to do in case of fire, Simon thought—Pray.

He sat down in the straight-backed chair. Three

books were on the table in front of him. A bible, a cheap composition book like the ones school-kids use, and a massive volume entitled *On Good and Evil* by Simon Agoropoulos. He had written that book thirty years ago, and it had branded him as a heretic.

Simon pulled the composition book toward him, opened it, and flipped through it to a clean page. At the top he wrote the date, "November 21, 1985."

He put the pen down and rubbed his eyes. He felt very tired. Sighing wearily, he picked up his pen again and started writing.

"It was a young girl today, about 19 or 20, I would guess. While the man who saw her, who was attacked by her in the night, admitted he had been drinking, from the way he told his story, I'm quite sure that he was not exaggerating. On the contrary, some of his friends were very skeptical and treated the whole thing as a joke. . . ."

The old man paused, thinking how strange human nature was. Men always made fun of what they could not comprehend, even when they were in danger of losing their own souls.

". . . so, if anything, I think the man probably played down the more frightening aspects of his experience.

"He mentioned several facts which cannot be overlooked, cannot, indeed, be explained in any natural fashion. First, the girl took on enormous strength, far beyond the capacity of her young body. She actually picked him up and threw him when he must have weighed twice as much as she. Secondly, she was able to move her body in unnatural ways, turning her head around to face directly backwards. Thirdly, and this is the most conclusive sign . . ."

Simon stopped again, looking over what he had written. There was something wrong with it, something off key. He had to read it over several times before he realized what it was. He had written that the girl threw the man, that the girl turned her head around. But it was obviously not the girl herself who had done these things. It had been something else, something controlling her. What had happened to the girl herself, to her soul, he did not know. But he knew she had not done those things. He thought for a moment how to reflect this fact in his writing, saw no easy way, and continued on as before.

". . . Thirdly, and this is the most conclusive sign, the man said her eyes glowed as if on fire. Surely all these things have only one meaning.

"The girl's body was found and I saw it for myself. The look of horror on the poor innocent's face was palpable. She must have seen into the bowels of hell."

Simon looked up from the composition book and shuddered as if trying to shake loose the memory of the girl's terror-struck face. He murmured a short prayer. He did it quickly, by rote and from long practice. Then he turned back to his diary.

"All this confirms in every particular what I learned from the dead girl's roommate. This is the second incident I have heard about and there will undoubtably be others.

"It is beginning at long last. The nightbroom is coming. My trial is at hand. Lord, I am so weary of waiting."

He wrote a few more minutes, then put down his pen and closed the composition book. He stayed in the chair while his fingers moved in circles around his tired eyes. His hands had the look of great age and great sensitivity. The waiting, he thought, had been the hardest part. He had been waiting for thirty years and was now so old he was afraid that when the trial came he would be too feeble to do his job. But it was coming soon now. He could see it in the night sky. He prayed that he would not fail.

His thoughts were interrupted by a soft, familiar mewing sound. Simon slid his chair back from the table and went into the kitchen to the back door. He opened the door a few inches and a jet black cat darted through.

The cat had started coming around several months ago. The old man was glad for its company. He bent over, feeling his back creak, and scooped it up off the floor. He sat down in the metal folding chair by the kitchen table and held the cat in his lap. He liked to stroke its midnight black fur.

"How can people see the devil in you, kitty?" he asked it. "All I can see is the freedom from the knowledge of good and evil. You are like man in the Garden of Eden, before he ate of the tree of knowledge, before the fall. You are innocent."

The black cat began to purr rhythmically as Simon rubbed it behind the ears. The sound made him smile, a serene, almost beatific look transforming his face, his clear blue eyes full of warmth and compassion. He truly loved his little friend.

"Well," he said at last, "I suppose you want your milk."

Simon never drank milk—it gave him indigestion—but since the black cat had started visiting him he always kept a quart in the refrigerator.

"Yes, milk is what you want, isn't it? You're not interested in a feeble old man."

The cat mewed in response and jumped to the floor. Simon gripped the hard edge of the table and unfolded his body from the chair. There was a twinge of pain in his chest. But he was always having twinges of pain there and he paid it no mind. His last bad attack had been over a year ago. He got the milk, set a bowl on the counter, and filled it full. The cat jumped up quickly on the counter, heading for the bowl of milk.

Simon scolded it gently. "Not up here, kitty."

Steadying himself with one hand, he bent over slowly and put the bowl on the floor. The cat's pink tongue was in it before he could straighten up again.

"Nice kitty," he whispered watching it lap up the milk.

Then his foot shot out in a sudden spasm and kicked the bowl over. The cat, hissing, jumped quickly away. Simon clutched at his chest. His face constricted in sudden pain and his lips drew back tight over his yellowed teeth. He staggered dizzily around the kitchen, clawing at his chest, struggling to breathe through the pain that cut into his heart like a hot knife. The startled cat looked from the man to the spilled milk and back up at the man again. The staggering man was dangerous, but there was good milk on the floor. The cat's hunger got the better of it. It crept up to the puddle of milk and hunched down low to lap it up.

His face turning red, Simon lurched crazily toward the refrigerator. The cat darted another look at him, then turned back to its milk. He hung with one arm on the refrigerator a moment, strange gurgling noise coming from him, then pushed off through the door to the front room. His head was pounding, screaming for oxygen. A monster had its sharp claws in his chest, sunk deep, twisting. He was almost blinded by the searing pain and when he reached the trestle table he could hardly see it. One hand still to his chest, he fumbled with the other over the top of the table for his bottle of pills. The cat was mewing behind him. Strangely, through the fiery hot hell of pain he felt sorry for the cat. It wanted more milk. Then his fingers finally closed around the pill bottle.

He lurched away from the table and fell back on his

small bed. The pain was so bad he couldn't work his hands to get the cap off the bottle. His fingers dug at it frantically and he remembered in sudden horror it had a child-proof cap. He had to PUSH DOWN AND TURN. But he couldn't do it! His eyes sought the large crucifix on the wall over his bed. *Dear Lord! Please!*

He had to push down and turn!

When he got the prescription at the drug store after his last attack, he had tried to open the bottle right there. It took him two minutes. He rang the bell for the pharmacist again and asked for a bottle that wasn't "child-proof."

"Can't," the pharmacist said laconically. "We're out of them."

He had meant to transfer the pills to another bottle, but never had.

His face was turning blue, his brain was screaming for oxygen, and still the monster had its sharp claws dug deep into his chest, only now it seemed to have an extra set of claws raking down his left arm. He struggled with the bottle, turning the cap. But it just went CLACK CLACK CLACK CLACK and refused to open. He couldn't turn it and keep it pushed down hard enough at the same time. Simon prayed. His head swimming, he prayed through the unbearable agony: *Please dear Lord please please let the bottle open dear Lord God.*

Finally the cap came off and pills spilled out all over. He felt for one of them and popped it into his mouth. Then he reached in under his shirt and grasped the small gold cross he always wore. The pain was getting still worse.

He knew he was blacking out, but he kept praying. The prayer was rambling, fragmented, and interrupted by bolts of lightning pain. He had to live! *Please Lord . . . . not now . . . I have waited . . . Dear God . . . . I have waited so long, Lord . . . My mission is just beginning. . . .*

A spasm of agony shot through him, making his hand jerk away from the cross. But still he prayed. *I need more time, Lord . . . just a little . . . . more . . . time . . .*

At the foot of the bed the black cat sat staring at him, mewing plaintively.

CHAPTER 8

Ted was convinced something monstrous was going on—and whatever it was, he knew he had only begun to scratch the surface. What he had learned, instead of answering questions, raised new ones. Joe Frantini's story didn't make any more sense than his own vision had. What could make a young woman's eyes fill with fire? What could give her the strength to heave a fully grown man through the air? What had killed her? The more Ted thought about it all, the more it seemed reality was coming unstuck.

The next day, he went to see Cindy Schultz, Billie Martin's roommate.

She lived in the Haight-Ashbury district in the middle of a block of tumble-down Victorians set so close together as to form an almost continuous row of buildings. The district still had not completely recovered from 1967's 'summer of love.' Though a lot of hard work had been done in some houses restoring the ornate Victorian facades, most of them were still run down and the whole area looked like a slum. Students lived there since it was one of the few places they could afford.

Ted found the house, then climbed the steep steps and knocked loudly. After a moment, the door opened to the length of the chain inside so that he could see a strip of

face—a bang of blond hair, a blue eye looking out warily, part of a small nose, some freckled skin, and half a
mouth.

"Cindy?" he asked. "Cindy Schultz?"

"I don't want to talk about it!" She tried to slam the
door, but Ted had put his foot in it.

"Please!" he implored her. "I know it must have been
very hard on you and I wouldn't bother you, but I'm
trying to stop the same thing from happening again!"

Cindy studied him a moment, her eye going up and
down.

"I'm trying to save someone's life! You've got to help
me!"

"Okay," she said at last. "Come on in."

Ted followed her up a dark stairway to the front room
of her apartment. There were boxes of books stacked up
near one wall. Some posters were on the floor—one of
Greece, another of Barry Manilow. Three bulging suit-
cases with clothes piled on top were near the door. There
was no furniture and the warped wooden floor was bare.

Ted looked at Cindy questioningly.

"I'm going home for a while," she said. "To get away.
You know . . ."

A small, unframed photograph was lying on one of
the boxes. Ted picked it up.

Cindy came up next to him. "That's Billie. It was behind a dresser and her parents missed it, I guess."

The picture showed a young woman smiling broadly,
dressed in white tennis clothes, holding a racket. She
seemed to radiate with health and vitality. Looking at it,
Ted felt a heavy sadness in his chest.

Cindy jerked away from him suddenly. "Billie had her
faults," she said thickly, on the verge of crying. "But she
didn't deserve what happened. I liked her a lot, actually."

"I'm sorry," Ted said, unable to think of anything better.

There was a heavy silence and then Cindy broke it. "Well, I suppose life goes on, doesn't it?" she said bravely. "There are some chairs in the kitchen if you'd like to sit down."

She led him to the kitchen and they sat down on old wooden chairs with peeling white paint. There was no table.

"I've got to find out what happened to Billie . . ." Ted let his voice trail off. Cindy was looking vacantly out the window as if she had forgotten he was there.

"Cindy?"

She turned to stare at him blankly. She was still in shock, he thought. Then her eyes focused on him and she seemed to come back from wherever she had been. She frowned.

"They had me under psychiatric observation at S. F. General," she said. "They wouldn't believe me. They said I was hysterical, seeing things. They said people's eyes couldn't have fire inside. They said Billie couldn't have jumped over the fence. They said—"

She stopped abruptly and looked out the window again, seeming to withdraw. Ted thought of his two years at the funny farm. "They" were always so sure of what could and could not happen. "They" always knew everything.

"I wouldn't bother you, Cindy," he said, "if there were any other way. I have to find out what happened to Billie! I'm afraid it could happen again. Can you tell me about it?"

Cindy looked around at him again, and sighed. "I was taking a shower," she began. "It was just after midnight."

* * *

Cindy was hoping the shower would revive her energy and keep her awake. She had been studying all evening for next day's economics exam and still had half the book to cover. Another last minute cram, she thought, standing under the hot spray and turning her face up directly into it. There was a whoosh of cold air.

"Hey! Close the door!" she yelled. She heard the door slam and then Billie's voice.

"Have you seen the flashlight, Cindy?"

Cindy poked her head out through the plastic shower curtain and blinked at her roommate. Billie had her heavy sweater on. "Where you going at this hour, Billie?"

"I heard something in the back yard," Billie said. "I'm going down to see what it is. But I can't find the flashlight."

"But it's after midnight! Do you think you should?"

"I'm sick and tired of those damn kids breaking things," Billie said firmly. Behind the rows of old houses was a jumble of small fenced backyards filled with debris and weeds. It was really sort of a no man's land down there, but Billie and Cindy had done a lot of work cleaning the junk out of their own small yard so they could have a little green space to themselves. But the neighborhood kids kept climbing over the old wooden fence, breaking it down more in the process, and making a mess out of their hard work. They had put some old lawn furniture down in the yard a week ago. It had lasted two days. Someone had broken the table and the two chairs had disappeared.

"Did you see anyone down there?" Cindy asked.

"No it's too dark. That's why I need the flashlight."

"I wouldn't go down there. You don't know who it might be."

"Oh come on, Cindy!" Billie said in a tone of exasperation. "I can handle a dumb kid or two."

"Some of the kids around here are pretty mean," Cindy replied doubtfully, still clutching the plastic shower curtain.

"Anyway, I'm going down. So where's the flashlight?"

Cindy shrugged. "Okay. It's your funeral. I think it's under the sink."

"Finally!" Billie turned to leave.

"Be careful!" Cindy said, adding, "I can see the headlines now: Co-ed Found Dead In Own Yard!"

Billie turned around again. "Don't get me all spooked! It's just a dumb kid!"

"Yeah, a dumb kid with a knife."

"Stop it!" Billie cried and left, leaving the door open behind her.

Swearing under her breath, Cindy climbed out of the shower dripping all over, pushed the door closed, and got back in. She spent a good ten minutes more under the hot water, relishing its massaging spray on her skin, before turning it for a quick blast of cold and jumping out. She dried herself off and wrapped a towel around her head, then opened the door a crack to let the steam escape. Feeling leisurely, she dusted herself with some bath powder while quietly humming to herself. Then, putting on her robe, she went out to see if Billie had caught anyone.

"Did you find anyone, Billie?" she asked, walking down the hall to the front room. There was no answer and no one in the front room. "Billie?" She went back to the kitchen. It was empty. "Billie! Where are you?" She went to the bedroom they shared and didn't find her.

Jesus Christ! Is she still outside? It's been ages!

An old wooden stairway ran from the kitchen down the outside of the house to the yard. Cindy opened the kitchen door and went out on the landing, thinking she was going to catch pneumonia in the cold air with only her robe on, and all because of Billie.

"Billie? Are you down there?" she shouted.

There was no answer. She went over to the railing and looked over. All she could see in the darkness was the flashlight lying on the ground, its beam orange and dim as if it had been left on too long. It was pointing at nothing.

"Billie! Where ARE you? What's going ON!" Only her own voice echoed back to her from the houses across the way. "If this is joke, its NOT funny! I'm going to catch pneumonia out here!"

She peered down into the darkness, straining her eyes to see. "Goddammit, Billie," she whispered to herself. "Where the hell are you?" As her eyes grew used to the darkness, she finally saw a movement.

"Is that you?" she called. "Billie?"

She blinked, trying to interpret the moving shapes in the darkness. They looked like bare legs. But there were more than two of them, it seemed. What the—? And now, as her eyes became accustomed to the lack of light, it looked like someone's bare ass down there. Huh? A bare ass, bobbing up and down, like . . . like . . .

Oh, God, no! NO!

"BILLIE!! BILLIE!!!" Screaming bloody murder, she tore down the stairs. Billie was being raped! It seemed to take hours to go down the two flights. She screamed all the way, hoping that if she screamed loud enough, the rapist would flee. Splinters from the wooden steps lanced into her bare feet, but she didn't notice them. She had to scream and shriek and wake people up to come running and scare the rapist away.

She would have kept running across the yard when she reached the bottom, but what she saw made her stop dead in her tracks and she involuntarily sucked in a lungful of air. Her pupils were dilated as far as possible and she could see perfectly. Billie was standing in the middle of the yard. She was naked, and her body was writhing in a slow, jerky pantomime. And something about her made Cindy want to stay away from her. She gripped the wooden rail of the stairway with all her might and watched transfixed as Billie moved, her long hair tossing in the air like a black shadow, her body twisting grotesquely into a thousand different shapes. Billie's back was to her, so she couldn't see her face.

She took a step backwards onto the bottom stair. Her mouth was wide open, but her screams had stopped. She wanted to turn and run, but she couldn't take her eyes from Billie's writhing form. She felt behind herself with her foot for the next step and lifted herself up on it backwards. She kept her eyes glued to Billie and shook her head slowly back and forth as Billie's movements slowed and then stopped altogether so that she stood deathly still, with her back to Cindy.

Cindy stared at her a moment longer and then found her voice. "Billie! What happened? Are you okay?"

Billie turned around slowly, moving with a strange stiffness. Her long hair obscured her face.

"Are you okay?" Cindy demanded, her voice cracking with fear.

Billie didn't answer her.

"BILLIE!! Please!! Say something!"

But Billie didn't say anything. Her long hair still a tangled mess in front of her face, she began walking slowly toward Cindy, moving strangely, like a machine. Cindy hesitated a moment, then took two steps down the stairs. At least Billie didn't seem to be hurt. Billie approached her slowly, seemingly oblivious to her nakedness and the cold.

"Are you okay, Billie? What happened?"

Still Billie did not answer. She continued straight toward Cindy, walking to within a few feet and then stopping short.

Cindy took a small step forward. "What happened?"
Nothing.

Cindy toyed nervously with the sleeve of her robe.
"Why won't you answer me?" she demanded plaintively.

Billie's hands went up and in a sudden movement
brushed the long hair away from her face.

Cindy's breath caught in her throat. Her heart
skipped a beat.

Billie was leering at her with a feral smile. Her eyes
held a dim gleam that pulsated slowly. As Cindy
watched transfixed, Billie came still closer—she didn't
walk, she simply moved. Her face seemed a separate
being, inhuman. No human face could wear such an evil
expression. Now the glimmer of light in her eyes
pulsated faster and brightened. Cindy could feel an evil
power radiating from them. They seemed to burn. She
tried to turn away, but could not. The terrible eyes held
her, dominated her with their fire. Looking into their
blazing brightness everything else seemed to slip away.
They seemed to speak to her, to reach into her very soul
and show her ages, eons, of cold crawling fear and white
hot terror, seas of wailing, tortured souls, misery and
misery without end. A feeling rose up in her like the vile,
nauseating stench of putrefaction. The incandescent
eyes held everything loathesome and malignant and unspeakable, everything hateful, everything obscene and
blasphemous. No sin was unknown to those eyes. No sin
was unthinkable to what belonged to those eyes.

It seemed like years, but could have been no more
than a minute before Cindy's legs turned to jelly and she
crumpled to the ground. And still she stared up at
Billie's hideous visage.

A man's voice came out of the night, shouting,
"What's going on? Who's there?"

The thing that had once been Billie Martin brought

forth a subhuman bellow. Its eyes flared crimson. It backed away from Cindy slowly, then turned and ran. It ran like the wind. It turned its glowing eyes up to the sky and fixed them on the tail of the comet hovering in the blackness. Then, as Cindy watched dazed and unbelieving, it jumped over the high back fence and disappeared into the night.

Cindy lay prostrate on the hard ground in shock, still feeling the horror of those fiery eyes inside her like a corrosive poison. Her body was working to expel it. Her bowels opened. Her bladder voided itself. Her stomach convulsed and spewed its contents from her mouth.

Later, when the police finally came, they found the body of a naked young man back by the fence tangled in the blackberry brambles. The police made her look at the body in spite of her protests, leading her back to where they had found him and playing their powerful flashlights over his face. His eyes were frozen open in stark terror. She turned away quickly. She had never seen him before.

She tried to tell them what had happened but it all came out rambling, incoherent, hysterical. They sent her off to the General Hospital for psychiatric observation.

"It was horrible. You can't imagine how horrible," Cindy said with a shudder when she had finished her story.

Unable to contain his nervous energy as Cindy related the fateful night's events, Ted had gotten up and started pacing back and forth in the small kitchen. Now he stopped in front of the chair he had been sitting in and asked, not really expecting an answer, not thinking Cindy would know, "What was it? What could possibly have happened to her?"

But he did get an answer, and it made his legs give way under him so that he sat down hard in the chair and stared at Cindy open-mouthed.

"She was possessed," Cindy said quietly. Then, seeing his stunned reaction, she added, "It's true."

"But there's no such thing!"

"There is such a thing. There are dark forces. They're real. Satan's power is real. I knew it the minute I looked into those eyes."

She got up and wandered aimlessly around the barren kitchen. "When Billie came charging at me I felt as if I was dying. I could feel the power that possessed her. It was like looking directly into hell. It was horrible! Her eyes were boring into me, turning my soul inside out! Only they weren't Billie's eyes—they were Satan's!"

Ted watched her moving around the kitchen and wondered if the experience had driven her mad.

"The dark forces are gathering," Cindy went on, talking very rapidly, running her words together. "They are getting stronger and stronger and they're going to take us over! It was Satan I saw in those burning eyes! I know it!"

She stopped abruptly and looked out the window, seeming to withdraw somewhere inside herself. Ted saw a small shudder run up her body.

He moved up behind her. "I know it was horrible," he said gently, "but you've got to realize it's not—"

She whirled around quickly. "It's true! I knew it when I saw Billie, but didn't want to admit it to myself. Then Simon explained it to me. He said—"

"Simon? Who is that?"

"He's an old man, a very wise—"

"An old man!" Ted exclaimed. "Does he have long white hair and piercing blue eyes?"

Cindy nodded. "Yes, that's him. Do you know him?"

"I've been trying to find him! Where is he?"

But Cindy didn't know where he was or where he lived. She didn't even know his last name.

"You must know something!" Ted cried desperately.

"I wish I could help you," Cindy said. "Believe me."

"All right. All right," Ted muttered, trying to calm himself. He paced around the barren room, then turned back to Cindy.

"He came to see you?"

"He was waiting for me here when I came back from the hospital. He wanted to know what had happened."

"And?"

Cindy sat down in the old wooden chair again. "I told him. And he told me he believed me. He said he knew I wasn't making it all up. He said Billie had been possessed, and the young man they found, too. I was sure he was right—I had known it all along though I couldn't admit it to myself."

"I don't understand," Ted said. "Things like that aren't real. Things like that don't happen—" He stopped. Those were the very words the psychiatrists at Hillsdale had used about his visions. No, he told himself, this wasn't the same at all. This was different! Satan wasn't real! Possession wasn't real! It was all superstition from the Dark Ages. And this was the end of the twentieth century!

Cindy broke in on his thoughts. "I know what you're thinking. It is almost impossible to believe. But I *saw* what happened to Billie."

"Yes, but . . ."

"Simon told me people often don't want to believe things they are afraid of. And that is Satan's greatest strength. Maybe you just don't want to believe it."

Maybe she is right, Ted thought. Maybe he was too afraid to admit he was dealing with powers he couldn't begin to comprehend. Maybe he was hiding from the truth. Maybe! Maybe! Maybe! He just didn't know!

He stood up. "And you have no idea of where I can find him?"

"I'm sorry."

"He didn't mention anything about where he lives? Maybe he mentioned something in passing about North Beach or the Mission District. Any clue would help!"

Cindy thought a moment, then shook her head. "I wish I could help you."

For the next two days, Ted wandered the streets of North Beach looking for the man called Simon. He knew Simon might not live there, but that was where he had seen him and he didn't know where else to look. He walked the streets for hours stopping every white-haired old man he came across, but it was never him. And all the while Cindy's voice rattled around inside his head, repeating a single word over and over again: *Possession*. But it was impossible! There was no such thing! Still, something had put the terrible fire in Billie Martin's eyes. Something had given her the strength to heave Joe Frantini in the air.

And something had killed her.

Possession.

He tried everything he could think of to find the old man. He went back to Emilio's to see Joe Frantini. The waiter had lost all desire to talk about the episode. But no, he finally admitted, the old man had not been back. Twice, Ted tried to make Lieutenant Bates realize how important Simon was, but the cop was as stubborn as before. Ted was consumed with frustration. He couldn't really explain his interest in the old man without revealing his vision and what Cindy had told him, and he knew Bates was the type who would throw him out on his ear at any mention of the supernatural.

In the evenings, he would give up his search and go home to be with Jill. He tried to keep his consuming fears closed up inside himself and to behave as naturally as possible. But Jill knew him too well and was too observant not to notice how depressed he was. He had also started drinking rather heavily.

One night she sat down with him on the couch and took the drink out of his hands. "What's wrong, Ted?"

He tried to smile. "Nothing. Why do you ask?"

"You know why I'm asking. Look at the lines on your face! You're worrying yourself to death. Can't you tell me what it is? I want to help."

"There's nothing wrong," he repeated stubbornly.

"Ted, please!"

"I tell you there's nothing wrong!" he said sharply. "Leave me alone!"

Jill bit nervously at her lower lip. She was looking at Ted intently, as if trying to read his mind. Finally, she said, "All right, Ted. Take your time. And remember I love you."

Ted nearly broke then. He realized he couldn't go on much longer.

At night, he would lie in bed beside her, unable to sleep, his mind in turmoil. He would think of what Joe Frantini had said—*She was something human once, but not any more.* And what Simon had said—*She won't be the last one, I'm afraid.* And what Cindy had said, the most frightening thing of all—*Possession.* And always, always, there was the memory of Billie Martin's dead body, swarmed by flies in that blindingly bright, stench-filled lot. And Jill, the way he had seen her in the vision, her face twisted and cruel, her eyes filled with flames stretching out like endless seas.

On Friday, after another futile day of searching for the old man, he made one last attempt to get Bates to act.

"Something is going on!" he insisted. "Something monstrous!"

His feet on his desk, Bates looked up at Ted with amusement. "Well! Something monstrous!" he said mockingly. "We've got monsters now!"

"Damn it, Bates! Open your eyes! It's—"

The phone rang. Bates picked it up. "Excuse me," he said, swivelling around in his chair.

Ted looked out the window. The sun was setting, he noticed. He had to get home to Jill. He was just wasting his time with Bates, he thought, clenching his fists in anger.

"Looks like we have another one," Bates said behind him.

Ted turned. He felt a chill run up his spine. "Another body?"

Bates shook his head. "No. Not yet, anyway. Another person with, quote, "glowing eyes." Some of the boys from Taraval station have her cornered. Maybe we'll get some answers now."

Ted immediately thought of Jill. His heart started pounding.

Bates got up. "Want to come along?"

It took Ted a moment to find his voice. "Y-yes, of course." It couldn't be Jill, he told himself. It wasn't night yet. It was just getting dark.

CHAPTER 9

Using his siren, Bates made it to the Taraval district from downtown in under fifteen minutes. Pulling in carelessly behind another cop car, he turned to Ted and said, "Here we are, Mr. Concerned Citizen."

Ignoring him, Ted opened his door and climbed out. Though the winter sun had just set, it might as well have been midnight. To his right, the ground rose sharply in steep lawns to houses perched high over the road. Electric light coming from their windows and front porches dissipated in the darkness. Across the road, the ground descended into the dense, tree-filled blackness of Stern Grove. He remembered how sunny and bright the day had been when he and Jill were married among those trees just two weeks ago. It seemed a different place now, dark and brooding, nearly unrecognizable. There was a good breeze, and overhead a canopy of low-lying clouds drifted silently through the black tree tops. The wind also brought random voices floating out of the darkness.

Bates spoke to him across the hood of the car. "It's a great night for spooks." He let out an unpleasant chuckle that seemed too loud in the muffled darkness. "Well, let's see what we can find out."

Ted followed him up the quiet road past two squad

cars. Bates looked around a moment, spotted a uniformed officer, and called him over. Over Bates's shoulder, up on the steep hill, Ted could see flashlight beams
playing back and forth behind one of the houses.

"What's your name?" Bates asked the other cop.

"Teel, sir." Teel's rugged face glowed red for an instant as he took a drag on his cigarette.

"What's the story, Teel? Seen any monsters yet?"

"Monsters, sir?"

Bates jerked his thumb over his shoulder at Ted. "Fellow here thinks we've got monsters." He turned to Ted.
"Or is it ghosts you're worried about?"

Ted clenched his fists at his side. He wanted to tell
Bates to go to hell. Instead, he said, "It's your fantasy.
You tell me."

Bates chuckled nastily and turned back to Teel.
"Well, what's the story, Teel? I haven't got all night to
waste."

Teel took a last puff on his cigarette and flicked it
away in a shower of sparks. He pointed up the hill to
where the flashlight beams moved in the darkness.

"An old woman named O'Hara lives there. She called
us about a half hour ago. There's a woman in her back
yard, naked, screaming obscenities."

"What about her eyes?" Ted asked.

"Mrs. O'Hara said her eyes were lit up like Christmas
tree lights. But I haven't been able to verify that."

"Didn't think you could," Bates said. "How many
men have you got up there?"

"Three others, besides me."

"And you haven't caught her yet?" Bates was in-
credulous.

Teel shook his head. "It's weird," he said, his voice
full of wonder. "It's like she's playing hide and seek with
us. We hear her screaming and rush over to where she
should be and she's not there. Then somebody catches a

glimpse of her someplace else and we close in on her and think we have her surrounded, and then she seems to vanish in thin air.''

"Jesus Christ!" Bates exploded. "I've got a bunch of *Keystone Kops* to work with!"

Ted took a step away and peered up at the house. Bates was obviously in no hurry, not taking it seriously. But Ted's stomach was doing flip-flops. What could be up there, he wondered, thinking of what Cindy had told him. He started up the stone steps that went up from the sidewalk and heard Bates's voice loud and peremptory behind him.

"Where do you think you're going? Come back here!"

Ted kept going up the steps. "I'm not a cop and I don't have to take your orders."

His feet slapping rapidly on the steps, Bates ran up to him with surprising speed and grabbed his arm. Ted could feel the other's breath as Bates hissed into his ear, "It is an offense to interfere with an officer in the performance of his duties."

Ted tried to yank his arm away, but Bates had a grip of steel. "It is an offense to disobey the lawful order of an officer!"

Ted grabbed the lieutenant's arm with his free hand and jerked it loose. "You seem to think this is all some hilarious joke!" he shouted angrily. "It's not! There are human beings involved!"

A high, quivering voice came down to the two men from the porch above. "Hello! Officer! Have you found Clarence yet?"

Ted looked up to see a stout old woman on the lighted porch. She was leaning on a thick cane.

"I do believe it's Mrs. O'Hara," Bates said with amusement. "Let's go see her, shall we?"

His face wooden, Ted stared mutely at the other. He was breathing hard and a growing rage was burning inside him. There was just enough light from the porch above to show the smirk on the cop's face. He wanted nothing so much as to wipe it off for him, but he followed him up the stairs to the old woman.

Just as they reached the top of the stairs, a high-pitched wailing laugh came out of the night. It wasn't a human laugh. It sounded like a hyena's. Then, a voice shouted thunderously: *"The Prince of Death is coming! Your lives are finished, you pieces of shit! You are shit! You come dropping out of god's asshole and your stench fills the world!"*

Ted and Bates froze in the eerie silence that followed the outburst.

"It's that horrid woman!" Mrs. O'Hara said, on the verge of tears. "She's been doing that all night. Shouting horrible things, blasphemy!"

The old woman turned her wrinkled face to Ted and peered at him through her thick glasses. "Have you found my Clarence?"

It was Bates who answered. Ted noticed his voice had lost its smug assurance. "Who is Clarence, ma'am? Your husband?"

"My husband?" The old woman shook her head nervously. "No, oh goodness no. Clarence is my dog."

"Your dog?"

"That horrid woman took him," fretted the old woman. "I had just let him out to make his mess and the poor thing had hardly finished when that woman ran out of the bushes and grabbed him. I saw her very clearly! Her eyes were on fire! On fire!"

"Well now," Bates said. "Don't you worry."

Ted couldn't bear it anymore. For some reason, Bates was stalling. He had to get away from him and find out what was going on. With a swift movement, he jumped down the porch steps.

He sprinted down the flagstone walk that ran close to

the house and was around the corner before Bates started yelling. The walk continued around the side of the house in a narrow space next to a high hedge and Ted raced down it to emerge in the back yard.

The yard was surprisingly deep. Light from the house extended into it for about ten feet and then gave way to the night. The yard was cluttered looking, packed with bushes and small fruit trees. A large white plaster bird bath seemed to glow in the center, and scattered about were plaster cupids, fawns and cherubs. The flower beds close to the house were trampled. Ted saw a uniformed cop approach the bird bath and dart his flashlight around some nearby bushes. Further back was another beam of light, but he couldn't see the person holding it.

He heard Bates's heavy feet pounding against the flagstone and moved quickly away from the house into the darkness near a small evergreen. An amazingly loud, sub-human cackle came out of the darkness at him, starting out low and rising higher and higher, sending his heart racing. He strained his eyes in the dim light but saw nothing. The eerie cackle stopped as abruptly as it had begun. Bates started yelling threats at him. He ignored the cop and turned around to where the flashlights were playing in the darkness. He could hear the other cops talking to each other in hoarse stage-whispers.

"See anything, Jack? I think she's near you." A voice said.

"No. I think she's over by Maxwell."

"She's not here," came a third voice, farther away. "Maybe—Wait! Wait!"

"What?"

"I saw a movement. Near you, Jack!"

"Where? I think—"

Jack was cut off as the impossible voice exploded out

of the darkness. It sounded like the growl of a vicious dog—a dog that could talk.

"Shit on Mary the whore-mother of god! Piss in her mouth! The Prince of Death is coming!"

Then the voice changed, so completely and so rapidly, it seemed it couldn't be coming from the same source. It was now high-pitched and breathily seductive.

"I'm all yours, boys, ripe and ready for fucking. Pull out your pricks and caress my cunt. Come! Come to me!"

Ted felt a series of convulsive shivers run up his spine. Was it possible that Cindy had told him the truth?

"What the hell is going on here?" he heard Bates explode behind him.

His heart racing, Ted moved further into the darkness, away from the tree he was under.

Another loud whisper came from the back of the yard, high-pitched and excited. "I see her! I see her!"

Another voice: "Where, Jack?"

"Back here! BACK HERE! HURRY!"

"Where *are* you?"

"I'm . . . I'm . . . Oh sweet Jesus! Her eyes! *Her eyes!!"*

"Jack! Where the hell are you? Jack!"

There was no answer. There was a sudden rush of movement and the sound of breaking branches as the flashlight beams moved jerkily in the darkness.

"Jack! Where are you?"

"Her eyes!! They're horrible! Oh, God!!"

"There she is!"

"Get her!"

"Look out!"

"Don't let her get away!"

"Look out! Behind you! *Behind you!"*

And then Ted saw her. She was racing right toward

him, a blur of naked white motion, a grotesquely fat woman with enormous swinging breasts and coal-hot eyes running at an impossible speed. Ted stood rooted to the ground, gaping in shock, his heart pounding in his chest. It could only have been a split second, she was moving her huge frame so fast, but it seemed longer— much, much longer. She fixed her burning red eyes on him and he was paralyzed, as motionless as the tree next to him. The blazing eyes, set deep in her fat face, seemed to reach into his brain and set it on fire. He felt as if he was going to die and in the next instant he felt as if he were already dead and the incandescent eyes boring into him were the terrible eyes of Death itself. A sea of terrifying emotions swept over him. In the middle of a breath, he choked on his own vomit, thrust up suddenly into his mouth, and now he was on the ground, retching in great, heaving spasms.

And then she was past him, gone into the night.

Behind him, he vaguely heard Bates yelling hysterically, "Stop her! Stop her, you clowns! STOP HER!"

But she was gone.

Teel saw her run into the darkness of Stern Grove. Bates regrouped his men for a search. They moved their squad cars across the road and aimed the spotlights mounted on them down the steep hill. But the Grove was vast, larger than several city blocks, and the naked woman had been running like the wind. It quickly became apparent that the search was hopeless. It was apparent to Ted, anyway—Bates was hell-bent on finding the woman and he kept his cops at it for nearly two hours before giving up. All during the search among the towering pines and spruce trees, Ted could hear the cop called Jack muttering. He was the only one besides Ted who had gotten a good look at the woman and her glowing evil eyes, and he was very shaken. He kept repeating the same phrase over and over, "I thought I was going to die!"

It was nearly midnight when Bates finally tired of the search. They all went back to Mrs. O'Hara's yard to check for evidence, and the cop named Maxwell found the dog in the big white bird bath. He called Bates and the others over. Ted crowded in with them and saw the carcass in bold relief in the harsh light of Maxwell's powerful flashlight. The sight made his empty stomach start heaving all over again.

Bates stared down at the gruesome sight a moment and then stepped back. He turned to Teel. "Get the old lady."

Horrified, Ted blurted, "You can't show her that! She loved that dog!"

"Shut up!" Bates snapped and then said to Teel, "Get the old lady, I said!"

Teel hesitated.

"That's an order!" Bates screamed, his face red with anger.

Ted grabbed the lieutenant's arm. "What do you think you're doing, for God's sake?" he demanded. "She's an old woman!"

Bates twisted away violently. The features on his livid face were twitching spasmodically, making Ted wonder if he had become unbalanced. "Shut the fuck up!" Bates snarled. "One more word and you'll spend the night in the can!"

Bates came back with Mrs. O'Hara tottering on her cane.

"Have you found my dog?" she asked piteously. "Have you found Clarence?"

"We think so," Bates said.

He quickly shoved Ted away from the bird bath. "Let

the lady have a look!"·

He took Mrs. O'Hara's elbow solicitously and moved her up close to the birdbath. "Is that your dog?"

The old woman stood deathly still a moment. Her voice was a high squeak. "Clarence?"

The poor dog didn't take up much room in the large white birdbath. It looked like the tiny head had been pulled from the body by brute force. Head and body lay a few inches apart on one side of the round shallow dish. The body was on its back, legs splayed, eviscerated, its bloody red guts spilling out of its stomach. The separated head stared up with open eyes. On the other side of the dish, a crude sign of some sort had been drawn by dipping a finger in the dog's blood, which had formed a small pool in the center.

It seemed to take Mrs. O'Hara some time to comprehend what she was seeing. For a moment, the world was utterly silent.

And then the old woman let out her horror. "Oh! Oh! Oh! Oh, my God! Oh!"

She turned her white, wrinkled face up to stare at the men around her and then her eyes rolled up into her head. *"Oh! Oh! Oh! O, my God!"*

Bates screamed, "Get her out of here!"

She started to keel over, the cane falling from her gnarled fingers. It was only luck that Maxwell was right behind her ready to catch her.

Ted wanted to smash his fist into Bates's face. It took every ounce of will power he possessed not to.

Holding the woman, Maxwell stared at Bates accusingly.

Bates was nearly hysterical. "I said, get her out of here! Get her *out of here!* And call an ambulance!"

The pitiful old woman looked tiny as Maxwell and another cop carried her back up to the house. Bates stared after them until they disappeared inside. Then he turned to Teel and pointed to the birdbath. "Well, Teel, what do—"

Teel turned sharply on his heel and walked away into the darkness.

"Bleeding hearts," Bates muttered furiously. "I had to find out if it was her dog, didn't I?"

Ted's hand clenched itself into a fist, but he kept it down at his side. He *needed* the damned bastard. After looking into the naked woman's horrible bright eyes, he knew that what Simon had told Cindy was the truth. The woman was possessed! Looking into her eyes had been like looking into hell itself. Even thinking about it now made him start to shake and sent his stomach churning.

"What's that?" Bates asked him.

Ted ignored the question. "Listen, Bates, it should be obvious by now that something's going on. I don't know what you think you're doing, clowning around, giving that poor woman a heart attack, but I tell you—"

"Shut up!" Bates screamed at him, sounding on the verge of crying.

Ted realized suddenly that the cop's eyes were pleading with him. The man was terrified! It wouldn't take much to push him over the edge.

"I—I've got to think! I've got to figure it out! Give me some time," Bates muttered, more to himself than Ted.

"You've got to find the old man I was telling you about," Ted said. "He knows what's going on! I've been looking for him, but I'm only one man. The police could find him in a day!"

"Yes, yes. The old man . . . What was his name?"

"Simon. I don't know his last name."

Bates looked up at the sky. He seemed to be trying very hard to control himself. In spite of himself, Ted felt sorry for him. It was a minute before Bates came back to his senses.

He pointed to the crude sign drawn in blood on the white plaster bird bath and asked, "What's that?"

Trying to ignore the butchered dog, Ted looked down at the blood-drawn sign. It consisted of a small circle near the dog's head and several lines that streamed away from the circle curving close to the rim of the shallow dish. The crude sign looked familiar somehow, reminded him of something. He stared hard at it, thinking he had seen something like it before, but where? He found himself thinking of his brother-in-law, Roger. But why Roger? And then it hit him. It wasn't Roger. It was Randy. Randy's T-shirt.

"Halley's Comet," he whispered.

"What?"

"Halley's Comet. It looks like a comet. That small circle is the head and those curved lines make the tail. It's a comet."

Bates squinted at it. "Yeah . . . it does look like a comet." He moved away from the bird bath. He slapped Ted on the back and let out an evil-sounding laugh. He seemed to be returning to his old self.

"Great!" he shouted. "A dead dog and a comet. I told you this city was the kook capital of the world! I bet that woman had something to do with that group I saw downtown this afternoon. They were screaming something about the comet being the end of the world. An omen of doom!"

An omen of doom, Ted thought. That's what Roger had said about the comet.

Bates followed him up to the house. "Just another loony gone berserk," the cop said. "I'd bet anything the woman was mixed up with those kooks downtown."

Ted stopped. "What are you talking about? What about her eyes? What about that voice!"

"Well, sure her voice was weird—so what?"

"But her eyes! The way they burned!"

Bates shook his head. "I didn't see her eyes."

"But I did. And that guy Jack did."

"Well, good for you!" Bates said sarcastically. "I didn't. And I'm the fellow that counts!"

"What's with you?" Ted demanded. "A minute ago you were scared witless. And now you're pretending nothing happened."

"I was upset, that's all. That old woman upset me, nearly dying on us."

"That's not all!" Ted insisted. "You know something monstrous is happening, but you won't admit it to yourself! It's something . . . diabolical and evil! It's. . ." Ted shook his head, at a loss for words.

"Diabolical and evil! Ho, ho! Now you've really flipped, Mr. Concerned Citizen! Why don't you go home and get some sleep!"

The ambulance was just pulling up, its red light flashing, when Ted left a few minutes later. He had spoken to Maxwell. Cursing Bates, the policeman told him that Mrs. O'Hara was in pretty bad condition, but it looked as if she would pull through.

He went down the steep stairway thinking he would walk home. He had a lot to think about and the night air would do him good.

He paused on the sidewalk and looked up. The low clouds were clearing to reveal a starry blackness, a moon three-quarters full, and above the moon and to the left, Halley's Comet. Its filmy tail swept away and up from the small, almost invisible head in a gentle curve. It had grown considerably in the past few days—every night it seemed to be getting longer.

An omen of doom, he thought.

Lieutenant Gregory Bates looked up at the comet a few minutes later. He had sent Teel and the others home after the ambulance had left and walked back to his car.

He opened the door, but he didn't get in. He stood staring up into the sky, trying to figure out some connection between the comet and the blood-drawn sign in the birdbath, between the butchered dog and the naked woman.

He was frightened.

As Ted had told him, as he already knew himself, something monstrous and evil was beginning. He had felt it in that bright cement lot when viewing the dead girl. And he had felt it tonight as soon as he had stepped out of his car in front of Mrs. O'Hara's house. He could feel it now. It was a cold, cold feeling and seemed to come out of the night to clutch his heart in its icy fingers. Looking up at the comet now made the feeling even stronger and sent his heart racing in protest. He looked down at his open car door and shut it without getting in.

He was frightened. He wondered why he could feel the coldness when none of the others seemed to. He wondered why the coldness, dreadful and frightening as it was, did not send him racing away from it but seemed to draw him toward it, seemed somehow compelling and urgent, seemed somehow to want *him*.

He was frightened, and because he was frightened he had tried to reassure himself with jokes and false bravado. He had not wanted to go into Mrs. O'Hara's back yard and confront the thing waiting there, so he had stalled with Teel, stalled with the concerned citizen, and stalled with the old woman. His fear had angered him, and he had taken out his anger on the old woman, forcing her to look at her decapitated dog. Now he felt small and mean and unworthy. And still frightened.

He patted his pocket nervously, looking for cigarettes. He felt he had never needed a smoke so badly, but he couldn't find his pack. He started turning his pockets out and then remembered. He had quit smoking two years ago.

But he still had his gun. Its hard weight pressed re-
assuringly against his side. There was no doubt in his
mind that he would use it, plunking the fat woman right
between the eyes if he had to.

She was still close by. He could feel her. He could feel
her terrible coldness coming out from the dark trees in
the grove, coming across the empty street at him. He
wondered again why he could feel it so strongly, so
clearly, when none of the others had. He wondered why
the icy fingers slipped themselves into *his* heart, wanting
him and not the others. And he wondered what would
happen to him this night.

In spite of his fear, he found himself moving away
from his car, crossing the deserted street to the dark
grove. And then he was moving down the steep bank
away from the safety of the road, in under the towering
spruce and pine trees. And with each step he took into
the darkness, he felt the grip of the icy fingers tighten
around his icy heart. His heart wanted to pound and
pound, but the cold fingers held it tight, controlled it
and pulled him forward. He wanted to turn around and
run back up the slippery bank toward the street lights,
but he continued down into the darkness, his legs working of their own accord, quickly and easily propelling
him forward.

He began thinking of his wife, how she was going to
yell at him when he finally got home to her (for he didn't
once admit to himself that he might not get home). She
would accuse him of whoring around again, out all
hours of the night with his cheap tarts as she called
them, getting God knows what filthy diseases. Tonight
at least, her accusation would be unjust, though it was
true enough that he had hardly married her when he
started being unfaithful. But tonight, he knew, he would
never make her believe what he was really doing. And he
would have to sit and take it, wait until her anger and

rage had spent itself so they could resume their sullen life together. These thoughts ran through his mind irrelevantly while his legs, unbidden, moved him ever forward, ever deeper into the trees. The icy fingers at his heart seemed to have relaxed their grip somewhat, as if surer now of his obedience. Or perhaps he was more used to the feeling. Perhaps he did not mind it so much.

The naked woman was not too far away now and he could feel her drawing him to her. He had known all along she was still in the grove and had pushed his men on to find her. But she had not wanted the others to find her. She only wanted him. She had waited for the others to leave, and then she had begun to draw him to her, sending out icy tendrils to grip his heart.

The trees became very dense, the ground around him pure black. He kept going forward in the darkness, feeling there was no need to see. And then the trees gave way and he was in a spacious clearing that seemed almost bright in the moonlight. There was something hazy and white in the middle of the clearing about a hundred feet away. It was the fat woman. The naked woman. Unthinking, he went toward her, seemed to float toward her slowly, his feet barely touching the ground, as if in a trance.

She was singing to him, singing an inhuman song of sounds that made no sense. Her voice was rising and falling in an eerie undulating wail that was both terrible and beautiful. He continued drifting toward her and the song swelled louder—floating now higher, now deeper, rising and falling like great ocean waves, and he was riding on the waves, being carried to her on the waves. And as he drew closer he saw how immensely fat she was. She was sitting on the ground, leaning back, holding her torso up with her arms behind her.

When he was half-way to her she turned her face to him. Her mouth was wide open and quivering with her undulating song. Her eyes were glowing like hot coals.

In spite of the ice in his heart, a fever rose in him and broke out in a hot prickly sweat under his clothes, as some part of himself full of revulsion and dread started screaming loudly in his head. He had to stop! He had to dig his heels into the earth and resist the force that was pulling him forward. But he kept drifting toward her and his eyes exploded in horror when he realized his body was no longer his to command. He wasn't floating to her on waves of sound but walking to her on his own two legs. He had to stop! But then another, darker part of himself told him no, told him not to resist, told him to go forward, floating on the terrible beauty of her wailing song. Sweat pouring from him and soaking his clothes, he warred with himself—something inside telling him to yield, to give in and float forward to the woman white in the moonlight, something else in him screaming at him to stop, to run away, to save himself.

But he could not stop.

He could not stop until he was just in front of her and she was looking up at him with her horrible glowing eyes, her singing mouth a perfect 0 in the round flesh of her face, the song floating out of it to hover in the air between them like sheets of burning ice.

And then he stopped. Stopped not because he wanted to, not because the screaming part of him full of dread had won control of his body, but simply because the icy fingers and wailing song no longer drew him forward. He stood deathly still in front of her and looked down into her burning eyes.

And her burning eyes locked on his and suddenly he was falling, falling headfirst into their glowing fires, falling so fast his clothes were stripped from him by the rushing wind, plunging down farther and farther, through miles and miles of space and an eternity of time, his naked body spinning, his mind leaving a long fading cry behind him. As he fell, he felt his life rushing out of him to join the wind. He was dying. Memories flew from his mind in the plummeting rush, memories and hopes and fears and loves were all stripped from him because he was dying.

And then he was in front of her again, standing firmly on the grass of the clearing in the moonlight, just as he had been before the fall. Only now he was naked, just as the fat woman was, his clothes strewn about the grass at his feet, his revolver glinting in the moonlight near his shoes. And she had stopped singing. She was lying on her back, her legs toward him and spread wide. Staring down at her, he thought hazily how immense she was, a mass of soft and yielding flesh, and her very immensity, the very abundance of her flesh, her quivering thighs and her full stomach and her massive melon breasts with their round egg nipples black in the moonlight made him want to sink himself in her, made him want to drown himself between her breasts and thighs. But to do so would risk death. The thought hit him very clearly. And then another realization came to him—her burning eyes were no longer locked on him and the icy fingers were gone from his heart. He could leave her if he chose.

He could leave her if he chose. Or he could drown himself in her soft and yielding flesh.

He stood before her, watching her move her body slowly up and down and licked his dry lips nervously. A soft sheen of sexual sweat glistened on her breasts and thighs. She started moaning desirously and lifted her hips into the air. He could smell the mustiness of the dark swatch of fur between her legs.

She lifted her arms up to him imploringly. "Come," she simpered, "Come to me."

Her voice was a strange hiss. It wasn't human. He knew it wasn't human. But it sent a current of desire racing up his spine. He looked down at himself and saw his penis jutting out tight and hard and throbbing with each beat of his racing heart.

No, he thought, *to do so would risk death.*

He could leave her if he chose.

He glanced over at his revolver on the grass. It was waiting for him to pick it up, its bluish metal shining softly in the moonlight.

"Come," she moaned in the voice that wasn't human, "Come to me."

Her arms were stretched up toward him and her fingers were grasping, closing on the air, wanting him. He looked at the sheen on her immense breasts. He looked down at the moist darkness between her thighs. His heart was pounding ferociously, pumping his penis so full of blood he felt it would soon burst.

He fell to his knees, fell on her hard, sank himself into the vastness of her yielding flesh, felt her swallowing him up, felt her hands like great bear claws locking themselves on his buttocks, felt her urging him on to thrust himself into her deeper and harder.

And then her vagina closed itself on his penis like a vise and a sound like nothing he had ever heard erupted from her next to his ears—an impossibly low laugh rumbling like massive rocks grinding together in the bowels of the earth. Terror clawing his heart, he jerked his head up and saw her glowing hot eyes radiating evil, saw her fat face twisted into a mask of deadly hate, saw her mouth form a hideous, monstrous, gaping smile. He tried to scream but no sound came out and the muscles of her vagina locked themselves on his penis in excruciating pain, and her monstrous laugh grew still louder, deeper, and her eyes blazed brighter, became twin volcanoes shooting flame, and he knew he was staring at death itself, Death, hideous and monstrous, grinning a gaping death's-head grin. He was being embraced by Death. Swallowed by Death with fiery eyes.

His own eyes bulged from his head with the horror of it. He tried to scream again and he tried to push himself away from her deadly hold, but her legs were wrapped around him now like thick pythons and his penis was wedged in her and held fast, and even to move an inch sent bolts of lightning agony shooting through it. So he thrashed with his legs and flailed away at her demonic face with his fists, beating her until her face was streaming with blood and still her monster laugh grew louder, filling him with its dread, filling the clearing, reaching up to the stars to fill the vast void of space with its rumbling thunder, and still her eyes shot flames, still her bloodied mouth held its gaping death's-head grin.

And now the icy coldness came again.

And he was shrieking now, bellowing and shrieking with the horror and agony of it as the coldness entered him through his anus and spread its icy tentacles through his bowels, sending his guts into convulsive cramping spasms of pure pain, sending his howling voice octaves higher in his agony before the torture suddenly stopped and the coldness moved down into his legs turning them numb, turning them into nothingness, dissolving them it seemed in a misty haze. And now the coldness was moving up into his chest and in some corner of his mind that could still think amidst the horror, he thought that when it reached his heart he would surely die, *prayed* that when it reached his heart he would surely die and end his torture.

As if reading his thoughts the monster Death-Woman grabbed his hair in her hands and jerked his head up so that he stared pop-eyed into the terrible fire of her glowing orbs and bellowed at him, "No! You will not die! We will use you! You will *not* die!"

The coldness reached his heart and he did not die. The icy tentacles were snaking their way slowly up his neck and into his head, *into his mind!* and he realized with sudden clarity what the coldness was. It was another *being!*

That thought flashed out just as the icy tendrils wrapped themselves around his soul.

His eyes started to flicker with an evil fire.

He fought with the thing in his soul, fought to keep his memories and hopes and fears and loves, fought to seize control of himself once again. His face began changing, rapidly alternating back and forth between the human and the demonic, terror and hatefulness supplanting each other on his features, his eyes alternately glowing and dimming, the fire there flickering as if in the wind.

Then, finally, his eyes surged with amber fire and swelled brighter and brighter. His face completely lost its look of terror, becoming hideously ecstatic, and his mouth pulled back, baring his teeth in a triumphant grin. Gregory Bates was transformed. A gruesome, cackling laugh came from him and his fiery eyes turned down to stare at the bloody face of the fat woman underneath him.

Their bodies were still wrapped together, but Gregory Bates found no pleasure in the voluptuousness of the woman for he could no longer feel pleasure. He roughly pushed himself away from the other's flesh and stood up, letting out a bellowing laugh toward the heavens. Since he could feel no pleasure, it was not a laugh of happiness or joy, but a mocking laugh of gloating triumph. He swept his evil eyes across the fat form of the woman now crouched on the grass like an ape. Turning from her with a fast, jerky motion, more quickly than Gregory Bates had ever moved before, he looked up into the night sky at the curved tail of Halley's Comet hovering in the void like a silver sword. He stared at it a long time while a dumb urge grew ever stronger within him.

Then he finally broke from his motionless pose to run off into the night, leaving the fat woman behind him.

He searched among the trees of the grove a long time before he came across the brown and white cat, its eyes gleaming yellow in the shadows. With a movement so swift it could not be seen, he scooped it up and ran with it to a rough wooden picnic table hidden among the trees. He placed one hand around the cat just above its shoulders and the other around the cat's head so that his thumbs were almost touching. Then he started pulling his hands apart. The cat's head tore away from its body in a great gush of hot steaming blood that spattered his naked body. Working quickly, he placed both parts on the picnic table and, dipping his finger into the bloody stump of the cat's neck, he drew a small circle on the wood with curved lines radiating out from it to one side. He stood back to admire his handiwork, then moved further away until he could see the comet through the trees.

Staring up at it, his eyes suddenly blazed brighter.

CHAPTER 10

Jill could still remember how when she was very young, hardly more than a baby, her father would give her a lollipop just so he could snatch it away again and watch her cry. It was always a tootsie-roll pop and he would wait until she had gotten her first taste and then grab it from her roughly. She would always try to control herself, fail, and burst into tears. As she grew up she came to realize that her father had some strange need to demonstrate his power over her. But the frustration and wide-eyed incomprehension she had felt at such capricious cruelty stayed painfully in her memory.

It was Friday night, November 23, 1985, and she was no longer an innocent child. Still, she had the same feeling of frustrated incomprehension. The more she thought about it, the more it seemed fate had finally given her love and happiness only to snatch them away again and watch her reaction with malicious glee. The man she loved was falling apart right before her eyes.

The lines of worry on his face seemed to grow deeper every day. He was drinking heavily. And sometimes, when he didn't know she was watching him, she would see him crying uncontrollably. He wouldn't tell her what was wrong, wouldn't talk to her at all if he could help it. But sometimes he would grab her fiercely and hold her in a vise-like grip as if he were afraid she would suddenly drop through the floor and disappear.

And now *he* had disappeared. He was usually waiting for her when she got home from work, but tonight he wasn't. She had waited dinner for him, and he still hadn't shown up. He hadn't even phoned her. Ordinarily she wouldn't have worried about it, but after the last few days, everything was a cause for worry.

There was a knock on the door. She ran and pulled it open.

"Ted!"

But it wasn't Ted. Frank Goldbaum stood in front of her. "Hi, Jill. I guess Ted isn't here."

"No, Frank. I don't know where he is." She took Frank's coat. "I've really been worried about him."

"So have I. He hasn't been in school all week, you know."

"He hasn't?" Jill sank into a chair. "I—I guess it shouldn't surprise me."

"People are starting to talk. He's supposed to come up for tenure soon. There's no way he's going to get it walking out on his classes." Frank sat down on the edge of Ted's overstuffed couch.

"He's frightened of something, Frank. At times, he seems absolutely beside himself with worry. And he won't talk to me at all! You're his best friend, Frank. Hasn't he said something to you?"

Frank looked down, avoiding Jill's eyes. "Well, I did have a strange talk with him Monday."

"What did he say?"

"The thing is," Frank said softly, "he made me promise not to tell you."

"Come on, Frank! I'm his wife! I love him!"

Frank quickly held up his hand. "Just a minute! I didn't say I wouldn't tell you!"

"I deserve to know what he told you!" Jill said evenly.

"I just don't know if telling you would do any good."

"What do you mean?"

"Well, he didn't make much sense, Jill. The story he told me was just crazy, just insane!"

"Insane!" Jill cried. "What are you talking about! Ted is *not* insane!"

"Hold on! I said what he told me sounded crazy."

Out of patience, Jill jumped up from her chair. "Well, what did he tell you?" she demanded.

"No, Jill. I don't think I should say. I did promise—"

"Frank!"

"It might just make matters worse, Jill! Let me talk to Ted myself first. If I can't get anywhere with him, then maybe I should tell you."

"You don't know what you're doing to me, Frank! I've been worried sick about Ted. It's just tearing me apart! What's happening to him? What?!"

"Jill—"

"You've got to tell me!" she cried, her face reddening, her eyes filling with tears.

Frank looked at her helplessly. "Sit down. It won't help getting yourself all worked up."

"You're the one who is getting me worked up!"

"Please, Jill. Sit down and I'll try to explain."

"All right!" Jill sat down.

"Ted came to see me in my office Monday," Frank told her. "He seemed very upset and said he had to talk to me. We went out to a bar by the beach. And he started telling me this story and, well, he made me promise not to tell you."

"You've told me that," Jill said coldly. "Get on with it. What did he say?"

"Well, to make a long story short, he thought you were in danger. He was afraid something horrible might happen to you."

Jill let out a nervous sigh. "What did he say, Frank!"

"He had some sort of nightmare." Frank paused. "Really, Jill, he was very upset, and I don't think he realized what he was saying. The fact is none of it made much sense. It all sounded crazy."

"He's not crazy!"

Frank squirmed on the couch. "I'm not an expert, Jill. But it sounded to me like Ted's having some sort of delusion. He needs help. Professional help!"

"What exactly did he think was going to happen to me?"

"It really didn't make any sense, Jill."

Jill gave up. She knew she wasn't going to get Frank to go any further. He would circle around it and circle around it, but he wasn't going to break his promise.

Frank left then, apologizing. "Try to talk to him, Jill. He needs help."

Closing the door after him, a sudden sob surprised her. She choked it back and told herself firmly, *One of us has to stay in control!* Blinking back the tears, she went into the kitchen and began mopping the floor. It was already clean, but mopping kept her hands busy and let her work off some of her anxiety.

Her thoughts turned to the man she had lived with before she had met Ted. Dan had been a bass guitarist with a local rock group. He was tall and thin, almost emaciated, very pale with long blonde hair. When she had first gotten involved with him, he had seemed to offer the excitement she craved at that point in her life. But over a period of months the excitment had turned to hell. All she could remember now were the fights and recriminations and scenes. He couldn't stay away from drugs. Uppers, downers—he took anything he could get his hands on. A thousand times, he promised her he would reform. It had almost become a daily ritual: "I'll stop, I promise. I'll stop tomorrow." But he never did.

She had stood by helplessly, watching him destroy himself.

She might still have been with him fighting the ritualized and futile battle if Elaine hadn't talked some sense into her. (Saved by her little sister—it hadn't done much for her opinion of herself.) Later, she had asked herself how she had possibly managed not to see what Dan was really like. How could she have been so blind?

She had met Ted only a short while after leaving Dan, and he had seemed so refreshing, so completely different from Dan, so stable. And now, if Frank was right, Ted was suffering from delusions.

She worked the mop faster. Frank was obviously no expert. He didn't know anything about psychology. But still. . . .

If only she knew what Ted had told him!

She went over the floor three times before realizing what she was doing.

Waiting for Ted, worrying about what to say to him, wondering if Frank was right—it all left her in a state of nervous exhaustion by the time Ted finally got back after midnight.

He came in looking haggard. Jill told herself to be calm. She couldn't yell at him the way she had yelled at Dan.

As evenly as she could, she said, "I was worried about you."

"I'm sorry, Jill." Ted brushed by her and went into the kitchen. She stood in the doorway watching as he poured himself a glass of straight whiskey.

He looked up at her guiltily. "I know you didn't bargain for this when you married me," he said, then took a gulp of whiskey.

She went in and took his hand and led him out of the kitchen to the living room. They sat down on the couch. Ted looked at her questioningly.

"I want to help you, darling," she said gently. "I know something is wrong. You haven't hidden it very well. Your drinking, the sudden fear I see in your eyes. Can't we talk about it?"

Ted took a big swallow of the drink. "There's nothing to talk about, honey. Everything's fine. Really."

"Frank was here a while ago."

"Oh?"

"He came to see you. He said he was worried about you."

"Oh really? That's strange." His hand shaking slightly, he took another sip of the whiskey. "What did he say?"

"He said that you came to see him last Monday, very upset. And that he had a strange conversation with you."

Ted looked down at his drink. Forcing herself to be patient, Jill didn't say anything more. She wanted to let him bring things out in the open himself. The silence dragged on and on. She watched his face intently, trying to glean any clue she could find. He seemed to be debating something inside himself.

After what seemed like ages, he finally spoke. "Did he tell you what we talked about?"

"No," Jill said. "He said you made him promise not to."

Ted sighed deeply. "Well, I guess it doesn't matter now. It's all over."

Jill was puzzled. "What's over?"

"I wasn't going to mention it. I didn't want to worry you." He took her hand and squeezed it. "But I guess I didn't succeed at that, did I? I should have told you right at the beginning."

"Told me what?" Jill blurted, losing her patience.

"Did I ever tell you my Uncle Bert died of cancer of the prostate?" he asked suddenly.

Jill shook her head.

"He did. And, well—for a while there were signs I might have it too."

"Cancer!" Jill exclaimed. "Oh Ted! You should have told me!"

"I didn't want to worry you. I tried to hide it from you—that's why I made Frank promise not to tell you—but I guess I didn't do too well."

"But—" Jill hesitated.

"What?"

"Frank said you . . ."

"What did he say?"

What had Frank said? Jill asked herself. Nothing, really! Only that Ted was worried about her. And that was only natural. All the rest of it was just accusations. Frank hadn't told her anything specific.

She kissed him. "Never mind," she said. "It doesn't matter. You're sure you're okay now?"

"Positive. The doctor says I have a very healthy prostate."

"What a relief! I just couldn't figure out what was wrong. You looked so preoccupied and worried all the time. And the way you were drinking! I was almost ready to believe anything!"

She had almost believed Frank. What was he trying to do, she wondered, making her doubt Ted's sanity? Ted hadn't been afraid of something happening to her. He had been afraid he had cancer. So why had Frank told her that whole cock-and-bull story?

"Anyway," Ted said. "There's nothing to worry about. It's all over now."

Yes, it was all over. She was so relieved, she didn't think to ask Ted where he had been all evening.

CHAPTER 11

Earlier that same night, Simon Agoropoulos sat in the luxury of a sleek Rolls Royce that purred smoothly up the circular drive of a Pacific Heights mansion. The limousine pulled to a stop under the mansion's front portico and Simon slid across the leather seat as the chauffeur jumped out and opened the door for him. Simon slowly eased his old frame out. The damp weather didn't help his ancient joints.

"Thank you, sir," the chauffeur murmured as Simon finally alighted and straightened up.

"No, thank you, Richard," Simon replied with a smile.

Declining Richard's offer of help, and unaware of the contrast of his threadbare look against the surrounding elegance, Simon went slowly up the wide, shallow steps. As he reached the massive front door, it swung open.

"Hello, Beth," he greeted the maid. "Is Mrs. Olson about?"

Beth made a small bow. "Yes, sir. "She's . . ."

"Simon!" Margaret Olson called out affectionately, coming down the hall to meet him.

Simon stepped inside. "Meg! How are you?"

They took each other's hands and leaned together to kiss. When they parted, their hands were still locked together. They looked at each other fondly.

Simon knew that Margaret Olson was at least several years past fifty, but she didn't look a day over forty. Her hair was still jet black except for a streak of white that ran back from her hairline. (And the streak had been there since she was twenty-five anyway.) Her skin was still firm and smooth, her figure trimly elegant. Dressed in expensive tweeds and a silk blouse and loaded with pearls, she looked exactly like what she was—a very rich woman in the highest reaches of society.

"How are you, Meg?" Simon repeated.

"I'm fine!" Meg said, her eyes sparkling. "The question should be, how are you? You gave me a terrible fright the other day."

She was referring to his latest attack, Simon knew. Only by the grace of God was he still alive. He thought sadly of the poor black cat. It had not come back to him since, and he missed its company.

"I survived it," he said. "That's the important thing."

Meg clicked her tongue at him reprovingly. "Well, we're going to have a talk about that!"

She led Simon down the hall to a long bright room she called the white room. The oriental carpet on the floor was predominantly blue, as was most of the furniture, but she had had all the dark wainscotting painted white after the death of her husband four years ago. In a way it was a sacrilege to paint over all that beautiful wood, she realized, but she had needed to brighten the place up. She had also taken away the heavy drapes from the french windows facing the garden, to let in all the light she possibly could. Her husband's death after a long and draining fight with cancer had left her deeply depressed, and redecorating the white room was just one of the many things she had tried to get herself out of her despair.

The result had been a pleasant, relaxed room. But it

hadn't helped pull her out of her depression.

There was a fire crackling in the fireplace. Simon sat down in one of the chairs in front of it while Meg took the other and rang for the maid.

"What would you like?" she asked.

"Some cognac would help my old bones, I think." Simon held his hands out to the fire.

Meg told the maid to bring two cognacs and turned back to Simon.

"I wish you'd come to your senses and move in here with me!"

"What would the neighbors think?" Simon asked, a twinkle in his eye.

"Oh posh! You know I don't give a damn what the neighbors think, any more than you!" Meg paused as the maid came back with the drinks, then continued, "There's no need for you to stay in that depressing set of rooms you have. I've got this whole mansion all to myself, with more rooms than I know what to do with. If you came here, you'd always have somebody around to help you in case of an emergency. I just hate to think of you all alone in that run-down fire trap!"

Simon stared into the fire a moment before replying. "We've been through all this before, Meg."

"A thousand times!" Meg agreed. "And a thousand times more until you come to your senses, you obstinate old mule!"

"Now Meg . . ."

"Well, really! What do your vows mean *now*, after all these years?"

"They mean a great deal," Simon replied seriously.

"But they kicked you out, Simon. They kicked you out!"

"Yes, they kicked me out—I didn't leave! I didn't break my vows. I still consider them to be as binding on me as on the day I took them."

"Do you think Bishop Sterling lives in poverty? Do you think the Pope lives in poverty? Of course not!"

"Meg! Enough!" Simon said sharply. "We've been through all this before. What anybody else does is not my concern. My concern is with my heart, my conscience, my God."

"But you're not a priest anymore!"

"In my own heart I am, Meg," Simon said quietly, not looking at her, but studying the dancing flames in front of him. "I took the vows and they are still binding on me."

Meg leaned forward in her chair. Her eyes showed the type of anger that only comes with deep love. "You know what you are, Simon? You're proud! And pride is a sin, isn't it?"

The truth of her accusation cut him deeply. He darted his eyes to her quickly and then back to the fire. He was full of pride, he thought. He had clung to his beliefs because of pride, and because of pride they had called him a heretic and expelled him. And still now, after all these years, the same feelings of pride still tormented him. Wasn't it pride to think you were God's vessel? Wasn't it simply *hubris* to think that you—out of all others—have been singled out to know the truth? Wasn't his insistence that he was still a priest simply a matter of stubborn pride? The accusation of pride filled him with doubts. Perhaps he was simply obsessed. Or simply mad.

Absorbed in his thoughts, he stared at the fire and swirled the cognac in his glass. The golden flames flickered and danced, seemed almost alive and full of magic.

Then he heard Meg's voice, soft and hesitant. "I'm sorry, Simon. I had no right to say that. You've been so good to me."

He looked over at her and smiled. "No. You were

right. I am proud. I need to have it beaten through my thick skull how proud I am."

"You're good," Meg said earnestly. "You're kind and wise and—"

"And too proud."

"You're a saint!"

"A saint?" Simon threw his head back and roared with laughter. "A saint! Oh, Meg! How funny you are! First you tell me I'm too proud and then you try to turn my head and swell my pride even further by calling me a saint!"

She blushed then. "Well," she said quietly, "You've been very good to me, that's all I know."

It had been Simon who had finally pulled her out of her depression following her husband's death. She was walking downtown about a month after the funeral, absorbed in black thoughts and not looking where she was going. She stepped off a curb against a red light. Someone grabbed her arm and pulled her back just before a minibus went barrelling past. She turned around to see an unprepossessing man, very neatly dressed but in clothes twenty years out of date. He looked very old, yet a strangely youthful energy seemed to come from him.

It was Simon. He had saved her life. She tried to thank him and walk away. (Perhaps to meet another bus at the next corner—she would never know whether it had been an intentional attempt at suicide.) But Simon wouldn't let her. He had looked at her for a moment with his penetrating blue eyes—it had made her feel he was searching her soul and reading her thoughts. Then he suggested they have coffee together. He had somehow sensed her needs in that instant and decided to take them on his own shoulders.

Well, they had talked for hours and she had found herself pouring out her soul to him in an outburst that was completely unlike her. But he had one of the most powerful personalities she had ever come in contact with. He was a man who saw differently from other people, and he had so much love and strength in him that he couldn't help but draw people to him, especially if they were lonely or frightened or confused. Over the next months, she and Simon had developed a bond between them that neither could have described. It was something stronger than friendship, almost like marriage. Her society friends could never get beyond his shabby exterior (which she had tried but found impossible to change) and had often asked what she saw in him. At first she had tried to explain, but soon had given it up. If they couldn't see it for themselves, it was useless to try to tell them.

Most of all, she thought, he was a man with a mission.

Simon brought her out of her thoughts. "Where's your cross?" he asked.

Her hand went to her throat and she smiled apologetically. "It doesn't really go with my pearls."

"You've got to wear it," Simon said urgently. "You've got to keep it on always. Your soul is more important than your pearls."

"Do you really think it's necessary?"

"Yes. I do."

Meg got up from her chair and went across the room to the french windows. She stared out at the garden, then turned to face her friend.

"I don't mean to doubt you, Simon," she said slowly, choosing her words carefully. "You've been very good to me. But . . . I do have doubts.

"And you think I do not?" he asked seriously. "I have doubts. I am *wracked* by doubts." He paused. "But I am asking only a little thing from you. Such a little thing—to wear a cross."

Meg sat down again on the edge of her chair. "But I feel like such a hypocrite. And one of the things you taught me—one of the many things—is the importance of honesty, of being honest especially with yourself."

"You do have to be honest with yourself," Simon answered. "You have to be completely honest. Are your doubts genuine, or only the product of fear? We doubt the things we fear, you know. A man has pains in his chest," Simon smiled deprecatingly, "but he doesn't go to a doctor. He doesn't want to know the truth! He doubts that the pains mean anything. Because he is afraid."

Meg tried to say something, but Simon cut her off. "It *is* coming, Meg! Things are already starting to happen. The forces of darkness are gathering. They are getting stronger day by day! I've told you what I've seen and what others have told me. Remember the girl I told you about? She was possessed, Meg. Possessed!"

He got up, went to Meg, and took her hand. "Get the cross, Meg. Get it now and put it around your neck and keep it on always! For the sake of your soul!"

Meg stared up at him with wide, frightened eyes. "All right, Simon," she said weakly. "All right."

"I too am filled with doubts," Simon muttered to himself as she left the room. "I have waited so long. So very long."

He had been waiting nearly half a century now, ever since his discovery of the manuscript. But he had not really discovered it, he thought. It had come to him, as if seeking him out, as if he were meant to have it.

In 1937, shortly after his ordination, he had gone to Egypt to do research on the ancient Coptic church, never dreaming his life would be irrevocably changed. He was in Alexandria walking through the crowded bazaar one particularly hot and dusty day when a man came up behind him and tugged on his sleeve. Feeling short-tempered because of the heat and the mass of sweaty people jamming the bazaar, he turned with his hand raised to shoo the man away. But before he could, the old man, bobbing his head obsequiously, thrust something into his stomach. Simon's hands took hold of it reflexively and he saw that it was a manuscript. Its extreme age was immediately apparent—a papyrus bundle, accordioned rather than bound like a modern book, crumbling to dust and filled with precise lines of handwritten ancient Greek. Simon had studied the language in his novitiate and a glance at the top leaf piqued his interest. It was titled, "On Good and Evil." He glanced up questioningly at the withered Egyptian. The old man was still bobbing his head and looking back and forth from the manuscript to Simon's eyes. Simon had wondered how he had gotten hold of such a treasure and thought he was probably a thief or grave robber. But it would be pointless to try going for the police. He had asked the Egyptian how much he wanted, his jaw falling open with the reply. Only five English pounds!

Simon had paid the man, who immediately had vanished in the surrounding throng. It was almost as if he had never been there, so fast did he disappear. And then Simon had felt like a fool. It had to be a forgery. The old Egyptian probably had a room full of the manuscripts, he thought ruefully. But he took it back with him to his airy white-washed room and examined it closely. The more he studied it, the surer he became that it was indeed authentic and very ancient—certainly no later than the second century A.D.

And his life began to change. In time it would seem that all his life until that moment had been a mere prelude.

He could still picture himself in his small white room on that first day, the fan overhead turning lazily as he pored over the manuscript with growing excitement. It contained familiar aspects of Manicheanism, Monophysitism, and Gnosticism, but the elements of these early and deviant Christian sects had been rearranged into something totally new. The views developed were presented so clearly, so cogently, and so powerfully that the words of the manuscript seemed to ring with truth! Simon was mesmerized.

When the sun went down that day, he did not notice it, but absent-mindedly got up, switched on the light, and went on reading. He read through the night, through the following dawn, and through the heat of the next day—not eating, not drinking, unable to take his eyes off the powerful words he read. He had found, it seemed, a truth he had been yearning for all his life.

He had always had severe and anxious doubts about the teachings of the Church, which the ancient papyrus bundle seemed to crystallize and, by some strange alchemy, to resolve.

His early doubts had involved reconciling the existence of evil with a perfectly good, all-powerful God. If God is supremely good and all-powerful, as the Church teaches, then he cannot do evil, ought not even to allow evil to exist. But evil obviously does exist.

The theologians of the Church attempted to solve this problem by using the concept of free will. God has given man free will, they said, and in giving man free will, He must obviously allow man to choose evil. Thus evil comes from free will.

But Simon had never been satisfied with this answer. Was Simon blind where others could see? Or did his damnable pride stand in the way of his accepting on faith a truth he could not make himself understand?

In reading the ancient words of the manuscript, he found order brought to his confusion. The fine lines of closely-written Greek seemed to blaze with the light of truth!

The manuscript explained that there was only one area in which the two opposing spheres of good and evil came together, and in that area alone could God indirectly work His will against the power of Satan. And where the spheres come together is in Man.

Man alone partakes of both the positive sphere of goodness and negative one of evil. Man is a creature somewhere between the two. Where God cannot do evil and Satan cannot do good, Man can do both good and evil. So man alone can cross the line between truth and error, light and darkness, goodness and evil.

Man is the battleground, Simon read, on which God and Satan contend. As man turns away from God, away from the good, Satan's sphere enlarges itself and God's sphere withdraws. And when occasionally—too rarely—man returns to God and His love, God's sphere waxes and Satan's wanes.

Simon's fingers trembled as he carefully turned over the accordioned pages of the manuscript. He was enthralled. He examined with fascination every fine point, every argument, every objection and rebuttal. The more he studied the long-hidden teachings, the more convinced he became of their truth.

Simon found an appendix at the back of the manuscript, different both in style and tone from the rest of the book. He could make little sense of it at first. It seemed to be a series of prophecies covering thousands of years, based on the doctrine of the shifting balance between the two opposing spheres. He paid little attention to it. It seemed so different from the rest of the manuscript. He thought it had probably been added later, by a different author.

It wasn't until ten years later that he would sit down to study the appendix seriously, and when he did he would realize it was the most important section of all.

But in that summer of 1937, his life changed direction radically. He made it his mission to translate the document and spread its truth as wide as he was able. It was a mission that led to the charge of heresy and to his expulsion from the Church.

He finished out his summer in Alexandria doing only the minimum on his original project and then set sail for New York. A storm overtook the ship in the middle of the Atlantic, but he hardly noticed it. While the ship pitched and tossed and the storm raged outside, sending the other passengers to their cabins, he sat in the deserted game room studying his precious manuscript and dreaming of how he would spread its message.

On reaching New York, his superior told him he was being assigned to Saint Joseph's College in Nebraska to teach philosophy and theology. It was just what he wanted. At the college he would have a library for his research and colleagues with whom he could discuss his momentous discovery.

In his heart, though, he knew he was becoming full of pride. He thought that when he published his great work, a translation and explanation of the manuscript, he would be hailed as the originator of a new era in the Church, a figure as bold and forceful as St. Thomas Aquinas. He had fantasies of meeting the Pope and of being elevated to high office.

He knew such thoughts were sinful and tried to control them. He attempted to expel them from his system with fasts and penances, sometimes praying on his knees on the hard floor of his room at the college until the pain shot up through his whole body—and once until he fainted from pain and hunger. But it did no good. His pride was like a spreading cancer, unstoppable, consuming him. And when his fall came, his pride became a great stone, crushing him under its weight.

His first years at St. Joseph's went smoothly enough, however. He didn't want to talk of the manuscript until he was sure he had translated it perfectly and understood every line, every word, every punctuation mark.

And except for confession, he kept hidden the agony of his swelling pride. Then, just before the war, he ventured to start discussing the ancient doctrines with his friends and colleagues. This caused no trouble at first. One could examine and discuss anything one wanted. There was perfect freedom in that regard as long as one did not subscribe to the beliefs one studied. As long as Simon kept his own excitement hidden, his friends were interested in his translation, agreeing with him that it was a significant historical document throwing some light on the early schisms within the new Church. But when he started passing around copies of his comments and explanations of the manuscript's doctrines it quickly became apparent that he was not merely examining the old manuscript, but adopting its teachings as his own. And there was no freedom in that regard.

He could still remember his first argument with Robert Marks, who taught Theology. They were sitting in Simon's room late at night, drinking a little sherry, and Simon had never seen his friend so agitated. He had just finished reading Simon's notes and comments.

"But you are taking the opinions of the manuscript as your own, Simon!" Robert had said in shock.

"I believe they are true, yes," Simon replied mildly.

"But those doctrines go against the teachings of the Church! They're heretical!"

"They are not heretical, Robert, just different."

"Don't be sophistical," Robert snapped crossly. "A doctrine different from the Church's is heretical!"

Simon very much wanted his friend to understand. "I am not concerned with what is heresy and what is not. I'm concerned with what is true."

Robert looked at Simon fearfully. "Be careful what you say! You are denying that God is all-powerful!"

"But that's just it!" Simon cried excitedly. "That's the beauty of it. The manuscript does not deny God's omnipotence. His power extends over everything real. He is all-powerful in the world of reality. But not in the opposite world. Not in the unreal sphere of the devil!"

"You are playing with fire!" the other barked.

"But—"

"I shouldn't even be listening to you!" Robert stood up abruptly and stormed out of the room.

A month later Simon was relieved of his teaching duties and forbidden contact with the students. He lived in limbo for another two months while they tried to decide what to do with him. Then began the long laborious process of defending his beliefs. The machinery of the Church ground slowly, but it ground finely. For a year Simon endured the questions of the five priests assigned to examine him. (They called it an examination. Simon called it an inquisition.) For a year he walked up the same winding stairs to the same small, bare room and sat across the table from them as they endlessly questioned him.

"We are trying to save your soul," one of the priests told him at the beginning. "The question is not whether the beliefs in this book of yours are heretical or not. Of course they are. The question is whether or not we can make you see the error of your path and bring you back to the Church. The Church can easily withstand your attacks on her. We are concerned with saving your soul."

Pearl Harbor was attacked, bringing America into one of the most destructive wars in history, and Simon's interrogation went on as if nothing had happened. The truth Simon thought he had found was treated as if it were a dread disease.

He tried to explain it to them a thousand times. God is truly all-powerful, he would tell them, but only in the sense in which, logically, he could be all-powerful, only in the sphere of existence. The opposite of that sphere was the opposite of God himself. It was a world of non existence, of darkness, of error and of hate. According to St. Thomas, God was the sum of all *positive* attributes and had nothing negative in His nature. How then could He hold sway over the negative realm, where His light could not penetrate, where his truth could not penetrate —a realm that was not truly real, but the opposite of reality.

Would God have sacrificed His only son if His power were truly able to cross the line between good and evil? Simon asked them. And he answered his question with a resounding No! Man was the only creature who partook of both good and evil, who could cross the line. And God made Christ, of man and God, to lead man to Himself in battle with the forces of darkness. Would He have let His only son die on the cross of human suffering if with a single command he could have defeated Satan? No!

They could never understand his point, those hooded men with cold eyes and ice in their veins. The endless inquisition continued from morning to night, week after week, month after month. He could never make them understand that he was questioning only a small part of the teachings of the Church. He was convinced they were frightened men of little faith. They seemed to think the Church was a house of cards and if they let him try to take out even a single one of those cards and replace it with another, the whole would come tumbling down. He had more faith than they! He thought of the Church as strong and built of brick. All he wanted to do was knock out one of the bricks and replace it with another, stronger one.

None of his arguments affected them in the least, as none of theirs affected him. At the end of a year, in the middle of the war, they sent him off to a monastery in Arizona, telling him to meditate and pray for guidance.

And they demanded his treasured manuscript, his translation of it, and every scrap of paper on which he had written. They got his translation and the notes, but Simon had forseen their demand and had hidden the manuscript. He smuggled it into the monastery with him and worked on it in the small hours of the night.

He redid his translation in secret and sent it off to be published. He knew what the result would be, but in his pride he thought he didn't care. When it became known what he had done, he was formally declared a heretic and defrocked. Though he had steeled himself against it in advance, the hurt was nevertheless unbearable.

And what was worst of all, no notice was taken of his translation. The shining new truth he had proclaimed was greeted with deafening silence and indifference.

He was crushed.

It wasn't until years later that he turned to the strange appendix once again and realized its true significance, the true purpose of his life.

Simon sighed now, staring into the low flames of Margaret Olson's fireplace. Well, he thought, it was all past history now, and in the end it would make no difference. The real battle was yet to come and coming very soon. He knew now that the real battle was not between himself and the Church, but between the two spheres, between God and Satan. Satan's preparations were beginning. He could see his malign effigy in the sky, and every night it grew bigger, closer.

He thought of the last lines of the cryptic appendix again.

When the nightbroom turns to blood, then will Satan come to enlarge his sphere.

Meet him clothed in your faith and battle him in righteousness.

Should Satan triumph, woe be unto Man. Hell

shall be made on Earth. Hell shall be made on Earth. Hell shall be made on Earth.

Margaret Olson came back and sat down in the chair opposite Simon. He looked approvingly at the small silver cross she now had around her neck.

"I put it on," she said.

Simon nodded. "You will be safe now. Or at least safer than you were without it."

"You've talked about it so much, Simon, I can't really believe it's finally going to happen. It seems like a fairy tale."

"The poor souls who have already fallen victim to Satan's power did not think it was a fairy tale, I'm sure."

"Are you sure that's what happened to them?"

"As sure as I can be, Meg."

Meg turned away to stare into the fire. It was almost out now. "I read a book about the beginnings of the Russian revolution the other day," she said quietly. "And I feel what they must have felt back then with the world crumbling about them, all the old rules being overturned. No stability. No security. Full of dread for the future."

She looked up at Simon, her eyes moist, the small lines in her face showing her age in that rare moment. "When, Simon? When? How much time do we have left?"

Simon was somber. "It has already begun, Meg. Satan is gathering his forces, as the possessions indicate. As for when the actual battle will take place, I don't know when that will be. It could be tomorrow. Or it could be next month. We just have to wait."

Simon hoped his heart would last long enough. He was convinced that his finding of the manuscript was no accident. He was meant to have some part in the coming battle.

Meg looked at her watch. "They should start arriving soon," she said.

"Yes. We'd better get ready."

A small group had grown up around Simon in the past few years. It met occasionally at Meg's house. They were people whom Simon had run across in various places (as he had found Meg on that street corner) and who were attracted by his magnetic personality and his kindness. He had never intended to form the group—it had just grown up around him. In their meetings, he would sometimes talk about the two spheres and the coming battle, telling them that they must prepare for it. In facing the challenge, faith was their strongest weapon. He was never sure how many in the group believed what he was talking about or even fully understood it. Many of them, he knew, were attracted to him and the group merely because it offered them an escape from loneliness and despair. There were misfits in the group, social outcasts, losers. Some had followed other prophets before him. And many would fail when the test came. But they were only human and that was humanity's lot. He had enough love for them all.

"Yes," he repeated. "We'd better get ready. There is a lot to do."

CHAPTER 12

On Saturday, before keeping her special appointment with Larry as she had promised, Jill talked Ted into going to Dominic's for a fancy breakfast to celebrate.

"Celebrate what?" Ted asked.

"Your clean bill of health!" she said happily.

At first Ted didn't want to go. He still seemed anxious and preoccupied. She supposed that was understandable, though—he must have been through hell the last few days, bottling up his worries about cancer. But it was all over now! And they had to celebrate. She teased him and wheedled and play acted at pouting until she got a big smile out of him.

"Okay!" he laughed. "I give up! Let's go to Dominic's."

The laugh meant a million dollars to Jill. For a while there it had seemed she would never see him happy again.

The breakfast at Dominic's was good, but the time went by too fast. Soon, unfortunately, it was time to go see Larry. She explained the situation to Ted, promising she'd be back in an hour, and drove off. She wished she could have spent the whole day with Ted, with no interruptions, but she had promised Larry she would go see him, so she would.

159

But she wasn't looking forward to it. Walking up the cracked driveway to Larry's converted garage, her spirits lost their glow. She hoped he wouldn't be in too bad a mood today, hoped he would keep his sexual advances to a minimum, hoped she could get his therapy over with and quickly leave.

Larry pulled the door open before she could knock. He had the biggest smile she had ever seen on him. "It's a beautiful day, isn't it?" he asked, and moved aside to let her enter.

Jill stood in the doorway a second, looking out. It was a beautiful day, sunny, not a cloud in the sky, and—wonder of wonders—almost warm.

"Yes, it is, isn't it?" she said, turning back to Larry and smiling in spite of herself in response to his huge grin.

Leaving the door open, Larry hopped on his crutch to the middle of the room.

"Look," he said pointing to the low coffee table.

Jill saw a jug of red wine, a loaf of sourdough bread, some Italian salami, and a hunk of cheese.

"What's all this for?" she asked.

Larry's grin widened still further. "What do you think? It's a beautiful day outside. You don't want to waste it inside here in my slum do you? I thought we could go up near the Golden Gate Bridge, get me some of that exercise you're always saying I need, and have a nice picnic."

He bent over the table and picked up the wine. "Come on! It'll be nice."

Jill had never seen him so happy or enthusiastic. She hated to hurt his feelings, but she just wasn't in the mood for a picnic with him—she wanted to get home to Ted. And she didn't want him to start getting ideas. He had to understand she was his therapist, nothing more.

"What about your therapy?" she asked.

Hopping to her energetically on his crutch, he put the wine in her hands. "We can come back here afterwards for that."

"You're still using your crutch too much," Jill said. "Try to use both legs and not hop so much."

Larry nodded. He was still smiling broadly. "Okay. You're the boss. Whatever you say goes—as long as we go on this picnic! I've really been looking forward to it." Very carefully, using both legs as much as he could, he went back to the table and picked up the bread, cheese, and salami. Stuffing them under his free arm, he walked slowly and carefully to the front door.

Jill didn't move.

"Well? What are you waiting for Jill?"

"Larry, I—"

"Oh come on! Loosen up! It'll be fun!"

Jill realized there was no way she was going to get out of this picnic without a big scene. And she didn't feel like going through that. Without much enthusiasm, she said, "All right, Larry. Just this once."

But it was a beautiful day. They drove up to the bridge in Jill's Toyota and parked in the lot under the approach ramps. Helping Larry unfold himself and get out of the car, Jill walked with him to the very edge of the high cliff and looked out across the bay.

"This is great, isn't it?" Larry said. He took a deep breath. "And smell the air!"

Jill inhaled the crisp ocean breeze and marvelled at the view. At her feet the rugged cliffs plummetted down hundreds of feet to the water below, the thick ice plant clinging to the rocks in a riot of red and purple and green. The blue waters of the bay were filled with the multicolored sails of a thousand boats. And as always, the huge red presence of the bridge was breathtaking. It seemed to leap away from the San Francisco cliffs to soar high over the water and slam smack into the solid headlands of Marin County on the other side. The hills of Marin—they were called hills in mountainous California, but in the East or Midwest they would have been considered genuine mountains, so huge and massive were they—were beginning to lose their barren brownness and take on a green tint with the winter rains.

It was all just gorgeous, Jill felt. Pulling a piece of wind-blown hair from her mouth, she asked Larry, "Where do you want your picnic?"

He moved carefully away from the cliff's edge and pointed up to the majestic bridge.

"Up there?" Jill asked incredulously. "On the bridge?"

"Sure! Before my accident, I used to go up there all the time. Haven't you ever been up there? There's a wide pedestrian walkway, you know."

Jill looked over at the metal-runged stairs leading up from the parking lot to the bridge. "Can you make it up those stairs?" she asked.

Larry smiled. "I can try!"

Jill marvelled at Larry's good cheer and enthusiasm. She just hoped it would last. His moods could change with surprising rapidity.

Larry did make it up the stairs. It was slow going, and his crutch got caught between the rungs once so that Jill had to help extricate it, but in a few minutes they were at the top. The bay was spread out below them on one side, and rushing cars whooshed by them on the other. Larry suggested they walk awhile and then sit down in the walkway for their picnic. It was wide enough so that they wouldn't block other walkers, he said.

They walked in silence slowly, side by side. Jill was glad she didn't suffer from vertigo. It was a long, long way down to the chilly water below—at least several hundred feet, she guessed. The bridge traffic was not heavy, the breeze and the height were actually exhilarating, and she felt more alive than she had in days. Part of it was the view, but most of it was the lightness she felt after the heavy worries about Ted had been lifted from her shoulders.

Larry started talking away at a mile a minute about some Kung-fu movie he had seen and Jill only half listened. But she thought if he could get to a movie theater on his own, if he could come out here and climb the steps to the bridge, he certainly didn't need to make her come out to see him on the weekends. She didn't mention this to him, though, not wanting to spoil his mood. He was happier than she had ever seen him.

They stopped a moment to look down over the railing at a big freighter steaming out of the bay, bound for some far away port. They they resumed walking.

Larry kept chattering away about the movie, seemingly intent on a scene-by-scene description of every kick and grunt. Jill's thoughts drifted to Ted. It had been a miserable week. Seeing Ted so upset and worried had made her ache. And it had come over him so suddenly! But the worst part of it all was the way he had withdrawn into himself and closed her out. Not being able to help, that was what had hurt most of all. It had made her feel so useless. Well, it was over now. And she could understand that he had been trying not to worry her, even though she had worried more not knowing what was the matter.

The only thing that still bothered her was Frank's strange visit. Why should he want to lie to her the way he did, saying Ted thought she was in danger, suggesting he was having delusions and losing his mind? Why? He was Ted's best friend, wasn't he? What was the point of such a vicious lie? It was vicious, there was no way to get around that. Vicious and cruel.

"Hey! Where you going?" Larry called out loudly behind her. She looked around and saw him twenty feet back.

She walked back to him. "I'm sorry, Larry. I was daydreaming."

"I bet you weren't listening to a word I was saying!"

Jill smiled sheepishly and shrugged her shoulders.

"Oh, what the hell!" Larry said. "It's a beautiful day, the sun is shining, the wind is blowing. I have a loaf of bread, a jug of wine, and thou. Not to mention some cheese and salami! What the hell! Let's eat, drink and be merry!"

Larry's exuberance helped revive Jill's spirits. She told herself to stop thinking and enjoy herself.

She helped Larry sit down, holding his free hand, feeling the surprising strength of his iron grip, and then sat down herself with the food and wine between them.

Larry unscrewed the metal cap from the wine bottle, put it to his lips, and took a drink. He put it down and wiped his lips with his hand, then looked at Jill guiltily. "I should have brought glasses, huh?"

Jill looked at the bread and the cheese. "You should have brought a knife," she said.

"No problem." Larry pulled something from his hip pocket and held it up close to Jill's face. "See?"

Jill looked at it. It didn't look like a knife. Then Larry's thumb moved suddenly, and the six–inch blade shot out under Jill's nose, just inches away. It was sharp and shiny in the sun. She involuntarily flinched back.

Larry smiled crookedly. "No problem," he repeated and grabbed the bread.

They ate in silence for awhile and then Larry asked her if she knew how many people had jumped from the bridge so far.

"Nearly a thousand!" he answered his own question. "It's going to hit a thousand soon. I read it in the paper." He made a diving motion with his hand. "Wheeeew—SPLAT!"

An image of a falling body appeared in Jill's mind, hitting the water as Larry shouted, "SPLAT!" It made her shiver a little.

She didn't want to think about it. "It's really beautiful up here. You were right, Larry. Great spot for a picnic."

Larry ignored her attempt to change the subject. "I think about jumping, sometimes," he said. "Actually, I think about jumping a lot!"

"Larry, don't—"

"It's true! Before the accident I used to come up here all the time. I'd look over the edge and think about what it would feel like. You have to make sure you hit the water right. Some people have lived through it, you know—not many, but some. Wouldn't that be a kicker? You think and think about it for days, maybe weeks, and you finally get up the courage to do it and they pull you from the water and you're still alive, but even worse off than before because every fucking bone in your body is broken."

Jill eyed him apprehensively. That strange look he'd had when he flashed the knife at her was coming back.

"Fuckers!" He spat the word out and took another pull of wine. "Why can't they just let the poor slobs drown? They want to die! Why do they have to pull them out and revive them and save their fucking, shitty lives?"

"Some people are glad when they live," Jill said quietly. "They realize afterwards how much life means to them."

"Yeah, and some people talk through their assholes."

"Come on Larry. I don't like to listen to talk like that. Please don't."

"Don't what?" Larry demanded. "Don't talk like there are a lot of fucked-up people in the world who

would be better off dead? It's true! You can't pretend
they don't exist. You can't pretend there aren't people
who have been shat on all their lives! You can't pretend
this world isn't a fucking shithole!"

Jill got to her feet. "Let's go back, Larry. I thought we
were going to have a nice time. I don't want to listen to
you rave."

Larry looked up at her, his scarred, disfigured face red
and malevolent. But then he smiled. "Hey, I'm sorry.
I'm always bum tripping you, aren't I?"

"Let's go, Larry."

"Hey, sit down! I'll be good, I promise!" He crossed
his hand in front of his heart. "Hope to die. Come on,
we still have some bread and cheese, and the wine's not
gone."

"Sometimes just being with you is exhausting, Larry."
Jill sat down again. "You're just so intense, you wear
people out."

Larry laughed. "You think it's exhausting for you?
Me, I have to be with myself all the time!"

Jill smiled, shaking her head. She supposed it was
true.

He reached out then and held her hand. She started to
draw it away, but he said, "Don't. I'm not going to try
anything. I just wanted to say I appreciate what you're
doing for me. I know I'm not an easy person to be
around and . . . well . . . Thank you." He let go of her
hand and smiled.

They left a few minutes later, going very slowly since
Larry's leg had stiffened up sitting on the cold metal
walkway.

When they got back to his place, Jill waited in the
dingy front room while he went into the back room to
change into his trunks for the therapy.

"I'll just be a minute," he said, disappearing through
the doorway.

Jill looked around the messy room and remembered

the mutilated nude foldout she had seen before. It didn't seem to be around now, thank God. Just thinking about it gave her the creeps. The bottle of wine, nearly empty, was sitting on the cluttered coffee table. She had taken two sips to be polite and Larry had drunk the rest. It didn't seem to affect him too much, though. Next to the bottle, his switch-blade was lying closed. He had popped it out at her purposely to frighten her, she thought angrily. She was glad she didn't have the ultrasound machine with her. Not doing that would cut a good twenty minutes off the session and let her get it over with quickly.

He seemed to be taking ages to change. She called out to him, "Aren't you ready yet?"

His voice came back from the other room sounding strange and husky. "In a minute. I'll be right there."

Her eyes went back to the switch-blade. A small shiver ran up her spine. She had gone out of her way to help him when she wanted to stay home with Ted, and all Larry could think of to do to show his appreciation was to frighten her with his damn knife.

She heard the thump of Larry's crutch on the floor and turned around. "Well, let's get—"

She broke off in mid-sentence, her breath taken away.

Larry was stark naked.

He was stark naked and his half-erect penis looked grotesquely red and huge next to his withered right leg. He was standing close to the coffee table, not far from the switch-blade, his ruddy penis bobbing slightly with his heart beat, a twisted, hideous smile pasted onto his disfigured face. His eyes were glassy, staring out brightly at her.

She felt like the air had been sucked out of the room. She couldn't breathe.

"Surprise, Jill." His voice was thick, husky. "Special treat for you today."

He took a hopping step forward, closer to the table,

closer to the knife. Jill looked back and forth from the knife to Larry, then took a quick step backwards.

"Larry! Don't!" she cried, her voice high and frightened.

The twisted leer on Larry's face grew bigger. "You always said you didn't think I was so ugly. Now's your chance to prove it."

He took another step closer to the table.

"No, Larry. No. Don't."

He was right next to the knife. All he had to do was bend over and pick it up. Afraid to take her eyes off him, she tried to picture the room in her mind. The door was probably about ten feet behind her. If she made a dash for it, he probably wouldn't be able to catch her. Probably.

Keeping her eyes glue to his naked, disfigured form, she bent down and picked up her purse.

"Hey! You're not leaving! You said you don't mind the way I look!" He took a quick jump forward.

Jill leaped backwards. Her legs hit a chair behind her and a high yelp came out of her as she tumbled over backwards with the chair, ending up with her legs high in the air.

"Hey!" Larry thumped heavily across the floor at her.

"No! Larry! NO!!" she screamed, rolling sideways off the chair, scrambling backward. "Larry! NO!"

He was over her now, his naked white body glistening with sweat, his eyes menacing, his mouth a snarl.

"You don't mind the way I look!" he shouted, lunging forward.

Jill thrust her leg out at him, hitting his crutch and knocking it out from under him. He fell forward toward her, bellowing with rage. Screaming, she rolled away as he came down next to her.

He hit the floor hard.

Jill scrambled to her feet. Shaking, her face drained

white, she ran to the door, flung it open, and ran out. As she raced to her car she could hear him behind her bellowing, roaring, cursing in rage and hate.

She jumped in her car and drove away, spinning the wheels. She ran through a stop sign, went two blocks, and pulled over to sit, shaking still, staring at nothing, thinking of what might have happened. That had been too close. Just too damn close.

By the time she got home, she had calmed down considerably and was berating herself for over-reacting. After all, he hadn't really done anything but take off his clothes and she had panicked immediately. If he had really intended to take her by force, he wouldn't have left his knife on the table, would he? A real rapist would have snuck up behind her and put the knife at her throat. If she hadn't panicked, if she had stayed calm and firmly told him to go back and put his clothes on, everything would have worked out all right. That's what she should have done.

If anything like that ever happens again, she told herself as she let herself in the front door, you have got to keep your cool, Jill. Don't panic!

The phone was ringing and she ran to answer it.

"Jill?" A man's voice.

"Yes. Who is it?"

"It's Frank. Is Ted in?"

Jill's hand tightened on the phone. "Frank! You have a lot of nerve calling now after last night!"

"What? What are you talking about?"

"You know damn well what I'm talking about!" Jill said angrily. "You lied to me last night! I don't know what sort of game you think you were playing, but—"

"Wait a minute now! Hold on! I didn't lie to you! What are you talking about?"

"Come off it, Frank! Ted told me what he talked to you about."

"He did?" Frank sounded surprised. "Then what's the matter? I don't understand."

"Cancer is not the same as a delusion, Frank!"

"Cancer! Maybe you'd better let me speak to Ted, Jill."

"I don't know what good that would do. Anyway, he's not here."

"I'm coming over, Jill. You've got it all wrong."

Frank arrived less than twenty minutes later. Jill let him in, saying, "You've got a lot of explaining to do, Frank."

She turned on her heel and went to sit down on the couch. She didn't offer Frank a seat, but he sat down anyway.

He looked at her nervously. "Ted isn't here?"

"No. He's at the university,"

"Are you sure?"

"What does it matter, Frank? He left me a note saying he was going to his office to catch up on his work."

"I just came from there, Jill. He wasn't in his office."

Jill examined Frank coldly. "Really, the university is a big place. Maybe he went to the library for something. Maybe he went to get some coffee! Why are you trying to fill my mind with doubts?"

"I'm not," Frank said. "I'm trying to figure out what's going on."

"That's what I'd like to know," Jill said. "Why did you tell me that cock-and-bull story last night?"

Frank lit a cigarette. "It wasn't a cock-and-bull story, Jill. What exactly did Ted tell you?"

"Oh, no! You're not going to play that game with me! Why don't you tell me your side! And it better be the truth!"

"All right. If that's the way you want it," Frank said, and proceeded to tell her of his long conversation with Ted at the bar.

Jill listened in silence. She was very skeptical when Frank began, snorting derisively when he first mentioned Ted's vision. But as Frank went on in his slow, scholarly way, piling detail on detail, she began to worry. It became harder and harder for her to believe that Frank was making it all up. Still, it was nearly impossible to believe the man Frank was talking about was her own husband! He had never once mentioned any of the things Frank was telling her. Ted had told her of his parents' and his sister's death, but never once had said anything about seeing their deaths in visions. The person Frank was describing was a madman or close to it!

By the time Frank was finished, she didn't know what to think!

"I tried to convince him to get some professional help, Jill, but he wouldn't listen to me." He looked at Jill for some sort of response, but she just sat toying with her wedding band, avoiding his eyes.

"What did Ted tell you?" he asked after a moment.

She looked up. Her eyes were red. "He said he was worried about cancer." She told him everything Ted had said to her.

"Well," Frank said, "I can't tell you who to believe, I guess. But there is one question you should ask yourself. Why would I lie to you? What possible reason could I have?"

"I—I don't know," Jill admitted weakly. She was feeling sick. It didn't occur to her that Ted really did have visions. As far as she could see, either Frank was a complete liar or Ted was a very ill person.

"I'm not making this up," Frank insisted. "Ted needs help. He needs professional help. It's not something you or I can deal with."

Frank sounded so sincere, Jill thought. And what reason could he have for making up such a story? He was Ted's best friend! But Ted wasn't insane! It wasn't pos-

sible. She knew him! She knew everything about him!
Or did she? He *was* a closed person. At times it seemed
he had a whole series of walls built up around himself to
keep people from seeing too deeply inside. *As if he had
a dark secret,* as Elaine had said. But really, he was just
shy, she told herself firmly. There had to be some mistake! Frank wasn't a liar, perhaps, but he must have
gotten things confused. Yes. That was it!

"There has to be some mistake!" she said. "You must
have gotten things mixed up, Frank. You must have
misunderstood him!"

Frank moved over next to her on the couch. "Jill, he
was as close to me as you are right now. We talked for
an hour. He said he saw you in a vision and something
horrible was happening to you and your eyes were glowing! I heard exactly what he said! And he didn't mention
one word about cancer. You can think I'm lying if you
want. But I'm not an idiot!"

"Okay, okay. But why would he tell you all that. Why
didn't he come to me?"

"Isn't that obvious?"

"No," Jill said. "It's not obvious. Not at all. I'm his
wife! If he needed help, he should have come to me."

"It was you he saw in what he calls his vision, Jill."

"But—"

"You don't understand—he really thinks that what he
saw is going to come true. He really thinks something's
going to happen to you and your eyes are going to start
glowing and you're going to turn into some sort of evil
monster!"

Jill sank back in a stunned daze. The full realization
of what Frank had told her was finally sinking in.

"He lost his parents," Frank continued, "and his little
sister. Now he thinks he's going to lose you."

Jill searched Frank's face for the smallest sign of de-
ceit or cunning but found none. He met her gaze levelly.

His features were full of concern.

"What should I do, Frank?" she asked.

"Get him to see somebody. I know it won't be easy. But he needs treatment by a competent psychiatrist."

Tears welled up in Jill's eyes and made shiny tracks down her cheeks. She wanted to scream.

Frank tried to give her hope, telling her there was probably a good chance Ted could be completely cured. He told her to be strong and have faith. It wasn't the end of the world. But no matter what he said, Jill just stared ahead blankly, her tears rolling down her cheeks. Finally, he realized he was just making things worse and left.

Jill waited unmoving on the couch for Ted to come home.

He came in just as the sun was setting, filling the living room with golden light. He kissed Jill on the forehead, then went into the kitchen and came back with a glass filled with whiskey.

"You're still drinking," Jill said. Her eyes had dried. Only by looking closely could Ted have told she had been crying.

"I'm exhausted. I have a lot of work to catch up on at school."

"Frank said he didn't see you there." Jill said evenly.

"Was he here again?" Ted asked, looking up from his drink. "What's he up to? Has he appointed himself my guardian?"

Jill ignored the remark. Trying to keep her voice steady, she asked, "What was that story about cancer you told me last night?"

"Huh? Come again?"

"Frank told me what you talked about on Monday. It wasn't cancer." Jill leaned forward and told Ted the things Frank had said—or she started to tell him, but he wouldn't let her finish.

He jumped up from his chair, shouting, "Damn that

Frank! I thought he was my friend!"

His face was red. The tendons on his neck stood out and his eyes seemed to bulge with anger. Looking at him, Jill suddenly thought of the way Larry had looked.

"Wait a minute!" Ted walked over to her. "You didn't believe him?" he asked as if he was scandalized. "Did you actually believe him?"

Startled by his accusing question, Jill blurted, "Well, yes . . . I did. I—"

"Oh God!" Ted sat down by her and taking her by the shoulders, turned her to face him directly. "I'm your husband, Jill! You hardly know Frank! How could you believe that garbage when I had already told you the truth?"

Flustered, confused, Jill stammered, "I—I d-don't know."

Ted kept her turned toward him, his hands firmly on her shoulders. She could see the anguish in his face.

"Please," he said, "Don't listen to Frank anymore. Don't even let him in here. I don't know what's happened to him. For some reason I can't begin to understand, he's all of a sudden got it in for me."

"I didn't believe him at first," Jill mumbled. "But he seemed so . . . sincere."

"Yes, he's good at that."

"Then all that stuff about your having visions was just—"

"Just his own strange fantasy, Jill."

He pulled her close and wrapped his arms tight around her. "Everything's okay, Jill," he whispered.

"I hope so," Jill said, snuggling closer.

"Oh, I almost forgot." He dug his hand into his pocket and pulled out a small blue box. "Here."

"What is it, Ted?"

"Open it and see."

Jill took the box and lifted the lid. "Oh, Ted!" she

exclaimed, picking up the heavy silver chain. As it came out of the box, it swung free, revealing a silver cross. Puzzled, she looked at Ted.

"Put it on," he urged.

"What's it for?"

"Nothing. It's just a present. Here." He took it from her and put it around her neck. "It looks nice."

She looked down at it between her breasts. "I don't understand," she said. "You haven't turned religious, have you?"

"A cross doesn't have to be religious. It's just jewelry. Don't you like it?"

"Of course, but—"

"Then wear it. Wear it all the time, if you love me."

CHAPTER 13

The phone rang twice. "Hello."

Ted cupped his hand over the mouthpiece so Jill couldn't hear. "It's Ted, Frank."

"Ted, I've been worried about you."

"Listen, Frank, if you say another word to Jill, I swear. . . .I swear. . ."

"Please, let me explain—"

"No! Just listen. If you see Jill again, I swear I'll kill you. I'll kill you, you understand?"

"Now, wait a minute—"

Ted slammed down the phone. Muttering to himself, he walked down the hall to the bedroom, where Jill was waiting for him.

Lieutenant Bates, still dressed in his impeccable blue suit, was holding up Billie Martin's naked body over his head, the body's arms and leg flopping about grotesquely. Bates was in a rage. Ted stared at him in awe. Bates was coming toward him holding the body in the air, shrieking at him. *This will happen to your wife, Mr. Concerned Citizen! To your beloved wife!* Then, suddenly, it wasn't Billie Martin's body Bates was holding up, but Jill's! It was Jill, naked, dead, swarmed by flies, and Bates was still walking toward him, holding her up, shouting. *Here she is! Your precious wife! Now it's hap-*

pened to her! Ted stared in horror as with a mighty lunge Bates heaved Jill's body high in the air at him and he saw her floating in space, her arms and legs twisting unnaturally, her hair fluttering in the wind. And then she landed on her feet in front of him. Her eyes were blazing and she looked like a demon out of hell.

She was holding something in her hands.

"What is it, Jill? What?"

She held it out toward him and he saw it was a small fluffy dog, its tail wagging merrily. He started to take it, but she drew it back next to her naked breasts. She took the dog's small head in her hands and started twisting, the tendons on her neck sticking out with the effort. She pulled the dogs head from its body in a great gush of blood that coated her breasts and belly. She held the dripping head up like a trophy, then threw it at him. Her eyes spitting fire, she tossed her head back and hellish laughter came shrieking out of her gaping mouth.

Ted bolted upright in bed, barely suppressing the scream that was lodged in his throat. Soaked with sweat, he stared into the darkness of the bedroom a moment, then turned to see the shadowy outline of Jill's sleeping form next to him. She was safe. It hadn't happened. Not yet.

He slipped naked from the bed, wrapped his robe around himself, and stumbled into the kitchen. He flicked on the light and, squinting against the sudden glare, went to the cabinet over the stove. The whiskey bottle was empty, but there was half a bottle of rum. He took it to the kitchen table with him, sat down, and took a long pull directly from the bottle. It made him shudder, but he quickly took another drink.

When he had finished half of what was there, the horrible feelings left over from the nightmare were mercifully blurred. It was something huge and monstrous—didn't Bates realize that? Dark, unimaginable forces

were at work! Two people had already died horribly—
and the fat woman! He recalled Joe Frantini's words.
*She was something that was human once, but not any-
more.*

Taking the bottle with him, he went out through the
dark living room, slid open the glass door to the
balcony, and stepped out. The cold penetrating his robe
seemed only a distant feeling. He took another pull from
the bottle, then looked up. Halley's comet was straight
overhead, its sweeping tail cutting through the starry
night like a knife. *An omen of doom.*

Possession, Cindy had said.

He had spent the day at the university library, as he
had told Jill in the note he left. He hadn't lied about
that, though he had lied about everything else. He had
gone into the stacks and pulled out every book he could
find on satanism and possession.

The feeling of death that had washed over him when
the obscene fat woman came charging at him convinced
him that what Simon had told Cindy was true.

He took the pile of books to a desk and sat down to
study them. A quick look was enough for most of the
books. There were only a few with real scientific merit.

Possession, he learned, was the control of a person's
soul by a devil or demon. Children were the most sus-
ceptible to attack, though anyone of any age could be
possessed. Documented cases—those witnessed by qual-
ified experts—were very very rare, it seemed. Most cases
of "possession" turned out to be hysteria or psychosis or
hoaxes. According to one book, there had only been two
dozen clear-cut cases of possession since the middle of
the last century. Another book put the figure at only ten.

Most possessions developed gradually. The explanation given for this was that it took time for the possessing spirit to weaken the victim's soul and assert its control over it. And even when that happened, there were

often periods in which the possessed person would regain control and seem cured. "In general," one author said, "The possession of a soul is not an easy matter for the demon. There is continual warfare between the victim and his or her tormentor. At times the possessed soul may even expel the offending spirit without the benefit of the rites of exorcism. Indeed, we may safely conclude that the possession of a soul is a very difficult task. Were it easy, instances of it would not be so rare."

This puzzled Ted. From what Cindy had told him, Billie Martin had been possessed in a matter of minutes. It seemed that she was completely overwhelmed before she even had a chance to fight back. And certainly the fat woman was under the complete and absolute control of whatever unimaginable being possessed her.

There were several signs of possession. The most common, but also the most unreliable, was the uncontrollable uttering of obscene and blasphemous language. This behavior, however, was also common in various forms of mental illness. A more reliable indication was the imitation by the victim of animal noises with uncanny power and precision, most often the grunting of a pig or the barking of a dog.

But the only conclusive signs of possession seemed to be those which involved supernatural abilities—such as superhuman strength and the ability to read minds and project thoughts. Possessed persons were known to have hurled objects several times their own weight. And at times they would project blasphemous and unclean thoughts into the minds of those trying to help them.

There were a number of case histories in the books. Ted read through them all. None of them made any mention of eyes that seemed to glow with fire.

The rites of exorcism were of no help in preventing possession, he learned. One author said there was no known way to prevent it. Another said the wearing of a cross was effective. But a third said the wearing of a cross was only sometimes helpful—only daily prayer and the purity of one's soul offered real protection.

Helpful or not, Ted decided, wearing a cross couldn't hurt. On his way home, he stopped off at a small jewelry store and bought the silver cross he had given Jill.

Now he stood on the balcony in the cold night, staring up at the awesome comet. What was happening now was something more than just possession, he thought. Possession was rare. Yet in just the last week there had been two cases—three if the dead boy found in Billie Martin's back yard had been possessed. And none of the cases he had read about mentioned anything like the horrible reality of the fire in the naked woman's eyes last night and the feeling of death that had washed over him.

Was it the comet?

He thought of the bloody finger-drawn sign.

None of it made any sense! There was an ounce of rum left in the bottle. He drained it and stumbled back inside.

The old man, Simon, held the key. If only he could find him! The gears of fate were turning, turning, drawing Jill closer and closer. And the cross wouldn't help. No matter what he tried, he knew his vision would come true.

No, that wasn't right, he told himself. There was a way to put Jill beyond fate's reach. There was a way to spare her the horror of the approaching darkness.

He went back to the bedroom. Standing in the doorway, he watched Jill's form rise and fall with her slow breathing. He thought of all the happy times they had spent together—the absurd way they had met, the joy of discovering each other's bodies, that day on the beach when they couldn't stop giggling, their wedding day. Sighing deeply, he went over to his side of the bed and picked up his pillow. The days of happiness were over forever.

He walked silently around the bed to Jill's side. She was curled up in a fetal position, lying on her side. Her long hair had fallen in front of her face. With trembling fingers, he carefully brushed it back. She didn't stir.

She looked so peaceful.

Ted's heart was pounding. He took the pillow firmly in both hands and raised it over her head. *There are worse things than death,* he told himself. *This is the only way!* Memories from the last few days swirled through his head one after the other. Jill as he had seen her in the vision, fighting something he couldn't see, shrieking in terror. The dead girl, Billie Martin, lying in that bright cement lot, flies buzzing around her, the area around her eyes darkened as if scorched by fire. Cindy's lips mouthing a single word: *POSSESSION.* The grotesque fat woman running at him with impossible speed, her mouth a gaping chasm, flames filling her eyes. And the wracking feeling of death that washed over him, the feeling that he was already dead and maggots were claiming his body.

There are worse things than death!

His heart was a raging beast, pounding madly. He held the pillow straight out in front of him, his arms rigid with tension.

DO IT! THERE ARE WORSE THINGS THAN DEATH! THERE IS SAFETY IN DEATH! DO IT! DO IT!!

Still holding the pillow out in front of himself, he turned quickly and walked out of the bedroom. He stumbled down the hall to the living room, fell on the couch and, sobbing, buried his head in the pillow.

* * *

Over the next several days Ted found it harder and harder to keep in control.

He knew he was beginning to crack and tried to cover it over by smothering Jill with attention. He took her to Trader Vic's for a sumptuous dinner one night. He bought her flowers and big boxes of See's candies. He took her to see *Beach Blanket Babylon,* an absurd show that had her laughing so hard that tears streamed down her cheeks. And he hugged her constantly, telling her over and over again how much he loved her.

He wanted to convince her that the stories Frank had told her weren't true and he wanted to assuage his tremendous guilt. He was failing her, he told himself. He couldn't bring himself to do what needed to be done to put her out of harm's way. When he thought of the horrid fat woman, he knew Jill would be better off with a quick and painless death. But he could not give her that gift.

On the surface, he kept up normal appearances, but underneath he was sinking deeper and deeper into despair.

On Monday he learned that Bates was officially listed as missing. While Jill was at work, he went out to the Taraval Station and found Teel.

"I think it got him," Teel said, puffing nervously on his cigarette.

"What do you mean?" Ted asked, though he knew the answer.

"Nobody's seen him since that night. Whatever got that woman got Bates too."

"What are you doing about it?"

"What can we do about it?" Teel asked. "The word has come down. Nobody is to talk about it at all. I shouldn't even be talking to you. They're trying to pretend everything is a-okay. Maxwell asked a few too many questions and found himself on furlough."

"Don't they realize—"

Teel cut him off. "They don't want to realize anything. They don't want to know. They're trying to pretend nothing ever happened."

Ted left Teel to spend the rest of the day wandering the streets looking for Simon. The next day he did the same thing and again came up empty-handed. On Wednesday, he went back to the Haight district to see Cindy Shultz.

He had forgotten she was moving out when he went to see her and found the place locked up tight, a "FOR RENT" sign in the window.

Every day at sunset, he would hurry home to keep watch over Jill and try to present a happy facade. But it was getting more and more difficult. Every night he would think: *It could happen tonight.* And every night he ended up drinking himself into a stupor. He tried to keep it hidden, but he knew Jill could tell.

On Thursday, Bates made the newspaper. His name leapt out at Ted from the front page. Picking the paper up from the counter where Jill had left it, Ted read the article quickly.

POLICE LIEUTENANT FOUND DEAD

The naked body of Lieutenant Gregory Bates of the San Francisco Police Department was found yesterday morning on the grassy slopes of the Presidio golf course. There were no wounds on the body, according to police. The cause of death has not yet been determined.

Bates, an eighteen-year veteran of the force, was reported missing by his wife Thelma (née Macpherson) last Sunday after he had failed to return home the previous night. Officer Bart Maxwell, the last man known to have seen him alive, refused to comment to reporters. The Police Information Office likewise refused to offer any information except to confirm that Lieutenant Bates had not reported for duty after his wife reported him missing. Information Officer George Bailey, when asked whether the death of Bates was connected to a number of similar occurences recently, issued a terse "no comment."

(But the Chronicle has learned that a number of mysterious incidents with similarities to the Bates case have recently taken place. See story on p. 19.)

The time of death was put at not more than twenty-four hours before the body was found yesterday morning, probably sometime Tuesday night. Police have not ruled out foul play.

Gregory Bates, 48, was born in Pittsburg and graduated from Union High School there. He served four years on the San Jose force before joining the SFPD. He was a member of the San Francisco Elks Club and was involved in many other community activities. . . .

Ted skipped the rest of the biographical sketch and turned to page 19.

NAKED BODIES FOUND

The discovery of the naked body of Lieutenant Gregory Bates (see story on p.1) is only the latest of a number of such gruesome incidents. So far, a total of six other bodies, all naked, have been found in the past ten days. Three of the bodies have been identified. They are:

Billie Martin, 19, a San Francisco State student whose body was found in a lot in back of a North Beach restaurant.

Samuel Hotchins, 39, a real estate salesman, was found last Monday in Golden Gate Park.

Louella Prescott, 60, a retired waitress. Her body was found in the Tenderloin a day later.

The unidentified bodies are those of a young teenaged boy found, remarkably enough, in the back yard of Billie Martin's apartment in the Haight-Ashbury; a middle-aged woman found on Sloat Boulevard; and an elderly man found behind the East Bay Bus Terminal.

The police have become increasingly tight-lipped as more and more bodies come to light, but the Chronicle has learned from a variety of sources who do not wish to be identified that the similarities among the cases are both striking and bizarre. One source said, "It's eerie. And I admit I'm a bit frightened by it. No one seems to be able to figure out what's happening."

According to our sources the first and most obvious similarity is that all the bodies were found completely naked. Secondly, none of the bodies showed any wounds. So far as has been determined, they all died the same way, of massive heart failure. Why such disparate people, some just teenagers, should all have died of heart failure, is said to baffle the medical examiners. Reportedly, they have found nothing in any of the bodies so far examined that would indicate poisoning. Another bizarre aspect of the cases is that all the bodies had strange marks darkening the skin around the eyes. And again, no explanation has been found for this.

Nor do the mysterious elements surrounding

these cases end there. A North Beach waiter reported seeing Billie Martin before her death. He claimed that Martin's eyes were "glowing like fire" and said she had superhuman strength. According to the waiter, Joe Frantini, the girl picked him up bodily and threw him through the air when he tried to help her. (One source told the Chronicle that the police have received other reports of people with "glowing eyes." But whether or not these reports were connected to any of the bodies discovered, the source could not say.)

There are also disturbing reports of similar cases outside of San Francisco. A quick check reveals reports of people with "glowing eyes" and/or the discovery of naked bodies in Sacramento, Stockton, Monterey, Santa Barbara, Los Angeles and outside of California in Chicago, Philadelphia and New York.

For a minute after finishing the article, Ted stared into space. Then he wadded the paper together, crushing it into a ball, and put it in the garbage bag under the sink.

"What is it?" he muttered. "What the hell is happening?"

The newspaper made him realize how obsessed he had become. He was like a man so intent on fighting the fire in his own house he doesn't see the city around him burning. It wasn't only Jill. Everyone was in danger.

Possession, Cindy had told him.

He grabbed his coat and drove downtown to the Chronicle Building at Fifth and Mission. After a frustrating runaround, he got the name of the reporter who had written about the bodies—George Mason. Mason, he was sure, realized the enormity of what was happening. He would want to help him find Simon.

He found the reporter covering a bloody ax murder in the outer Mission. He was a short man with thinning hair and a bristly black mustache.

"Oh, that," Mason said when Ted told him of his interest in the story. "Yeah, that made a good story."

"I think we can help each other." Ted said. He felt a splitting headache coming on. He had to stop his drinking, he thought as he quickly told the reporter about Simon. "I'm sure he knows what it's all about!"

"Yeah?" Mason didn't seem impressed. "What's his name? Maybe I'll talk to him."

Ted had to wait for a sudden wave of dizziness to pass before answering. It seemed as if Mason was at the far end of a long, hazy tunnel. "I only know his first name," Ted had to force the words out. "That's the point. If we work together we can find him—"

"Hey! I can't spend my time on a wild goose chase like that! I'm a working reporter."

"Damn it, I thought you understood!" Ted shouted through the sharpening pain. "Something monstrous is going on! We've *got* to find that old man!"

"So, if you find him, I'll talk to him," Mason said.

Ted turned away from him quickly.

"Listen," Mason called out after him as he walked away, "the story was good copy. It sold some newspapers. As far as I'm concerned, that's it. Understand?"

Mason's voice seemed to echo in his skull as Ted forced himself to keep putting one foot in front of the other. The pain had turned to throbbing hammer blows two inches in from his ears.

It's going to happen again! he thought, panic rising inside him.

The glare from the sidewalk was becoming excruciating. Holding his hands over his eyes, he staggered forward until he came to an alley. He took a few steps into it, then collapsed in a doorway.

To the people walking by, he was just another drunk.

Someone with a sledge hammer was pounding on the inside of his skull. The pain of it was excruciating and he bit his lip to keep from screaming. A small trickle of blood ran down his chin. His hands pressing against the side of his head, he lay in the doorway trying to will it to stop, trying to believe that it wasn't really happening.

A hissing roar rose up to accompany the incessant pounding and together both swelled to an impossible crescendo. Then, abruptly, both ceased, and he felt like he was floating in an infinite black void. Images, sounds, and smells he could not understand drifted into his mind out of the nothingness. Colors formed themselves into pulsating shapes and slowly—so slowly he could hardly see the change—resolved themselves into a face.

It was the old man. Simon.

His wrinkled face with its pale, translucent skin floated in the darkness. The old man began speaking. Ted understood the words rather than heard them.

You must find me. It is very important. You must find me!

Ted heard himself answering with a strange calm. *I have looked all over for you. What is your name? Where do you live?*

The old man looked troubled. *You must find me. There is not much time left. It is coming.*

How? How can I find you?

But there was no answer. The old face began spinning, faster and faster. It receded to a distant point and then disappeared in the blackness.

A sudden coldness swept over Ted, chilling him to the bone. The world was black and void. He could see nothing, hear nothing, feel nothing but the numbing coldness. Then a sound came to him from far away. As he strained to listen it seemed to come closer. It grew louder and he realized it was laughter—evil, inhuman laughter.

(The laugh of a demon, laughter from hell, cold, cruel, bloody laughter, swelling louder and louder, crashing into his ears, shaking his whole body, booming like thunder.)

And now a tiny figure in the distance, naked.

Jill.

The hellish laughter was coming from her! Her mouth stretched wide like a gaping black chasm, she floated closer out of the void. Her eyes were like twin fires shooting flame. And over her head (in the sky?) a sinuous beam of red light writhed like a snake.

Suddenly, she was right in front of him and dancing obscenely in her nakedness. She threw her head back, her hair flying. The horrible laughter came spilling out of her shrieking mouth and seemed to split the air with its violence.

Behind her, the void started giving way to a brilliant glow.

She turned, pounded her feet on the earth, and threw up her hands over her head. The glow exploded into a roaring wall of fire. It's immense size dwarfed her. She was a tiny dancing silhouette before the monstrous flames.

Now she turned again and reached out. It seemed to Ted that if he reached out to he would touch her.

I am with her, he thought.

He was with her in the vision. He could not see himself, but he knew, somehow, he was there with her. She wasn't ten feet away from him. She looked like nothing human—only a grotesque caricature of a woman.

He felt something in his hand. What? It felt heavy, metallic. He tried to make himself look down to see it, but could not. Yet it was important.

Very important.

The hellish caricature of Jill danced up to him, whirling like a dervish, her eyes filled with fire, her face a mask of evil, and he lifted the heavy hard thing in his hand. Somehow, it was very important.

The flaming wall roared. The heavy thing in his hand was very heavy.

What is it?

The question dissolved in his mind. Darkness spread like black ink over the sheets of fire. Jill faded away into mists.

There was nothing for a while and then Simon's words came back to him, understood rather than heard.

You must find me! There is not much time left. It is coming.

He screamed. The terrified sound came raw out of his throat. Then he was being shaken. He opened his eyes and saw a crowd of people gathered around him. An old man was kneeling down beside him, holding his shoulders.

He had a mane of white hair. It was Simon!

The old man turned his head away and spoke to someone behind him. He was speaking Spanish. When he turned back, Ted saw that it wasn't Simon. He didn't look at all like Simon.

Hurriedly, Ted got to his feet and pushed through the circle of people.

He wandered around in a daze for nearly an hour, then went into a bar. He sat in a booth in back and drank until the world was only a distant blur.

It was pitch dark when he walked bleary-eyed into the street. He looked at his watch. Seven-thirty. Jill was all alone!

It took him too long to remember where he had left his car. It was after eight when he found it. He got in and sped home.

The house was dark. It seemed almost heavy in its emptiness.

"Jill!" he called out. "Where are you?"

The room swallowed the sound of his voice. There was no answer.

"Jill!" he yelled. "Jill."

She had to be home! He turned on all the lights in the living room, then ran to the kitchen and turned on the lights there. It was clean and empty. The off-white cabinets stared back at him mutely.

"Jill! Jill!!" He ran down the hall and went from room to room, turning on all the lights until the whole place was as bright as a movie set and still he couldn't believe she wasn't there. His thoughts screaming in his mind, he wandered back unsteadily to the living room. Jill couldn't be out in the night! Not with fate's hellish forces there lurking, waiting to jump out of the shadows and destroy her!

He stood stock still, staring out the windows at the black night, then turned quickly and ran back down the hall to the bedroom. He had already looked for her there, but in his panic he refused to accept that. Anything seemed possible but the simple fact that she was out in the dark night. But the room was still empty. Then he thought of the bathroom. He hadn't looked there before. He slammed back the door and flipped on the light. The towels and shiny blue tile greeted him in silence.

He had been trying to keep his terror bottled up for days now and could contain it no longer. It all came rushing out, overwhelming the small part of his mind that was still rational. Screaming, he rushed out of the bathroom to his study.

"Jill! Stop hiding. I know you're here! Please, come out!" He threw open the closet door. "Jill! Please!"

He ran back to the spare bedroom where they had

stored all the boxes left over from moving. He started pushing the boxes out of the way, throwing them in the air. "Jill!" he shrieked as a box went flying. He grabbed another box and threw it in the air. And another box. "Where are you!" And then in a frenzy he picked up box after box and heaved each one against the wall until there were none left to throw and he stood panting heavily, staring wild-eyed around the room.

"JILL!!!"

His desperate cry faded away slowly. Then came another voice.

"Oh, God! Ted!"

He turned around. It was Jill.

He rushed to her, throwing his arms around her. Jill dropped the bag of groceries she had brought in with her as he collapsed on her, his sudden weight making her stagger backwards.

"Ted! What is it!" she cried.

But he didn't answer her. He was a dead weight in her arms. She eased him slowly to the floor. His face was slack and ashen.

Frightened as she was, Jill didn't panic. She knew he had just fainted. She ran and got a seat cushion from the living room sofa, brought it back, and stuffed it under his legs to make the blood go back to his head.

The phone rang. It was probably Penny, she thought, calling for a ride to their dance class. She let the phone ring, and kneeled down to stroke Ted's hair.

After a minute, his eyes blinked. He moaned and tried to sit up.

Jill pushed him back down. "Just lie still a while longer."

His eyes focused on her. He stared at her a moment and then asked, his voice slurred, "Where's your cross?"

"Huh?"

"Your cross! Why aren't you wearing it?"

"Does it matter? What happened, Ted?"

Ted sat up. "You ought to be wearing it," he said firmly.

Jill helped him to his feet. "I don't understand what's going on, Ted! I come home and hear you screaming and rush back here and the store room's a mess and you fall into my arms and faint—and then you ask me why I'm not wearing that damned cross!"

"Please, Jill," Ted said, slumping back against the wall, "just get it and put it on."

"No! I'm going crazy trying to figure you out, Ted!"

"All right. I'll get it for you." Ted went into the bedroom and came back the silver cross in his hands. Sighing, Jill gave in and let him put it on her.

"There. I'm wearing it," she said. "Now can you please tell me what's going on?"

"I'm sorry," Ted said, brushing by her to walk quickly down the hall.

Stifling an impulse to scream after him, Jill bit her lip and knelt down to gather up the groceries. She stuffed them back into the bag and went into the kitchen.

Ted was looking in the cabinet over the stove where they kept the liquor. He didn't seem to realize she was behind him watching. He was muttering to himself under his breath, looking frantically through the cabinet. His whole body was shaking. He looked horribly like a paper puppet on a string, Jill thought. Dan used to get the shakes like that too, she remembered, when he needed a fix.

Ted pulled out an unopened bottle of gin. He could hardly get the cap off, but eventually he managed it and put the bottle to his lips for a quick shot, then poured out a large amount into a tall water glass. Setting the bottle down with a thud, he turned around with the glass in his hand.

His eyes were wild. "I—I d-didn't know you were there."

Jill was too shocked to move or speak. She looked back and forth from the gin in his hand to his ashen face. She knew it was Ted in front of her, but she didn't see him. She saw Dan. She saw Dan that day she had come home and found him at the kitchen table, his belt wrapped tightly around his upper arm, its end between his teeth, a needle sticking into the obscenely bulging vein of his arm. She saw Dan the way he had looked up at her then, surprised, his face the color of chalk, his eyes wild and desperate. But it wasn't Dan. It was *Ted* with the same wild look in his eyes! It was Ted! It was Ted destroying himself!

She would have yelled at him then, yelled and screamed and ripped the gin glass from his hand and slapped him hard across the face, screaming she couldn't let him destroy himself. She would have fought and yelled and argued, telling him she couldn't stand to watch what he was doing to himself. She would have told him he was killing himself! She would have told him he couldn't possibly hate himself so much as to do what he was doing.

She would have told him all the things she had told Dan.

Except they hadn't worked with Dan. They had made Dan hide away from her. They had made Dan hate her.

Instead, she went up to him and put her hand on his arm. She said as calmly as she could, "Please, don't start drinking again. You've been drinking so much lately."

Ted dropped his eyes from hers to look down at the glass in his hand. He was hurting her terribly, he knew. But he needed the gin. He needed it to forget. He wanted to stop his tortured soul from screaming out loud.

But the way she was looking at him, her eyes pleading

with him, taking another drink would be like slapping her in the face.

He put the glass down on the counter.

Relieved, Jill stood up on her toes and kissed him on his cheek. "Thank you," she whispered.

"I don't want to hurt you, Jill," he said pathetically. He looked over nervously at the glass of gin. He longed for it.

Jill put her arm through his and urged him gently away from the counter. "You're shaking," she said. "Let's go in and sit down in the living room. I'll fix you some coffee."

She was exerting a gentle pressure on his arm, but the glass of gin seemed to hold him like a magnet. Jill was pulling him away from it, but its pull seemed even stronger. He couldn't stop himself. He had to forget how he had seen her, her face twisted and evil, her eyes shooting flames. He lifted his arm away from Jill's hold, turning to pick of the glass, and drained it quickly.

"I'm sorry!" he blurted, reaching for the bottle.

But Jill was too quick for him. She grabbed the bottle away.

"Please," he said. "I need it." He knew how pathetic he sounded and hated himself for it.

Holding the bottle behind her back, Jill faced him defiantly. "Can't we talk?" she asked. "Can't you tell me why you need it so badly?"

I need it because I'm a failure, Ted thought. *I need it because fate is closing in on you and I can't do anything to stop it.*

"I need it," was all he said in a whining tone. God! How he hated himself!

"You're destroying yourself," Jill said evenly.

"I know."

Ted held out his arms to her imploringly. He was destroying himself and Jill too. He hated himself with a deep passion. And because he hated himself, he had to have that bottle!

Lunging forward, he grabbed Jill's arm with one hand and twisted the bottle away from her with the other. The sudden movement, though, made him lose his balance and he instinctively reached out to grab Jill. He regained his balance, but she went flying. She fell down hard on the side of her hip.

He backed away from her slowly, guiltily clutching the bottle, staring at the look of shock and surprise on her upturned face.

Slowly, her hip aching, she picked herself up from the floor. Ted seemed a motionless statue in front of her, wild despair and guilt frozen upon his features. He took a staggering step toward her. The bottle slipped from his fingers. It seemed a long time before it hit the floor. There was a loud smash and pieces of glass flew everywhere. And then he was in her arms, bent over, burying his head at the base of her neck.

She held his heaving shoulders tightly.

"It's okay," she soothed, still in shock herself. "It's okay. I'm here."

Ted struggled to keep his mind a blank. He felt if he started thinking now he would go mad. Jill had left the paper bag of groceries on the kitchen table. He glued his eyes to it, trying to concentrate his whole being on it. *Don't think!* It was brown and bulky, rolled over and crinkled at the top. It was a little wet where Jill's hand had held it. He concentrated on every detail, not daring to move his eyes, not daring to think.

Look at the bag!

Don't think!

It's a brown bag. It's full of groceries. There is a little tear in it. It is rolled over at the top.

DON'T THINK!

But he saw Simon's weathered old face, ringed with

with hair. *You must find me! There is not much time left. It is coming!*

Don't think! Damn it, don't think!

But in spite of himself, he remembered the naked fat woman charging at him like a demon from hell and the dead girl, lying in the bright cement lot covered by flies.

Look at the bag! Don't think!

But he remembered Simon being thrown back against him at Emilio's and Simon dropping the paper bag he was carrying.

The paper bag! It had a name on it!

He moved away from Jill as if forgetting she was there and stared at the bag. The men at Emilio's had rushed out when that man came in telling them he had found the dead girl. They had knocked Simon against him, making him drop a bag he was carrying. He had picked it up and handed it back to the old man.

Behind him, Jill said, "Ted, please—"

"Quiet!" Ted shouted, not taking his eyes from the bag. He tried to picture the bag Simon was carrying. It had the name of a store printed on it.

"Ted, come on, please—"

"Shush!"

What was the name? What?

HENSON'S

"Oh, God! Yes! Henson's!"

Jill stared after him dumbly as he ran from the kitchen.

He raced down the hall to the telephone, pulled the directory out from under it and flipped through it almost afraid to hope. But there it was. HENSON'S TOBACCO listed in bold print. It was on Turk Street in the Tenderloin.

Of course! There were thousands of old people struggling to survive in that run-down area. And Simon probably stopped in that store regularly. They probably knew him there!

He went to the closet and got his coat.

"Where are you going?" Jill asked.

"To find someone who can help us."

"What?"

"I can't explain now. Please Jill, whatever happens, don't go out. Stay inside. And wear the cross I gave you."

He rushed out the door.

CHAPTER 14

San Francisco's Tenderloin was a grimy area whose flop houses and cheap residential hotels attracted old people who could not afford to live anywhere else. The aged moved in to mix with the dope pushers, the male and female prostitutes, and the winos—all of society's discards.

Henson's was hardly more than a hole in the wall of a run-down building next to a pornographic movie theater. There was room in the tobacco and magazine shop only to take about five steps inside, turn around carefully, and walk out again. A shrivelled old woman was wedged into a small booth on one side of the store, surrounded by racks of candy and chewing gum. She hardly had room to move in the cramped space and rested her arms on the glass counter because there was no other place to put them.

It was raining when Ted arrived. Dripping, he hurried into the tiny shop and asked the woman if she knew Simon. The name wasn't familiar to her, she said. He described the old man.

"We're swarming with old people here," she said. "Just waiting to die, seems like sometimes. Don't go dripping all over the magazines, now."

Thick stacks of Time and Newsweek were on the floor

at Ted's feet. Both had pictures of Halley's Comet on their covers. Ted stepped back away from them.

He decided he would wait there all night for Simon. And if he didn't show up, he would wait all day tomorrow. He had no choice.

But he was worried about leaving Jill alone. He asked the woman behind the counter if there was a phone. She pointed out the door.

Huddling under the small awning to keep out of the rain, he phoned home. The phone rang at least a dozen times before Jill finally answered it.

"It's Ted, Jill. Thank God you're home. I was afraid you'd gone out. I—"

"I was out." Jill's voice sounded hard, controlled. "I went out and walked in the rain to think. I just got back."

"Please, don't go out again," Ted said desperately. "You don't know what might happen. You've got to stay inside at night. Are you wearing the cross?"

"Listen Ted. You need help! Frank was right all along."

Ted slumped back against the wall. "I can explain everything Jill. It's not what you think! Please!" He broke off abruptly.

A white-haired old man was walking down the street toward him, hatless in the rain, his shabby coat collar pulled up tight under his chin. It was . . .

Jill's voice came over the phone. "You've got to face facts, Ted. Something's happened to you. You're not the man I married anymore. But I still love you and want to help you if you'll let me—"

Ted let the phone fall away from his ear. It was Simon coming down the street!

"I can explain everything, Jill!" he yelled into the phone. "Just wait till I get home!"

Slamming down the phone, he ran down the sidewalk

and grabbed the old man by the elbow. "Simon!" he cried.

The man started and turned fearfully, as if he thought he was being mugged.

Ted started talking. The rain was pouring down in torrents and Simon was gaping at him open-mouthed, but Ted didn't notice. Everything that had been pent up inside him just came exploding out.

It was a minute before Simon got over his surprise and put a stop to it. The rain was dripping down inside his collar, soaking him to the bone. He broke in when Ted paused for a breath and shouted over the splattering rain and hissing traffic, "Calm down, young man! Have we met before?"

Ted nodded, his eyes drinking in the sight of the old man. Never had anyone looked so beautiful.

"Yes, we have met," he said. "At Emilio's remember? They knocked you back against me and you dropped your bag. That's how I found you! I wanted to talk to you then, but looking at that girl made me sick and I had to leave and by the time I got back you had disappeared. I can't believe I finally found you! It's been a nightmare. Oh God—"

"All right!" Simon shouted. "You've found me. Now let's get out of the rain!"

They hurried to Simon's apartment, which was just around the corner. Going up the dingy stairs, Simon had to stop twice to catch his breath. They took off their soaking coats, then Simon turned to Ted.

"I believe you mentioned something about having visions?"

"That's right," Ted said uncertainly. Now that he had found Simon, he was afraid the old man wouldn't believe him. "I know it sounds crazy, but it's the truth. You've got to believe me!"

"Oh, I believe you," Simon said kindly.

"You do?"

"Yes. You see, I've been waiting for you."

Ted stared. "I don't understand."

"I'll explain in a bit. First, let's get some hot tea before we both catch cold."

They went into the small kitchen, where Simon put on a pot of water to boil. "Now, I want you to tell me about this vision you had."

"I've had two now."

"All right, tell me both of them. Try to remember everything."

"But I don't understand! What did you mean you've been waiting for me?"

"First, tell me about what you saw in your visions."

Sipping his tea, Ted went over his visions as carefully as he could. He was sure there were some details he had forgotten, he said, but the most important things, the most terrifying things, were still vivid in his mind.

Simon listened patiently, interrupting Ted only twice. The first time was when he mentioned the strange beam of blood-red light that had appeared in both visions.

"Wait a minute," Simon said. "Tell me that again."

Ted described the arc of red light again, then waited for Simon to respond.

But the old man merely grunted, "Go on."

Simon didn't interrupt again until Ted came to the wall of fire in the second vision.

"He shall come in fire," Simon intoned mysteriously.

"What?"

"I'll explain later. Go on.

"There's not much left," Ted continued. "What sticks out most strongly in my mind was something I was holding in my hand. I don't know why it should seem so important, but it does. It was something heavy and hard, but I don't know what it was. Yet I feel sure it was crucial, somehow. It's the last thing I remember from the vision."

Ted waited nervously for Simon to say something, but the old man was staring at his teacup, lost in thought. Then he looked up at Ted, and his eyes were moist with tears.

"So, you've finally come," he said. "I have been waiting such a long, long time."

Before Ted could ask what he was talking about, Simon started talking about the ancient book to which he had devoted most of his life.

Simon had been stung by his expulsion from the priesthood, but kept his hopes pinned on the publication of his translation of *On Good and Evil*. With great anticipation, he awaited the acclaim and controversy he was sure would come. He waited in vain. The book went unnoticed. It sold less than a thousand copies.

He finally had to admit the truth to himself. The book was a failure and he was a beaten man. He had lost his vocation. He had no money, no friends, no job, no home.

Taking odd jobs where he could find them along the road, he wandered from Arizona to California. He spent the summer of 1950 in the San Juaquin valley picking lettuce. The pride that had tormented him for so long was finally gone.

Then his hopes revived. He met a man in Fresno who believed in him. Jim Snyder was astounded to find the man who had written *On Good and Evil* picking lettuce. A deeply religious man, Snyder had read the book when it had first come out and thought Simon a genius. To help spread Simon's message, he gave him a half-hour radio program on the local station he owned, paying Simon a salary more appropriate to a star.

Simon used the program to spread the teachings of the ancient manuscript on the nature of good and evil, always stressing what he thought was its most important message. While man depends on God in fighting evil, even more importantly God depends on man, and man must help God in His struggles against Satan.

But the response to the program was hardly more encouraging than the response to his book had been, and Simon was not too unhappy when he lost his job after two years when Snyder sold the station.

For several years after that, he had sold shoes in Santa Barbara.

He had always thought the manuscript had come to him that day in Egypt as part of God's purpose. He had staked his faith on that. But after the failure of his book and radio program he realized he had only been suffering the delusions of pride and vanity. He was no different than a thousand other false prophets, he told himself. He wasn't meant to spread God's word. He was meant to sell shoes.

One evening he came home from the shoe store and pulled out the fragile manuscript from the box he kept it in under his bed. Holding it in his trembling hands, he wondered why he still kept it, dragging it around with him from town to town. The dream was dead. He would never make a new life for himself unless he put it all behind him. He would destroy the ancient papyrus bundle with its fine lines of Greek. He took it out to the incinerator in the back yard and stuffed it in. In a way, he thought, it was like committing suicide.

And he couldn't commit suicide. He couldn't light the match he held in his trembling fingers.

He pulled the soot-covered pages from the incinerator and ran back inside.

There had to be something he had missed! It couldn't have been a delusion! He couldn't let the dream die. He had to give it one more chance!

If there was something he had missed, it had to be in the only part of the manuscript he had not gone over with a fine-toothed comb—the section at the end he called the appendix. Not sure what to make of it, he had not even mentioned it in his book.

And so, for the first time, he turned to the mystical and visionary section at the end and studied it seriously. It contained a series of cryptic prophecies that seemed to cover nearly two thousand years. The basic theme of the prophecies seemed based on the teachings of the first part of the manuscript, the thesis of the two spheres of God and Satan, reality and unreality. The two spheres were in a constant struggle and according to the mysterious author, changes in the balance between the two would be mirrored in the history of the world.

> God and Satan contend through
> the instrument of man.
> As man needs God,
> so God needs man.
> Man holds the balance between
> God and Satan.
> And one man can tip the balance
> for heaven or for hell.

At first Simon had a great deal of trouble deciphering the cryptic passages containing the prophecies. But as he did manage to figure them out one by one, he discovered to his awe that all of the predictions had come true.

> In the fifth out of the East they shall come
> overrunning Christendom. Their leader shall begin
> and end with the first, and shall come with the
> nightbroom.

After some puzzling, Simon realized this passage referred to the hordes of Attila the Hun, which swept out of Asia, the east, to overrun Christian Europe in the fifth century. Attila's name began and ended with the first letter of the alphabet. And he did come in the fifth century. As for the "nightbroom," Simon couldn't figure it out.

Other passages foretold the collapse of the Roman Empire and the coming of the Dark Ages; the establishment of the Frankish Empire in the beginning of the ninth century; the Great Schism within the Church in the eleventh century; and the battle of Hastings and the Norman Conquest. The discovery of the new world was foretold as well as the rise of the United States, World War I, the Russian revolution, and World War II.

And every prophecy had come true but the last. It's time was yet to come, but it was the darkest of all and the most fearsome.

> Come the century of blood and death,
> The twentieth near the twenty-first,
> When the nightbroom turns to blood,
> Then will Satan come!
> The heavens shall shake.
> The sky will roar.
> God and Satan warring for
> Possession of the earth,
> Man shall choose either
> Heaven or Hell.

Simon pondered this last prophecy for some time. Its portent chilled him. Though a battle between God and Satan was foretold, the form it would take and, more importantly, its outcome were not revealed. It seemed that the last and most important prophecy was deliberately left obscure. Why?

And there was the mysterious reference to the night-broom again. The nightbroom was mentioned often throughout the manuscript, usually in terms of some catastrophe. It puzzled Simon. When he first came across it, he interpreted it as a symbol of the dark sphere, of Satan. But that was just a guess. He knew there was more to it than that.

He spent weeks trying to figure out the strange reference. He was sure it was significant, and became even more sure as he mulled it over.

He never would have figured it out if he hadn't been lying in bed one night unable to sleep listening to a late night talk show on astronomy. He was nearly asleep when the words "broom stars" popped into his head. He bolted upright and turned to the radio. The ancients sometimes called comets "broom stars," he learned.

The next morning, he skipped work at the shoe store and went to the local library to take out a book on astronomy. Flipping through it to the chapter on comets, he sat down to read.

> Records of comets go back at least to 500 BC. The ancient Greeks called comets "hairy stars". Indeed, the word comet comes from the Greek *kometes,* meaning the "hairy one." Others, such as the Chinese, compared the tail of a comet not to hair, but to the straw of a broom, and called comets "broom stars."
>
> Because of their spectacular appearance, comets have attracted attention since the dawn of history. Fiery, brilliant, with a tail that can stretch halfway across the night sky, the appearance of a comet cannot fail to inspire awe in those who witness it. For primitive peoples, the sight of a comet in the heavens was a terrible portent announcing the wrath of the gods.

Often white, sometimes yellow or even blood red, a comet may hover in the night sky for days, weeks, even months. During this time the comet may wax brighter or grow dim; its tail may swell or shrink or sometimes split into as many as five separate tails; sudden jets may shoot out from the head toward the sun; rarely, the whole comet may fragment into two or three separate comets. No wonder then that for the greatest part of recorded history, comets instilled terror as omens of war, pestilence, the death of kings and the overthrow of kingdoms. No wonder comets were synonymous with evil and called by some in the middle ages "Satan's tail."

The most notorious comet in this regard is Halley's Comet. Astronomical calculations show that again and again during times of catastrophe, Halley's Comet appeared in the sky. From the time of Attila the Hun in 456 A.D. and the Norman Conquest in 1066 to more modern times Halley's Comet has returned like clockwork, bringing disaster with it every time . . .

The nightbroom was Halley's Comet! Taking the book with him, Simon rushed home and got out the manuscript. Yes! Every time the nightbroom was mentioned in the ancient prophecies, according the the book, Halley's Comet had appeared in the sky. And its next appearance would be late in 1985 and the early part of 1986.

Then will Satan come!

Looking up from the crackled old manuscript, Simon suddenly knew why he had found it so many years ago in Egypt. There was a purpose behind it, though not the one he had thought. He wasn't meant to spread the teachings of the two spheres, or reconstruct the Church, or make himself famous by publishing a book. No, the significance of the manuscript was not in its teachings, but in its prophecies. Especially in its last prophecy. He was destined, he knew, to take part in the coming battle.

He was meant to warn the world! Satan was coming!

He went down to the shoe store to tell the manager he was quitting, so that he could devote full time to his message. But as he walked through the door, he heard a warning voice coming from a long-forgotten part of his mind.

Your pride is returning, Simon. Be careful.

And the voice was right, he realized. It was only his pride that told him he was the one to warn the world. Perhaps the ancient manuscript had come to him for a purpose—and he still believed that it had—even so, he did not know what that purpose was. It was his pride that made him presume he knew God's will. If God truly had a role for him to play in the coming battle, then He would show him that role in time.

He would wait, he decided. He would beat down his pride and vanity and wait for God to reveal Himself.

He made that decision in the summer of 1960.

"And it has been twenty-five years now," Simon sighed. "But you have finally come, as I knew you would."

"I still don't understand how you could know I would come see you." Ted said.

"Wait. I will explain in a minute." Simon stood up. "You know what happened to that poor girl, Billie Martin, and the others, don't you?"

Ted nodded. "I spoke to the girl's roommate and she told me you had been to see her. I couldn't make much sense of it then. I think I understand more now, but it still seems fantastical. Sometimes I just can't believe it's all real."

"It is real," Simon answered forcibly. "The dark sphere of negation is real. Satan is real—as real as the comet which we see growing ever larger in the sky. It is the nightbroom, Satan's effigy."

"But . . . that manuscript—how can you be so sure of it?"

Simon smiled. "It is interesting that you should ask that question, considering you have proved the manuscript's truth."

"Me? How?"

"Your visions, Ted. Remember the prophecy—'When the nightbroom turns to blood, then will Satan come.'"

"But what does it mean?" Ted asked in frustration.

"You still don't know? What you saw in your vision —you called it a beam of red light, I believe—was the nightbroom. When the comet turns to the color of blood, the battle will start."

Ted just stared at the old man as the truth of what he had been told sunk in.

"In a way," Simon continued, "The war has already begun. The recent possessions leave no doubt about that. Satan is gathering his forces for the assault, taking over the souls of as many mortals as he can. But the real battle will come when the nightbroom turns to the red color of blood. Exactly when that will be or how it will happen, I don't know. But it *is* coming soon. Satan is now in the sky! And if Satan wins, all the misery of the worst wars and famines will seem like nothing. I cannot even begin to imagine the horror of it, because the world will literally become hell. Satan will rule the world!"

"It can't be," Ted moaned.

"It is only recently that mankind has tried to ignore the dark side of reality, Ted, as any anthropology book will tell you. But Satan and his dark forces have always been with us. As the Bible says, their name is legion. Throughout most of history, the forces of darkness have been in a weak and disorganized state because they have been far removed from their source of power—Satan. That is why most possessions in the past have been in small children and even then possessions were quite rare. But now Satan is at hand. We can see his effigy, the nightbroom, right over our heads. And he is even now strengthening his demonic forces—for Satan gives them their power just as God strengthens those who choose to accept Him. And now his demons are gaining strength daily, possessing people almost at will. The battle is at hand, Ted! You must be strong!"

"But I'm not strong," Ted said, and the weakness of his voice seemed to prove it.

"You will become strong, Ted. You must! A tremendous burden has been placed on your shoulders."

"On my shoulders?"

"I told you I knew you would come, Ted," Simon reminded him. "There is a part of the last prophecy I haven't told you about yet. Come."

Getting up, Simon beckoned Ted to follow him. He went to the front room where his manuscript, brown with age, lay on the trestle table. He picked it up carefully.

Ted could smell its extreme age.

"You're an orphan, aren't you?" Simon asked him.

"I never said—"

"I know you never mentioned it. But you are." The old man's penetrating blue eyes stared intently at Ted.

Troubled, he replied nervously, "I am, yes."

Simon nodded. He put the manuscript down on the table again and carefully opened it up. "Look," he said.

Ted leaned over close to him and looked down at the spidery lines of ancient Greek.

"Let me translate it for you," Simon said. "These are the last lines of the last prophecy—the one that is yet to come."

Moving a finger along the closely written lines, the old man began to read aloud:

"A child of tragedy, an orphan, shall see in visions . . . the coming of the nightbroom—The balance of the spheres will be unstrung—and Satan's power will overflow its bounds—The burden will be heavy, yet the orphan must not fail—for in his mortal hands he shall hold—the world's final fate."

Straightening up, Simon turned to face Ted. "You see? I knew you would come. It was prophesied two thousand years ago."

"But . . . what does it mean?"

"You know what it means."

"But I . . . No. I don't." Turning away, Ted sat down on Simon's bed and held his head in his hands.

The old man put his hand on Ted's shoulder. "It means you have to be strong. And you must have faith. Faith in God, but most of all faith in yourself."

"No . . . no . . . no . . ."

"You have a crucial role in God's plan, Ted. In the battle against Satan, you hold the world's fate in your hands."

Ted looked up at the old man. His eyes were red. "You may want a part in God's plan," he said bitterly, "but I don't."

He jumped up, went over to the table, and grabbed the manuscript.

"You see this?" he demanded, waving it in the air.

"Please!" Simon cried. "Be careful!"

"You and your precious manuscript! Do you have any idea what it means?"

"Please! Don't hurt it!" Simon reached for the ancient pages, but Ted jerked them away.

"I'll tell you what it means!" he shouted angrily. "It means my whole life has been a sham!"

"No!" Simon protested. "You are part of God's plan!"

"Yes! Exactly! That's all I am—a part of God's plan. Do you have any idea what it felt like when you translated that passage, seeing my life described on pages two thousand years old? Two thousand years ago it was determined that I should see my parents die in a plane crash! My life was plotted out and nothing I could do made any difference!"

"Ted—"

"Well, this is what I think of God's plan!" Ted screamed, ripping the manuscript in half. He threw the pieces at the wall. The pages fluttered in the air. "Let God get somebody else to save the world! I don't want the job!"

Simon stared in horror at the pieces of his life's devotion scattered about on the floor. Falling on his knees, he began to gather them together.

"I don't care about the world," Ted said bitterly. "All I care about is Jill. Jill is the world to me. She is all that matters."

Simon got to his feet and put the pieces of his manuscript on the table, spreading them out with loving hands.

"Ted," he said, turning around, "you are a part of God's plan. Please don't try to fight it."

"I tell you I don't care! I don't want to be a part of His damn plan!"

"But you may not have any choice. Not if you want to save your wife."

"There's only one way I can be sure of helping her."

"What do you mean?"

Ted ignored the question. "What do you know about these possessions?" he asked.

"Very little, I'm afraid. I haven't been able to find out much."

"I got Jill a cross. Will that protect her?"

"It will help, but there is no guarantee. Satan's power is growing stronger every day."

"Then what can I do?" Ted asked fiercely.

"I am not sure, Ted. I think you will have to wait and see."

"Wait!" Ted shouted. "What are you talking about! Wait for Jill to be possessed like that dead girl we saw? Wait until it's too late?"

"Wait for God to reveal the rest of His plan, Ted. You must have faith!"

"My visions always come true. I suppose that is part of God's plan, too."

"Maybe it is," Simon said thoughtfully. "But maybe it will be different this time. We must wait for God to reveal Himself."

"I can't wait!"

"But what else can you do?"

"Only one thing. I can strike first." Ted grabbed his coat.

"Where are you going?" Simon asked, alarmed at Ted's manner.

"Home. There is only one way to protect Jill. I only hope I have the courage."

CHAPTER 15

It was well after midnight when Ted got back. The house was dark. He let himself in and went quietly down the hall to the bedroom.

A line of light from the hall made a diagonal slash across the bed. Jill was sprawled out on her back, twisted in the covers as if her sleep was restless and disturbed. Ted went up close to her. She wasn't wearing the cross he had given her. He stood looking at her a long time, then went to the kitchen and poured himself a stiff drink.

He took it with him out on the balcony, where looking up he could see the long, blazing tail of Halley's Comet.

The nightbroom.
Satan's effigy.

The feathery line of fire was still a pale white. As long as it stayed white, Jill was safe. But soon it would turn red—the color of blood—and all hell would break loose.

Finishing his drink, he went back to the kitchen and poured himself another. He drank it quickly, turned out the light, and went back to the bedroom.

Jill had shifted position on the bed, but she was still lying on her back. He could see her pretty face clearly. A frown creased her brow.

217

He picked up a pillow that had fallen on the floor.

His heart pounding, he wondered, *Is this too part of God's plan? Am I merely acting out directions laid down since the dawn of time?*

It suddenly seemed to him that if he reached out he would be able to peel away the surface of the world like so much wallpaper and reveal underneath the true reality of fate—the black machines whose gears and cogs ground out man's destiny. A person could think and struggle and sweat his heart out trying. It made no difference. The inhuman machine of fate would ultimately decide his success or failure.

But death puts you beyond fate's reach. In death you are invincible.

Jill stirred. A small, plaintive moan escaped her lips.

Ted held his breath, waiting for her to quiet. He crept up next to her head and held the pillow out. His heart was pounding hammer blows. His hands were shaking.

It won't hurt. It will be painless. Painless.

And afterwards she will be safe forever.

Slowly, almost imperceptibly, he lowered the pillow over Jill's face.

It's the only way! You must strike first! You must! Before the nightbroom turns to blood! She will be safe forever!

DO IT! DO IT NOW!

Jill rolled away. Her eyes opened. "Who is it? Ted?"

He froze.

She reached over and turned on the small table lamp by the bed. "Ted! What are you doing?"

The pillow was still in his hands. "I . . . I . . . wanted to save you, b-but I couldn't."

"What are you talking about?" She got out of bed and took the pillow.

Ted just shook his head, then turned and wandered out of the room, his steps slow and heavy.

A tear ran down Jill's cheek. Tomorrow, she decided, she was going to get some help.

"It's not really ethical," Dr. Alex Spinneli told Jill the next evening as she drove him to their flat. "And it probably won't work."

Jill glanced at the distinguished-looking psychiatrist. "I've got to try *something!* I just can't sit by and watch Ted fall apart!"

She had known Alex for several years. He was a resident at Hamilton Hospital, where she worked. If there was anyone she could trust, she felt, it was he. But he was very reluctant to do what she asked.

"I still have reservations, Jill," he said now. "A psychiatrist is not supposed to go poking his nose where he's not wanted. And I still think you should tell him right away what I am. He's going to guess anyway, probably."

"I know him, Alex. If I tell him you're a psychiatrist, he'll close up tight as a clam. Please, try it my way."

They found Ted sitting in the kitchen, a bottle of whiskey in one hand, a glass in the other. He looked horrible. His cheeks were sunken and grey, his eyes red and bleary. He didn't seem to notice when they came into the room.

"Ted?" Jill whispered.

He started and looked up. It took a while for his eyes to focus. His head was swaying back and forth.

"I . . . I brought a friend home for dinner," Jill went on quickly. "I hope you don't mind."

"Hi, Ted," the psychiatrist said. "I'm Alex Spinneli."

He held out his hand. Ted made no move to shake it. Instead, he took another drink.

"Well!" Jill said. "I guess I'd better get busy cooking! Why don't you two get acquainted?"

Taking off her coat, she made an ostentatious display

of getting food out of the refrigerator and rattling pots and pans.

Alex sat down across from Ted. "Well, how's it going, Ted?"

Ted gave him a bleary look, as if to ask what this man was doing sitting across from him, and then went back to staring at his drink.

Alex fidgeted with his tie. "Well, look—I guess that was a stupid question. I mean, obviously it's not going very well the way you're drinking." He paused. Ted wasn't responding. "I used to do a lot of drinking myself. Sometimes I'd get to feeling so down, it seemed the only thing I could do was drink until I couldn't think any more."

Alex eyed Ted carefully. He couldn't even tell if he was listening.

"Is that the way it is with you, Ted?" He asked.

Ted still didn't reply.

"Sometimes it feels pretty lonely, doesn't it?"

Jill was watching intently. *Please listen to him, Ted,* she thought. She tried to will the thought into his head. *Please! Listen to him!*

Alex put both elbows on the table and leaned a bit closer to Ted. "That's all right, you don't have to say anything if you don't want to. What I'd like you to understand though is you're not really as alone as you feel. There are people who want to help—"

"Who the hell do you think you are?" Ted asked suddenly. His voice was hard and mean.

"Ted, he's just—" Jill broke in, but Alex raised his hand to silence her.

"I'm just somebody who wants to help you if you'll let me."

His eyes squinting, Ted stared at the man. "You're a doctor, a head doctor, right?"

"Perhaps I should have told you right away, yes—"

"Well, I don't want your help. Get out!"

Jill took a step forward. "Ted! Please!"

"Get out!" Ted shouted. "I didn't ask for your help. The help I need you can't even begin to give me! Get out!"

He stood up and leaned over the table threateningly, glowering at the doctor.

Jill grabbed his arm. "Listen to him, Ted! Please! Don't you realize what you're doing to yourself! You need help, Ted! Please!"

Ted ignored her. "Get the hell out of here!" he yelled at the doctor. "NOW!"

"All right," Alex said, standing up.

Jill tried to say something more, but the doctor put his hand on her shoulder and led her to the front door.

"I'm sorry," she said, fighting back tears.

"Don't apologize," Alex said. "The biggest step is realizing you need help. I'm not surprised at what happened."

Jill nodded her head numbly and closed the door behind him. She leaned back against it, her mind a confusing whirl of fear and anger. The anger came out on top. She dashed to the kitchen, brushed by Ted to the liquor cabinet, and flung its door open with a bang. She grabbed the bottles and took them to the sink. Shaking with anger, she started pouring them down the drain.

"It has got to stop, Ted! It has got to stop!"

Ted ran over to her. "What are you doing? Stop it!"

"NO!" she shouted, emptying a bottle and throwing it in the trash. "I've had enough Ted! I can't let you destroy yourself!"

"Stop it!" he hissed, grabbing her arm.

"Let go!" she screamed. She knew she was getting hysterical but the momentum of her emotions was too strong to stop. Ted was destroying himself! He was destroying them both! Screaming inarticulately, she wrenched her arm free from Ted's grip in a sudden jerk, and grabbed another bottle.

"Stop it!" Ted howled, pushing her back and raising his fist in the air.

To her horror, he brought it down at her face.

She screamed.

Ted froze, and grief-filled horror appeared on his own face.

He was going to hit me! The thought pounded in Jill's mind again and again. He was going to hit me! She shot one last desperate look at him and ran. Ted called out to her, but she kept on running. She ran to the bedroom and locked the door.

She didn't come out again until a little before eight, having changed into her jeans and a loose-fitting shirt. Going into the living room, she could see Ted still sitting at the kitchen table with his back to her.

She paused, trying to decide if she should just sneak out and avoid an argument. But she didn't want to upset him any more than necessary. She knew he hadn't meant to hit her earlier. He had stopped when he realized what he was doing.

She went to the kitchen doorway. "I'm going out to my dance class now," she said to his back. "I'll be back by eleven."

He turned around. He looked terrible, his eyes blood-shot, his face pasty, and with that blank look that comes from drinking too much.

He stared at her a moment, trying to focus his eyes on her. "What?" he asked finally, his voice dead, toneless.

She repeated herself. The way he looked, it was all she could do to hold back the tears. Then, thinking of what Frank had told her about Ted's 'visions,' she added, "Don't worry Ted. Nothing's going to happen to me."

It seemed to take awhile for her words to sink in past the booze. When he finally understood what she had said, his eyes widened. "No, Jill. Don't. Stay home."

Going up to him, she kissed him lightly on the forehead. "I'll be okay, Ted. I promise."

Then, because she was starting to cry in spite of herself, she turned away quickly, heading for the front door.

Ted caught up with her halfway across the living room, grabbing her elbow. "Please, Jill! You know I don't like you to go out at night!"

"I've got to, Ted," she said quietly. "I can't stay home and watch you drink yourself to death."

"No, Jill," he said anxiously. "You can't go out."

His eyes were pleading with her so desperately, she suddenly felt unsure of her resolve. It wouldn't be the end of the world if she stayed home.

But what good would it do?

Ted tightened his hold on her arm and he moved back, trying to pull her with him. The clawing feeling made her feel claustrophobic. She'd go crazy if she had to stay home with him.

"I've got to get out of this house," she said, pulling away. "Can't you see that? Can't you understand? I've got to get away from the feeling of doom you've filled the place with."

She started to turn away, but he grabbed her again.

"Okay, okay," he said hurriedly. "I'll go with you, then."

"No," she answered, losing her patience. "Is your brain so full of booze you can't see? I don't want you to go with me! I'm trying to get away from you! Can't you see that?"

The words were hardly out of her mouth when she wished she could take them back. He looked like she had slapped him across the face. She turned away quickly, ran to the door, flung it open, and rushed down to steps to her car, crying all the way.

* * *

Ted stood immobile in the middle of the room, looking out the open door into the black night. Then, hearing Jill's car door slam shut, he ran out to the top of the
steps and yelled down, "Jill! JILL! You don't know
what can happen! YOU DON'T KNOW! JILL!!"

But she couldn't hear him, or didn't want to. The engine started and the headlights flashed on. He ran down
the steps, reaching the street just as her car pulled away.

He ran up the street to where his own car was parked.
It took his shaking hand too long to unlock the door.
Jumping in and smashing his key into the ignition, he
saw her red tail lights disappear around the corner. In
his rush, he popped the clutch out too quickly and
stalled the engine.

"Dammit! Get a grip on yourself!"

On the second try he pulled away smoothly, then
pushed down hard on the gas. His engine whined.
Reaching the corner, he squealed around it on two
wheels and saw an empty street rising up in front of him.

He raced up to the crest of the hill and saw a pair of
red lights disappearing down over another hill two
blocks ahead. Was that her? He didn't know. Screaming
down the hill, his car bottomed out in the trough at its
base and then raced up the next hill. His wheels left the
road when he reached the top and the street dropped out
from under him. The car came down with a bone-jarring
suddenness and he slammed on the brakes.

Jill's car was at the bottom, stopped at a red light. He
could read her license plate—JILL-2.

He came to a stop in the middle of the street, halfway
up the hill behind her. His hands were shaking on the
steering wheel, adrenaline was pumping through his
body, and his head was throbbing with whiskey, feeling
ready to explode.

He knew she wouldn't go back with him. The only

thing to do was to follow her and keep an eye on her. He wished he knew where her class was held. He hoped she wouldn't look too closely into her rear-view mirror.

The light turned green. He took his foot off the brake and followed Jill as she made a left turn.

He tailed her car up and down the hilly streets, wondering where she could possibly be going. She was heading east, through industrial districts and deserted streets that seemed to get worse and worse-looking with each block. They skirted the base of Potrero Hill, and for a while the streets seemed to improve as they went through residential neighborhoods. But then they were back in among the looming dark warehouses and broken-down deserted factories, driving on streets lined with broken glass and old tires and winos passed out in doorways.

It looked like she was heading for the Bayview district. But that was nothing but warehouses and public housing and slums. It was one of the roughest neighborhoods in the city, close to the shipyards on the bay. What the hell was a dance class doing there?

Then his heart started pounding with fear. He had his window open a crack and the wind was coming in, full of the fishy, salty smell of the bay. The same smell that had come to him in the first vision.

He followed Jill around a corner, and then her car quickly slowed to a crawl, as if she were looking for a parking space. He had to step on the brakes quickly in order to stay a good way behind her. He followed her at her slow pace down the poorly lit, depressingly poor street, past a knot of teenagers standing on a corner and laughing. In the middle of the next block, she slowed even more in front of an old warehouse. It seemed the only building around that had any lights on. Every space in front of it was filled with cars and trucks and tractor-trailers. She kept going past it. Ted turned off his head-

lights and crept along behind her—not too close. She
came to the end of the block, traversed the cross street,
and pulled in behind a trailor sitting on its jacks. Ted
pulled his car to a stop when she got out. He wanted to
jump out of the car and tell her to go back home with
him, but he knew it would be useless. He could barely
see her in the dim yellow light of the only street lamp as
she crossed the road and started walking back toward
him, toward the lit-up warehouse on the other side of
the street. He wanted to look up to see the color of the
comet, but was afraid to take his eyes off her.

She reached the warehouse safely and quickly went
inside. Ted realized he had stopped breathing and took
in a deep breath. It smelled strongly of the bay.

He leaned forward and looked up through the windshield at the sky. It was overcast and the low-lying
clouds were lit up with a vaguely yellow glow by the
city's lights.

It could happen tonight! It could happen at any time!

Putting his car in gear, he drove forward to find a
place to park. He had to go up to the next block, beyond
Jill's car, before he found a space. He got out and
looked up again at the sky. He wished he could see the
comet! *(The nightbroom, Simon called it. Satan's effigy.)*
He walked back toward the warehouse, the chilling
breeze from the bay cutting through his shirt. He had
rushed out with no coat.

The warehouse windows were almost opaque with
grime and dirt, but he could see through them in places
where the dirt had been rubbed off by others with
curious eyes. He saw a long, bare, high-ceilinged room,
much brighter than he had expected from the dim light
that came through the windows. There were a lot of
women in leotards, jeans, and shorts. Some were on the
floor doing stretching exercises, others were doing high
leaps in the air, and some were standing around talking.

It took him a while to spot Jill, but he finally did, in her jeans and loose shirt, her long hair tied in a bun on the top of her head. She was doing toe touches.

He moved away from the window, satisfied that she was safe inside. As long as she was inside, out of the dark night, away from the salt smell of the bay, she would be safe. Before heading back to his car to wait, he looked over at the kids at the corner of the other end of the block. They were talking, laughing, jiving and, it seemed, doing no harm.

Going back to his car, he realized it was facing the wrong way for him to watch the warehouse. He turned it around and shut off the motor to wait.

He had a lot of time to think, sitting in his cold car, and his thoughts were mostly about what Simon had told him. *Satan. The dark side. The coming battle between good and evil. The nightbroom.* Deep inside himself, perhaps, he believed Simon. But on the surface of his mind—where he verbalized his thoughts, where reason was more important than instinct and the tool of logic could even make you doubt whether grass was green or the sky blue—he rationalized, telling himself this was the tail end of the twentieth century, that the world of demons had long ago been explained away as the product of man's subconscious.

(And that was it, wasn't it? The dark world had been explained away, but not explained. It had been swept under the rug of rationality—it hadn't been faced squarely and dealt with.)

But still, the very idea of a dark world of evil was absurd. Wasn't it?

And so his mind tied itself into knots of confusion.

But in his gut, where instinct reigned supreme, there was no confusion. In his gut, he *believed.* In his gut, he was terrified.

He thought of the last lines of the prophecy: *For in his*

mortal hands he shall hold the world's final fate.

It wasn't true! He wasn't strong enough. He couldn't even control his own fate, much less the world's.

What was it Simon had said? *If Satan wins, all the misery of the worst wars and famines will seem like nothing, because the world will literally become hell. Satan will rule the world.*

The real battle will start when the nightbroom turns to the red color of blood.

Shivering, he leaned forward to look up at the sky. His view was blurred by a fine mist that had deposited itself on his windshield as the heavy clouds overhead released their moisture in a fine foggy drizzle. It was nine-thirty, and in the hour and a half he had been waiting, the foggy mist had gotten heavier and heavier. He reached out now and turned on the windshield wipers. Their first few strokes mixed the water and grime on the glass into a milky white film, but after a minute the glass become relatively clean.

Still, he could see nothing above but the clouds.

A while later, impatient for Jill's return, he got out of the car and walked through the wet and foggy night to the warehouse. The mist had settled on the window panes there, too, and he had to wipe one with his sleeve in order to see in. A long line of women going through a rather complicated series of steps stretched away from him. It took him a while to spot Jill. She was at the far end of the line. She was safe.

But for how long? It could happen at any time.

He stepped back from the window and looked up at the sky almost expecting to see the comet blazing redly. But there was nothing save a vaguely yellow glow. The clouds were so low now he couldn't really see them. He was in them.

There was a sudden burst of shouting and laughter behind him. He whirled around, his heart leaping in his throat. It was just the gang of kids down the street that he had passed earlier when he first came. They were very close together now, as if crowding around for a look at something. Their shouting swelled louder and then cut off abruptly, leaving dead silence. And in the moment of silence Ted heard a small sound like breaking glass. Then the kids broke away, running in all directions, scattering, shouting and whooping as they disappeared into the soft, foggy shadows.

For a second, Ted wondered what they had done. But his worried mind could not hold the thought for long and he turned back to peer in the window. The women were still practicing.

He wished the night was over. And he wished the air wasn't so heavy with the salty smell of the bay—the same smell that had come to him in the first vision. In spite of the cold, fear came pouring out through his skin in beads of sweat, turning his skin clammy, soaking his shirt.

He took a last look through the window, then walked back to his car and got in. A minute later he heard the sound of wailing sirens growing louder and got out again. Looking down the street toward the warehouse, he saw a car with a flashing red light come around a corner, its siren screaming, and pull to a stop. Then came a huge fire truck, its lights flashing in counterpoint to the car's. It came to a stop behind the car. Their sirens both slowed to a low growl and then stopped. But their red lights kept turning, sending out revolving beams of red light.

Ted realized what the kids had been up to. They had pulled a fire alarm. It must have been the silent type connected directly to the fire house, because no ringing alarm had gone off. He thought perhaps he should tell them it was only a false alarm.

But the warehouse doors opened, and women started

streaming out. A few stopped to look down the street at
the activity of the firemen, but most hurried directly to
their cars to get out of the cold night. He walked halfway down the block, expecting to see Jill emerge any
second. Woman after woman came out, bathed in the
strobing red light of the fire truck, and he didn't see Jill.
Cars started up, pulled away from the parking spaces
and turned down a side street to avoid the fire truck, and
still Jill didn't emerge.

A few more women came straggling out of the warehouse. Jill wasn't among them.

Ted stood near a parked van and glued his eyes to the
warehouse door. His stomach was convulsing and he
tasted acid bile in his mouth. Where the hell was she?

The last car pulled away. The red-lit street was
deserted.

Down the street, firemen were using their powerful
flashlights to check in doorways and windows for a fire
that wasn't there.

Where the hell is she?

Panic rising in him, Ted started across the street for
the warehouse. He hadn't taken five steps when Jill
finally came out with another woman. They stood just in
front of the door talking and laughing. Ted moved back
across the street into a shadow cast by a large truck. It
would do no good to rush up to her now. She would
move away from him, the way she was feeling. Besides,
he could keep an eye on her from where he was. He just
wanted her to stop talking and get out of the night with
its salt-air smell—to get into her car and drive home.

But she wasn't moving. She was pointing down the
street to the fire truck.

Get in your car! Ted urged her mentally.

She and the other woman moved apart. The other
woman turned and started heading up the street in Ted's

direction. But Jill was going the other way! Toward the fire truck!

What are you doing? Come back!

Ted took a few hesitant steps after her, his legs seeming almost too heavy to move. He wanted to run after her, but suddenly he froze in terror.

Jill was fifty yards away from him, standing in the middle of the street, facing away from him. And over her head the revolving beam from the fire truck made a red band of pulsating light in the foggy air.

It wasn't the comet he had seen in the vision!

He was unable to move for a second. Then his terror exploded from him in a long, harrowing scream.

The scream seemed to crack the world.

Jill turned around.

Ted started running but his legs seemed too heavy and he couldn't move fast enough.

Time had slowed to a crawl.

Something seemed to move at Jill, something like a dark shadow in the fog and he heard her screaming now, screaming and screaming, and he couldn't see what it was—just a darkness in the foggy air and he couldn't run fast enough. She was struggling, shrieking, and her hair fell from the bun on top of her head and started whipping around.

And then she stopped struggling. Stopped screaming.

He finally reached her, grabbing on to her shoulders and spinning her around with his momentum before he could stop himself. She started yelling at him in rage.

Her eyes were shiny and bright red.

He stared at her in horror. Her face was twisted in rage and her eyes were glowing. She was yelling, yelling.

"He stole my purse! He stole my purse!"

The words were just senseless sounds to Ted. He dug his fingers into her shoulders and savagely pulled her to himself, crushing her in his arms.

"Stop it!" she cried. "Stop it!"

It took all her strength to push him away. "He stole my purse! A man in a black cape! He stole my purse!"

As her words began to sink in, Ted stared at her open-mouthed. "What?"

"A man in a black cape sneaked up behind me," she said shakily. "He grabbed my purse, Ted. He stole it!"

Her eyes were still red, pulsating. It was from the red light of the fire truck.

"Y-your p-purse?" Ted stuttered.

A voice came from behind him. "Is everything okay here?"

"Someone stole my purse!" Jill said.

Turning, Ted saw a fireman in heavy rubber clothes.

"But you're okay now?" The fireman asked.

"I-I'm okay," Jill said.

Ted turned back to look at Jill dumbly. His mind was swirling. *Is this what I saw in the vision? Is this it? The salt smell. The beam of red light. Jill with glowing red eyes. Is THIS what I saw?*

"You might try looking for it," the fireman told Jill. "You won't get your money back, of course, but you might get your driver's license and keys. We'll keep an eye out for it too."

"Thanks," Jill replied. "We will look for it."

As the fireman walked away, she turned to Ted. "God, that scared the life out of me. I'm still feeling shaky." She paused. "What are you doing here? Did you follow me?"

"Yeah, I followed you." Ted said. "But it's over, now. It's all over, Jill."

Jill looked puzzled.

Ted sighed. "It's hard to explain. I know Frank told you about my vision. Well, it's all over. I know it's been hell for you lately. But I'll make it up to you. I promise."

He took her in his arms and kissed her.

She searched his face intently. "I don't understand. Is it really all over? You mean you don't think you saw me in a vision any more?"

"I can't talk about it now. I'll explain later. Let's go home, Jill."

"All right, Ted. But I want to look for my purse."

Up the street, the fire truck and the car pulled away.

"It could be anywhere, Jill."

"I know. But I want to try."

They walked up the street and came to an alley. "I think he ran in there," Jill said.

They went into the alley.

"It's pitch black in here," Ted said, feeling his way along. "Even if it's here, we won't be able to see it."

Jill's voice came out of the darkness next to him. "I guess you're right."

"Let's go back."

They turned around. Someone was standing at the entrance to the alley—just a black silhouette against the pale light of the street beyond.

Jill squeezed Ted's hand tightly. "It might be him!" she whispered.

Before Ted could answer, the black form started moving toward them. Where its eyes should have been, two glowing pools radiated a fiery light.

CHAPTER 16

"Where's your cross?" Ted hissed urgently.

"I don't have it."

The black shape came down the alley toward them. Jill couldn't understand what she was seeing—why there were two blazing disks where the eyes should have been. But she knew one thing. She was frightened. She had to get out of there!

She acted.

She acted before she could think, before Ted could restrain her. Letting go of his hand, she started running —not away from the dark man, but *toward* him, toward the alley's entrance and, she hoped, escape.

"Jill!" Ted yelled behind her. "NO!" But she was gone.

She tried to dodge around the sinister shape, but she wasn't quick enough. The man grabbed her.

"NO!!!" she shrieked.

But she was in his crushing grip and staring up into his hideous, boiling hot eyes, like molten lava. They bore into her, seemed to penetrate her very being to fill her with tortured agony.

Then something hit her a glancing blow on the side, knocking her breath out of her, and she was falling. She slammed into a wall and fell to the ground.

Ted had charged up the alley at full speed, knocking into her and the dark man, separating them. His momentum carried the man in front of him as they tumbled over each other out into the dimly lit street.

The light revealed the man's nakedness. Bellowing with animal rage, his eyes burning with supernatural fire, he leaped to his feet as if he weighed nothing. Ted tried to scramble away from him. But the naked man kicked him in the stomach before he could move more than an inch. Still roaring like an enraged gorilla, the man planted another kick in Ted's side.

Jill came staggering out of the alley to see Ted being picked up by his hair. Ted was screaming in agony and the naked man was holding him by his hair with one hand as if he were a paper doll.

This can't be happening! she thought. *It isn't real!*

Then the man saw her. Dropping Ted to the ground, he turned to her and threw back his head and let out a thunderous, evil laugh.

She cringed back in horror against the side of the building as the naked man advanced on her slowly. The hellish laughter coming from him seemed to shake the ground. His eyes were pulsating brighter and brighter. She felt as if his eyes were raping her.

Her knees gave way under her and she sank to the ground. The naked man come up in front of her, towering over her, and turned his glowing eyes down to leer at her.

His eyes were so compelling and dominating, Jill didn't see Ted come up behind him and get knocked away again with a single swipe of the man's arm. She could see nothing but his fiery eyes. They held her. They dominated her.

They seemed to possess her.

Nothing existed but those blazing eyes and the roaring laughter.

Then, dimly, she was aware of arms around her, aware of being picked up and carried. Somewhere in the back of her mind a part of herself was trying to get through to her to tell her to fight, to scream, to save herself, but the voice seemed very far away, far beyond the burning eyes that captivated her, filling her being with their power.

The naked man carried her into the black shadows of the alley.

Ted lay unconscious in the street. His head had smacked against the pavement when the naked man knocked him over.

Then, groggily, he blinked his eyes open and saw the pale foggy sky. And faces. Three black kids were staring down at him.

"What was that thing, man?" one of them asked.

Ted's ears were ringing. The boys voiced seemed to be coming from a deep well. Where was he? Who were these kids?

"That was some dude! He didn't have no clothes!" a boy said, excitedly.

"And he got your girl, man!" another boy said.

"My girl?" Painfully, every part of his body throbbing in protest, Ted sat up. He saw where he was. He remembered.

He jumped to his feet. "Where did he take her?" he demanded.

"Up that alley!" said the tallest boy. Around his neck, he was wearing a gold cross.

Ted grabbed it.

"Hey!" the boy shouted.

"I need it!" Ted yelled, ripping it away with a swift jerk that broke the chain.

"You can't do that!" the boy shouted, but Ted was already running up the alley.

The dim light from the street gave out as soon as he

entered the narrow space between two buildings. He
didn't know what he was going to do. He had the cross
clutched in his hand and just ran. He tripped over something and fell flat on his face in the darkness. He picked
himself up and kept going. A low, low moaning noise
was coming out of the blackness in front of him.

It stopped abruptly as he approached it. He saw two
pale spots of amber and charged at them holding the
small cross in front of him.

Jill was trying to break free of the incandescent eyes
that held her. While a part of herself had already been
conquered, another part struggled valiantly against the
evil presence trying to possess her. That part of herself
was frantically screaming: *Hold on to your self! You are
a human being! A human being! Don't let go of your humanity! Hold it! Tighter! Tighter!*

She was lying naked on the hard cold pavement. The
naked man stood over her, compelling her to look into
the fire of his eyes, forcing her to yield her will, her humanity, her selfhood to him. She tried to turn away but
could not. Slowly, piece by piece, she felt her self slip-
ping away.

Then the spell was broken, the burning pools of fire
losing their hold. She felt another presence. A good
presence.

The dark man had turned away. His hellish eyes were
now on Ted.

Ted held the tiny gold cross in front of him like a
shield. It seemed a puny thing, but it was all he had! He
thrust it out in front of himself at the two glowing orbs,
the only things he could see in the pitch black night.

"Demon!" he shouted. "I have the cross! In the name
of God—"

The dark man's hellish laughter exploded in the air,
drowning out Ted's words. The fiery disks moved closer.

"It is the orphan!" the dark man roared. "THE OR-PHAN!!"

The words seemed to hit Ted like a physical blow.

"THE ORPHAN HAS COME TO DO BATTLE!" The dark man laughed contemptuously.

Now his voice was like the hiss of a snake. "You watched your parents die, didn't you, orphan? You watched your sister's slaughter!"

"No," Ted whispered. "No . . . No . . ."

A wailing scream rose up to pierce the darkness.

"Jill!" Ted cried, unable to see her. "Where are you?"

"YES, JILL!" the dark man boomed. "YOU WILL WATCH HER DIE TOO!"

"NO!"

"YOUR PARENTS! YOUR SISTER! *YOUR WIFE!* HER DEATH WILL BE THE MOST HOR-RIBLE OF ALL! THE FIRES OF HELL WILL SHINE FROM HER EYES, TOO!"

"Ted! Ted!" It was Jill's horror-stricken voice.

Ted whirled around in her direction. But he still couldn't see her. The glowing eyes suddenly jumped in front of him, blocking his path.

"Ted!" she cried again.

"Save her, Ted!" the evil voice mocked. *"You cannot! Your parents! Your sister! Your wife!"*

It was all true, Ted thought feverishly. He was impo-tent, doomed to fail since the dawn of time. A mere pup-pet dangling from fate's strings. His visions, his parents and sister, Jill's horrible fate, all were simply moves in an eternal chess game.

But I'm not going to accept it! I'm not going to give in!

He lunged at the evil being in front of him. The golden cross in his hand struck the dark man's shoulder. To his astonishment, a shower of sparks exploded from the spot. The dark man's eyes flashed in red-hot rage. He roared like a wounded bull. Ted staggered blindly after him trying to plant the cross on him again. Swinging his arm in front of himself, he met nothing but thin air.

The demon-man had disappeared.

Ted blinked at the darkness. Where was he? Then the dark man's roar erupted behind him. He turned to meet a crushing blow on the side of his head. It sent him reeling backwards, his head spinning. The cross fell from his hands as he hit the ground.

The dark man's roaring laughter reverberated up and down the alley. Ted groped for the cross. It was his only hope! His hand touched something.

"Jill!" he cried, pulling her to him. She was sobbing uncontrollably. He realized from the touch of her skin that she was naked.

"HOLD HER WHILE YOU CAN, ORPHAN!" the dark man howled.

"The cross, Jill!" Ted hissed at her. "We've got to find it."

A flickering light suddenly filled the alley.

"What *the hell* is going on here?" It was the boy Ted had taken the cross from. He was holding a cigarette lighter over his head. The two other kids stood uncertainly behind him. One had a knife.

Jill thrust something into Ted's hand. It was the cross. The dark man had his back to him, looking at the newcomers. Ted leaped up and thrust the cross between his shoulder blades. There a flash like lightning. The dark man jumped high in the air.

"Run, Jill!" Ted yelled. "Get out of here!"

The dark man's leap was awesome. He went twenty feet through the air to come down next to the three boys. They fell back on each other in astonishment, the tall boy dropping his lighter into a pile of refuse. It exploded in flames.

Jill was still on the ground. Ted yanked her to her feet. "RUN!"

He gave her a shove and she started running down the alley. But the dark man jumped in front of her, blocking her path. Screaming, she stopped herself and started backing up uncertainly.

"YOU ARE MINE!" the dark man bellowed, closing in on her.

Ted charged him once again. But the demon-man made another mighty leap in the air, over his head, and came down behind him. Ted spun around just in time to press the cross against his naked chest as the man came at him. Sparks and smoke filled the air. The dark man flew into the air yet again.

The boy with a knife threw it quickly. It sank into the soft flesh of the dark man's belly. He fell into the flaming pile of debris. He howled and twisted, and then went motionless.

Jill ran into Ted's arms. Together they stood staring in awe at the burning form and the leaping yellow flames. The three boys moved next to them.

"What was it?" the tall one asked.

"Something. . . . something from hell," Ted whispered. He held out the cross. "You can have it back now."

The boy took it. "Nobody's going to believe this."

"We'd better get out of here," Ted said, leading Jill, still dazed, back to her pile of clothes at the end of the alley. He helped her into her coat, and then picked up her other things. "Come on, let's hurry."

The boys were still staring in awe at the burning man.

"You'd better pull the fire alarm again," Ted said. "For real, this time."

The boy who had thrown the knife fell to the ground howling in agony.

"Hey!"

"What the—"

Writhing on the round, the boy screamed shrilly. His eyes started to flicker with a yellow light.

"Oh, God!" Ted cried. "It's trying to get into him!" Give me the cross!"

He turned to the tall boy. "Come on!"

The boy dug in his pocket and pulled out the cross. Ted grabbed it away from him. Falling on his knees, he pressed it against the writhing boy's forehead.

The boy's wails doubled. He thrashed around violently.

"You're hurting him!" the tall boy shouted.

Ignoring him, Ted kept the cross pressed to the poor boy's head. There were no sparks, so he supposed the demon hadn't gotten full possession yet. But the boy's wide eyes were glowing dimly.

"Please, dear God," Ted begged.

The boy's eyes started to dim. His struggles subsided.

After a moment, he spoke. "What . . . w-what happened?"

Ted took the cross away. "Get out of here! All of you! As fast as you can." He pulled the boy to his feet, grabbed Jill's hand, and started running, the others following. He didn't stop until he was down the block by his car. "Don't go near that alley!" he told the boys. "And when the firemen get here, warn them too."

He opened the door and helped Jill in the car, then turned back to the boys. "And thanks."

"Nobody's ever going to believe it."

"Maybe not now," Ted said. "But in a few days, everybody is going to know about it."

He looked up at the sky. The clouds were breaking up. Halley's Comet loomed like a silver sword among the stars. "In a few days . . . or sooner."

On the way home, Jill started coming out of the numbing haze that had mercifully enveloped her. As the memory of the horror she had been through returned, she began to shake. She put her hands over her face and rocked back and forth in the car seat, moaning sorrowfully.

"It's over, now," Ted said tenderly. "You're safe, Jill. It's over."

But it wasn't over, Jill felt. Her system was poisoned. She had walked through hell, it seemed, and the feeling of hell was still inside her. A monstrous evil had entered her, violating her very being. Her insides felt defiled, unclean. Nothing in her life could have prepared her for the face to face confrontation with pure indescribable evil she had experienced.

"Jill . . . Jill . . ." Ted repeated helplessly.

"Oh, God!" she wailed. "It was horrible! It was . . ." But she couldn't continue. She simply sat crying the terror out until they got home and Ted took her hand and led her indoors.

He tried to take her in his arms and comfort her, but she felt so unclean, so defiled, she couldn't bear him to touch her. She pushed him away and ran to the bathroom. Throwing off her coat, which was all she was wearing, she got in the shower and turned it on hard.

She just felt so *filthy!*

She spent half an hour scrubbing herself. When she got out her skin was red and raw. She still had the feeling of evil inside her, but it wasn't so overpowering anymore, as if she would contaminate anything she touched.

Ted was sitting on the bed, waiting for her with a clean robe.

"Is that what you saw, Ted? Is that what you told Frank about? It was real?"

"Yes," Ted said wearily, "It was real."

She sat down next to him. "You should have told me!"

He shook his head. "Would you have believed me? Would it have helped?"

Jill considered the question thoughtfully. "I guess not." Even now it seemed hard to believe. Even now with the feeling of evil still throbbing inside her it seemed as if what had happened couldn't have happened. But it had happened. And she didn't have to ask Ted what it was. She knew better than he, for she had looked into its burning eyes—*the eyes of a demon*. No, she never would have believed him.

"But it's all over now, isn't it?" she asked.

"I, uh . . ." Ted looked into her frightened eyes. It wasn't all over, he knew. Even if what had happened that night was what he had seen in the first vision—and he didn't think it was—there was still the second vision. *The wall of fire and Jill dancing obscenely, her naked skin glistening in the firelight.*

Jill grabbed his hand. "It *is* over!" She said fiercely. "Isn't it?"

"I hope so," he whispered. "I hope so."

He gave her a hug, then went to the window and pulled back the curtains. The comet was huge, stretching its tail halfway across the sky.

"When the nightbroom turns to blood." he muttered to himself.

"What?" Jill asked, coming up beside him.

"Nothing." *It's not over. In fact, it hasn't even begun.*

"Get dressed," he said. "We have to go see an old man." *There has to be a way to save her!* he told himself firmly.

(He repeated the thought over and over, as if repetition would make it true.)

Jill looked at him questioningly.

"He's an ex-priest, Jill," he told her. "He can help us.

I *hope* he can help us."

"I don't understand, Ted," Jill said uncertainly.

Ted held her tight. "It's not over, Jill. It's only just beginning and you're still in great danger."

She looked up at him fearfully. "B-but your vision . . . You said it's already come true!"

"No, Jill, it hasn't come true. Not yet."

"Then . . . then, what's going to happen to me?"

You don't want to know, Ted thought, wrapping his arms tighter around her. *Oh God, you don't want to know!*

"Get dressed," he said. "And wear your cross."

It was still dark out when they knocked on Simon's door. The old man met them in a threadbare robe and slippers, his white hair all dishevelled from sleep.

"Ted!" he exclaimed. "Thank the Lord! I've been so worried! When you ran out the other night, I was afraid you would do something rash."

"I didn't have the courage," Ted said, still not sure Jill wouldn't be better off in the nothingness of death.

"Thank God you've come back! I didn't know where to find you!" Simon turned to Jill, peering at her closely. "And you must be . . ."

"Jill," she said, taken by the old man's kindly blue eyes—eyes that seemed very wise. "We must have gotten you out of bed."

"That doesn't matter," Simon replied, leading them into his cramped apartment. "Nothing matters now except the battle! Nothing!"

He sat down on the unmade bed. "It is coming soon! We have very little time left. The comet is huge! I stayed up half the night watching it. It seemed to float among the stars like a frozen shriek, just waiting, biding its time. It seemed to radiate evil!"

Simon was becoming more and more agitated. Now he jumped up from the bed. "Satan's power is increasing at a tremendous rate! He is taking over the souls of people all over the country! Have you seen the papers? There are reports from France, Italy, India—all over. Of course, they don't know what it is, or if they do, they won't come right out and say it. But it's obvious to anyone who knows about these matters! People all over the world are falling to Satan's power! And every hour, every minute, Satan's effigy comes closer, spreading its tail across the sky! And the real battle hasn't even started!"

Simon turned to Ted suddenly, moving so close Ted could feel his moist breath. "And you, Ted, you hold the world's fate in your hands!"

"But I still don't understand what I can do!" Ted cried. "You said God has a plan for me! What is it? You must know! What are you holding back?"

Jill had been watching this interchange with growing frustration and bewilderment. Now she burst out, "Will somebody tell me what this is all about? Please!!"

"Just a minute, Jill!" Ted said, still looking intently at Simon. "You must know more than you've told me, Simon! You must!"

"You know everything, Ted," Simon said weakly. He moved away from the younger man and sat on his bed again. "I've told you everything I know."

"I don't believe you!"

"Often it is better not to know the future," Simon said, barely speaking above a whisper. "You know that better than anyone, Ted. You of all people should realize that knowing the future does more harm than good."

"I was right, then!" Ted cried. "You do know more than you've told me!"

"Yes. When I read you the last prophecy the other night, I left out a part." Simon looked up at Ted pleadingly. "You don't want to know, Ted. It will be easier for you if you don't know. Please—"

"I *do* want to know! And you're going to tell me!"

"All right," Simon sighed wearily. He went over to the trestle table where the pieces of the manuscript lay. He hadn't been able to put them together again after Ted ripped them up. His hands trembling, he sorted through the pile, then picked up a page.

"Ted, I beg you—"

"No, Simon. Just read it."

Simon read slowly, translating as he went along. "A child of tragedy, an orphan, shall see in visions the coming of the nightbroom . . . The balance of the spheres will be unstrung . . . and Satan's power will overflow its bounds . . . The burden will be heavy, yet the orphan must not fail . . . for in his mortal hands he shall hold . . . the world's final fate . . ."

Simon looked up. "Ted, please—"

"Finish it!" Ted shouted. "I've got to know!"

"A choice must he make of his own free will . . . For God or Satan, for heaven or hell . . . Will he kill his love? . . . Or will mankind crown the King of Hell?"

"That's all," Simon said, looking up. "I don't know what it means."

Ted said, "Yes, you do! You know as well as I what it means!"

"*I* don't!" Jill interrupted. She went over to Ted. "What is it, darling? I haven't understood ten words since we got here!"

Ted stared at her unable to speak. Then, without warning, his legs gave way under him and he sat down hard on Simon's unmade bed. He covered his face with his hands.

"Ted!" Jill cried.

Simon took her arm. "Let him alone," he said gently, leading her to the easy chair and sitting her down. "I will try to explain things to you."

He pulled up a chair and sat down. "A tremendous

battle is almost upon us now—the most important in history. This battle, Jill, will not be a battle between nations for possession of a piece of land. It will be a battle between two opposing forces for possession of the whole world! Preparations for the fight are already being made. Perhaps you have read in the papers of some strange incidents, people disappearing, people with superhuman strength, people with eyes of fire."

"You don't have to explain that," Jill said. "It nearly happened to me."

"What?" Simon was taken aback.

"It was a naked man, and his eyes were like fire, just as you said. I felt I was looking into hell itself. Ted saved my life!"

"I didn't!" Ted shouted, jumping up. "It was meant to happen that way! Don't you see? It wasn't my vision!"

"But—"

"Nothing I do matters! Nothing any of us does matters! Fate is just toying with us! Whatever happens now was determined by a toss of dice at the beginning of time!"

"No, Ted," Jill said evenly. "You were strong and brave! You saved my life!"

"I didn't!" Ted insisted, slumping down on the bed again.

Jill wanted to go to him, but Simon restrained her. "Let me finish telling you what I know," he said. "Then you can talk to him. The man was possessed by a demon strengthened by Satan's power. Even now we can see Satan's effigy in the night sky."

"I don't understand," Jill said.

"It's the comet, Jill. Since the dawn of time Satan has been wandering in the black voids of space—and every time he came close to earth he unleashed his power against us. And now he is back again. It is not us poor mortals Satan wants, really. We are merely the instruments in the fight against his real adversary, God. Do you understand what I'm saying?"

"I'm not sure," Jill said. "I don't think I do."

Simon explained the teachings of the ancient manuscript on the two spheres, and how man existed halfway between them. "The universe is a balance, Jill," he went on. "A balance between good and evil, God and Satan. And the balance is always precarious and unstable—sometimes good is more powerful, sometimes evil. Now, picture a balancing scale, one side holding good and the other holding evil. And put mankind right in the center, on the crossbar between then. If we who sit in the center go toward the good side, it will be heavier, and if toward the evil, it will be heavier. You see?"

"I think so," Jill said, her brow furrowed in concentration.

"Good. This is the important point: It is we ordinary men and women who sit in the center of the balance who determine the course of history for good or evil. If Satan's power grows, it is because we made it grow by our evil actions. If God's power grows, it is also because we made it grow. You see, though we depend on God, He in turn depends on us!"

"I think I understand," Jill said slowly. "You're saying God needs our help to fight against Satan."

"Exactly! And we must not fail this time! Satan wants nothing less than the soul of every person on this planet! He wants to make the earth hell!"

Jill sat back in her chair trying to comprehend the enormity of what Simon was saying. It was truly awesome. To make hell on earth! She thought of the horror she experienced multiplied a billion-fold and shuddered.

"And it's coming soon?" she asked.

"Yes. It is prophesied that Satan will launch his attack when the nightbroom—the comet—turns to the color of blood."

"What will happen then?"

Simon shook his head. "I cannot say. I don't know how the attack will proceed."

"You said earlier that the world's fate was in Ted's hands."

"Yes."

"Why? I don't understand."

"I cannot tell you why," Simon answered. "I only know that it is so." He got up and picked up some of the crumbling pieces of the manuscript from the trestle table.

"These are pieces of a book nearly two thousand years old," he said. He told Jill how he had devoted most of his life to the ancient manuscript and explained its prophecies.

"And you think Ted is the orphan mentioned in the last prophecy?" Jill asked. She glanced over at her husband. He was still sitting on the unmade bed, his head hung down.

"I am sure he is the one." Simon replied.

"But . . . but why?" Jill was bewildered.

"As I said before, I cannot tell you *why*. God works in His own ways. He has chosen Ted for a crucial role in His fight against Satan. Why he chose him and not someone else, I cannot tell you."

Jill still wasn't satisfied. "What was that part you read, about Ted having to choose, and something about killing his love?"

Simon looked over at Ted, who was still on the bed, seemingly oblivious to the conversation.

"What does it mean?" Jill asked.

Simon hesitated a moment longer before replying. Then he sighed deeply and faced Jill squarely.

"Sometimes," he said, "there is what I call a window

in time—when the balance between the two spheres is so delicate and unstable that one person, if placed in the right position, can tilt the world one way or the other, for good or evil. When the nightbroom, the comet, turns to the color of blood, a window in time will open and then close after a few minutes or a few hours—I don't know how long—but what happens in that short period will determine the world's fate for thousands of years. That is when the battle between God and Satan will take place. And I think the passage I read means that Ted is somehow going to be the decisive factor in the battle. What he does will determine the winner, whether God or Satan."

"And the part about killing his love?" Jill's voice was barely a whisper.

Simon spoke now as if every word caused him deep pain. "God is not cruel, Jill. He is love! But sometimes He demands sacrifices—even as He sacrificed His only son! It is not something He wants . . ."

"It's about me, isn't it? Ted might have to choose between me and . . . and God."

"It could mean so many things, Jill. So many things."

"I see."

Jill sank back in her chair. Her eyes had a faraway look. For a long time, no one spoke.

Then Ted got up from the bed and fell on his knees in front of her. The sun had come up a while before. A thin beam came through the tiny window over the table and shone on his face.

"Oh, Jill! I love you so much! You mean more than God or anything! If I have to choose, I—"

Jill put her fingers softly on Ted's lips. "I'm a bit confused by all this, Ted. But if it's all really true and you do have to decide between me and God, you mustn't think I am so important. You must do what you have to do."

"No! You don't know what you're saying!"

"I think I do, Ted. Last night I saw into the eyes of something made of pure evil, something so cruel and hateful and obscene that even to look on it was torture. I know what is at stake! We cannot let that evil loose upon the world, Ted."

"But Jill! I love you! Nothing else matters to me! Nothing!!"

"I hope that's not really true, Ted. I know it's not really true. There are millions, billions, of people in this world. You cannot forsake them. You cannot deliver them into Satan's possession, especially not because of your love for me."

"What are you talking about, Jill? I love you! I can't forsake you!"

Jill's eyes took on a distant look again, as if she were looking beyond her surroundings to something hidden.

"And what would your love be worth, if purchased at the expense of mankind?" she asked. "No Ted, you cannot think like that. Looking into that—that thing's eyes last night, I found out what evil really is. I got such a feeling of greed and grasping desperation—it was a being so consumed with itself and its own desires it was blinded to anything or anybody outside itself. That's what evil is, Ted! And if we forsake the rest of the world for ourselves, we too will become evil!"

She ran her hand through Ted's hair. "Do you understand?"

"I don't know," he said shakily. "I don't know."

Simon looked at Jill with deep respect. "You are a very wise woman."

Ted looked from Jill to the old man, then back to Jill. "I'm not strong enough," he cried. "I won't be able to make the right choice! I don't have the strength!"

"I have faith in you, darling," Jill said.

"And you must have faith in yourself, Ted," Simon

said firmly. "And faith in God, too!"

Leaning forward, Ted rested his head on Jill's lap. She tried to comfort him, though she was terrified herself. For a long time, no one spoke.

Then Simon broke the heavy silence. "We must pray for strength," he said. "There is a church not far from here where I often go. We must go there and beg God to give us strength."

Outside it was grey, cold, and windy. They hurried through the city streets to a small church several blocks from Simon's apartment. Ted and Jill sat together in back. His mind seething with turmoil, Ted was too upset to pray. He thought hard, but his thinking got him nowhere. Beside him Jill sat with her eyes closed, whispering quietly at times, praying silently at others. Simon knelt down in front under the altar and prayed fervently for Ted. They spent nearly an hour there and when they left, Jill felt a little less frightened. Ted felt no better than before. He still felt himself a plaything of forces he could not even begin to comprehend.

Jill was ahead of the others going up the stairs on the way back, and she was the first to see the sign on Simon's door. She let out a shriek, but quickly stifled it. Ted and Simon rushed up beside her.

Drawn in bright red blood was a small circle with lines streaming up and away from it. Ted recognized it immediately as the same comet symbol he had seen in Mrs. O'Hara's bird bath. Just in front of the door was a headless rat the size of a cat.

Simon hadn't seen such a sign before, but he knew what it was. "When the nightbroom turns to blood . . ." he murmured.

"They know about us," Ted whispered.

An old woman came out of her apartment across from Simon's and looked at the three of them wide-eyed.

"I've never seen nothing like it in my life!" she said, pulling her yellow housecoat tighter around herself.

"What happened, Mrs. Matlock?" Simon asked. "Did you see?"

"Seems like the world's falling to pieces, I tell you," Mrs. Matlock said. "I heard this terrible commotion out in the hall and opened my door a crack. And there was this naked man! He was holding a squealing rat—that rat right there!—big as a house it looked! I could hardly believe my eyes when he pulled the thing's head off! I tell you I shut my door again right quick and pulled all the bolts!"

"It's a good thing you did," Simon said.

"I tell you something's going on! You can feel it! Haven't you noticed it?"

"Noticed what?"

"It's a heavy feeling, like something in the air. Like just before a big storm bursts. Something's not right! And I'm not the only one! Everybody's frightened. Why, this morning I went down to do my shopping and I could see it on the faces of the people in the street! They're frightened! They can feel it too, the heaviness. It kind of sits right in your chest, a dreadful feeling, I tell you! Something's not right!"

"Something's just not right, I tell you!" Mrs. Matlock repeated. Then she turned around and locked herself in her apartment.

"It's true," Jill said. "I didn't think of it before, but when we were going to church everybody we passed seemed frightened. No one would look you in the eye." She put her hands to her breast. "And she was right about the feeling too. It is a sort of heaviness, a feeling of dread. Don't you feel it?"

Simon nodded. "Yes, I feel it too. Satan is drawing closer. The time is almost upon us."

Ted was staring at the bloody door. "They know

about you, Simon. It wasn't just coincidence the demon picked your door."

"No, it wasn't coincidence," Simon agreed. "Satan knows I have some role in God's plan. He's going to do everything in his power to get at me, somehow."

"And they know about me," Ted said. "The demon that attacked Jill last night knew who I was! He knew about my parents and my sister! And . . . and Jill!"

He looked at Simon pleadingly. "What are we going to do?"

"We can only wait," Simon said. "And pray."

CHAPTER 17

The feeling of dread Mrs. Matlock had described lowered itself over the land like a blanket of heavy fog.

People were frightened—of what, they knew not—but frightened they were. People who hadn't had a religious thought in ten years reacted to the feeling by praying or dusting off the old family Bible to read. Others simply locked themselves indoors like Mrs. Matlock and stared at the walls, nervously waiting for whatever was to come. Some left work to return home to their families. Mothers called their children home from school.

Something was worming its way into people's hearts and lodging there.

And in the envious, the greedy, the spiteful, long-buried desires were being resurrected. Old wounds suddenly felt fresh and new, kindling the urge for revenge. The greedy threw off inhibitions to mug and steal. The warped gave full range to their twisted desires and lured little girls into dark corners to perpetrate unspeakable crimes. Arsonists torched buildings. Men murdered their wives. Parents beat their children. Every form of human evil came rising to the surface.

Those possessed by Satan and his demons—more than a hundred in San Francisco alone, and thousands across the globe—waited for nightfall.

Jill and Ted were waiting, too, in Simon's small apartment, listening to the old man's whispered prayers. Ted had picked up the decapitated rat by its tail and dropped it in a wastebarrel on the landing. Jill had found bucket and sponge and washed off the door. And now they were simply waiting, the feeling of cold dread in their hearts growing stronger and heavier.

They had talked very little since entering the stuffy apartment, each preoccupied with his own thoughts. Now Ted could stand the silence no longer. The feeling in his chest was growing to seem like a pale copy of what he had felt looking into the glowing eyes of the possessed fat woman.

"What are we doing?" he burst out suddenly, making the others start nervously. "We don't know what we're doing! We're just sitting here! Why aren't we out doing something!"

"We're waiting, Ted," Simon told him.

"Waiting for what?!"

"We are waiting for God to reveal his plan. He has a plan for us and we must wait until he makes it clear."

"A plan!" Ted said bitterly. "You're grasping at straws and you know it!"

"Please, darling," Jill urged him. "We must have faith!"

"I have no faith!"

"God *does* have a plan!" Simon repeated forcefully. "The old manuscript and its prophecies, your visions— God must have a plan!"

"I hope you're wrong, Simon! For Jill's sake. . ."

Sobbing, Ted turned away from them.

Simon tried to comfort him. "God is love, Ted. We can't be sure of what the prophecy means. Whatever happens, you must do what is right."

Ted tried to say something, but sobbing choked his throat.

"Listen, Ted," Simon went on. "I am only an old man and I have made a lot of mistakes in my life. But there is one thing I am sure of. God never requires us to do evil in order to achieve good. Never! Forget about the prophecy, and when the time comes, do what is right!"

"But how will I know?" Ted asked desperately.

Jill answered him. "You will feel it, Ted. You will know."

"Feel it?"

"You can feel the difference between good and evil," Jill said, remembering the horrible eyes in the night. "It is not something you need to think about. Follow your feelings."

But it wasn't only the prophecy Ted was thinking of. He was also remembering what he had seen in his visions. And his visions always came true.

He slumped down on the bed and sat there awhile in silence.

Then he went over to the small window.

"It's getting dark," he said. "I want you to go back home now, Jill."

"No! I want to be with you!"

"That's just it! You shouldn't be with me! You're safer away from me!"

"But why?"

"Don't you see? According to the prophecy, I'm going to have to make a choice between . . . well, you know. But if you're not with me, maybe I won't have to make that choice!" He was also thinking of his second vision. In the second vision, he knew he was with her, holding that heavy thing in his hand. If they stayed apart, maybe it would somehow short-circuit the course of events.

"Please, Jill," he said. "Let me take you home."

She looked uncertainly at Simon.

The old man shrugged. "I don't have anything better to suggest. But—"

"But what?" she asked.

"Frankly, I don't think it will make much difference."

"Maybe not," Ted said. "But we can't just sit here! We've got to try something!"

He looked at Jill pleadingly.

"All right," she said at last. "You can take me home."

"You'll be safer."

Simon went with them. The city streets were nearly deserted. Those few who were out walked hurriedly, with their heads down, anxious to reach their destinations and get inside.

Ted checked all the windows in their apartment to make sure they were locked.

"Don't let anyone in, Jill—no matter what," he told her. "And don't go out—no matter what."

She nodded. "I understand."

"And don't take your cross off—not even for a minute."

"I'll be okay," she said bravely. "Ted?"

"What?"

"Is . . . is it going to happen tonight?"

"I don't know."

"That dreadful feeling . . . it's getting stronger." *Don't start crying now!* she told herself. *You've got to be strong! You can't let Ted see how frightened you are!*

She and Ted stood gazing at each other a moment, then rushed together. Simon, who had been watching them from the door, turned away as they hugged each other fiercely.

"Oh, Jill!" Ted sobbed thickly, "I love you so much!!"

She pressed herself against him hard. "I love you,"

she whispered with trembling emotion as she fought back her own tears.

They started to break apart several times, but each time came back together as if invisible lines of force held them close. They both knew that this might be their last moment together. Both were afraid of letting it end.

They let the seconds stretch into minutes, and the minutes pile up until finally they moved apart and regarded each other at arm's length. Their faces were streaked with tears.

"Well," Ted said at last, "I guess . . ."

"Yes. . ."

"You'll be safer alone."

"I understand."

"Don't go out, no matter what. If . . . if it happens, it will be outside. So you've got to stay inside here!"

"I know darling. I won't go out and I'll keep this cross on."

"Well, I guess Simon and I should go now . . ."

"I have faith in you, Ted. I know you'll make the right choice."

Jill turned away and bit on the back of her hand to keep from bursting into tears. Ted started to go to her, but Simon restrained him.

"Don't make it harder on yourself," the old man said gently.

Ted let himself be led to the front door and out into the night. Pausing at the top of the stairs, he heard Jill locking the door behind him. The image of her tearful face was still vivid in his mind. If he saw her again, he knew, her eyes would be filled with a terrible fire.

"Come on, Ted," Simon said, starting down the steps.

Ted started to follow him, then halted. "Look!" he said, pointing to the eastern sky. "It's the comet."

The comet was just coming up over the eastern horizon. It looked impossibly huge.

"Satan . . ." Simon whispered.

"It's white!" Ted said. "It's still white!" Maybe it wouldn't be tonight, he thought hopefully, and he could spend a few more precious hours with Jill. *Please, don't let it be tonight! Dear God, give us a little more time together! Don't let it be tonight!*

But the dreadful feeling in his chest, pressing against his heart like a heavy weight, told him his prayer had little chance of being answered.

Simon and he got into his car. They rode in silence back toward the Tenderloin and Simon's apartment. They were nearly there, when Simon turned to face Ted.

"I almost forgot," he said, "I have a meeting later tonight. Worrying about you and Jill made it slip my mind. It's at the house of a friend of mine in Pacific Heights. I'll tell you how to get there."

"What are you talking about?" Ted asked with bewilderment. "A meeting? How can you think about that when—"

"You don't understand," Simon interrupted. "They may be able to help us. It's a small group of people who know about the nightbroom. I didn't know how else to prepare for the battle, so I gathered these people together just to be ready."

"And they can help us? How?"

"Frankly, I'm not sure," Simon said slowly, "Like you, I wanted to do something, but I didn't know what." He had thought perhaps his small group had been part of God's plan for him and he had encouraged them, thinking that in time God would reveal what He wished them to do.

The old man explained this to Ted, adding, "God still may give us a sign Ted."

"All right," Ted said without enthusiasm. "Tell me how to get there."

Simon gave him directions to Meg Olson's mansion.

Ted did a U-turn and went to Van Ness Ave. for the drive to Pacific Heights. *Please,* he prayed, *don't let it be tonight! Give us just a little more time!*

The night seemed especially dark—as if the air were filled with black ink. The streets were mostly deserted.

There was no denying it was a strange night. A strange, strange, night! Larry thought. People were fuckin' freaked out of their gourds! If you looked at 'em sideways, why they were liable to run away in terror. Not that there were many people out on the streets now, but those few that were—hurrying by with fear written all over them—they were fucking freaked out of their gourds!

But when the hell was the goddamn bus going to show up? It was damn cold standing out in the windy wet air. And the cold was shooting right into his leg, cramping the damaged muscles into tight knots. If he had a car, if he could goddamn drive a car, he wouldn't need the stupid bus, and wouldn't have to standing out on the corner in the cold, leaning on his crutch.

But he had to wait. The bus would come. It *had* to come! Because he needed it for his plan.

It was a good plan. Oh yes! A really nice plan he had been working on for a while now.

A little surprise for that bitch, Jill.

The wet wind changed direction, coming around to whip Larry in the face, making the skin sting a little. He swiveled on his crutch to turn away from it and saw a man hurrying toward him on the sidewalk. The man had his head hunched down into his coat and was bent over to stare at the sidewalk as if he were afraid to look up. Afraid he would see a boogy man. His eyes narrowing into mean slits, Larry watched him. He was keeping close to the buildings, as if they offered him safety, taking rapid frightened steps. Larry was out by the curb. He waited till the man was even with him, then took a deep breath and yelled, as loud as he could,

"BOO!!"

The man let out a high yelp and jumped, hitting his shoulder against the brick wall. His eyes bulged out at Larry a second and then he ran.

Larry's loud guffaws followed him down the street.

OH, YES! People were fucking freaked! Out of their gourds! Fucking Freaked!

And you couldn't deny it. It was a *strange, strange* night! There was something in the air. Something that came inside you, cold and dreadful. And it was making people freak out of their everloving gourds, making 'em shit in their pants. It was a weird feeling that seemed to come from nowhere and everywhere.

He could feel it, just like everyone else. And when it first had started, earlier in the day, he had been freaked! Just like everyone else.

It was like he had swallowed an ice cube, he thought, and it had gotten stuck half way down. And it made him real nervous. It had really freaked him. But after a few minutes, it had begun to feel good. And all his fear had gone away. It made him feel *strong* like snorting a good long line of cocaine!

It made him feel *powerful!*

It made him feel there was something, somewhere, that liked him, that understood him. Not someone— something. Something that wanted him, like nobody had ever wanted him before.

It made his forget his disfigured face and twisted, too-short leg. It made him feel *strong* and *powerful* and it gave him the courage to finally put his plan into action.

A little surprise for that fucking bitch!

Before the cold feeling had lodged itself in his chest, his plan had been kept on a shelf in the back of his mind —only to be brought out and looked at in moments of fantasy. Sometimes he thought of it while he masturbated. He would hold his shiny switch-blade with one hand and beat off with the other and think about Jill. Think about what he would do to her with his shiny switch-blade.

Picture the blood flowing.

He would punish her for humiliating him, running away the way she did like he was some loathesome thing.

But it had just been a plan gathering dust and he knew he would never work up the rage to do it.

Until tonight!

Until tonight when that strange cold feeling came stealing into him, frightening him at first and then re-assuring him.

Making him feel *strong* and *powerful!*

The bus was coming out of the night.

It pulled to a stop with screeching brakes. The door opened and Larry looked up at the driver. He was fucking freaked out of his gourd too!

Larry used his powerful arms to pull himself aboard.

"Nice night, ain't it?" he said.

Every window of Meg Olson's imposing white mansion blazed with light as Ted and Simon drove up.

Meg met them at the door. She was extravagantly dressed in an evening gown. Her hair had been done up with a diamond tiara, but the tiara was now askew and her hair was dangling loosely in wisps. Her low cut gown revealed melon breasts that heaved with emotion.

"Thank God you've come!" she cried. "I've been trying to call you!"

"What happened?" Simon asked with alarm.

"I've been so stupid! Richard, the chauffeur, has been missing since last night, but I didn't think anything of it as it's happened before.

Leading the two men inside, she continued talking rapidly. "I was going to call the police, but I realized that would be useless and tried to get you instead. I didn't know what else to do! Thank God, you're here! I'm frightened, Simon! Frightened!"

"Of course you are," the old man said. "So are we all!" Simon guided her to a plush blue chair and sat her down, then sat down in a chair next to her. Ted perched on the arm of the sofa.

"Now tell me," Simon said, "What happened?"

"Well, I was up in my dressing room with Beth, my maid. We were playing dress-up like school girls. We both felt this heavy, depressing coldness and were trying to cheer ourselves up. It's a horrible, dreadful feeling Simon! I can still feel it!"

"I feel it too," he said. "Please, go on."

Meg sighed heavily, trying to calm herself. "Beth was just putting the tiara on me when we heard this inhuman sound. It was singing, eerily beautiful in a way, but inhuman and cold. It chilled me even more and seemed to add to the feeling of impending doom choking my chest. It sounded as if it were coming from the garden. Beth and I looked at each other for a moment, frozen, and then I said I had better go see what it was. But Beth said she would go. She seemed strange somehow, with her eyes glazed over. She said it very slowly, as if there could be no argument—"I will go"—and walked right out of the room in a sort of trance. Oh, I was so stupid! I shouldn't have let her go! I should have known what it was! But I wasn't thinking straight. The sound was getting louder and louder, rising and falling like waves on a beach, and it was very compelling in a way. I went back to my dressing table and just sort of stared at myself in the mirror. After a moment, the sound suddenly stopped. And then there was this horrible scream. It was Beth! It sounded like she was being murdered!"

Meg's hand went to her breast. "I jumped up and ran downstairs. The quickest way to the garden is through this room so I ran in here. The french doors were wide open and the screams were coming through them clearly. I guess I panicked because I just froze in the middle of the room, afraid to go out. The screams stopped and there was nothing for a moment. Then Beth screamed again, much worse than before. It was a blood-curdling scream of pure terror, as if her insides were being ripped out. That got me moving. I rushed out the open doors and just as I got outside, the screams sort of died away like a record winding down and I froze again, I'm afraid, just outside the doors. And then I heard these strange animal sounds—grunting noises. I took a few steps forward, and realized the sounds were coming from my left. I took a few more steps and then I saw them! I saw them!!"

"Them? Simon asked. "There was someone with Beth?"

"Yes! It was Richard! And they were like two dogs! They were naked, and Beth was down on her hands and knees and Richard was on top of her, humping her like a dog!! I don't know what I started shouting then, but I started shouting. I couldn't imagine Richard raping anyone, but there he was—in my own garden! I was still quite a way away from them and I started running at them, shouting something or other about rape and the police, when they both turned their heads around toward me. I saw their eyes! They were bright red! They were on fire! They were still locked together like dogs and they just stared at me with their glowing red eyes! They didn't move! They just stared at me! And then they started laughing, and it was a horrible, ghoulish, inhuman sound. Then Richard pulled himself out of Beth and stood up facing me. And he started singing!

"It was the same singing I had heard before, and it

seemed to penetrate me. It was as if he was coming inside me with the song, raping me, and what was so terrifying, I wanted to give into it! It was so compelling—the sound of it, the rhythm of it. I felt myself going all hot and Richard was coming toward me slowly, his naked body glistening in the light from the house, his penis monstrously huge. I just stood there, watching him come to me, his undulating song sending waves up inside me.

"And then I don't know how I did it—maybe it was because Beth started laughing in a horrid cackle—but I suddenly reached for the cross you made me wear. My hand went up to it instinctively and it seemed to break the spell. But Richard started singing louder, at a tremendous volume that seemed to vibrate the ground. I don't know how to describe it—it was sort of like tug-of-war for a minute. The cross seemed to take on a power and fight against the song. And I started backing away, still holding the cross as tight as I could. Every step was a tremendous effort. I had to put my whole being and will into taking each step. When I finally reached the house, Richard abruptly stopped the song and ran away. I looked for Beth, but she was gone too!"

She sat back in her chair. Her face was flushed and her breasts were still heaving, nearly spilling out of the gown.

"I went out there again," she continued. "It was after I tried calling you. I found Beth's clothes strewn on the lawn. They weren't ripped or anything. She must have taken them off herself. And the cross I gave her was there too. She must have taken it off also."

Simon nodded. "No doubt Beth felt the song's compulsion more strongly than you did, Meg."

"But what happened to her?" Ted asked.

"She was possessed through the use of sexual congress," Simon explained. "During intercourse, people's souls are unguarded and receptive, and that makes it easier for a demon to gain possession of them. One of the partners must already be possessed, and the demon in that person entices the other into sex. Demons have no sex, of course, so it works either way. A man can be used to possess a woman or the other way around."

"Is that what's been happening to people?" Ted asked, horrified.

"I suspected it was when I talked to Billy Martin's roommate, who said the poor girl had been raped. But I couldn't be sure until now. I suppose it appeals to the evil nature of a demon to use the act of creation in a perverted way to destroy someone."

"And that's what will happen to Jill," Ted muttered to himself in horror.

"You saved my life, Simon, for the second time," Meg said. "If you hadn't insisted I wear that cross, what happened to poor Beth would have happened to me. Do you think she is suffering much?"

"I don't know. It would depend on how much of her own personality she can manage to hold onto. If the demon totally suppresses her soul, she won't be aware of what is happening to her. But if—" Simon broke off to look over at Ted, who had gotten off the arm of the sofa.

He was staring in horror at the french doors.

"What is it?" Meg cried, jumping up.

A naked woman was pressed up against the glass panes of the doors. Her legs were spread wide and bent at the knees and her arms were up over her head. Her breasts were two flattened circles. Her face, also pressed against the glass, was distorted and grotesquely in-human.

Her eyes were wide open and burning with white-hot fire.

"It's Beth!" Meg shrieked. "Dear God! Beth!!" She started forward, going to her young maid.

"No, Meg!" Simon grabbed her arm.

There was a wrenching sound of wood against metal and then a sharp crack. The french door crashed into the room, its glass shattering, shards flying everywhere. Meg stumbled back screaming. Simon reached into his coat and pulled out a large cross. Ted took a step forward, then froze, staring in disbelief.

The naked maid now stood on the fallen door, hands on her hips, her jaw thrust out aggressively. Her burning eyes went from one person to the next radiating hatred and contempt. Her face looked like a wolf's or a hyena's, with a bloodthirsty grin baring gleaming white teeth. Foul, inhuman laughter rumbled out of her.

Ted thought it sounded like the laughter he used to hear in the dead of night at the mental hospital—the laughter of madness. Only this was much, much worse. Unthinking, he took a step toward the demon-woman, his hands clenching themselves into fists.

Simon shouted over the terrible laughter, "Stop, demon! In the name of Christ!" He thrust out the cross. "In the name of Christ, begone!"

The demon-woman turned her fiery eyes on him and bellowed like thunder, "IN THE NAME OF SATAN!! IN THE NAME OF SATAN, WHO IS COMING!!"

The brilliant eyes suddenly swelled still brighter, becoming balls of pure fire so bright they blotted out the face in which they were set.

"SATAN! COME TO US! SATAN!!"

Simon tried to shout over the demon's thunderous voice. Their two voices rose in the air and battled.

"In the name of Christ our Lord . . ."

"IN THE NAME OF SATAN . . ."

". . . we pray to thee, oh God, to deliver us . . ."

". . . OUR LORD OF DARKNESS WE PRAY TO THEE!! COME TO US! SATAN!! COME TO US!!"

". . . deliver us from this serpent of death . . ."

"YOU WILL DIE TONIGHT, OLD MAN! YOU HAVE SINNED IN PRIDE AND YOU WILL DIE!!"

". . . deliver us, oh Lord, from thine enemy . . ."

"KING OF DARKNESS, EMPEROR OF HELL, SATAN, COME TO US!!"

Ted took another step forward toward the hellish thing. His head was swimming, his vision was consumed by the wolf-faced demon. His arms were straight out in front of him, grasping the air.

The demon whirled to face him. "YOUR BRIDE SHALL BECOME SATAN'S BRIDE! SHE IS DAMNED! THE PIG IS DAMNED!"

His face contorted by blind fury, Ted lunged, his grasping fingers instinctively finding the demon-woman's neck and closing tight.

Screaming "NO! NO! NO!" he bore down, his fingers pushing deep into the cold flesh. His eyes bulging insanely, his neck tendons popping out, he squeezed with all his might.

Meg was shrieking and Simon was shouting something to him, but he couldn't hear it.

And then he was in the air. *He was in the air!* He was over the demon-woman's head struggling helplessly, held up by her small hands. And the bellowing laughter was now impossibly loud, flooding the room with its thunder.

The demon-woman threw him. He flew twenty feet through the air to smash against the grandfather clock in a jangle of gongs and bellowing laughter.

"YOUR PIG IS DAMNED!! YOU CANNOT HELP HER, YOU MISERABLE SCUM!! SHE BELONGS TO SATAN!! BY SATAN SHE WILL BE POSSESSED!!!"

Now, incredibly, Simon's voice rang out, seeming to split the air with its power. *"IN THE NAME OF CHRIST OUR SAVIOR! DELIVER US, OH LORD,*

*FROM THIS SERPENT OF DEATH, THIS CRAWL-
ING WORM OF HATRED!! DELIVER US!!"*

The demon jumped high in the air, flipping over in a
backwards somersault to land on its feet on the broken
door.

*"DELIVER US, OH LORD, FROM THIS FOUL
MINION OF YOUR ENEMY, FROM THIS JACKAL
OF WICKEDNESS, THIS BLASPHEMOUS
SNAKE!! IN THE NAME OF CHRIST, OUR
SAVIOR, DELIVER US!!!"*

As Simon continued shouting, the demon's face
changed. The fire left its eyes to be replaced by aching
horror. And Beth, the young maid, once more appeared.

"Help me!" she cried. "Oh please, please help me!
Help me!"

Simon came toward her, but even as he did so she
jumped in the air again doing another backward somersault. Coming down, her eyes were glowing, her face
once more twisted and evil and inhuman.

Simon flinched back.

"HELP ME!!" the demon bellowed mockingly. "OH,
SIMON! HELP ME! HELP ME!"

As if pulled by an invisible string, the demon jumped
backward out of the doorway and into the black night.

Simon gaped at the spot where the demon had been,
then, hearing Ted moan, went over to where he lay next
to the remains of the clock.

With Meg helping, the old man helped Ted to stand
up. Every part of his body was screaming in pain. He
was hardly able to breathe against the agony.

"You shouldn't have tried what you did," Simon told
him. "You would not have killed the demon, which cannot die, but Beth. And then the demon might have tried
to possess one of us."

"We've got to go after her," Ted rasped, "and catch
her."

"You can't kill her, Ted."

"Not to kill her . . . to catch her."

"But why?" Simon asked.

Ted shook his head. He waited until he could breathe easier and then answered. "Satan, the demons—they know all about us, but we know next to nothing about them! We've got to catch her and question her!"

"How?" Meg asked.

"I don't know, but we've got to try!"

"Ted, we'll never find her," Simon said.

"We won't if we stand around arguing about it! If you don't want to help, I'll do it on my own."

Leaving Simon and Meg staring after him, Ted walked over the fallen door and out into the night. He checked the grounds of the mansion and saw nothing.

"I'll go looking for her in my car," he said, coming back inside. "I hope she hasn't gotten far."

"All right, Ted," Simon sighed, "I'll go with you."

"What about our meeting, Simon?" Meg asked.

"We'll be back in a while, one way or the other. Ask them to wait."

Meg grabbed Simon's hand as he went out the front door after Ted. "Don't go," she pleaded. "You're too old for this."

"No, Meg. It's what I have waited for nearly all my life."

It was a wild, windy night, and bitterly cold. Thick clouds now flew by overhead, seeming to brush the tree tops that swayed in the wind.

Before getting in his car, Ted looked for the comet. But the clouds made it impossible to see. It was a good sign, he thought. In his vision, the sky had been perfectly clear with the comet's red tail easily visible. It wouldn't happen tonight he told himself. It *couldn't* happen tonight!

Simon thrust something in his hand. It was a cross attached to a beaded chain.

"What about you?" he asked.

"I have another." Simon indicated the larger cross he was wearing around his neck.

They circled the block around Meg's mansion and saw not a living soul. The streets were deserted. Ted wondered how many people were huddling in their houses trying to escape the cold feeling of dread. Nearly everyone, it seemed.

He turned down another street, going slowly, peering into the darkness, sweeping his eyes from one side of the road to the other. High hedges and brick walls hid the elegant mansions of San Francisco's rich. If Beth was not out on the street, but behind the high walls, they would never find her. Still, he had to try. He had to do something!

Simon sat beside him, clutching his cross and whispering prayers.

"Do you see anything?" he asked the old man.

"No."

They came to the last row of houses before the land ended in cliffs high above the ocean. To the west, the red towers of the Golden Gate Bridge loomed against the night sky, and the park-like Presidio army base was black with trees. The wind came in off the ocean, howling eerily through the trees and telephone wires like the wailing laments of a thousand lost souls.

They came to a dead end. Ted did a U-turn, then turned onto the road that led through the Presidio. It was starting to seem hopeless. The possessed woman could be anywhere, he knew.

Then Simon shouted, "Look! Up ahead!"

There was a bouncing light-colored shape far ahead. It was moving fast. His heart pounding in his chest, Ted stepped on the gas. A moment later his headlights caught the naked figure.

"It's her!" he hissed.

She was running ahead of them along the side of the road, her legs and arms nothing but a blur. Ted pulled closer until she was just fifty feet ahead of them.

Glancing down at the speedometer, he whispered in awe, "I can't believe it!"

He was going thirty-five mph and still the possessed woman was in front of them. He sped up to forty and was pulling up alongside her when she pulled away again.

"God in Heaven!" Simon shouted. "You'll kill her!"

"What?"

"Like the others. Her heart will explode! It is still a human body—whatever possesses it!"

Ted put on the brakes to slow for a sharp turn in the road. She shot ahead. Coming out of the turn, he speeded up to her again. Just as he got even with her, she veered away from the road and plunged down the steep bank that fell away from the road.

"We've lost her," Simon said as she disappeared.

"NO!"

Ted stomped on the brakes and the car screeched to a halt. "You wait here!" he shouted, jumping out.

Simon shouted after him, but he ignored the old man and bounded down into the trees of the rock-covered bank. It was too dark to see more than shadows. Ted could only pray he didn't trip over a rock or fallen branch or run into a tree. He knew the slope ended in precipitous cliffs over the ocean. If he tripped and started to roll down, he wouldn't stop until he hit the water hundreds of feet below.

He jumped sideways in broad leaps a good way down the bank before fear got the better of him and he stumbled to a halt, finally grabbing a tree branch to break his downward momentum. The thumping concussion of the ocean pounding against the rocks below came up and mixed with the howl of the wind. Hanging on to the branch with one hand, panting for breath, he looked around him. Behind him, the hill rose steeply to the road. Below, it descended another twenty feet and then he could see nothing but air. On either side of him were trees. The possessed woman was nowhere to be seen. Guessing, he headed to his left, in a line parallel to the cliff.

He had gone a hundred laborious feet when he heard it. A high, vibrating sound, eerie and compelling and horribly beautiful. Meg Olson had described a sound like it only an hour earlier, but his mind did not connect the description with what he was hearing now. The sound rose above the hissing wind and the muffled pounding of the ocean, cutting through those sounds like a shark fin through water. He stopped and stood deathly still. Turning his head this way and that, he judged the sound to be coming from below, near the edge of the cliff.

The sound swept over him in waves, rising and falling, soaring and swooping, seeming at times to lift him from the ground. A sort of queasy mixture of fear and excitement filled his stomach, the same mixture he had once felt as a small boy going into the fun house at the county fair, its dark and spooky entrance both forbidding and enticing.

He hesitated a moment longer, then turned and picked his way down the steep ground toward the quivering sound. It was becoming harder and harder for him to think straight. The undulating sound came through the howling air with terrible beauty, reaching into his very soul and seeming to guide his movements down the treacherous hillside.

He came to a big boulder blocking his path, but the sound pulled him forward relentlessly. It pulled him around the boulder to the very edge of the cliff high above the ocean waves. He had to hug his belly against the rock and slowly inch his way around. He did not look down at the distant surf because he had no fear of falling. The sound filled him, mesmerized him.

Inch by inch, feeling the way with his feet, he edged around the boulder. And then he saw the demon-woman on another large boulder not twenty feet away. Her naked body was etched in gray against the darker sky. Her glowing eyes lighted her face. Her hands were stretched high into the night, her back arched to thrust her breasts in front of her, and her terrible song floated up in the wind to fill Ted with its compelling urgency.

Ted gazed up at her with awe, his mind empty except for the waves of her song. Over her head the Pacific wind was blowing away the clouds to reveal the starry firmament—and the long curved tail of Halley's Comet. It was blood red.

Ted did not see it. His whole being was concentrated on the naked woman in front of him.

CHAPTER 18

Larry stared at his reflection in the glass of the phone booth. The harsh fluorescent light coming down from the top seemed to accentuate the tight distortion of his scarred features. He smiled at himself, a weird, twisted smile, and laughed.

"You're a gruesome motherfucker!!"

Outside it was nearly pitch black. There was just a glow from the freeway over his head where a few cars rushed by onto the Golden Gate Bridge heading for Marin county. The parking lot was empty. A lonely deserted spot, perfect for his plan.

He held the phone to his ear with one hand and dialed with the other, then picked up his knife from the aluminum shelf. He felt the fine keenness of the blade.

Little surprise for you, Jill!

He listened to the phone ring six times, then slammed the receiver back on its hook with a force that made the bells jangle. His dime clinked down to the coin return.

The fucking bitch better not have shafted me! he thought irrationally, as if Jill should know he was phoning her—as if she should have been cooperating in his little surprise for her. If she wasn't going to answer, he told himself, he would have to track her down and peel off her skin layer by layer.

Layer By Layer!

She could have it any way she wanted it—fast and neat and quick, or layer by layer, slow and excruciating. It was all up to her. All she had to do was answer her goddamn phone!

He put the tip of the knife against the glass and pushed the blade back inside the handle. Putting it down on the shelf, he got his dime, put it in again, picked up the phone, and dialed.

You just better pray. Better pray you answer. Peel your skin if you don't. Layer by layer.

The phone rang once.

Peel your skin, bitch!

It rang again.

Slice by slice!

A third time.

Scream by scream!

There was a click. Jill's voice. "Hello?"

Larry felt his throat constrict. He forced the words out anyway.

"Hi Jill. It's Larry."

She decided right, he thought. *Now she can get it neat and quick! IF SHE BEHAVES HERSELF!*

Her voice was wary. "Larry? What are you calling for? I don't feel like talking."

"I just wanted to tell you something," he replied, picking up the knife again. He pressed the button and the blade shot out. "I've been feeling real bad about what happened. Real bad!"

"Well, you shouldn't have done it."

"Yeah, I know. I know I shouldn't have. I feel real bad. I felt real bad right after it happened. I'm feeling really depressed, you know? I just don't know what to do."

"I'm sorry, Larry. But . . . listen, do you think we

could talk about it some other time! I don't—"

"The thing is, Jill, I'm just feeling so bad. You know —suicidal. I think I'm feeling suicidal."

Eat it up, bitch! Eat it up!

"Don't talk like that!" Jill said sharply.

"I just can't help myself!" Larry whined. "After what I did . . . you know . . ."

Eat it up!

"You didn't really do anything. I shouldn't have panicked, I guess."

"But I was going to do something. Something bad! And I think maybe I just don't deserve to live!" Larry choked out a sob. "Do you think you could come over here?"

Eat it, Bitch! Eat it up!

Jill hesitated. "Now? I can't, Larry."

"You're the only person I can talk to and I'm just feeling so bad!"

"Can't we just talk about it over the phone? I can't go out tonight."

"I don't know, man. I just . . . just don't know. I'm wondering if it's worth it anyway." Larry turned the knife back and forth, back and forth, watching the shimmer of the fluorescent light play along its sharp edge. First he was going to fuck her and then, to be fair (he had to be fair!) he was going to let his knife fuck her. "Maybe we should just say good-bye, you know? And . . . and you can forget you ever knew me."

"No, Larry! Listen—"

"You know where I am?"

"Aren't you at home?"

"No. I'm at the bridge."

"You're at the bridge?"

"Yeah. Like I told you the other day, that's the way I want to go."

Eat it up! Come on, baby, eat it up!

"Listen, Larry!" Jill shouted with alarm. "Don't do anything!"

She's eating it! "But I'm just feeling so bad. If I could just see you. Just talk to you a little. But maybe, if you don't want to come, we can just say goodbye. I mean—"

"NO! Listen. Stay right where you are."

She's eating it. She ate it!

"And don't do anything! I'll come right over!"

She ate it all up!!

"That would be nice, Jill. But like I said, if you don't want to—"

"I do want to! Larry, please don't do anything until I get there!"

"Okay, sure. I'll be waiting for you."

"Good. Good. Y-you wait for me and I'll be right over there as fast as I can."

"Thanks, Jill." *Thanks, bitch!* "Oh, Jill . . . Don't call the cops or anything. If I see a cop, I'm gonna jump. No cops. Understand?"

"I—I understand. No cops. I'll be there as soon as I can."

"I'll be waiting."

Smiling crookedly, Larry dropped the receiver back on the hook.

She ate it! She ate it all up!

That strange feeling in his chest was stronger than ever now, flooding him with feelings of power and strength!

He held his glistening knife up and kissed it. "We're going to have a nice little fucking session, you and I," he said insanely. "First me. And then you." *

He slid back the phone booth door and was knocked off balance by a ferocious gust of wind. Sand hit him in the face like sharp needles. Looking out, he saw a paper cup fly by, a blurred streak. A tree branch rolled along the ground.

"Jesus Christ!" he whispered to himself. "Looks like we're gonna have a fucking tornado or something!"

Halley's Comet hung in the sky like a bloody sword.

Jill hung up the phone, starting nervously when the whole house shook under the brunt of a sudden gust. It felt like a small earthquake and she put her hand to the wall to steady herself. The wind had been building and building for the last half hour, rattling the windows and whining through every chink and crack in the house, making her teeth ache. But the howling wind was nothing compared to the feeling in her chest—lodged there like an alien presence and radiating dread.

She felt like finding an enormous rock and hiding under it.

It had been several hours now since Ted had left her alone to pace nervously through the empty house. She was frightened and jumpy and emotionally exhausted. When the phone first had started ringing she had frozen in terror and had simply stared at it until it stopped. Then it had started ringing again, and she had told herself it was just a phone for heaven sakes and it might be Ted calling.

But it was Larry.

And he was going to commit suicide if she didn't go see him at the bridge. Or was he? Maybe he was just playing some nasty trick on her. Maybe he wasn't at the bridge at all!

She turned back to the phone and dialed Larry's number. She let it ring and ring. There was no answer. Of course, he could be there and purposely not answering it, thinking she might call to check up on him.

If only she knew what to do!

Ted had pleaded with her not to go out. No matter what!

And she didn't want to go out, goddamn it! Something monstrous and evil was brewing! A battle between God and Satan, Simon had said. She thought of the demon's eyes boring into her. She still felt dirty inside, defiled! She just couldn't go out!

She just couldn't!

But what if he really is going to jump?

He's not! He's just playing some trick!

But what if?

She felt like screaming! And if the wind didn't stop howling she was going to go insane! She couldn't even think!

Then just stay home, dammit! Larry is not your responsibility! You're not supposed to leave the house! No matter what! An unspeakable horror is waiting for you out there! You can't go out!

But what if he really was going to jump?

She picked up the phone again. She was trembling so badly it took her three tries before she could dial Larry's number correctly. She let it ring a full two minutes before giving up.

"Larry, if this is just some trick!" she cried aloud.

She had no choice, she realized. Maybe he *was* just trying to pull something. But she couldn't take that chance! If he did jump, she would never be able to live with herself! And she had the cross Ted had given her. It would protect her. She would go out and get Larry and drag him right back here!

She went to the front closet and started pulling on her coat. And then she stopped. She didn't have her car! It was still where she had left it last night, at the dance class. How could she go to Larry if she didn't have her car?

You can call a taxi.

"No," she muttered to herself, "They wouldn't want to drive on a night like this."

But maybe they will. You can't be sure.

She wished her conscience would just shut up! Pulling off her coat again, she went down the hall to the phone. She got out the phone book and flipped through the yellow pages to the taxi companies.

She crossed her fingers, hoping no one would agree to come out.

CHAPTER 19

Ted was balanced precariously on two jagged rocks at the edge of the cliff. A false step or sudden gust of wind would quickly send him plunging down into the foaming waves hundreds of feet below. But he was only dimly aware of the height as he stared open-mouthed at the naked figure on the boulder in front of him. The demon-woman's undulating song, high and pure and inhuman, came through the night to fill his soul. And her eyes, even twenty feet away from him as she was, seemed to look through his own eyes to the back of his head. Fear clutched at his heart, but the feeling was far away, as if in a dream.

The quivering song and glowing hot eyes drew him forward.

Unable to look away from the form in front of him to find a secure footing, he took a step. His foot hovered in the air a moment, instinctively waiting to feel resistance on a level with his other foot. But there was none. It went down into a space between the rocks. His arms gyrating wildly in reflex, he started falling. The whole world seemed to be tilting away from him. Then his chest came down hard on a slab of stone and his head was out over empty space and he was staring down at the ocean hundreds of feet below. Pain shot through him like lightning and for a moment the sounds of this world came back to him, the muffled thunder of the surf, the whining, howling sound of the wind. It was like suddenly waking from a dream. He wondered where he was, what had happened to him, what he was trying to do. The puzzlement lasted for only a second before memory returned and with it, terror.

Keeping on his belly, he pushed himself back away from the edge. And then the demon song came to him again, so high and powerful it made his body vibrate like a ringing glass. It was terrible, but it was also beautiful and compelling. He squirmed around on the rocks, turning over on his back. The naked demon had come closer. She was standing over him so close that if he stretched out his leg he would touch her. And her eyes were brighter than ever, her song more terrible and beautiful than ever, coming out of her oval mouth to hover in the air like a shimmering rainbow of sound and captivate him with its frightening beauty. He thought vaguely that he should block his ears from its luring urgency. He started to raise his hands to his ears, but the waves of sound were rising and falling, sweeping over him one after another, and he forgot what he was doing.

And her eyes were burning with ancient fire, older than man, older than the world. He tried not to look at their fiery brightness, but that was impossible. It was as if thin lines of forces came out of the two burning pools to turn his head up at them.

And suddenly he was falling, falling headfirst into their brilliant light, plunging down through the fires, through miles and miles of space and an eternity of time. He felt himself spinning in the void, tumbling over and over, his mind leaving a long fading cry of terror behind him. Memories flew from him in the plummetting rush, memories of his parents, of his sister, of Jill—memories and hopes and fears were all stripped from him in his headlong fall through eternity.

And then he found himself back on the high cliff over the Pacific, the demon-woman standing in front of him. He was standing up now, facing her. And he was as naked as she, his clothes strewn around the rocks, the cross Simon had given him lying forgotten near a shoe. He stared at her dumbly and did not shrink back when she reached out to take his hand, her fingers colder than ice. Her mouth still quivering with her terrible, beautiful song, her eyes still lighting her face with their ancient glow, she led him by the hand away from the precipice to a flat rock near a wind-blown tree. The ever-present wind whipped around his naked body, sapping it of its warmth, but he did not notice it. He felt hot and feverish.

She let go of his hand and lay down on the flat rock, her legs toward him, her burning eyes fixed on his. Abruptly she stopped her singing and the sound of the wind and surf seemed like silence.

He stared down at her naked form. Except for her face, which glowed with the fire in her eyes, her body was all rounded gray shadows, voluptuous and desirous. He tried to think, to fathom what was happening, but his thoughts disintegrated when still half-formed. He tried to find some memory, any memory, that would tell him who he was. But his mind felt like cotton wool, soft and amorphous. She was moving her hips up and down with a slow, sinuous rhythm. The fever in him rose, bursting out on his skin in droplets of fine sweat.

Her hands went to the insides of her thighs.

"Fuck me."

Her voice was like the hiss of escaping steam.

"Fuck me."

His penis was jutting out straight and hard. He tried to think. Her hips were vibrating up and down in ecstasy.

He wanted her.

"Take me. Fuck me."

Then another voice, frightened. "Ted! Ted!!"

The sound of his name sent Ted's mind swirling in confusion. He didn't realize what he was hearing, whose voice it was, only that it was a voice, not that it was calling his own name.

"FUCK ME!" The demon-woman hissed urgently, her eyes blazing brighter.

The voice came again, louder, desperate. "Ted! Don't look at her! TED!!"

He tried to piece the sounds together, to understand their meaning. Before he could, the demon-woman sat up on the rock, her eyes shooting angry flames, and started singing her compelling song again, high and wailing in its terrible beauty. His mind ceased its uncertain groping as the waves of sound washed into it.

Breathing hard, shaking from the cold, Simon was easing his way around the large boulder Ted passed just minutes before. His heart was pounding explosively in his chest, but he couldn't think about that. He clung to the rock and inched his feet forward carefully on the treacherous cliff's edge. He could see them both—the demon-woman sitting on the rock, and Ted, naked, with an erection, standing motionless in front of her.

His cheek pressed against the rough surface of the boulder, he called out again. "TED!! In the name of God! Don't look at her!"

At the mention of God, the demon-woman jumped to her feet as if gravity had no hold over her. Her face twisted in rage and though it didn't seem possible, her eyes became still brighter, bathing Ted and the area around him in their eerie light.

Her voice was like the roar of a passing train. "GET AWAY, OLD MAN! THIS ONE IS MINE! MINE!!"

Simon had slid his way around the boulder and was

standing now on solid ground. He had his large cross at arm's length in front of him. He shouted over the wind, "The Lord is my shepherd: I shall not want. He maketh me . . ."

"GET AWAY, OLD MAN!!" the she-devil bellowed in hideous rage, rending the air. "He is mine!! MINE!!"

". . . He leadeth me beside still waters; he restoreth my soul . . ."

The demon-woman choked in fury, howling, bellowing like a bull. Simon saw Ted suddenly jerk away, as if the spell was broken, and kept shouting as loud as he could,

"Though I walk through the valley of the shadow of death, I shall fear no evil, for thou art with me . . ."

Ted moved back away from the raging demon and turned uncertainly to face the old man.

". . . Thy rod and thy staff, they comfort me . . ."

In a paroxysm of rage, the demon leaped high into the air—

". . . Thou preparest a table before me. . ."

—and came down with her feet on Ted's shoulders, sending him reeling back to the very edge of the precipice. Then her body slammed into his, knocking him down. Heedless of the danger, Simon stumbled toward them over the jagged rocks. Ted was flat on his back, his head tilted back out of sight over the edge. The demon woman crouched over him, grabbed his penis and squatted down to try thrusting it inside her. But it was flaccid. She was ranting curses so fast the words melded together in a single long ejaculation of blasphemy.

"JESUSFUCKMARYWHORESHITONGOD DAMNFUCKCUNTJESUSWHOREMARY . . ."

She was still squatting over Ted's prostrate form, working frantically on his penis, when Simon thrust his cross out flat against her bare back. There was an explosion of crackling electricity around it and the smell of burning flesh. A spasmodic roar of rage erupted from the demon, seeming to echo back from the ocean to split the very heavens. She leaped high, leaving a trail of urine in the air behind her, and seemed to disappear in the night.

Then her horrible thundering bellow came from behind Simon and he whirled around to see her on top of the big boulder he had eased around earlier.

"Begone, evil serpent! In the name of Christ, our Saviour! BEGONE!!"

The she-devil leaped in the air at him. Simon thrust his cross high up to meet her as she came down. She landed on it between her breasts, bolts of lightning shooting out around it, crackling, hissing, spewing blinding flames. She hung there a moment as if she hardly had weight and then, writhing, fell to the rocks at his feet. Green vomit exploded from her mouth. Her bowels voided themselves. He stared at her in frozen horror a moment. Then she jumped up, and squealing like a thousand rats, darted away into the darkness.

Simon stood where he was, turning his head around to either side as far as it would go, looking, waiting, expecting her to come back any minute. If she did, she would win, he thought. His heart felt like it was tearing itself from his chest. He waited for a minute, then another minute, and his laboring heart began to slow. After a while, he felt safe and issued a silent prayer to God. Then he picked his way over the rocks to where Ted lay unconscious.

The scarred muscles of Larry's twisted leg were cramping badly from the cold and lack of movement. He was waiting in the phone booth on the edge of the parking lot, keeping its door open just enough to keep the flourescent light off. He hadn't planned to wait in the booth. He had planned to wait behind some of the supporting pillars under the freeway, but the wind was so cold and biting he had stayed in the booth mumbling to himself, playing impatiently with his switch blade. Now he pushed the door closed and the light flickered on, painfully bright after the darkness. He looked at his watch. It was after one a.m. He nudged the door open again and the light blinked out.

Come on, bitch! What's taking you so long? Me and my knife, we're waiting!

The parking lot was still deserted and the nearby freeway carried fewer and fewer cars to the bridge—the late hour and violent winds and the cold, dreadful feeling all conspiring to keep people from driving. Overhead was the comet, its tail huge, dwarfing even the massive presence of the bridge. Looking up at it through the smudged glass of the booth, Larry wondered what had happened to change its color from silvery white to blood red.

The strange feeling in his chest was stronger than ever, making him feel strong and powerful still. Yet in spite of that, the sight of the comet made him shudder.

Where the fuck is that bitch?

He was tired of waiting for her. She had already left her house, he knew, because he had phoned back and gotten no answer. So she was on her way.

Hurry up! Me and my knife, we've got a little surprise! First I'm going to fuck you and then my knife is going to fuck you!

His anticipation had built up to such an unbearable pitch he now wanted nothing so much as to just get it over with.

Meg Olson's maid Beth, possessed by a demon older than the world, was running over the rocks where San Francisco ended at the ocean. She was running with inhuman speed and inhuman indifference to the cold.

Beth's mind no longer activated the arms and legs of her own body. A bare flicker was all that remained of her soul, a dim awareness of far off memories, hopes and dreams—and a faint feeling of choking horror. In possession of her soul was the subhuman, brutish spirit that possessed her. The demon was in constant agony, in constant war with itself and every other being but Satan, because its own nature closed it off forever from the sight of God and redemption. And because of its constant agony, it nourished a perpetual rage. That rage found release only in evil—pure, indescribable evil.

Beth's body was a gruesome sight now. Simon had scarred it front and back with the hateful sign of the cross and it had used its fingers to rip away the flesh around the sign between its breasts, obliterating it. It could not reach the one on its back and so it had rubbed against a rough tree until the flesh was worn away, leaving muscles and bones protruding. It felt the excruciating pain of it in Beth's soul, but not as its own pain.

And now it was guiding Beth's body rapidly over the rocks that swept around to the Golden Gate Bridge. Beth's eyes glowed with the timeless fires of hell. Her face was twisted with hate. And the demon in her was following a dumb urge that was growing stronger by the minute, impelling it to the bridge. Satan, the Lord of Darkness, Prince of Death, King of Hell, its source of power, was coming! Soon he would establish his kingdom of hell on earth.

Larry kept playing the scene over and over in his mind —how he would lure Jill into the dark recesses under the on-ramp to the bridge. How he would flash his knife at her and watch her cringe with terror. How she would beg and plead with him hysterically. How he would force her to undress herself. Or no—maybe he would cut her clothes from her with the knife, snip, snip, snip. And how he would rape her, savoring every minute of her terror. And afterward, how he would let his knife caress her, let his knife rape her.

He laughed insanely.

He looked up at the blood red comet—it was hard to keep his eyes off it—and shivered. There was something about it, some power to it he could not understand. He had sure picked a strange, strange, night to do his little number on Jill! Yessiree!

Forcing himself to look away from the looming red presence in the sky, he saw someone running into the deserted parking lot.

Jill!

He yanked the phone booth door open and hobbled out into the wind with his crutch. He had to squint against the stinging sand thrown up by the wind. He kept his knife out of sight behind his back.

Yes. She was running right for him!

Then his jaw dropped open. She was naked! What the hell? She was running with incredible speed! As she came closer, he realized it wasn't Jill. *It never rains but it pours,* he thought. Maybe he would get two of them tonight! His fingers played excitedly over the blade of his knife. She was coming straight toward him, the howling wind whipping her hair around her face.

As she passed under a light on the freeway on-ramp, he saw the gruesome wound between her breasts, extending half way down her belly. His blood turned to ice. And now she was out of the light, still coming toward him and he saw her eyes glowing like twin coals. His heart pounding in terror. he whipped his knife out in front of him and screamed.

"Keep away from me! Keep away!!" It was a high, whining scream, full of abject terror.

Her strength was unbelievable, the speed of her movements impossible, and he had no chance to use his knife before he found himself being thrown backward on the ground. His crutch went flying, but he managed to keep hold of the shiny switch-blade. Bellowing like a mad bull, the demon-woman leaped on top of him. She came down flat on his chest, her hands grabbing for his throat. He drove the knife deep into her back and a sound erupted from her like nothing he had ever heard. In stark terror, he wrenched the knife out of her and drove it in again and again and again, and each stab made her shriek to split the heavens.

Finally, she stopped moving. His head spinning deliriously, Larry pushed her off himself. His mind was like a broken record *(What—What—What—What—)* as he watched her fall away in strange angles, totally loose-jointed. Then blood started spurting, somehow in delayed reaction, from all the knife wounds. *(What—What —What—What—)* It went all over, on her, on the ground, on Larry. He crabbed backwards on the hard gravel away from it. He half expected the body to start moving again and kept his eyes glued to it.

Panting, he propped himself up on his elbows. Blood was no longer spurting from the dead body, but oozing out slowly. His knife was still embedded in her back from his last desperate thrust.

Not daring to look away lest the heinous thing suddenly come back to life, he pushed himself along the ground further from it. Then the effort became too much and he stopped. He saw a vague mist rise up from the body, faintly luminescent in the dark night. Strangely, the strong wind did not blow it away. It hovered over the body a moment, then to Larry's horror started moving toward him.

He scrambled backwards across the ground. But it still floated toward him. Frantically he struggled to his feet. He turned to run, but his leg buckled under him and he fell to the ground, shrieking in horror.

The strange glowing mist surrounded him.

He screamed in agony. He could feel icy fingers thrusting deep into his brain. In some far corner of his mind he told himself this couldn't be happening. But the thought was smothered. He struggled against the icy tentacles, instinctively trying to force them out, but he was not strong enough.

His eyes started to glow with an evil radiance.

The demon was a bit confused—as always after entering a new body. There was still a lingering scream of terror in the soul it now possessed, and the demon savored its warmth. After a while, it made its new body stand up. The withered leg at first made it difficult to walk, but it concentrated its power into the atrophied muscles and was soon able to use the leg well enough.

It turned Larry's now fiery eyes up to the sky to look at the enormous red comet hung like a frozen shriek among the stars. Satan, the King of Hell, was coming!

"COME MY MASTER! COME!" It roared, then howled in glee like a demented wolf.

And then again it felt the dumb urge it had felt before pulling it toward the bridge.

The taxi swung into the parking lot, its headlights just missing Beth's blood-soaked body with Larry's knife sticking out the back. Jill bit at her lip nervously as she peered out the back window trying to spot Larry.

The taxi lurched to a stop. "That's $7.50 plus tip," the driver said.

"Wait," Jill said. "I don't see him. Can you drive up to the end?"

"Listen, lady. I didn't want to bring you out here in the first place—"

"Please!" Jill begged.

"What a night!" the driver muttered, putting the cab in gear.

Jill searched the surrounding darkness as the taxi rolled forward. Larry was nowhere to be seen.

"Can you honk the horn?"

"What?"

"Honk the horn! Maybe he'll hear it."

The driver leaned against his horn. "Satisfied?"

"Thank you. Do you see anybody?"

"I don't see nothing but the spooky night. Now let's get out of here. I shouldn't have come out here to begin with. Something's not right tonight. I can feel it! Something's just not right!"

Jill rolled down the window and stuck her head out into the stinging wind. "Larry!" she yelled.

The wind seemed to swallow the sound. All she could see was darkness. Where the hell was he?

She pulled her head back inside. "Wait for me. I'm going to look for him."

"Hey, no offense, but I want my money first!"

"I'll just be a minute!"

"The money first!" the driver shouted, swinging around and holding out his hand.

"Will you wait for me?"

"Yeah! I just don't want you disappearing on me!"

"All right." She handed him ten dollars, then pushed the door open and got out, the wind ripping it out of her hand and slamming it shut. Her hair lashed her face like thousands of tiny whips as she walked away from the cab and stared into the shadows for Larry. Where the hell was he?

Maybe he was under the approach ramp trying to get out of the wind, she thought, walking toward it. Then she stopped. If he was anywhere around, he should have seen her by now!

"LARRY!" Sounding small and inadequate, her yell swept away in the rushing wind.

He couldn't be here! It was all a twisted, sadistic joke!

She turned around to see the taxi pulling away.

"No!" she yelled, running after it. "Come back! COME BACK!"

She tripped, falling down hard and skinning her hands. Helplessly, she watched the taxi speed away and disappear into the night.

"Oh God!" she moaned, picking herself up. She had never felt so alone in her life! Clutching fearfully at the cross Ted had given her, she turned to look up at the bridge. Her eyes didn't stop on the flood-lit towers, but kept moving up to the blood-red streak of gleaming color in the sky above. Her eyes widened in awe and fear. The comet was huge! Monstrous! Just looking at it made her stomach knot, and it seemed to flood her mind with horrible thoughts of agony and terror and death. It made the ever-present heaviness pressing against her heart even stronger and more sinister. What was it Simon had said? *When the nightbroom turns to blood.*

Oh God! It's going to happen tonight! It's tonight!

She ripped her eyes away from the awesome sight. She had to think! She should never have come out here! Never!

Don't panic!

Think!

She looked up at the bridge again, carefully avoiding the blazing red comet.

Think!

She would go up the stairway to the bridge and calmly flag down a passing car. *Yes.* And she would ask them to take her home. *Yes.*

Leaning crazily against the wind, she started off toward the stairway. Everything would be all right, she told herself. She could flag down a car and be safely home in half an hour.

If there are any cars.

No, don't think that! There have to be at least a few!

As she reached the stairs, the wind eased a little, blocked by the cement and steel undergirding of the bridge. But at the top, the wind seemed stronger than ever. And the bridge was deserted. There wasn't a single car in sight! *Don't panic!* She looked around. The toll booths behind her were dark and empty. They stopped collecting tolls at midnight, she remembered.

Don't panic! Don't panic!

Turning around again, she saw someone moving far out on the bridge—a solitary figure.

Larry! She had forgotten all about him! At least she wasn't alone! There was another human being to help her!

"LARRY!" The yell tore from her throat painfully and was swallowed by the wind. He was never going to hear her over the screaming gale! She started to jog as fast as she could against the wind.

"LARRY!" she called again painfully. "LARRY!!"

He was still moving away from her, though she was running as fast as she could. And something was wrong. Something was strange about him. He was moving too quickly. And he didn't have his crutch! What the—?

She stopped and took a deep breath. Putting everything she had into it, she roared out his name again.

"LARRY!!!"

Thank God! He hears me! He's stopping!

CHAPTER 20

Simon knelt down by Ted's unconscious form at the edge of the cliff and pulled him back so that his head was no longer hanging over empty space. Even in the darkness he could see that the young man's body was covered with bruises.

Ted moaned, the sound coming out low and faint. Then his eyes opened. A look of terror swept over his face.

"It's all right," Simon soothed. "She is gone. You're safe now."

Ted shook his head. There was hardly a cloud to be seen now and the blood-red tail of the comet stretched like a long wound across the heavens. He pushed himself up.

"It's happening!" he wailed. "Simon! Look!"

The old man looked up and his eyes widened in awe. He crossed himself quickly. "God preserve us," he murmured. "I should have known!"

"What?"

"I'm an old man, Ted. You must forgive me! I wasn't thinking straight. The comet will reach conjunction with earth in a few hours! I should have realized it would happen when the comet came closest to us!

Ted started pulling on his clothes. "Jill! My vision! I've got to—"

"She is safe at home, Ted!"

"I've got to go to her!"

"No! Ted! Listen to me!"

"I've got to go to her! *My visions always come true!*" Ted started climbing back to his car.

Simon hurried after him. "You said yourself she was safer alone!" he shouted. "Ted! Please! Listen to me!"

But Ted was beyond listening. Simon didn't catch up to him until they reached the car. He grabbed Ted and shook him.

"Ted! You said yourself she was safer alone!"

Ted let out a harrowing moan. "Yes . . . You're right." He stared at Simon with bulging eyes.

"You've got to be strong," The old man told him. "I may not be with you when the time comes."

"What do you mean? I need you!"

"I'm an old man, Ted. You heard what the demon said earlier. I may die tonight."

"No!" Ted cried. "I need you!"

"Listen to me! You hold the world's fate in your hands! You must be strong! The danger point will come when the comet reaches conjunction with earth. The window in time I talked about before will open up, unsettling the balance between the two spheres of good and evil. *You have to hold the balance until the window closes again!*"

"How can I hold the balance? How?"

"I'm sorry, Ted. I don't know. But you must find a way!" Simon was miserable. He had waited all his life for this moment and now that it was here, he felt lost and frightened. He had no idea what to do.

Ted was staring up at the huge, blood-colored comet.

"Come on, Ted," Simon said gently. "We should go back now. My group should be waiting for us at Meg's."

In a daze, Ted got in the car. He waited for Simon, then did a sharp U-turn. *Jill is safer alone,* he told himself. *She is safer alone!* He repeated it over and over, trying his best to believe it.

Simon sat quietly in the seat next to him and nervously fingered his cross. He still did not know what his role in God's plan was. If he had a role to play, why didn't he know what it was? The battle was beginning! He looked over at Ted, his profile a gray shadow. He felt in his bones, instinctively, that he should stick by this young man. He had to be patient, he told himself. He had to wait—

"Look!" Ted shouted, interrupting his thoughts.

A naked man was running like the wind in front of them, his pale skin caught in Ted's headlights.

"It's another one!" Ted hissed, speeding up.

"Let him go," Simon urged. "We should get back to Meg's."

"No!" Ted shouted. "This one we're going to catch!"

Simon fell against the door as Ted swerved sharply around a tight bend, the tires squealing. Then he fell across toward Ted as they went around another bend in the twisting road.

Ted stared in frustration at the naked figure running in front of him. If the road weren't so winding, he could easily overtake the man, he thought, But the twists and turns made it impossible for him to go over thirty. Then they went around another bend and the road opened up. Ted stepped on the gas, sending the car up to forty, and pulled alongside the naked figure.

The man turned his face to them as they pulled along side. He was grinning dementedly. His eyes were bright with the fires of hell.

Suddenly he disappeared, turning down a road that forked away. Ted slammed on the brakes, throwing Simon forward, and screeched to a stop, overshooting the turn off.

"Ted!" Simon shouted. "Let's go back to Meg's!"

"No!" Ted yelled, putting the car in reverse. "We're going to catch him!"

He backed up, then sped into the side road, which led to the Golden Gate bridge, not half a mile away.

How can he walk without his crutch? Jill wondered, staring at Larry's distant figure. He looked like a tiny speck compared to the massive towers of the bridge soaring over him. And the amber light of the fog lamps made him seem vaguely unreal.

He had heard her over the howling wind and stopped, but he wasn't coming back to her now. He was just staying where he was, waiting for her to walk to him. What was he doing? Why didn't he come? Where was his crutch?

She didn't want to walk out there, fighting the fury of the wind every step of the way, couldn't he realize that? She didn't want to be out in this hellish night at all! Couldn't he feel the heavy, dreadful coldness?

Maybe he's still going to jump!

She cupped her hands to her mouth and yelled, "LAAAA—" The yell was hardly out of her mouth when she broke off coughing. Her throat was raw.

Dammit, Larry! Come here! Please!

She gave up. He was the only other human being around! Running her hand along the ice-cold railing, she started walking toward him. She walked as fast as she could, keeping her head down, trying to keep the stinging, bitterly cold wind off her face and out of her eyes. She stopped twice to cling to the railing for dear life when the raging wind threatened to pick her up and toss her over the side. And each time she stopped she looked up to see Larry standing stock still, like a department store mannequin, waiting as if he had all the time in the world. *Damn him anyway!* He had gotten her into this fix. She had come out to help him and now that she needed help, he wasn't budging.

Damn him, anyway!

As she got closer, he seemed to get more unreal in the amber fog lights. But the wind was too strong to look at him for long and she put her head down and kept walking, clutching at the rail with one hand and at her silver cross with the other. She didn't think of how he could help her. He was another human being and on this hellish night, she just needed to be with someone. Mostly she was trying not to think of what had happened to her the night before and how horrible it had been. And she was trying not to think that the same thing, *or something even worse,* could happen to her tonight.

As she finally got close to him, he turned his back to her. *God! That's just like him!* she thought. She came up behind him, stopping just two feet away. There were stains on his pants—dark, brownish red spots, like dried blood.

She shouted over the roaring wind, "Dammit, Larry! You wanted me to come! At least talk to me! I'm frightened out of my mind!"

Slowly, so slowly it seemed to take minutes, he began turning around. Again Jill wondered what had happened to his crutch, how he could walk all the way out on the bridge without it.

"What's the idea . . ." she began, and then she saw his glowing white-hot eyes radiating evil, his scarred and disfigured face even more hideous than before. She stopped breathing.

A bolt of lightning flashed from nowhere out of the cloudless night sky and struck the closest bridge tower. She felt the bridge shake under her and the tremendous clap of thunder thudding in her chest. But she hardly noticed the occurrence.

Two eyes burning with fire older than man were staring at her out of a grotesquely inhuman face, its lips snaked back into a hideous, diabolical smile. She couldn't understand what she was seeing. It was a nightmare come out of the wind! She wanted to run, but her legs had melted away into the cold night. She wanted to look away, yet the gruesome face held her. The nostrils were flaring like a mad bull's. The eyes were incredibly wide, burning with the heat of hell, making her feel as though she was dying, making her feel she was already dead, her body decomposing, crawling with maggots.

She screamed.

The gods hurled another bolt of lightning out of the raging sky, its blue-white light exploding with the power of a bomb, its thunder slamming into her like a flying brick wall.

Not realizing what she was doing, acting instinctively, she took a step backwards. Larry reached out to grab her, digging his icy fingers into her wrist.

He laughed dementedly over the roar of the wind, his evil eyes bearing down on her.

NO, no, no, I don't want to die don't want to die don't want to die, no, please, no, don't want to die, no please, no, don't want to die . . .

His hellish mouth stretched open wide and a sound came out of it—a deep, deep sound, vibrating on the wind. She didn't really hear it, but felt it come into her like waves, felt it break over her hypnotically, rythmically, mesmerizing her. It came inside her, penetrating her, wave after wave, rising and falling, rising and falling, making a hot fever rise up in her.

No. Don't. No . . .

But the demon's song was invincible and swept into her relentlessly, filling her up with its power.

She was falling. Falling headlong into fathomless burning eyes, careening down, down, down, without end, through miles and miles of eternity.

"It's going toward the bridge!" Ted shouted as the two red towers came into view.

Trying to keep pace with the racing demon, he fought to control the car against the driving force of the wind as he came up on the approach ramp to the bridge.

He was doing fifty, and still the demon flew ahead of him!

"Slow down!" Simon shouted. "The toll booths are coming up!"

Ted jerked his foot off the gas, but not soon enough. The car was still going too fast to hold the road against the cross winds and make it through the narrow lanes between the booths. A gust came against the car, pushing it sideways.

"Look out!" Simon cried.

Ted slammed on the brakes, sending the car fish-tailing at one of the booths.

"Oh God!"

Ted spun the steering wheel around. The car skidded with its rear wheels sliding forward. It crashed sideways into the rubber barrier. Simon was thrown over, almost landing on Ted, and then the car bounced off, hitting the barrier on the other side, still moving forward, and the old man went flying back.

Somehow they ended up on the other side of the toll booths.

"Are you okay?" Ted shouted.

"Yes, yes," Simon trembled.

Ted stepped on the gas, heading onto the deserted bridge in pursuit of the racing demon. In the sky he could see the blood-red comet tail, huge and monstrous. It dwarfed the towers of the bridge, having doubled in size in the last half hour.

"Look!" Simon shouted. "Just up ahead!"

A naked man and woman were standing on the walk-way. The man's burning eyes showed that he was possessed. The woman's hair was flying in the wind, obscuring her face.

Ted's heart raced—he knew who it was. His visions always came true! He would run up to her and watch her eyes start to burn and her face twist and contort itself into a demonic vision of pure evil. She would be as good as dead. Or worse. There were worse things than death! Much worse!

He brought the car to a jarring halt right next to them as the naked man he had been chasing raced ahead.

"Jill! Jill!" he screamed, jumping out of the car.

He started to leap over the low railing to the walkway, but Simon caught his arm.

"Don't get too close!" he shouted over the wind. He held his large cross out in front of him.

Shaking with terror, praying it wouldn't be her but knowing it would, Ted went over the rail. The demon in Larry turned his head toward him, abruptly shutting off the wailing song. His eyes flared brighter in raging anger. Jill was standing in front of him naked and unmoving, in a trance. He reached out swiftly and grabbed her to him.

The sound that came out of him then was not a voice, but a thundering snarl of pure hatred.

"You will die this night, old man! You cannot win! Satan will crush you!"

Staring at Jill and nearly crazy with fear and anger, Ted moved forward. Simon lurched to catch his coat and pulled back hard.

It's coming true, Ted thought. *It is all coming true!*

"THE BITCH IS MINE!" the demon roared out of Larry's twisted mouth, its voice now like a howling wolf's.

Holding his cross out in front of him, Simon started praying, yelling loudly. But unlike the demon's, his voice was swallowed up in the gale-force wind.

"PRAY, OLD MAN! PRAY! YOU WILL DIE TO-NIGHT!" The demon bellowed.

There arose a tremendous roar in the air. More than the wind—it was as if a screaming jet was taking off right over their heads! Ted and Simon looked up in unison. The demon turned his glowing eyes to the sky too.

The comet's blood-red tail was writhing like an enormous snake, growing before their eyes. It was coming down out of the heavens at them!

Suddenly the entire sky exploded in a swirling cauldron. Bands of red and yellow and orange spiraled out in a huge vortex that engulfed the sky. The demon's eyes pulsated brighter at the amazing spectacle. Ted and Simon gaped in horrified silence, transfixed, struck dumb. Only Jill, still in a trance, did not look up.

The sky was a sea of flame, bubbling and seething, and now it began spinning. Its center started lowering, turning into a tornado of flame. Lighting crackled around it. The wind, impossibly, became even more ferocious. The bridge started swaying. And still the great funnel of swirling flame descended in a deafening roar.

"Dear God!" Simon yelled. "It's happening! It's Satan come to earth!"

The demon roared with a triumphant laugh, "IT *IS* SATAN! SATAN!! SATAN, YOU HAVE COME FOR YOUR KINGDOM!"

The demon went into an uncontrollable frenzy, crowing and howling and laughing. Seeming to forget the mortals nearby, he raised his hands to the sky and screamed, "SATAN!! COME TO US!! COME TO TAKE YOUR KINGDOM!!"

Bracing himself against the raging gale, Ted looked away from the tornado to the demon, then to Jill, then nervously back to the demon again. The hellish thing was ranting wildly in triumph at Satan's coming. Jill stood two feet behind him, staring vacantly at nothing, her long hair whipping in the incredible gale. Ted thought of running to her and pulling her quickly away. But the demon might swirl around suddenly and catch her. She might fall over the side. It was too dangerous.

Perhaps he could rush the demon, pushing him over the side! The water was hundreds of feet below. Could it fly? He didn't know. His heart pounding ferociously in his chest, he looked back at Jill, beautiful in spite of the dumb horror on her face.

He took a step toward the demon and froze. What if he should fail?

The monstrous tornado of fire moved down out of the sky and struck the high headlands of Marin County across the bridge. There was a tremendous burst of lightning around where it touched, like an enormous string of firecrackers being set off at its base. Then the rest of the sky cleared suddenly, the fire disappearing, to reveal that the tornado of fire was really the comet's tail!

The demon shrieked wildly, thumping his chest, howling in an orgiastic frenzy.

"SATAN IS COMING!! SATAN IS HERE!! SATAN IS HERE!!"

Ted's mind screamed at him to act. *Rush the monster and heave it over! Do it! Now! Before it's too late!*

But what if he should fail? The demon might lash out at the last instant and pull Jill after it.

There are worse things than death! Do it! You must act!

As if his body were an alien thing, Ted forced himself to move closer to the demonic presence. The bridge lurched in a sudden gust, making Jill fall back against the railing. His heart leaped in his throat.

DO IT! NOW!!

He turned to glance quickly at Simon, seeking some sign of strength and encouragement. But the old man, his white hair whipping in the blowing gale, was oblivious to him. He was staring in awe at the fire, which now seemed a giant pillar of flame, his lips moving rapidly in prayer.

The demon had moved away from Jill, bellowing in ecstasy at the monstrous tower of fire that snaked up in the sky to become the comet's tail.

DO IT! NOW!! NOW!! NOW!!

Ted rushed at the hellish thing, holding his arms straight out. Not thinking of his own safety, he ignored the raging wind and the swaying bridge under his feet, and used every ounce of his strength as he slammed into the demon's back. Caught by surprise, it roared in horrible rage. But Ted's momentum kept him going, taking the demon in front of him. It smashed against the railing, then jacknifed.

In an instant it was gone, its roars of hate fading away into the howling night.

For a moment, Ted was stunned by his success—unbelieving, almost expecting the demon to float up again on the wind. Then he ran to Jill and swept her into his arms.

I DID IT, he thought. *I DID IT! I STOPPED THE VISION FROM COMING TRUE!*

"You're safe! Safe!" he cried, crushing her tight. Her skin was like ice. Coming out of the spell, she burst into tears against his shoulder and shivered violently.

Her coat was pressed against the rungs of the railing by the wind. He grabbed it and wrapped it around her, then pulled her close again, covering her with kisses.

He heard Simon shouting at him over the wind, but ignored him. "It's all over now," he said, burying his face in her hair. You're safe now. Safe."

It seemed to him he had accomplished nothing short of a miracle. Since the dawn of time, Jill had been destined to fall into Satan's power. But he had stopped it!

Staggering against the howling gale, Simon came up to them. He grabbed Ted's hair and roughly turned his head toward himself.

"What have you done?!" he demanded, his face red with anger.

Ted looked at him stupidly, uncomprehendingly. What had he done? He had killed the demon! He had saved Jill! That's what he had done! But he said nothing. He could not find words.

"Hurry! We've got to get away from here!" Simon yelled.

"But, but I k-killed it!" Ted stammered.

"You *can't* kill a demon! You killed the man it possessed! Not the demon! It can possess one of us now!"

Ted looked at Simon in horror.

"Your vision can still come true!"

The words hit Ted like a blow. He moaned pitifully.

Simon had taken his cross off. He pulled Jill away from Ted and slipped the chain over her head. "This will help protect her! Now let's get out of here!"

Jill's frightened eyes went to Ted. She spoke for the first time. "I—I d-don't understand."

But there was no time to explain. Simon was heading back toward the car. Ted grabbed Jill's arm and pulled her along with him after the old man.

"Hurry!" he shouted.

Ahead of them, Simon screamed out in sudden agony. Ted watched in horror as he fell to the ground, the wind rolling him over and over until he stopped against the railing. He was surrounded by a glowing mist. His withered old arms and legs were flailing wildly.

"He gave me his cross!" Jill shouted.

"Keep it!" Ted cried. "Don't take it off!"

"You can't let him die!" With a sudden motion, Jill

jerked the cross down, breaking the chain. She thrust it
out at Ted.

"Take it!"

Ted didn't move.

"Take it!" she yelled. "You can't let him die!"

Ted took the cross and ran over to the old man, falling on his knees beside him. Simon was babbling in-
coherently, his face contorted in terror. His eyes were
beginning to flicker with light. Ted pressed the cross
against his forehead, creating a small shower of electric
sparks. The old man let out a horrible shriek, a piercing
wail of agony that made Ted jerk the cross away again.
He took a wild look around at Jill standing in the wind
behind him and then put the cross back on Simon's forehead. Ignoring the crackling sparks, he started shouting
the twenty-third psalm. It was all he could think of to
do.

"Though I walk through the valley of the shadow of
death, I shall fear no evil. Thy rod and thy staff, they
comfort me . . ."

Simon's flickering eyes began to dim. Ted kept the
cross pressed to his forehead and shouted his lungs out.

"Thou preparest a table before me in the presence of
my enemies. Thou anointest my head with oil . . ."

Simon's struggles subsided. The crackling white
sparks died away.

". . . and I shall dwell in the house of the Lord—"

Behind him, Jill let out a screaming wail, high and
pure and horrible.

Ted whipped around and his body turned to stone. *It
was his vision!* Jill, her face frozen in terror, was writhing
in a macabre dance, throwing off her coat. Over her
head the blazing red comet tail descended to the hills of
Marin. She was fighting something, something he
couldn't see. The wind pushed her dancing over to the

rail and held her there as she struggled with flailing arms against the invisible demon. Her cries of terror stabbed like a dagger through Ted's heart.

Breaking through his paralysis, Ted leaped to his feet. But the ferocious wind caught him and sent him flying. He landed on the deck of the bridge with a bone-crushing jar. The cross escaped from his fingers and went skidding away. He scrambled after it frantically on his hands and knees, grabbing it just before it could go over the side. He jumped up and turned to Jill again.

And what he saw turned him to jelly, making his body useless in his abject terror.

Her eyes were burning brighter and brighter. Her face was changing from human to inhuman as she fought with the demon within her. The eyes dimmed, then burned brighter. Her mouth twisted itself into a leering grin.

"Jill!" he screamed, holding the cross up. But it was too late. Her eyes were now glowing steadily with the timeless fires of hell. Her face was a contorted mask of loathesome horror. She opened her mouth wide and roared with inhuman laughter.

Ted staggered toward her, the cross out in front of him. She stood where she was in her nakedness, roaring with laughter, her eyes shining with evil venom. Ted approached her slowly, then lunged forward quickly with the cross, trying to press it against her. But she leaped up in the air as if she weighed nothing. Still screaming horrendous shrieks of maniacal laughter, she smashed her foot against his head with such force Ted flew backwards ten feet to fall near Simon's prostrate form.

She started to go toward him, but then looked back over her shoulder to the tremendous pillar of fire on the Marin headlands, still swirling and blazing with the light of the sun.

"IT IS SATAN!!" she roared.

Turning, she started running toward the column of fire.

"SATAN!! SATAN!! I AM COMING!!!"

Ted swam spinning into dark unconsciousness.

Delirious and triumphant with evil joy, the demon worked the muscles of Jill's lithe body, running over the bridge toward the comet tail now planted as a pillar of fire on the hills of Marin. It felt strange in its new body —the third it had possessed that day—but it knew the feeling would pass. There were occasional attempts by the soul to push it out but the attempts were feeble and easily overcome. It enjoyed the feeling of the soul's terror. But its thoughts were directed toward Satan.

Satan was coming at long last!

The demon raced Jill's body along the asphalt surface of the bridge, cutting through the violent wind like a bird, barely touching her feet to the ground. How glorious Satan was that its power should grow so strong! Soon Satan would manifest himself, borne in the great pillar of fire ahead. The demon used its new human eyes to drink in the sight thirstily. The immense tornado grew from the hills in a blaze of swirling light—it stretched up and up, higher and higher into the night, joining with Satan's blood-red tail in the deep blackness of space. At its base, lightning flashed around it, its thunder reverberating from hill to hill.

Let the pitiful mortals behold Satan's power! the demon thought. Let them shake in awe at the sight of his doings! Let them pray to their God! It will do no good! SATAN IS COMING!

The demon worked the legs of its new body harder, in anticipation of his lord's imminent arrival. A sharp pain grew in the human's chest, next to her thumping heart.

And terror once more welled up—clawing, crying terror! The demon forced the body to laugh a horrible, chilling, inhuman laugh.

Terror. Yes, terror. But wait my pretty human. Wait! There is more terror to come!

CHAPTER 21

Jill's face floated in a random pattern through the swirling blackness. She looked as Ted had last seen her. Her eyes blazed with hell fire. Her features were hideous and hateful. He tried to call to her. Her mouth opened in a horrible grimace. A torrent of maggots streamed out.

He screamed.

His eyes blinked open, revealing the red tower of the bridge looming over him and the comet that was like a bleeding wound in the sky. His ears picked up the roaring wind. He felt the cold bridge against his body.

He sat up in a daze. One thought—one horrible, horrible thought—formed itself in his mind and screamed its awful truth at him.

His vision had come true!

He got to his feet and hardly knowing what he was doing, started walking toward the awesome spout of fire in the distance. He gripped the rail and put one foot in front of the other mechanically.

His vision had come true!

"TED!"

He stopped at the sound of his name. It barely rose above the wind. Turning, he saw Simon crumpled on the cold walkway. *Simon! Oh, God! Yes! Simon will help me!*

He raced back to the white-haired old man and knelt down beside him. Simon was breathing hard, his chest laboring, the air whistling in his throat. "Listen, Ted," he rasped.

"It's happened!" Ted cried. "The vision came true! It's got Jill! You've got to help me save her!" His voice rose hysterically. "You've got to help me save her!"

"Listen to me!" Simon cried, straining to make his voice stronger. Ted looked down at the old, wrinkled face, saw the pain in it, and realized Simon was dying. *But he can't die! Not now!*

Simon reached up a bony hand and clutched Ted's coat fiercely, surprising him with his desperate strength. His blue eyes seemed to pop from their sockets. His voice was full of a lifetime of determination.

"You must stop Satan!" he said. "He will make the world his hell! You must stop him!"

Simon searched his face for an answer, but Ted could not speak. Terror for Jill, terror for Simon, terror for himself filled his soul.

His face cringing in agony, Simon shook in a spasm of coughing. His hand fell weakly from Ted's coat.

"Don't die!" Ted shouted. "You've got to live!"

The old man's face was turning blue. His chest was heaving in agony. He spoke with great effort.

"You can do it, Ted."

"How?" Ted wailed.

"The group . . . get my group . . . at . . . Meg's . . ." Simon stopped, gasping for breath. Ted lifted his head up and cradled it in his arms.

"And then what? Don't die! I need you!"

"Remember . . . it is all in . . . in the . . . balance . . . and one man . . . can . . . tip . . . the balance . . ."

"But what should I do!" Ted screamed hysterically. "It's got Jill already!"

A strange transformation came over the old man. The

pain left his face and his blue lips turned peaceful. He looked almost beautiful. He seemed to be listening to something far away. A small smile curled his lips.

"Yes," he whispered. "My mission is . . . finished . . . now . . ."

"You've got to live!" Ted cried. "I don't know what to do!"

"One man . . . can . . . tip . . . the . . . balance," Simon repeated, quoting from the ancient manuscript that had come to him so many years ago. He felt as if he were floating now, in his last moment. Everything seemed very clear to him, bathed in light as clean and shimmering as the early morning sun. His part in God's plan was now completed. He *had* been too proud, he realized, for his role in God's plan was only as a guidepost, to send Ted off in the right direction.

He looked up at Ted's anguished face. There was no pride in the young man, only fear and helplessness.

Simon tried to speak, but his strength was almost gone. Ted put his ear down next to his mouth.

"It's your . . . turn . . . now . . ." He wheezed. "It's . . . all . . . in . . . the . . . balance . . . have . . . faith . . . one . . . man . . . can . . . tip . . . the . . . balance . . . between . . . good . . . and . . . evil . . . one . . . man . . ."

Simon's heaving chest stopped its labors. The old man went limp.

Ted stroked the fine dry parchment skin of Simon's cheek. "I needed you," he whispered.

But the old man was dead. Ted laid his head down on the walkway and pulled himself to his feet. He felt drained of all feeling and emotion. There seemed nothing left in him, nothing at all.

"NO!" he shouted, raising his fists to the sky. "NO! NO! NO! NO!"

The wind picked up his denying words and swept them away into nothingness. He was all alone. He felt so tiny, only a toy soldier with his fists raised, dwarfed by the enormous bridge and the giant pillar of fire towering in the sky.

Jill was possessed by a being of unimaginable horror. Satan was coming to earth from the nightbroom. And the one person who could help lay dead at his feet. He was all alone.

He looked inside himself for something solid to cling to and found nothing. He had no strength. He had never been strong. He had always failed the people who needed him. *He had always failed!* Jill was lost. He could never save her now.

"NO!" he cried again. "NO!"

Jill was *not* lost! Not yet! Simon had believed in him! One man can tip the balance! Simon had told him. The old man had believed in him! He had to hold onto that belief, no matter what!

Simon's cross was lying a few feet away, its chain caught in the railing. He ran to pick it up and clutched it to his chest.

One man can tip the balance!

He took one last look at Simon's crumpled body, the wind rippling his white hair, his face still serene, beautiful. Then he ran back to his car. A police car sped by him, ignoring him, heading toward the pillar of fire. Another followed in its wake, its siren wailing. All hell was about to break loose! He *had* to stop it! It was his only hope for saving Jill! He climbed into his car and swung around back to the city. *One man can tip the balance!* he told himself again and again as he sped across the bridge, leaving the tornado of fire behind him.

There was one more act still to be played out, he knew. Only his first vision had come true so far, and the stage was now set for the second. *Jill, naked in front of the awesome spout of flame, dancing obscenely, her eyes radiating evil power. And something in his hand, some-*

thing important, something hard and heavy. That was
what he had seen—that was all he had seen! And there
was hope in that! Because he had not seen how it would
end! So anything was still possible! It was all in the balance, Simon had told him. And he could still tip the
balance! Jill's fate was not sealed! Not yet!

But the prophecy . . . *A choice he must make of his own
free will. For God or Satan, heaven or hell. Will he kill his
love? Or will mankind crown the King of Hell?*

The prophecy!

*No! Don't think about that! Don't think about that!
DON'T THINK ABOUT THAT!*

*Simon believed in you! Think about that! Simon be-
lieved in you!*

As he left the bridge, a fire truck whizzed past him
heading for Marin. He realized they had no idea what
was happening. A fire truck against Satan! Only he and
a few others, the people in Simon's mysterious group,
knew what was at stake.

Now a knot of people were running toward him. They
were naked. As they passed him, he saw how their eyes
glowed, how their faces were contorted into evil shapes.
They were running toward the pillar of fire, he realized.
The demons were gathering strength moment by moment.

They ran past his car, ignoring him, running like the
wind toward their lord and master. He shuddered. Fear
ate away at his insides like acid. Could he really stop
Satan himself and all the forces of Hell?

"One man can tip the balance!" he shouted out loud.
He repeated the phrase over and over again at the top of
his lungs all the way to Meg Olson's mansion.

The violent wind had not abated. It was rattling the
many-paned windows of Meg Olson's ornate library,
hissing and whining through cracks in the casements.

Meg had asked all the people in the group to wait for
Simon's return. She had herded them into the library—
the white room, where they usually met, was a shambles.
Only two-thirds of the group had shown up. It was, after
all, a terrifying night.

Ted went into the library, closed the door behind himself, and stopped dead in his tracks. Was this Simon's
group? he asked himself in stunned disbelief. Were these
the people who were supposed to help him?

They were scattered over chairs and a sofa, and on the
floor along one wall. Many were old and feeble. One
bald man near Ted looked palsied. Another was wheezing and coughing. An aged woman in an absurd flowered hat sat on the sofa crying quietly to herself. And the
younger ones didn't look much better. A young man
was slumped down in the corner, his chin resting on his
chest, his eyes staring vacantly as though he were spaced
out on drugs or alcohol. A girl with blonde hair to her
waist was holding her sides and rocking back and forth
on her haunches like an autistic hild. Even the smell of
the room was one of decay and hopeless despair.

Meg came up to him. As nervous and frightened as
she obviously was, she seemed a tower of strength compared to the others.

"Where's Simon?" she asked.

Ted pulled her close and whispered into her ear, so no
one else would hear, "He's dead."

For a moment, he thought she was going to be hysterical. But she pulled herself together and, taking him by
the elbow, she guided him out into the hall.

She shut the door behind them. "Dead! How? He
can't be!"

"I'm sorry, Meg. He was possessed. There's no time
to explain. He told me to go to his group." He pointed
his thumb at the library door. "Is that them?"

"It's most of them, all that would come." She

clumped back against the door. "Oh, poor Simon! What are we going to do?"

"I—I don't know," he admitted. "Simon must have had a plan! Didn't he ever tell you what he expected?"

Meg shook her head slowly. "He never told us all that much. He never said what his plans were. I—I don't think he had any."

"Oh, God!"

"He just made us feel good. That was all. He touched each of our lives in a different way and we just sort of formed this group around him."

"But he said he told you about his old manuscript and the prophecy of Satan's coming!"

"He did. But he never told us what he expected us to do when the time came. And to tell the truth, most of us didn't really believe him. We listened to him out of respect, because he made us feel better about ourselves, made us feel worth something, but we never knew what to make of his talk about the battle between good and evil. All he said was that we would soon face a great trial and that we must have faith—faith in God, but more importantly, faith in ourselves."

Ted felt sick. Pushing down the clawing despair that was rising in his throat, he tried to think. It was all in the balance, Simon had told him. And he told him to get the group. But now what? He had no idea what to do.

Except—

He thought of the second vision. He was standing in front of the monstrous tower of fire staring at Jill, something hard and heavy in his hand. That meant he was going over the bridge to the pillar. And if he was going, he had to take the group with him. It was a first step, at least. He would worry about what came next after he got there.

Meg was crying softly beside him. "I could never

decide whether Simon was a saint or a madman. I never—"

"He was a saint, I hope!" Ted cut her off. "We've wasted enough time. We're going to meet Satan head on!"

Meg gasped. "What?!"

"I'll explain." He opened the library door and stepped in, Meg coming in behind him. He surveyed the cowering people, whose eyes were all on him, watching him fearfully. The room was deadly silent.

He tried to speak, but could not find his voice. *You could be leading these poor people to their deaths*, he thought. *You don't know what you're doing! Admit it! You have always failed the people who needed you! Always!*

He felt his hands trembling. His knees were ready to give way. He wanted a drink. He badly wanted a drink! He looked at the young man in the corner, his face pale and vacant. *I'm no better than he is!*

Meg broke the tense silence. "I—I've got the crosses Simon brought," she said, picking up a box from behind the desk and setting it down on top.

Ted looked at her, hoping she would keep talking and cover over his fear. But she just stared back at him.

He found his voice. "Yes . . . Good . . . The crosses . . ." He turned to face the others. "Everyone should take a cross."

"Simon brought these over a week ago," Meg added. "He said we would need them when the time came."

"I want to know what's going on!" a fat, middle-aged woman demanded loudly. "Where is Simon? Why isn't he here?"

"Yes!" another voice came from the back of the room. "Where's Simon?"

Ted had known he would face this moment and had planned to say that Simon was waiting for them on the other side of the bridge. He knew they would panic if he told them the truth. But now his resolution seemed to drain away entirely. He seemed to crumple up before their eyes. "He died a while ago," he said. "Simon is dead."

"What? Dead!"

"Dear God!"

A swelling babble of frightened voices filled the library. And all at once the crowd seemed to break for the door, as if stampeding from a burning room.

Ted stumbled back against the door ahead of them, blocking their exit. "No! Please!" he shouted, holding up his hands. "Please! Be calm!"

He turned wildly to Meg, but she was as frightened as he. Hands were pulling at him, trying to get him away from the door.

"Please!" he yelled again. "Don't be frightened!" But he knew it was hopeless. He was too weak! Simon had counted on him, but he didn't have the strength. Tears of despair were streaming down his cheeks. Soul-destroying images flashed through his mind—of his parents, of his little sister, of Jill. It was hopeless! Jill was doomed! The whole world was doomed! He wasn't strong enough!

The frightened people crowded around him, pushing and shoving to get out the door. Hands came at him, grabbing him, pulling him.

"No! Wait!" he begged. "Please!"

Another hand laid hold of him.

"Let us out!"

"We have no business being here!"

"We don't know you!"

They were all babbling in his ears, trying to pull him away from the door. He leaned back with all his weight, not knowing how to hold them, but not willing to let them leave. Then a young, teenaged girl pushed her way roughly through the others.

In the press of bodies she was thrown up against him. She put her hands to his chest and pushed herself back.

"It is you!" she exclaimed, straining against the jostling crowd. "I thought so! Don't you remember?"

"Let us go!" a man shouted above the others.

Struggling to keep his back against the door, Ted yanked his arm away from a grasping hand and looked down wildly at her fresh, innocent face. Irrelevantly, absurdly, he started going through the catalogue of his students in the university.

"I'm Becky!" she said. "From the bar out by the beach? You helped me get away from Johnny!"

"I want to go home!" an old woman cried.

"Let us out of here!"

Ted stared down at the girl in a daze. Meg Olson started yelling at people and pushing her way through the crowd trying to get people away from the door.

"You were the only one in the whole bar who would even lift a finger to help me!" Becky shouted over the others.

Ted's mind started clicking. He remembered the man with the gold ring in his ear. He remembered the humiliation of getting knocked out in the parking lot, the feeling of failure.

"The guy didn't catch up to you?" he croaked.

"No! I got away! Didn't you realize that?"

Meg Olson had managed to get a few people away, thinning the crowd that still was crushing in on Ted and Becky. Becky turned around now and pushed back the young man behind her.

"Listen, everybody!" she shouted. "This man is my friend! He helped me when nobody else would! Listen to what he has to say!"

The frightened voices in the room kept going.

"Listen to him!" Becky shouted. "LISTEN!"

Slowly, the hubbub of voices died down, leaving only the howling sound of the wind and the rattling windows. Several people returned to their seats. Others remained standing in a circle around Ted.

Seeing Becky again worked a remarkable change in Ted. He thought he had failed her, too that day in the bar. But he had helped her! And there was something else too. She said that he was the only one in the whole place who had even tried to help her. That was the thing. He had tried!

The important thing was to try! Jill was depending on him! If he let his fear overwhelm him and stop him from even trying, she would certainly be lost!

"Now listen to me!" he shouted forcefully. "Simon sent me to you with his last words! He told you about the battle between good and evil, and how the world is a balance. You've seen the fire in the sky and the comet's bloody red tail! Satan is coming and we must meet him head on! We must go to the pillar of fire!

"Oh no!" cried the woman in the flowered hat. "Simon never told us it was going to be so terrifying!" She shook her head violently. "It's too dangerous! I saw that whirlwind of fire! It's not for us to try and stop it!"

"It is for us!" Ted insisted. "Who else is going to do it?"

"She's right," a young man said, the one who looked drunk. He got up from the floor. "We can't do anything. We're just ordinary people!"

"Yes, we're just ordinary people!" Ted agreed. "But Simon told me that it is we ordinary men and women who determine the world's fate! Don't you understand what is happening? It is Satan himself! Satan! We will all be doomed anyway if we don't act now! Satan is trying to take over the earth—literally to make it a living hell! Simon brought you all together just to meet this challenge! No one else will do it for you! Didn't Simon tell you that you must have faith in yourselves? Didn't he tell you that you would have to face a great trial of your faith?"

There was an uncertain murmur.

"Didn't he tell you that?" Ted demanded again, his face red, his voice hoarse.

"He told us all that," the woman in the hat answered. "But we never believed him! No, we never did! We never did!"

"You didn't believe him!" Ted shouted angrily. "I'll bet you believed him when he gave you his kindness! You believed him when he told you that you were not forgotten! You believed him when he told you that you were worth something, when he gave you his compassion and his strength! I bet you believed him then all right! Yes, you believed him then!"

The woman shook her head nervously. "I'm just so frightened.

"I'm frightened, too!" Ted replied.

Becky took a step forward. "I joined Simon's group only two weeks ago," she said. "But I know what he taught us. We have to have faith in ourselves! How can you forget him so quickly?"

Ted went to the box of crosses on the desk and picked it up. "We're wasting time!" he shouted. "Everybody take one of these crosses!"

Ted started walking toward the others when a tremendous shaking arose in the house. The lights dimmed, flickering. Several people screamed. The lights brightened again, then the library windows shattered under the sudden onslaught of the raging gale outside. The wind rammed into the room, knocking the older people over, sending the chandelier swaying. The lights went out completely.

"There's no time to lose!" Ted shouted into the darkness over the screams. "Those of you who have faith in yourselves come with me! We'll pass out the crosses on the way. The rest of you can go to hell!''

Hoping he would not be alone, he stumbled out of the darkened house to his car. But even if no one else followed, he would have to go anyway. He had already wasted too much time. Meg Olson came out behind him, fighting the raging wind, and then others appeared. All in all, out of the twenty people there, about a dozen came to join him. He crammed five of them into his car and Meg Olson took the rest in her Rolls Royce.

The battle between God and Satan now seemed to be churning the very heavens, unhinging the natural laws of the world. Lightning was flashing in blue-white bolts out of the cloudless sky. Repeated cracks of thunder sounded. The wind was now at hurricane force. And in the distance, the sky glowed with the unnatural light of Satan's tornado of fire.

Ted had to grip the steering wheel with all his strength and fight constantly to keep the car on the road. Tree branches flew by in the air, windows shattered in the houses they passed, and power lines fell in showers of sparks. The frightened people in the car with him sat tight-lipped and silent, seemingly resigned to their fates. Strangely, Ted realized he himself was calm, calmer than he had been in weeks. In convincing the others of the need for faith, he had also convinced himself. He was still gripped by fear, but felt now at least that he could break through the fear into action. He had been mired in a swamp, thrashing around without direction, his struggles only making him sink deeper and deeper into the paralyzing muck. Now that the moment demanded action, he felt himself on solid ground with a clear sense of direction. While the danger now was greater than ever, it seemed to him he might actually break through fate's snare and save Jill.

(If it isn't already too late! No! Don't think about that

or all your strength will unravel!!)

As all these thoughts passed through his mind, he never once thought of his personal safety. He knew of course he was walking into the jaws of hell. Yet that knowledge seemed irrelevant compared to the task at hand and to his love for Jill. She had brought him out of his dark and lonely valley. She had made it possible for him to love again. She was such a good, good person! He loved her so much! How horrible it was that—*No! Don't think about that!*

As he approached the bridge, with Meg's Rolls keeping close behind him, he left the protective cover of trees and houses and came out onto the high promontory. The wind, its power now unchecked, slammed into the car and sent it skidding giddily across the pavement. Several of his passengers screamed. The man in the brown coat seated next to him shouted at him hysterically.

"Turn back! For God's sake, turn back!"

Ted, his knuckles white on the steering wheel, wrenched the car back to the middle of the road. "We can't turn back," he yelled over the screaming wind. "We've got to keep on! For Simon's sake! For the sake of our own souls!"

The man in the brown coat sat back, staring straight ahead, his jaws clamped shut, his hands locked on a cheap cross he had pulled from the box. Ted wondered whether he would have turned back—the fear in his belly was like acid—had it not been for Jill. None of the others, he reminded himself, had the immediate personal stake in this that he did. He looked up in his rear-view mirror. The people in the back seat were sitting mutely, wooden faced. The Rolls was veering wildly across the road, but following still. He said a silent prayer of thanks for Meg.

The entrance to the bridge was blocked by two police cars, pulled sideways in front of the deserted toll booths, their red beacons turning, blinking. Ted braked to a stop. A cop came lurching toward him out of one of the booths. He was hardly walking at all—the wind was pushing him. He fell against Ted's car and grabbed onto the door handle for dear life.

"Are you crazy!" he shouted as Ted rolled down the window a crack, letting the wind sweep into the car. "Get away from here!"

"We've got to get through!" Ted shouted back.

"You can't get through! The damn bridge could come down any minute!"

Ted pointed through the windshield at the raging pillar of fire stretching out of sight in the sky. "We know what that thing is! You've got to let us through to stop it!"

The cop looked at him as if he were insane. But the cop also knew he didn't have a clue in hell as to what was going on. Still, his orders were to keep everyone away.

He turned to look at Meg's Rolls pulling up.

"They're with me!" Ted yelled at him. "Listen to me! You have got to let us through! It's the only way to stop that thing! The only way!"

The cop shook his head. "But the bridge—"

"We'll take our chances!" Ted shouted hoarsely. "Now let us through! For God's sake, let us through!"

The cop examined the desperation on Ted's face a second. "It's your funeral," he yelled. "I hope you know what you're doing!"

So do I, Ted thought. *So do I.*

The cop let go of the door handle, took a step, and was immediately blown off his feet. The wind rolled him along the pavement several yards before he managed to stop himself. He didn't try standing up, but crawled to his squad car, then reached up to open the door, and pulled himself in.

"He's right!" someone in back yelled. "We'll get ourselves killed!"

Ted ignored the remark and put the car in gear as the squad car backed away. He eased through the narrow lane slowly, Meg following in her Rolls. He started to speed up, then immediately let up on the accelerator. With the police car in the way before, he had not been able to see the surface of the bridge. Now he could, and his face went white. The man next to him murmured, "Jesus Christ Almighty!" The red towers still loomed overhead, enormous and strong and unmoving, but the deck of the bridge itself was swaying, rolling, and buckling as if made of rubber. The sound it made was unreal, grinding and groaning as shrieking metal rubbed against metal.

What tremendous powers were being unleashed! Ted felt puny and insignificant. Just a moment ago he had told the cop he could stop the spout of hell fire. But how! With their tiny crosses? This was a battle between unfathomable forces! A battle that was turning nature upside down and in which mortals were mere pawns. Two whole worlds were colliding, God's and Satan's. What was it Simon had said? Man is the battleground on which good and evil contend.

The car pitching on the bridge, he turned to the man beside him and then quickly craned around to look at the people in back. Even in the orange light of the hell fire, their faces were pale. Their eyes did not meet his, but stared straight ahead, glassy with fear. He turned back to look at the bridge and the awesome pillar towering over it. What chance did they have?

The man next to him opened his mouth. Ted thought

he would start screaming, but instead he began speaking in a sing-song chant. Ted could just hear the words over the hurricane winds and the awful groaning of the bridge.

"Yea, though I walk through the valley of the shadow of death, I shall fear no evil . . ."

The man's voice grew louder. Ted joined in the recitation of the psalm, shouting out his lungs, shouting out his terror, smothering his horror in the words of King David's song.

"For thou art with me, thy rod and thy staff, they comfort me . . ."

Still shouting out the psalm, Ted eased the car forward on the terrifying bridge. It felt like some mammoth beast filled with angry rage. The very elements were conspiring to keep them from Satan's pillar of fire. The wind tore across the car, sending it skidding this way and that while underneath them the bridge buckled and shook, the terrible sound of its guts grinding together, sending shudders through the car. Their faces white with cold fear, the passengers were bounced around the car.

As they moved further onto the bridge, the car was tossed so violently that recitation of the psalm became impossible. They had to clamp their jaws tight lest the bucking car cause their teeth to snap together and bite off their tongues. They fell over each other uncontrollably. Their heads smashed against the roof. And when they reached the middle of the bridge, Ted thought surely they would never make it. Between the two great towers the deck had the greatest freedom of movement and the car careened madly about, from one side to the other across all five lanes, one moment flying through the air, the next thudding down hard, and more than once coming up against the rails and bouncing off. It was impossible to drive or steer. Ted simply struggled with the wheel and prayed. He tried to keep track of the Rolls behind him, but it was useless. He prayed that Meg was following.

And then the world turned upside down.

The bridge seemed to drop out from under them. The car floated in thin air a moment and then, coming down, was met by the bridge deck lurching up again. Car and bridge slammed together, the car bounced up, caught the wind, began tipping, and came down on its side. The screaming passengers fell on top on one another in a mass of flailing arms and legs. Stunned but unhurt, Ted fought the writhing bodies around him, trying to pull himself up to the door on the top side. The car was rocking violently back and forth, threatening to turn upside down and crush the people inside.

Someone's knee rammed into Ted's stomach. Pushing it ruthlessly away in spite of the howls of its owner, Ted reached up to the steering wheel, grabbed it tight, and managed to yank himself above the others. But the shift in weight seemed to unbalance the car, tipping it dizzily, almost flipping it on its back. The screams became deafening. Ted froze. When the car rocked back, his hand found the door handle, and he pushed the door open. The wind tore it from him and wrenched it back on its hinges.

The car went rocking again, increasing the panicky yells from its hysterical occupants. Again, Ted froze motionless. Afraid his weight would tip the car over, he waited until it seemed to stabilize. Then with his hands on the door frame, he quickly pulled himself up. He scrambled out and over the side, falling head first and just managing to catch himself with his hands and turn his fall into an awkward somersault on the buckling bridge deck.

Fighting the hurricane gales, he got to his knees and saw the Rolls coming toward him at a crawl. The Rolls, much heavier than his light import, was doing better in the wind, though it still bounced crazily on the moving deck. He risked lifting one arm from the ground to wave at it to stop, then held onto the drive shaft of his car and carefully stood up. He looked through the open door at the terrified people still clumped up against the doors at the bottom.

"Don't panic!" he yelled, realizing the command was absurd. "One at a time now! Get yourselves out! The Rolls is waiting."

He reached his arm in and grabbed a woman's hand. Carefully, afraid the car would tip over, he helped her up to the opening. She had a gash on her forehead. Blood was dripping everywhere. She looked at him accusingly.

"Hurry!" Ted ordered. She pulled herself out with Ted's help, then dropped down to the pavement and fell on her hands and knees.

"Don't stand up!" Ted yelled, afraid the wind would catch her. "Crawl to the Rolls!"

The back door of the Rolls opened. Becky started to get out. He waved her back. She couldn't help and he had enough people to worry about already. Slowly, the woman crawled over to Meg's car and the back door opened again. She disappeared inside.

One by one, he helped the others out and told them to crawl over to the Rolls. When the last one had made it, he dropped to his knees himself and fought against the wind to crawl over the writhing bridge deck to the limousine. His car, empty of its ballast, tipped over on its back, crushing the roof.

The last two people from his car, a younger man and an older man, were still crouched down by the side of the Rolls, waiting to get in. But the car was packed tight. Becky had the back door open, straining with all her might to keep the wind from yanking it out of her hands.

"There's no more room!" she yelled.

"Make room!" Ted shouted back. He tapped the older man on the shoulder. "Get yourself in there!"

There were already nearly a dozen people in the car, crammed on top of each other. Ted could see heads and feet pressed up against the windows. The older man was having a hard time forcing his way in. Ted put his hands on his buttocks and pushed.

"Make room in there! Hurry!"

The man made it inside. Ted turned to the other. "Your turn!"

He looked at Ted wild-eyed a moment, then began clawing his way over people. Ted grabbed him and pushed. There were screams of protest, but Ted ignored them and kept pushing. The black-haired woman who had gone in first started sliding out the open door again. Ted grabbed her shoulders and shoved her back.

The Rolls was now jammed from floor to ceiling with bodies. A muffled voice was screaming hysterically, "I can't breathe! I can't breathe!"

There was nothing to be done about it. Ted realized, however, that every inch of space was taken up. There was certainly no room for him.

He started heaving against the door to push it closed against the mass of people.

"Wait," Becky cried. "What about you!"

He told her to roll down the front and back windows, and then, with a final heave, pushed the door shut. He put one arm in through the front window and the other through the back. Struggling against the sea of people, he forced his arms to come together and lock around the middle post, flattening himself against the side of the car. "Let's go!" he grunted.

"What are you doing?" Becky yelled, aghast.

"Hanging on! Tell Meg to get moving!"

The Rolls started forward with a jerk and Ted lifted

his feet from the ground, wedging them onto a tiny strip of molding along the side. The bridge was still heaving and tossing like a wild beast and he was jerked cruelly back and forth. He tried to keep his head pressed against the car, but could not, and his cheek banged against the metal with bone-crushing force. He gritted his teeth against the pain and prayed.

Every ten yards of progress seemed to take hours. Ted's arms at first throbbed with pain and then turned numb. He felt blood oozing down his face from the repeated bashings against the car's roof. Once he started to lose his grip, but someone's hand came out the window and grabbed him so that he was able to force his numb arms tighter together. Then a ferocious gust of wind came slamming against the car, heaving it sideways just as the bridge tilted underneath it. Ted screamed in horror as the car skidded and he saw the walkway railing coming at him, ready to crush him against the car. But Meg regained control with only inches to spare and the car veered away.

Through it all, Ted held on and prayed.

CHAPTER 22

As the over-laden Rolls Royce passed under the second tower of the bridge, the raging beast under it quieted its struggles. The wind began to lose some of its savagery, too, Ted noticed gratefully. The numbness had left his arms and they were pulsating with pain again, but he closed his mind to it. The worst part was over for now, he told himself. Meg had gotten them through. He felt a surge of admiration for her strength and determination.

They left the bridge and came to the freeway cut into the rocky cliffs. The winds suddenly died away to nothing. It was like the eye of a hurricane, Ted thought—all around, a circle of raging violence, but calmness and serenity in the center. Except in the center of *this* unnatural and rainless hurricane a pillar of hellfire towered into the night.

Meg started to slow the car to a stop. He yelled in through the window, "Keep going! I'll hold on!"

He looked up at the pillar of fire. It came from the very top of the mountainous headlands, extending up and up to merge with the bloody red tail of the comet. Or, rather, he thought, the comet was sending down its awful fire to the earth below. He was awed by its immensity, its supernatural light, its swirling colors—and

its horror. A road was cut into the hillside just below it.
He could make out the fire truck that had passed him
earlier and a number of cars.

That was where they had to go.

Jill raised her arms high in a gesture of victory and
roared with triumph. Her eyes were burning with the
fires of hell. The demon within her felt full of power now
that it had brought her to Satan's pillar. The seething
spout of fire roared up in front of her. The flames did
not dance and flicker like earthly fire, but undulated
rhythmically, shimmering with diamond-bright light.
The space around the pillar was freezing cold, as if all
the heat had been sucked out of the air, and patches of
frost had formed on the ground. And though the demon
in Jill did not notice it, there was a feeling in the coldness
—a feeling of death in the coldness.

Close to the column's base, nearly in the flames, stood
two naked men and a naked woman. Their eyes were hot
coals and their bodies were emaciated, as if they had
been starved for weeks. Their feet were bloody messes
and their faces wore the look of the insane. Jill could not
know it, but she looked nearly the same. They were facing the hellish flames and beating their fists against their
breasts, wailing like animals being led to slaughter.

Jill could not resist as the demon within her made her
approach the towering pillar. She could not resist as her
fists began pummelling her breasts and she too began
wailing to the heavens in horror and agony.

Within minutes, more of the possessed came running
up to the summit. Soon the fiery column was encircled
by men and women and children, all beating themselves
unmercifully and crying out in horrible, soul-destroying,
bellows.

It was a ritual of torture, to help the nightbroom's
fiery tail give birth to the monster it contained. They

were laboring to bring forth their lord and master, Satan, the Prince of Darkness. But somewhere in the brutish backwaters of their minds, the demons knew the battle was not yet won. The window in time had opened. The balance was upset. The nightbroom had sent down its awful fire. But the one ingredient necessary for Satan's triumph was still missing. Only one thing could tip the balance between good and evil. Only Man, they knew, partaking of both good and evil, could make the necessary choice for Satan's triumph. They were waiting for a man, unpossessed, with a free will. He would make the choice: for heaven or for hell.

The narrow road Ted had seen followed the contours of the mountainous headlands, climbing up to within a hundred yards of the highest summit before levelling off and coming to a dead end. Above it, the blazing pillar rose into the night. Below, far in the distance, the lights of San Francisco could be seen through the cables of the Golden Gate Bridge.

The fire engine that had passed Ted on the bridge had come roaring up the dirt road like an enraged mechanical beast. A water truck had followed in its dusty wake. The half-dozen firemen had jumped off quickly and there had been a burst of rapid and precise activity. Hose segments had been unrolled one after another. Nozzles had been attached. The water truck had been readied for pumping. Everything had been prepared. But then nothing happened. The black-clothed firemen looked at each other uncertainly in the eerie light that bathed the road, then turned to gaze up in open-mouthed awe and fear at the brilliant, unearthly fire spout.

Jack Krober, the engine driver, fingered the gold crucifix he wore around his neck and murmured, "Mother of God!"

He had a feeling he wasn't going to make it through this night. He could only remember one time in his life when he had had a similar feeling. He had run into a burning apartment building to save a bed-ridden old woman. He had found her quickly enough, but with all the smoke and flames he had become disoriented, unable to find his way back out. The fear he had felt then —the seeming knowledge in the pit of his stomach that this was finally it—had been strong. But it had been nothing compared to what he was feeling now. This was pure dread, coiled like a snake around his heart. He thought of his wife waiting for him at home, of his three-year-old daughter. And he tried to think of whether he had mailed in his last life insurance premium. He couldn't remember doing it. But he must have, he told himself.

"What do you think it is?" his buddy Pete asked him in a trembling voice.

Krober's eyes followed the blazing column of fire all the way up to the bloody-red comet head. "I don't know," he whispered. "It's something this world has never seen before."

A moment later, three Highway Patrol cars came speeding up the road in close formation. Captain John Subic jumped out of the lead car and looked up at the flaming pillar. Its base was hidden by the curve of the hill, but he knew there were people up there. Naked people who had run ahead of him at an impossible speed before veering off the road to follow a ridge to the summit.

He let out a moan of fear, but quickly swallowed it, hoping no one had heard. "Perkins!" he barked. "Go up there and tell me what you see!"

Perkins, a baby-faced rookie, hesitated uncertainly. "Sir?"

"You heard me! Go on up there!"

Perkins looked up at the swirling tornado of fire. He should have gone off duty an hour earlier to meet his fiancee. They had planned a late dinner together. He thought of her now wistfully, but hesitated only a moment longer before pulling out his revolver and scrambling up the hillside. He had been on the force for only six months and felt a need to prove himself, to show he was just as brave as the older men. He didn't realize that the veterans were just as afraid as he was, that the only difference between them was that the older men had learned to hide it.

As Perkins disappeared from sight, Captain Subic reached into his patrol car and grabbed the microphone. "Subic here!"

The dispatcher's familiar southern drawl crackled through the radio. "What the hell is going on up there, Captain?"

"I can't answer that," Subic said tersely. "Whatever it is, we're going to have our hands full. Send me help!"

By the time the groaning Rolls Royce came lumbering up the narrow road with Ted still clinging precariously to the outside Meg's crushed passengers were screaming in panic for her to let them out. But she kept going along the road as far as she could, finally pulling to a stop behind a patrol car parked diagonally across the road, blocking it.

Ted quickly extricated his throbbing arms and jumped off. His left cheek was bruised and bloody from repeatedly banging against the car's roof. He glanced at the cops, wondering if they thought their weapons would do any good against Satan, then swept his eyes around to the massive hillside. Its every feature was thrown into sharp relief by the pillar's supernatural light. The barren ground, strewn with rocks and rutted by deep gulleys, rose gradually from the road, then

abruptly ascended to the summit, which looked as if a
great hand had flattened it as easily as if it were a sand
mountain on a beach. He could not see the possessed
people at the pillar's base, but he knew Jill was up there.

The news of Simon's death had been a hard blow for
Meg, and the cold feeling of death pressing against her
heart was stronger than ever. She was just barely keeping herself under control, but she seemed calm and
business-like as she tried to help the people coming from
her limousine.

The odd collection of humanity that Simon had gathered around himself struggled to get out. One of the first
was Robert Jameson, whose brown coat seemed a
permanent fixture. Pushing fifty, he had a bald spot on
the back of his head and large, sad eyes. He had di-
vorced his wife ten years ago after her third affair and
never remarried. A loan company accountant, he had
been sitting on a park bench one day, a bottle of whiskey
between his knees, when Simon had sat down beside
him. He had found himself pouring out his life story to
this total stranger whose sympathetic face encouraged
confidences.

Robert Jameson fell to his knees as the people behind
him pushed over him. He got to his feet and pulled his
brown overcoat tighter against the unnatural cold and
moved away from the Rolls in a daze. He was puzzled
by what he had done crossing the bridge, reciting the
twenty-third psalm as he sat next to Ted in the bucking
car. Why had he done it? How had he done it? If someone had asked him, he would have said he didn't even
know the psalm! Yet it had come out of him perfectly
memorized. He looked up at the soaring pillar and realized with surprise that he was not afraid. He knew he
should be terrified. But all his fear had left him when he
started reciting the psalm.

Sheila Jacks, who had looked at Ted so accusingly

when he had pulled her from his overturned car, was pushed out from the Rolls headfirst, screaming obscenities. Meg caught her by the shoulders and helped her to stand up. Pushing Meg's hands away, she moved back from the others, trying to keep her distance from them. Her face showed the toll life had taken on her—though she was only thirty, she looked much older. At sixteen she had become an unwed mother and her life since then had been a constant battle for pennies to support her daughter. She worked as a cashier at the local Safeway, and it was there she had met the strange old man called Simon.

This night seemed to her a confirmation. Life had long ago taught her the reality of evil. She could even lie awake at nights and feel its presence as it oozed out of the woodwork and surrounded her bed. Yes, evil was real, she thought, looking up at the blazing column of fire. You could feel it! And you were powerless against it. She wondered suddenly why she had come here. She could have stayed with the others who had remained behind at Meg's. There was nothing anyone could do. It was all hopeless! When were people going to realize that?

Carl Rosen came out of the Rolls just behind her. Tall, thin and awkward, with bulging buck teeth and thick eyeglasses that doubled the size of his eyes, he had just turned eighteen. He lived with his widowed mother in a cramped one-bedroom apartment and thought of Simon as the father he just vaguely remembered. Carl was a near-genius, though no one but Simon had ever bothered to notice.

He looked up at the monstrous pillar with grim satisfaction. This was it, he thought, the retribution of hell finally come to punish the world—and long overdue, in his opinion. The end of the world! He knew he would die along with everyone else of course, but that too gave him a certain comfort. It was over! *Finally,* it was all over! And the whole world was getting exactly what it deserved.

As people continued to fall out of the Rolls, Ted pulled Meg away. "There's no need for you to stay, Meg. You and the others should leave. It was a mistake to bring you."

Meg's confusion was plain. "But you wanted us to come! You said Simon told you to bring us!"

Ted looked at the odd collection of people. They looked so pathetic! They seemed so irrelevant! He knew what he had to do—and they were not a part of it. He said, "Simon was *dying,* Meg! He was grasping at straws, wanting to feel he had a role in God's plan, however small. And I was hiding from the truth."

"But I don't understand!" Meg cried.

He looked up at the towering spout of hellfire. "I've got to go up there alone. No one else can do it!" He began walking across the road.

Meg chased after him and grabbed his arm. "Ted! You're not making sense!"

"Simon must have told you about the prophecy, Meg!" He could almost hear Simon's voice now. *The burden will be heavy, yet the orphan must not fail. For in his mortal hands he shall hold the world's final fate.*

"Yes, but—"

"I am the orphan, Meg!" he cried. "I've tried to hide from it, but all along I knew what I had to do! I can't hide from it any longer! My wife is up there! My love! I've got to choose between God and Satan. I'm the only one who can do it!"

"No, Ted! We can help you! We can—"

"Don't you understand? I've got to tip the balance between good and evil! I've got to kill my love or mankind will crown the king of hell!"

"I can't escape it, Meg!" he shouted, backing away

from her. He shifted his weight from foot to foot, hesitating a moment, then turned and scrambled up the bank of raw earth cut into the hillside above the road. Stunned speechless, Meg could only stare after him. At the top of the bank, he stopped to pull Simon's cross from his pocket. Holding it in front of himself like a shield, he glanced down at Meg, then turned around and began to pick his way over the rugged terrain.

There is only fate, he thought. *It waits for you, biding its time, until finally you have to confront it.*

Meg watched him until he disappeared from view into a small gulley. He had looked, she thought, like a man walking to the gallows.

Becky came running up to her. "What's Ted doing? Why didn't he wait for us?"

"Why didn't he wait?" Becky asked again.

"Oh, God!" Meg cried, as the truth finally hit home. "He's going to kill his wife!"

At the road's end, Captain John Subic looked up at the swirling pillar for the hundredth time. He was tense and frightened, worried about Perkins. The young rookie should have come back by now. If he had sent him to his death, he would never be able to forgive himself. His appeal for assistance had been answered by three cars full of deputies from the County Sheriff's Department. But Subic had lost his nerve—there was a horrible feeling like death next to his heart—and was uncertain about what to do. His men and the deputies milled about, waiting for his orders.

"Maybe I'd better radio headquarters again," he said to no one in particular, "and ask for instructions."

Above the road, halfway to the summit, a dark figure could be seen. It was Ted, clawing his way upward at a frantic pace. The walls of the ravine he was in rose up on either side of him. Large boulders loomed over him like dark sentinels. He was short of breath, panting heavily, and his legs ached from piledriving up the loose gravel.

He felt as if time were drawing him forward, pulling him toward the horrible convergence of events he knew lay ahead. He would go up over the crest and there the raging fire would blaze in front of him. Something hard and heavy would be in his hand, something very important. Jill would come rushing toward him, the fires of damnation burning in her eyes. And then—then he would have to choose.

With each step he took he rushed faster and faster until finally his screaming lungs forced him to stop. He leaned against a large boulder and clutched Simon's cross to his chest. For a moment he could hear nothing but his own gasping breath. Then, as his panting subsided, he heard coming down from above something that with his breathing suggested a rushing river. He held his breath and the sound turned into what seemed to him cries from a slaughter house—a melding of heart-rending screams and high, piercing wails punctuated by deep bellows of agony. It was a monstrous symphony of torture!

Reflexively, his hand tightened on the cross. He looked up at the swirling river of fire soaring over him. It seemed to take up half the sky. He pushed off from the boulder and shakily stumbled on, trying not to think that some of the agonized cries he heard were Jill's.

He ran blindly up the ravine until it ended. He tried to scramble up the steep wall, but the gravel was too loose and he kept sliding back. For a moment, like a rat in a maze, he stared wildly about, then ran back down to where the walls sloped up more gently and clawed his way up on all fours. He came out on the sloping ridge Jill had run up earlier and into the full glare of the immense fiery pillar. On his right, the Pacific gleamed far below. The narrow fire road was to his left, the people

on it all but invisible. But he noticed none of this. Shielding his eyes with his hand, he looked up along the ridge.
He strained to spot Jill against the brilliant glare, but the
pillar's base and the possessed people ringing it were still
hidden from view.

A screaming voice came out of the night. "Keep away
from me! *Keep away!*"

He turned slightly and as his eyes adjusted to the
glare, saw a man on the ridge above him. It was Perkins,
the young rookie. His baby face was twisted by madness. And he was pointing his revolver straight at Ted.

"You're not going to fill me with your hell fire!" Perkins shrieked. "Keep away, I said! I'll shoot!"

Ted froze, eyeing the gun warily. "I—I'm not one of
them," he said, trying to sound firm yet understanding.
"Look, I have no fire in my eyes." He began walking
slowly. "Don't be afraid."

"Keep away!" Perkins screamed, stepping backwards. "Stop!" He was holding the revolver in both
hands, his arms straight and stiff.

Ted slowed, but did not stop. "I have a cross," he said
softly, holding it up. "I'm not one of them. I won't hurt
you." He continued talking in soothing tones, trying to
be firm yet gentle, trying to talk to the crazed patrolman
the way he had seen the psychiatrists at Hillsdale deal
with their patients.

He walked up close enough now to see the tears
streaming down the young man's face. He could smell
Perkins' cold sweat. Perkins stank of fear.

The gun was trembling in his hands. "Stop!" he cried.
"I'll shoot!"

Still edging closer, Ted pointed at the blazing summit.
"You went up there, didn't you? You saw them."

"They were torturing themselves! They were screaming! It was horrible!"

Ted was now within reaching distance of the terrified

patrolman. He kept his eyes on the gun. His body was tense, coiled, ready to jump. "You're safe now," he said. "It's okay." His hand was slowly moving up to take hold of the revolver.

"Their eyes!" Perkins howled. "Oh, God! Their eyes. . ."

Ted took hold of the gun barrel. "You're safe now. It's all over."

Perkins began muttering nonsense sounds in the sing-song voice of a small child. He didn't resist as Ted pulled the gun from his grasp.

"It's all over!" Ted repeated urgently. "It's all right! You're safe!"

But the young patrolman could not hear him. He fell to his knees, his arms hanging loosely at his side. His face seemed to break apart like a jig-saw puzzle and he began alternately to scream and cry in great, choking sobs.

Ted turned away—the pull of time drawing him toward the summit was stronger than ever. He thought of his last vision. He could almost see Jill standing before him, her eyes burning with the power of hell. He could almost see the wall of fire roaring up behind her. And the thing that had seemed so important, the hard and heavy thing in his hand. Simon's cross.

No!

The gun!

It hit him like a blow. He had Simon's cross in one hand, but the cop's gun was in the other! He stared at the gleaming blue-black revolver. That was the terribly important thing he had felt himself holding! The gun! He knew now there could be no mistake about the prophecy. It was coming true! The awful knowledge of it sent him reeling. He let out a quivering moan and shoved the cross in his jacket pocket.

When he looked up again, someone was standing above him on the ridge. It was Jill! The roaring pillar seemed like a wall of fire behind her, its light electrifying her jumbled mass of hair. She threw her head back, raised her arms against the raging flames, pounded her feet in triumph, and roared with laughter. Her skin was drawn tightly over her skull. Her mouth was a gaping chasm. It was not Jill he saw—though he knew it was she—but something unimaginably evil, the hideous visage of the demon that possessed her. She fell forward on her stomach and slithered down the hill like an undulating snake. He stared in horror as she jumped up, landing on her feet only ten feet away. She stared back at him out of her burning eyes, then approached him in slow, deliberate steps, arms on her hips, elbows out. Her naked skin glistened in the fiery tornado's unnatural light.

She stopped right in front of him and stood with her legs apart and her breasts thrust out. Her seething eyes bore into him like cutting torches. Her leering mouth opened in a triumphant laugh and the demon's voice came bellowing out like thunder.

"SO! You have come, orphan! And you are alone! The old man is dead! I told you he would die this night!"

Ted felt a sudden sense of dislocation as past and present merged together, what his eyes saw now converging with what his mind had seen earlier. Then he ripped his eyes away from her—from the thing that had been the woman he loved—and looked at the gun lying in the palm of his hand. Everything was coming true! The vision, the prophecy, everything!

As if reading his thoughts, the demon nodded and howled with laughter. The terrible eyes mocked him. "Yes! It has all come true! And now, orphan, you hold the world's fate in your hands!"

The voice was like the hiss of escaping steam. Ted could only stare in horror as he tried to piece his exploding mind together.

The demon jumped high in the air, flipped over, and landed on its feet again. Sweeping its arm toward the blazing column of fire, it thundered. "Now comes SATAN! The KING OF HELL will be born in that fiery crucible! AND ONLY YOU CAN STOP HIM, ORPHAN!" The demon leaned forward, and pushed Jill's grinning face to within inches of Ted's. "YOU MUST KILL HER! YOU MUST KILL YOUR LOVE!"

Ted swayed back as if the winds of death were blowing against him. He had known this moment would come ever since Simon had read him the prophecy. This fate had been stalking him all his life. He looked down at the heavy black revolver, the instrument of death, then back up at the thing that had once been Jill.

"No!" he cried in futile rebellion. "She is innocent! Innocent!"

The demon backed away, dancing in hideous ecstasy. "You are too weak!" it crowed in triumph. "Too weak, Orphan! Man has always given us our power! Man always chooses evil, because man is too weak to make the sacrifices good requires! You must kill your love! The nightbroom will wither like a vine in the desert! Satan will be stopped!"

Ted's face was white. His eyes bulged in horror. Since he had been pulled from his mother's womb, his whole life had been directed to this moment, to this fate. But he could not do it!

"I love her!" he yelled. "I cannot kill her!"

"Then the balance will be unhinged!" the demon hissed, specks of froth flying from its mouth. "Satan will cross the abyss between his dark sphere and the human plane! Within that mighty column he shall manifest himself! Because you are too weak! TOO WEAK!!"

The demon jumped high in the air, cackling in delirious glee. "SATAN! LORD OF DARKNESS! COME TO US! THE ORPHAN IS TOO WEAK!"

Now the demon made Jill lunge forward suddenly. It made her grab Ted's hand with unhuman strength and thrust the gun barrel into her mouth. It made her burning eyes taunt him.

Screaming, Ted yanked the gun back, broke away from the grinning monster, and ran. He fled down the sloping ridge, not knowing where he was running to, but running as hard as he could. The demon followed only inches behind, keeping pace with him. Its toes were barely touching the ground. It's head—Jill's head—was stretched forward over his shoulder and it was hissing into his ear. "You must kill her! You must! But you cannot! You must! You cannot! You must! You cannot! You must!"

Ted raced down the ridge, trying to shake the monster loose, but it stuck to him with shadow-like perfection. He came to the ravine he had climbed up earlier, but didn't go down it. Instead, he veered to his left, going down another ridge that branched away toward the ocean. The demon raced behind him, chanting its horrible litany over and over. "You must! You cannot! You must! You cannot!"

The ridge flattened into an elongated plateau that ended in a cliff high over the ocean. Ted stumbled to a halt. He had to escape! But there was no escape—only a sheer drop to the ocean hundreds of feet below. He lurched away from the cliff and turned around. Jill was there waiting for him, blocking his path.

The demonic eyes burned with malicious glee. "A choice he must make of his own free will," the demon quoted. "Will he kill his love? Or will mankind crown the King of Hell?" It was Simon's voice! The demon was imitating it perfectly. Simon's gentle voice!

And he knew he had to shoot her. *I have to kill her!*
The revolver was a burning hot iron in his hand. *I have to kill her!* His body trembled in terror. *I have to kill her!*

He lifted up the gun. He slid back the safety catch.
Slowly, against his will, he stretched out his arm.

I have to kill her!

"You can have her back!" the demon said, its voice
now soft, creeping into his ears and purring seductively.
"Do not shoot and I will give her back to you!"

"You're lying!" Ted screamed, the gun shaking in his
hands. "Jill is gone!"

"You can have her back! I promise!"

"What are *your* promises worth? She is gone!"

"No! She is here still. I have her soul imprisoned, but
she may yet come back. Look! Her body is unharmed!"
Her hands moved obscenely over her breasts. "I have
saved her for you!"

"No! It's a lie!" Ted shrieked. He was going insane!

"I will *show* you!" the demon roared.

And in an instant, the fire was gone from Jill's eyes.
Her face went completely slack, becoming unformed,
like the waxen faces of the dead. Then, as Ted watched,
humanity slowly returned to her features. Her eyes
stared ahead unseeing a moment longer, then came alive
with terrible pain.

She spoke, her voice seeming to float from far away,
as if borne on the wind. "So cold . . . so much pain . . .
so much . . . help me . . . help . . . the pain . . ."

It was *her* voice! Ted lowered the revolver and lurched
forward to take her in his arms.

"STOP!" the demon commanded, its fire leaping into
her eyes. "You must choose first! God or Satan! You
must choose!"

"I can't!" Ted cried, falling to his knees. "I can't!"

The demon bent over him, bearing down. Once again,

Simon's voice came out of Jill's mouth. "A choice he must make of his own free will. For God or Satan, for heaven or for hell!"

Ted could only gape at the monster.

"Hurry!" it bellowed. "Your time is running out! You must choose!"

Struggling to keep the pieces of his mind together, Ted thought of what Jill had told him. *You will do the right thing, Ted. You will know. You will feel it.* And Simon's last words. *Have faith. One man can tip the balance.* But at what cost?! To kill the one he loves? Hearing Jill's voice again had nearly destroyed him. He wanted her back! He didn't care about anything else! He didn't care! He loved her! But he knew the demon was lying. He would *never* get her back!

"Choose!" the demon demanded.

"I choose God," he screamed, leaping to his feet and thrusting out the pistol.

The demon's eyes flared, turning crimson. "You cannot shoot her! You are too weak!"

"I can!"

"Then do it! Shoot her!" The demon planted Jill in front of him, legs apart, a motionless target. Her lips wore an ecstatic grin. "Do it! Kill your love!"

Trying to hold it still, he gripped the gun in both hands. He could see nothing but the burning red eyes, feel nothing but the heavy revolver. He sighted along the shiny pistol, aiming straight at the grinning mouth. The face that had once held so much love now looked like nothing so much as a skull.

There is nothing of Jill in that face, in that body! Jill is gone! Your love is gone!

PULL THE TRIGGER! SHOOT HER!

He was sweating from every pore. He was shaking. His whole body quivered in rebellion. He could not do it!

YOU MUST! SHOOT! PULL THE TRIGGER!

It seemed someone had thrown a switch somewhere, stopping time. Jill's vulpine face was rigid in delirious triumph. Her searing eyes bore into his. She stood only inches away from the cold steel pointing straight at her face. There was no sound, no movement at all. Man and demon were locked in a silent tableau.

Something was wrong!

He could feel it! Something was very wrong! He shifted his eyes to the gun, then back to the demonic face.

"You *want* me to shoot!" he cried. "You *want* me to kill her!"

"YOU FOOL!" The demon thundered. It lunged forward, raising its fists in fury. Ted flinched back reflexively, crouching down and lifting his arm to ward off the blows. But the demon quickly backed off. It's rage turned to ferocious glee.

"The orphan is too weak!" it cackled to the sky. "The worm lies to himself! He cannot face the truth! He cannot do what his God requires!"

"No!" Ted cried. "No! You've turned everything backwards. You want me to kill her! You want me to tip the balance! But for Satan, not God! Killing her wouldn't stop Satan. *It would bring him!*"

"Remember the prophecy!" the demon howled, overflowing with anger again.

He thought of the ancient words. *Will he kill his love? Or will mankind crown the King of Hell?* "Dear God!" he shouted. "It must have been a warning! All along it was a warning *not* to kill my love!"

He reared back, swinging the pistol around behind him, then lunged forward and heaved it over the demon's head far into the night. "It was a trick! A trick!! Dear God!"

He had no chance to protect himself this time. The

demon was like a rabid dog. Its fist slammed into the side of his head like a sledge hammer and all of a sudden his feet were no longer under him. He flew sideways, coming down hard on the rocky ground close to the cliff's edge. The demon came at him again and he scrambled back desperately, coming to the precipice. He could feel the demon's fury pouring out. One more blow would send him plunging toward the ocean. He ripped Simon's cross from his pocket and wildly thrust it out as the enraged being charged.

"Keep back!" he yelled. And then he was struck dumb. The demon had stopped, seemingly frozen.

It was the cross! The cross!

It was rimmed and criss-crossed with thin spider web lines of the purest blue light he had ever seen. Even as he watched, they grew thicker, brighter. The light was beautiful! What was it? What had happened? He looked up at the demon and saw the fear in its burning eyes.

"The choice," he whispered. His heart was galloping. "I made the right choice! I made the right choice!" The cross was now glowing brilliantly, beautifully. Brandishing it at the demon, he jumped to his feet. "You mortal fool! That will not protect you!" But even as it spoke, the demon backed away, cringing.

"I made the right choice!" Ted shouted. Tears were streaming down his cheeks. "I threw the gun away! I stayed on the right side of the balance!"

Backing away, hate and rage and fear flooding its features, the demon stared at the shining cross as if it were something unspeakably obscene—as if the very light of it were painful.

"You wanted me to kill her!" Ted moved forward, stalking the demon, pushing it back. The brilliant cross lit up his face. "Kill her and stop Satan, you said! That is the way the devil always tempts man, isn't it? Do *this* evil, the devil says, and I will spare you a scourge a thousand times worse. But evil can never counter evil. Evil can only add to evil!"

The demon reared back, howling in fury, and swung its fist at the cross. But it couldn't touch the glowing object. Its arm stopped in mid air, as if meeting an invisible shield.

"No!" it screamed as Ted shoved the cross closer. "Keep it away! I will let you have her back!"

"I will have her back!" Ted roared. "Leave her! NOW!" He charged forward with the cross. The demon leaped away, then turned to run, but instead fell to the ground as if its powers had fled from it.

"This is how I will defeat you!" Ted shouted, straddling the thrashing demon. "Not with a gun, but with a cross!"

As he brought it down at the demon, the miraculous cross started bucking madly, as if an invisible hand had grabbed hold of it to force it back. He struggled against the repelling force, pressing the cross down with all his might.

"Leave her!" he commanded the demon. "Go back to your eternal hell!"

"I will make you kill her yet!" the demon snarled. "You will kill her yet!"

And even as the demon spoke Ted felt spikes being driven into his head. He cried out in agony, but managed to keep hold of the wildly bucking cross. It seemed his clothes were on fire and he was being burned alive.

"Leave her!" he shrieked through his agony.

The demon's eyes started to dim. It was writhing like a nailed insect. "No . . . no . . . stop . . ." it croaked weakly, its voice sounding hollow, distant. "Stop . . . I will . . . give her . . . back." Ted pressed down on the shaking cross with all his might, trying to force it still closer. A stream of urine shot out from between Jill's flailing legs. Her bowels opened, expelling watery yellow excrement.

The agony flooding through Ted began to subside. The bucking cross lost some of its violence and he forced it closer to Jill's face, pressing it down, down. "Get out of her! Leave her, demon! Get out!"

Her face began changing rapidly. She scowled. Laughed, Cried. She began grunting like a pig. Then she squawked like a chicken. Her eyes flashed to white hot intensity, then dimmed again, leaving only the faintest glimmer. The cross was brilliant now, bathing her in its pure light. And slowly, slowly, she began to look human once again.

Ted could feel her emerging presence! He managed to press the cross still closer, only inches away. "Jill! Force it out! Look at the cross! The cross!"

Her mouth opened wide and green-yellow vomit spewed out, splattering the shining cross, which suddenly started jerking up ferociously as the demon made a last desperate attempt to push it away. Then, just as suddenly, the invisible hand gripping it let go. The pain coursing through Ted's body disappeared. The glimmer of fire in Jill's eyes vanished.

She lay on the ground limp and motionless. He met no resistance now as he lowered the cross and gently touched it to her forehead.

"Jill . . ." he whispered. "Jill . . ."

A luminescent mist rose from her and began moving toward him. He quickly waved the brilliant cross at it. It dissolved. He fell on his knees and stroked her forehead. It seemed freezingly cold to his touch. For a terrifying moment he thought she was dead. Then her eyes blinked open and she let out a wailing, soul-wrenching cry of terror. But it was a *human* sound, expressing *human* emotion! Dropping the cross, he pulled her to himself, wrapping his arms around her. He cried with gratitude and relief. She was alive! Alive!

He took off his jacket and wrapped it around her. She was shivering violently and her breathing was rapid and shallow. "You're safe now, darling," he whispered lovingly, taking her in his arms again. "I made the right choice. You're going to be okay."

He started sobbing uncontrollably. The prophecy had come true and she was still alive! Even now, he could hardly believe it had happened. She had been to hell and back, and now she was going to be all right, he told himself, refusing to admit any other possibility. She was going to be all right!

He took the jacket sleeve and gently wiped away the vomit from her chin. She looked pale and gaunt. There were dark bruises all over her. Her lips were caked with blood. Her long hair was thickly matted.

She began mumbling deliriously—something about Satan and the pillar of fire.

"Oh, darling!" he murmured. "I love you! I love you!"

"Satan . . ." she mumbled. "Satan is coming . . . the nightbroom . . . you must stop him . . ."

"No, Jill! It's over!" he soothed her. "You're safe!"

Her eyes fluttered open again. She lifted her arm and caressed his cheek. "Ted . . ."

"Darling! You're all right!"

Her arm fell back down limply. "Satan is coming," she said weakly. "You've got . . . to stop him . . ."

"No, darling. It's all over. You're safe now." He couldn't stop crying!

"It's not over . . . the demon . . . I saw in his mind . . . Satan is coming . . ."

Ted thought she was still delirious. "Hush, now," he whispered stroking her cheek.

She looked at him imploringly. "Please, Ted . . ." she

whispered, straining to speak. "Listen to me . . . . Satan isn't stopped yet. You've got to get the others . . . . Show them your cross . . . ."

Ted stared at her as the slow realization came over him that she wasn't delirious! "What are you trying to say?" he asked, suddenly frightened.

"You've got to hurry . . . get the others and . . . surround the pillar . . ." she broke off, coughing. "Once Satan is formed . . . in the fire . . . it will be too late . . ."

"I don't understand! I threw the gun away! The cross started glowing! I made the right choice!"

"I can't explain, Ted . . . You must hurry! Satan is coming!"

Ted looked up at the swirling tornado of fire. It seemed larger than ever, blocking out most of the sky. He didn't understand it, but he knew Jill was right. The battle wasn't over! He grabbed the glowing cross and laid it on her breast, then scooped her into his arms.

"No . . ." she protested. "You've got . . . to leave me."

"I can't leave you!" he shouted, struggling to his feet, lifting her up. She was very weak from the night's ordeal and she seemed a dead weight in his arms.

"You can't take me with you . . . There's no time! Get the others . . . show them your cross . . . they will follow you . . ."

He stumbled slowly up the ridge, staggering under her weight. "I'm not going to leave you! You are all that matters to me!

She fought against him feebly. "You've got to put me down," she whispered painfully. "I don't matter, Ted. Not compared to the whole world! Satan is coming!" Even as she spoke, the swirling pillar of fire started pulsating spasmodically. "Look! It's starting already . . . You've got to leave me . . . Please!"

He looked into the sky. The blood-red comet tail was

contorting on itself in a thousand shapes. And as he watched, it began contracting rhythmically along its length, as if laboring to give birth. The bloody redness of the comet's tail began seeping into the pillar of fire, staining its flames.

"It's Satan!" Jill cried, struggling against him with surprising strength. "Put me down! Hurry!"

Ted gently eased her to the ground. He felt like his heart was being ripped out, but he knew he had to do it. "Take the cross," he said, folding her limp fingers around it. "It will protect you!" It was still glowing brightly.

Jill shook her head. "You need it, Ted. That . . . is your power . . . . Show it to the others . . . and they will follow you."

"No—"

"You must take it!"

"Dear God! You're killing me, Jill!" He took the cross back and stood up.

"Hurry!"

"I love you!" he cried, then turned away and began running.

In the sky, the column of hellfire was raging.

CHAPTER 23

"We've got to make a stand!" Meg Olson shouted for at least the tenth time. "We've got to go up there! We can't just stay here like sheep waiting to be slaughtered!"

Standing on the back of the giant fire engine, looking out over the fearful faces of the crowd, she searched for a sign, any sign, of courage. She had waited as long as she could for Ted to return. But finally, sorrowfully, she had come to the conclusion that he was not going to come back. And when the nightbroom had begun pulsating, pumping its blood-red color down into the pillar, slowly at first, then faster and faster, she had been forced to act. She'd told Becky to take the box of crosses they had brought and to pass them out, and then she had climbed up on the back of the fire engine.

"Please!" she begged. "We've got to make a stand against evil! If we don't act, we are lost! We've got to go up there!"

"We can't do anything!" Sheila Jacks shouted. Pointing up at the soaring tornado, she demanded, "How can we fight *that?*"

"I don't know!" Meg answered. "But we've got to try!"

"It's the end of the world!" Carl Rosen yelled. Behind

his thick glasses he looked strangely satisfied. "We might as well accept it!"

"You don't know what you're saying!" Meg cried.

The engine driver, Jack Krober, climbed up next to her. "She's right!" he yelled. "I've got a wife and daughter and you all probably have family, people you care about. We've got to think about them! We've got to try!"

"What slop!" Carl Rosen yelled angrily. "It's hopeless! We're only getting what we deserve!"

The crowd started babbling fearfully as everyone tried to speak at once. Meg tried to shout over the hubbub, but she was drowned out. Then, suddenly, the crowd quieted.

Ted was standing on top of the steep bank over the road, holding his cross up high like a beacon. Its bright glow rained down on him and the ground around him. He looked, Meg thought, like an angry messenger from the gods. The crowd was stunned, their upturned faces filled with awe at the sight of the shining cross.

"Listen to me!" he shouted commandingly, his voice coming from someplace deep inside himself, a place he had just discovered. "Satan is coming! We must stop him! And we *can* stop him!" He thrust the cross higher. "Our power is greater than his!"

"Mother of God!" Jack Krober whispered in awe. "It's a miracle!"

"I know you are filled with terror," Ted continued. "But that is what Satan wants! He feeds on our fear of him! Satan wants us to cringe in terror—that is what gives him his power! But if we conquer our fear, our power will be stronger than his!" He shook the glowing cross. "And this is the proof! This is our power! It is in us! It is in you! Each and every one of you!"

Meg looked down at her own cross and saw that it was starting to shimmer with the same pure light as

Ted's. She nearly dropped it in her stunned disbelief, but quickly tightened her grip.

She jumped down from the fire engine and quickly climbed the steep bank up to Ted. "W-what is it?" she stuttered breathlessly.

"It is *you,* Meg!" He took her arm and lifted it up so that she was holding the cross high over her head. "This is our power!" he thundered. "It is in each and every one of us! You must only look for it and you will find it!"

Other crosses started to glow now—specks of diamond pure light scattered throughout the crowd, islands of brilliance in the sea of faces. A warm feeling of peace and serenity flooded through Jack Krober as his cross started to shine. He began crying. Carl Rosen's cross started glimmering faintly. He stared at it in disbelief. How was it possible? he wondered, as strange feeling of hope and strength swept through him. Captain John Subic didn't know whether to laugh or cry, whether to be happy or frightened. It just wasn't real! But his cross, too, was becoming radiant with pure blue light.

Looking down on them all, Ted felt he was witnessing a rebirth. "Hurry!" he shouted. "We must surround the pillar before Satan is born into it! Hurry!"

Sheila Jacks broke from the crowd and scrambled up the bank. It seemed she had been waiting for this moment all her life! She had always known the reality of evil and now she knew there was another power. As she neared the top, Ted grabbed her hand and pulled her up. Bob Jameson, his brown overcoat fluttering, climbed up slowly after her. He had expected something like this. He didn't know why, but he had.

"Come on, now," Ted shouted, "The rest of you! We must all go up there!"

Carl Rosen was next, pushing back his thick glasses as he reached to top of the bank, his face flushed with excitement. Kissing his cross, Jack Krober jumped down from the fire engine and climbed up the steep bank with ease. Captain Subic, his revolver in one hand and a shining cross in the other, yelled for his men to follow him, and climbed up after Krober.

Ted grabbed the gun away as he neared the top. "Weapons can't defeat Satan! Tell your men to leave their guns!"

"Are you crazy?" Subic glared at him angrily.

Ted held his cross up in the cop's face. It was much brighter than any of the others. "*This* is our power! Tell your men to leave their guns!"

Subic stared at the brilliant cross a moment, then looked down at the one shimmering in his hand and said, "I guess you're right!" He turned to his men and told them to throw away their weapons.

Ted faced those still hesitating on the road. "Hurry! Our power is greater than Satan's! We can stop him! Come on!" He was forced back up the hill as they came surging up all at once. He went a little way further up the hill, then turned back to face them. "Remember! Satan feeds on our fear of him! We must banish our fear! We must have faith!"

Holding his cross high, he turned to lead them up the hill when a howling voice came booming out of the night. "ORPHAN! ORPHAN!!"

Screams exploded from the crowd. Ted whirled around and saw, standing on a large rock, a naked man —a demon with fiery bright eyes. It seemed to have appeared out of nowhere!

"YOU WILL DIE, ORPHAN! YOU CANNOT DEFEAT SATAN! YOU WILL BURN IN HELL!"

With a mighty leap, the naked demon flew into the air. Ted had no chance to move. He could only lift his chining cross up at the thing as it came shrieking down, its arms and legs flailing in the air. He braced himself for the impact, but as it came down into the glowing halo surrounding his cross, the demon disappeared in a burst of flame.

He gaped into space at the spot where it had been, then came to his senses and turned back to the stunned crowd. "Our power is greater than Satan's!" he shouted triumphantly.

He charged up the hill and the crowd surged after him, their glowing crosses forming a long oval cluster of diamonds on the hillside. Meg and Jack Krober were in the lead, with Becky just behind them. Bob Jameson, wheezing, unused to the exertion, fell back to the tail of the crowd. Carl Rosen ran back to him, took his hand, and helped him on.

"Don't worry, Bob," Carl said with fierce determination. "We're going to beat that thing! We're going to win!"

Ted ignored his aching legs and screaming lungs and pounded his way up the hillside. The light from the cross seemed to be guiding his way. The paralyzing fear that had held him in its grip for so long had left him. He had been so consumed with the power of evil, he knew, that he had forgotten the power of good. In the moment he had confronted the denom in Jill, ready to shoot her, he had looked inside himself, and instead of the hollowness he had always felt before, he had found a solid feeling, a feeling telling him not to be afraid. His fear dispelled, he could see the demon in Jill for what it was—not colored and distorted by his terror of it, but as it really was —a miserable being that needed his fear of it, that lived off his fear of it. That was what gave evil its power! Fear! His love for Jill had been twisted into fear, but he had regained that love again! The crimson tower of fire soared into the night, taking up the sky, but the sight of it no longer filled him with dread. He felt nearly invincible now.

Finally, half-way to the summit and the roaring spout

of hellfire, his starving lungs forced him to stop. Gasping for air, he looked back and the crowd strung out on the hillside below him, their crosses lighting up the night.

"Hurry!" he yelled. "Hurry!"

In the column of fire, Satan was beginning to manifest himself. This was the moment foretold in the ancient manuscript Simon had found so many years ago. Satan was crossing the awful abyss between his dark sphere of negation and the human plane. The pillar's flames were slowly coagulating, coming together, thickening into a monstrous shape. A single clawed hand gradually formed in the fire, finger by finger. The vague outlines of a misshapen head shimmered in the flames. Slowly, Satan was being born.

Panting for breath, Ted pushed on up the hillside, at times clawing his up on on his hands and knees, grabbing rocks, shrubs, anything he could to pull himself up. Krober, still fresh, had gone ahead of him. Subic and several other patrolmen and deputies were right behind him. Meg and the others trailed behind.

Suddenly Krober yelled "Look out!"

Lined up above him on the hillside were a dozen naked beings—a dozen pairs of burning, searing eyes set in a dozen tormented faces. They had once been husbands and wives, fathers and daughters, sons and mothers, but now they were monsters, half-human, half-devil. They stood in a line, blocking the crowd's path. Then, abruptly, they began wailing and beating themselves, creating a tableau of naked misery and suffering beyond comprehension. One bellowing man began pulling out his hair in bloody handfulls. A young woman started shrieking and beating her breasts. A boy threw himself to the ground repeatedly. Each one committed some unspeakable horror. Their baying howls and their screams and their shrieking moans piled higher and higher, fighting for supremacy.

As they started down the hill toward the crowd, Jack Krober scrambled back to Ted. "What are they doing?" he demanded, his voice shaking.

"Fear is their weapon! They're trying to fill us with terror. But we can't let them!" He jumped to his feet, facing the crowd below. "Don't give in to fear! We can beat them!"

As the demons came down at them—a walking wall of torture and horror, Ted and Krober lined up with Subic and his men to meet them head on. Gritting their teeth, planting their feet firmly on the ground, they held out their shining crosses like shields. As the demons came down the hill at them, the air between the two lines seemed to boil with the contending forces of good and evil. Ted's line held steady at first, but the wailing torture became too much for them. It clawed into their hearts to fill them with dread and they had to fall back step by step. They yielded their ground slowly at first, but as the wailing of the demon's increased in frenzy, their slow retreat threatened to turn into rout.

"We've got to help them!" Meg cried. "Hurry!"

She and Becky moved up to join the disintegrating line and others quickly followed. As more and more people came up behind them, the retreating front line slowed, then stopped, and then began pushing back up the hill. The demons increased their furious bellowing and their horrible torture. One man began chewing on his arm—eating it!—and shrieking in agony with each bite. Another jabbed his thumbs straight into his eyes, releasing fountains of blood. But the crowd pressed on, moving like a great sparkling wave, carrying the demons in front of them. They reached the point where the demons had first appeared and continued pushing up the hillside.

Yielding their ground slowly, inch by inch, the demons moved backwards to a relatively flat area. The crowd kept on after them, holding their crosses high.

But now, from the summit, streaming down out of the blinding glare of Satan's pillar, came more naked demons. They came in twos and threes, running down the hillside at an incredible speed, to join in the line of torture. The wailing tumult became deafening. It blew against the advancing crowd like a gale, forcing them to stop in their tracks.

Ted and Meg stood side by side in the front line, not ten feet from the hellish throng. Jack Krober and Captain Subic were next to them, and just behind them were Sheila Jacks and Becky, together with most of the firemen and the police. The wailing bedlam seemed like a physical force, pushing them back. They had to lean against it, digging their feet into the ground. They were holding their own, but Ted realized they had to do more. Satan was forming in the column of fire! They had to reach the summit before the monster's birth was complete!

He shouted into Krober's ear, "When I give the word, fall back to your left. Tell the man next to you!"

As Krober edged over to the cop on his left, Ted turned to Meg and told her to fall back to her right. But there was no way to pass the word to everyone in the crowd. He just had to have faith that things would work out. He knew his idea was risky, but he couldn't dwell on that—there wasn't time!

"Now!" he yelled.

The front line of people split apart, half of them falling back to the left and the other half to the right. The mob of naked demons charged forward into the breach. People tumbled back screaming in horror. Carl Rosen was pushed into a backward somersault. His glasses went flying and were trampled. Sheila Jacks had her cross knocked from her and only retrieved it an instant before a possessed man came charging at her. She lifted up the shining cross and the naked demon jumped back, howling in anger.

It was near chaos, but things were working out the way Ted had hoped. The demons had come charging into the midst of the crowd and were now almost surrounded by the glowing crosses. But all would be lost if he didn't quickly gain control of the frightened people.

"Don't panic!" he yelled. "Hold on to your crosses! They will protect you!"

He grabbed Krober's sleeve. "We've got to surround them! Get some people up there!" He pointed to the top section, where the crosses were thinnest. "Move!"

Krober ran off and started grabbing people from the thickest part of the crowd. Ted ran down the hill to another section where the demons were threatening to break through. Becky was the only one keeping them contained. She alone had stood her ground while those about her had fallen back screaming in horror. A young cop was quivering in abject fear, his cross at his side. Ted slapped him on the back, told him to hold up the cross, and pushed him up toward Becky. He shoved several more people into the gap, then ran up next to her himself and thrust out his radiant crucifix at the bellowing monsters.

The demons were completely encircled. They jumped into the air in raging spasms, howled like rabid dogs, flailed and pummelled themselves unmercifully. Yet the people ringing them held steadfast.

"We're beating them!" Meg shouted, watching her cross grow still brighter, become almost blinding.

A giant amoeba seemed to be throbbing on the hillside, its perimeter a brilliant necklace of sparkling diamonds. The pure blue light from the crosses suffused the air and seemed to cover the wailing bellows of the demons like a quieting mist.

The circle began closing in slowly, inch by inch. Her face flushed, horror and hope alternating on her features, Sheila Jacks fought forward with relentless determination. She felt as if all the evil in the world were in that demonic mob and if they tried hard enough they could squeeze it out of existence. Becky moved up with Ted, focusing on her cross with fierce concentration to block out the horror of the demons. Bit by bit, step by step, she pressed against the evil force.

As the circle tightened around them, the demons were pressed closer and closer until they formed a solid mass in the center. And still the crosses ringing them swelled brighter. And still the people pushed in at them. They beat their breasts in defiance and rage, roaring like apes. They pounded their feet on the ground in a thumping frenzy. But their rage seemed impotent as the surrounding ring of crosses moved in at them. They fell back over themselves and some were lifted from the ground by the press of other naked bodies. Writhing together, they became an animal with a hundred arms and a hundred legs and a hundred burning eyes.

The thunderous bellowing rose higher and higher, yet when the sound reached the surrounding people, it was muffled and seemed to come from far away. And now, on the outer edge of the mob, the demons' eyes began to lose their fire!

"We're doing it!" Becky cried.

Yet in the flaming column above, Satan's form was thickening. Two monstrous eyes could be seen in the crimson flames. A pair of clawed hands moved sinuously.

The crowd pressed in tighter on the writhing pile of naked flesh. It seemed nothing could stop them now. The repelling force of evil was weakening quickly. One by one, the naked demons fell to the ground, the fire disappearing from their eyes. One of the first was a young boy and after a moment he began crawling on his stomach away from the mob toward Becky and Ted. Becky screamed as he approached her.

"Don't be afraid!" Ted shouted. "The demon in him has gone!"

No longer possessed, the boy was not repelled by the shining crosses. Moaning in pain, he crawled toward Ted and Becky slowly. His small body was a mass of bruises. Blood streamed from several wounds, leaving a trail on the hard ground behind him. Pulling himself laboriously forward, he stopped at Ted's feet. Ted scooped him up in his arms, broke away from the circle, and laid him down on the ground a few feet away. He quickly ran back next to Becky. He wished he could have done something for the boy, but there was no time!

Others now began crawling out from the pile of bodies. An emaciated woman with a battered, bloody face. A bald man who pulled himself forward with one arm, the other only a bloody mass of flesh. The man whose hair had been pulled out, leaving his scalp an open wound. Others, like the man who had gouged out his own eyes, lay dying where the demons had left them.

The repelling force of evil gradually diminished; then, as the last pair of eyes went blank, the force disappeared entirely and the encircling crowd rushed in. The carnage was horrible. Sobbing uncontrollably, Sheila Jacks fell on her knees next to a dying girl who reminded her of her daughter. Becky tried frantically to stanch the blood gushing from the leg of a teenaged boy, but it was a futile effort. Nearly blinded by tears, Ted pulled her away. "We can't help them! There's no time! Satan is already coming into the pillar!"

A vaguely humanoid shape could be seen in the towering flames, sharply defined in spots, still strangely diffuse in others. Satan was coming to life. Two monstrous yellow eyes were now set in a wolfish head. The clawed hands now had long sinewy arms to go with them. The rest of the misshapen body was still coagulating in the flames, but it was growing more defined and solid by the minute.

The long, angular wolf-head turned to look down on the tiny mortals and its yellow eyes opened wider, bearing down on them with seeming contempt and sending arrows of terror to pierce their breasts.

There was no time to help the naked, moaning people still suffering the ravages the demons had inflicted. The crowd hurried after Ted and Becky over to the ridge that led to the summit. The air seemed strangely calm now, and as they moved away from the moaning victims the only sound they could hear was a soaring hiss coming from the flaming pillar. It almost seemed like silence after the wailing bedlam of the demons. Grabbing rocks and small shrubs, Ted pulled himself up the steep side of the ridge. It took every bit of determination he had not to go running down the other side to the spot where he had left Jill. He could only pray that she was all right and climb on. Becky followed him without hesitation and Krober, Captain Subic, and Meg came right after her. Carl Rosen, nearly sightless without his glasses, helped Bob Jameson and was guided by him in turn. The carnage they had witnessed did not deter any of them. If anything, they were more determined than ever to make their stand against the evil power that had made such torture possible.

With Satan's disembodied head leering down at them, they climbed up the ridge in the full glare of the enormous spout of flame. The light from their crosses, which had once seemed so bright, now looked pale and weak. The soaring hiss of the flames had grown to a thunderous roar. Ted felt he was on the rim of an erupting volcano. He was about to come face to face with Satan himself.

He paused just below the crest, waiting for the others.

"All right!" he yelled when they arrived. "We're going up now! We don't know what we're going to find, but remember—fear is Satan's greatest weapon. Our fear gives him his strength. We've got to surround him, just the way we did the demons! We can beat him as we beat them if we hold strong and don't give into our fear!"

He ran up to the crest. He seemed only a black silhouette against the fiery pillar. "Hold onto your crosses! They will protect you!"

He charged to the summit while the crowd surged after him. They came to a broad, nearly oval plateau twice the size of a football field. In its center, wider than a large mansion, the blazing pillar soared into the sky. Its crimson flames leaped and danced. In them, Satan's half-formed figure loomed like a colossus.

The crowd split into two threads like a small army of ants and headed for opposite sides of the pillar. Captain Subic and his men ran with graceful speed, holding their crosses like guns—the weapons they used more often. Krober and Ted raced ahead of the other line, around the further side of the monstrous column. They kept their distance from it, staying close to the edge of the plateau. When the two lines joined, Ted broke away and ran around to the opposite side to make sure the pillar was surrounded. He saw Bob Jameson, his brown coat flapping behind him, fall into place next to Carl Rosen and he moved in beside him, completing the circle. Once again, they had the evil surrounded. Yet now their crosses seemed puny weapons against a raging inferno. It was Satan himself they stood against, and his looming dark shape dwarfed them into insignificance.

Satan's upper torso and head were now solid, rising above the still shadowy outlines of his legs. Horns like spikes came from the crown of his black skull. Canine teeth gleamed in his mouth. A long, black, arrow-tipped tail whipped the flames furiously. The monster from hell, Satan, the Lord of Death, was completing his long journey from the sphere of darkness to the human plane.

He opened his long wolf's mouth and rent the air with his roar, making the very ground shake under the feet of the tiny humans surrounding him. Yet they held steadfast. There was a swath of bare ground fifty-feet wide between them and the column. At a signal from Ted, they began moving in, tightening the circle, but almost immediately, they came against the repelling force of evil that radiated out from the pillar. Horror clawed its way into their hearts. Each step became more difficult, and after making only small progress, they were stopped dead, as though they had come up against an invisible wall. Their shining crosses began to shake wildly. Satan's roars repeatedly shook the earth.

Ted struggled savagely, digging his heels into the ground, leaning forward with all his weight, but he could not move an inch closer to the fiery pillar. Then, suddenly, he realized to his horror that he was being pushed backwards! The flaming pillar was expanding! Its repelling force was pushing the circle out!

Meg felt as if a pair of enormous arms had grabbed her. To Jack Krober, it seemed someone was using a battering ram against his stomach. The pressing force was irresistible, and all around the circle people began to give ground despite their valiant struggles. Grunting furiously, veins popping out on his forehead, Ted pounded his feet into the ground, but still he slipped backwards. Their glowing crosses seemed impotent against this embodiment of evil, the King of Hell! If the satanic pillar kept expanding, he knew, they were doomed. Soon they would be pushed off the high plateau altogether, and those on the west side, where he was, would plunge hundreds of feet to the rocky beach below.

"Dear God!" he pleaded as he stumbled back. "Save us! We need your help!"

He, Bob Jameson, and Carl Rosen were only ten feet away from the cliff's edge. They fought wildly against the evil force, their muscles bulging, their eyes popping, tears streaming down their cheeks. But still they were pushed back, their feet scraping on the hard ground, closer and closer to the cliff's edge.

As he had on the bridge, Bob Jameson began shouting the twenty-third psalm. But still he stumbled backwards.

Satan's thunderous roars now turned to howling laughter, contemptuous of the pitiful humans surrounding him. His arrow-tipped tail whipped the flames of his pillar furiously, seeming to make it swell outward even faster.

Ted fought uselessly to hold his place against the relentless force. Not even a yard now separated him from plunging death. Simon's cross bucked wildly in his hands, its glow seeming pale and weak against the raging wall of fire coming at him. Ted felt betrayed. He had made the right choice! But it was all for nothing! His feet slipped against the ground and he was pushed back another foot.

There had to be a way to crush Satan! There had to be! What had happened to the power of their crosses? Coming up onto the plateau, his cross radiant, he had felt invincible. But now it seemed Satan was the invincible one! His grotesque form was now nearly solid in the flames. Perhaps evil was the true reality and goodness only an illusion! In a moment, they would be shoved from the plateau like crumbs from a table. They would plunge to their deaths on the rocky beach below still pathetically holding their crosses. And the howling laughter of fate would reverberate in their ears all the way down.

His feet scraped backwards again. Only inches remained between him and thin air. Next to him, Carl Rosen began screaming.

"Help us!" Ted cried. "Help us, Lord! Help us!"

In an instant the crosses swelled brighter all around the circle. A halo of pure blue light spread out from each one. Ted could hardly believe what he was seeing as the halos stretched out and came together, merging with one another, forming a solid band of light enveloping the people and their crosses—making a ring of light that encircled Satan's pillar.

And there was a Presence in the light!

Ted felt a gentle, caressing pressure that made his skin tingle, and he began sobbing with the wonder of it. It seemed like a warm wind, he thought, blowing against his back and counteracting the evil pressure radiating out from the pillar. He looked around the circle. Carl Rosen had stopped his screams. He was crying, his face filled with awe. Sheila Jacks held her cross high over her head in triumph. Jack Krober was trying to pray, but it seemed he could not find his voice. He simply shook his head in awe. Meg was holding her cross high and laughing and crying at the same time. Looking from face to face, Ted felt a swelling sense of exaltation. It was truly a miracle!

In the whirlwind from hell, Satan bellowed in raging anger. His yellow eyes squinted to points and his clawed hands beat against his hairy breast. His tail slashed the flames. The thunder of his anger shook the ground and sent shivers through the surrounding circle. But in spite of the monster's rage, the circle now held steadfast.

Letting out a cry of triumph, Ted pressed forward against the wall of evil and felt it yield. Others, too, now started pushing inward and the circle began to tighten.

They still had to fight hard against the evil pressure, their crosses bucking wildly. The Presence in the ring of light enveloping them was only just enough to tip the balance—to give them courage and hope. But they all knew they could not be stopped now. You could see it in their faces, in the way they fought, in the tears of joy streaming down their cheeks.

The King of Death shook his fists in frenzied rage, trying to break his way out of the flames. But the lower parts of his hideous legs were still mere shadows—he could not yet escape his womb of hellfire. He had nearly completed his journey across the terrible abyss between his world and the human plane. But his mighty pillar was narrowing before he could culminate his birth.

"We're winning!" Ted cried exultantly. "We're beating him!" He thought of what Simon had told him. It truly was ordinary men and women who held the balance between good and evil.

The knees and thighs of Satan's monstrous form started dissolving in the flames. Straining with all their might, holding their crosses high like beacons, the people pressed in closer. Meg was crying freely now. Her tears just wouldn't stop. She was letting out the soul-destroying doubts and life-denying feelings that had nearly consumed her since her husband's agonizing death. And she was crying for Simon too—that he was not here to witness this miracle, this confirmation of his life and affirmation of his faith. Not far from her, his eyes reflecting its fire, Jack Krober looked up at the soaring column. He had never thought he would live through the night, and yet he had not hesitated to throw his lot in with the others. He wondered if his wife and daughter would believe what he had to tell them, that there is a power for good in this world! And if we look hard enough, we can find it. But first, we must look in ourselves!

Slowly, triumphantly, they pushed inward and the electric ring of light tightened around the pillar. Satan's form was melting. Everything below his shoulders had disappeared. His head and arms hovered impotently in the flames, but still he roared. The pillar narrowed to a width of only twenty yards across and still the crowd pressed in. Bob Jameson kept repeating the psalm over and over, hoarsely now, but still with every ounce of feeling he possessed. And he too, like so many of the others, was crying freely in awe and wonder, weeping for a life full of doubts. Carl Rosen had joined in the psalm when Jameson's voice began to falter. It didn't matter to him that with his glasses broken he could see no more than a blur—he could *feel* what was happening. Confident of his strength, he pressed hard against the wall of evil.

But now, unseen by anyone in the crowd, someone came running onto the summit from below. It was the young rookie, Perkins, and he had found another gun to replace the one Ted had taken from him. His smooth, pink face was twisted by madness. He aimed the gun and the hovering spectre of Satan's head and fired three times. The shots rang out loudly.

The pillar of fire flashed brighter, swelling outward!

"Dear God!" Ted screamed. "No! NO!" He whirled around, saw the young cop, and broke into a headlong run. Perkins squeezed off two more shots at the Satanic head, and again the pillar surged outward.

"Stop!" Ted yelled. "No! Stop it!"

Perkins simply stared at him as Ted came charging, hitting him head on. They fell together on the ground, tumbling over and over. Ted pushed himself up, grabbed the gun away before Perkins could react, and flung it out over the cliff.

Lifting his glowing cross, he shouted, "This is our

power! Don't you see? Evil can only add to evil! This is
our power!"

But Perkins could only gaze at him vacantly. He was
beyond understanding now. Ted put his arm on the
young man's shoulder. "Don't be afraid," he whispered.
"It's all right now."

Ted looked back at the pillar and saw Satan's arms
and clawed hands dissolve in the flames. The once
mighty column still soared into the night, but was only
a few feet across at its base now. The encircling crowd
had held fast when the shots rang out, keeping it contained. Satan's head hung disembodied in the fire, its
outlines melting away. Its horns and pointed ears disappeared, and then its mouth and snout. Soon there were
only two yellow, hate-filled eyes staring out wrathfully,
and then they too flickered away into the flames.

A moment later a strong wind began blowing. The
fiery tornado lifted up from the ground and started re-
ceding slowly into the sky. A mighty cheer came from
the crowd.

"We've done it!" Meg cried.

"Dear God! We won!" Becky shouted.

As the funnel of fire rose higher, the wind became
stronger and stronger, scattering the crowd. The band of
blue light vanished when the circle broke, and people
dropped to the ground to keep from being blown over.
Ted crouched down, shielding his eyes with his hand
against the stinging wind, and watched as the swirling
tornado rose into the night, returning to the bloody-red
nightbroom from whence it came. When he looked
down again, the glow was gone from his cross.

The battle was over.

Now he had only one thought—to find Jill. The others were lying flat on the ground to get out of the wind
storm, but he had to find Jill! He left Perkins and, lean-

ing crazily into the raging gale, ran and stumbled across the broad plateau to the ridge that led down to the road. With the vicious wind tugging at him, he plunged recklessly down the rocky slope in broad leaps and jumps. He was nearly a third of the way down when a sudden gust hit him broadside, nearly lifting him from the ground. He lost his balance and fell, rolling over and over down the ridge. He slammed into a large boulder, hitting his head hard. Only one thought lingered as darkness closed in on him and he lost consciousness.

I love you, Jill! I love you!

EPILOGUE

He was swimming up through cold black spaces toward a distant and hazy light. But every time he got close to the shimmering light, something happened to push him back down and he had to start swimming up all over again. Sometimes, when he was close to the light and before he was pushed down, he would hear busy sounds—sounds of people walking on a hard floor, of doors opening and closing, and voices, some loud, some soft. And pictures would come to him out of the dark spaces. Simon opening a door. Simon and Jill talking. Jill walking up to him and smiling. And he would struggle harder than ever to reach the shimmering light. It seemed he never would, though. It seemed he was doomed to spend the rest of his existence swimming upward toward the distant white light.

Finally he did break through to the surface and his eyes opened. He saw a white ceiling with a large fluorescent light fixture hanging from it. He was surrounded by white curtains. He was in bed covered by a white sheet drawn up and tucked under his chin. The only other things he could see were his left arm, which was on top of the sheet, and the clear plastic tube running up from the joint of his elbow to a bottle hanging by the side of his bed.

He tried to push himself up, but a wave of dizziness

swept over him and he fell back on his pillow. His eyes closed again. Just before the black spaces reclaimed him, he pictured Jill, beautiful and smiling. Something had happened to her. Something horrible.

When he woke up again, the tube was gone from his arm. A woman with a streak of white running through her hair was sitting on the foot of his bed. She was dressed expensively and looked coolly elegant.

She smiled. "Welcome back."

Ted blinked at her blearily. Memories were flooding his mind. The swirling pillar of fire. The naked demons. Jill . . . He bolted up in bed. "Jill!" he cried. "Oh, Meg, I've got to find her!"

She put out a restraining hand. "It's okay, Ted. I've seen her!"

"What? She's alive?!"

Meg nodded.

"I've got to see her! Dear God! She's alive!" He tried to get out of bed.

"Calm down!" Meg gently pushed him back down on his pillow. "She isn't here, Ted. They took her to another hospital. I think she's going to be all right."

Ted squeezed her hand hard. "Oh, Meg! Did you talk to her?"

"No. They had her under a lot of medication and she was barely conscious. But I spoke to her doctor. He thinks she's going to pull through."

"Oh, God!" Tears of joy and relief streamed down his cheeks. "I've got to see her, Meg! I've got to!"

"But Ted, you can't leave here! You're not strong enough!"

"Please, Meg! You can arrange something! I've got to see her!"

"All right," she sighed. "I'll speak to your doctor."

She returned several hours later with a burly attendant pushing a wheelchair. The attendant wheeled Ted out to the ambulance entrance, shifted him to a stretcher, and loaded him into an ambulance. Meg climbed in beside him.

"Now try to stay calm," she said, as they moved off. "The doctor said you were still very weak."

"I'll try," he sighed. "How long was I out?"

"Two days."

"And what about the others? Becky and the people from Simon's group. Are they okay?"

"Becky's fine. She's staying with me, now. A few people, like you, ended up in the hospital, but mostly with minor injuries. We were still in the circle when the wind came up so suddenly and it knocked us about pretty badly. It's a miracle we all made it down alive." She paused a moment, deep in thought. "Yes," she said quietly, "it probably was a miracle." She stopped again. "I wonder if people will ever believe it."

"What do you mean?" Ted asked.

"I'll get you a newspaper later. You should see the stories! They're bending over backwards to explain it away! Atmospheric phenomena and all that rot! Mass hallucinations, one professor said."

"You mean they don't realize what it was?" He couldn't believe it!

"They *refuse* to understand! Oh, there's tons about it in the papers! They're full of pictures and everything. After all, thousands of people saw the pillar, and the storms before and after were real enough! They can't deny that! But something *in* the pillar? Certainly not! It was a mass hallucination! And as for the rest of it, you can take your pick of explanations. Secret weapons. Sunspots. Flying saucers. Anything but the truth!"

"Then no one knows . . . except us."

"No, that's the tragedy. No one knows. No one will ever know, but us."

"We can't let that happen, Meg!" Ted said earnestly. "We have to tell them what it was all about!"

"We can tell them," Meg replied. "But will they lis-

ten? They haven't so far! I don't think they want to
know!"

At the hospital, Ted was lifted off the stretcher, put in
a wheelchair, and wheeled inside.

"Would you like me to wait?" Meg asked when they
reached Jill's room.

"Yes, please."

Meg held the door open. The attendant wheeled Ted
in next to the bed and then left. The heavy door sighed
to a close, leaving a soft hum coming from the ventila-
tion system as the only sound in the room.

Ted couldn't talk. There was something in his throat
blocking the words. But it didn't matter, because the
tears in his eyes were speaking for him. And Jill's eyes
were crying too. They looked at each other, neither of
them able to say a word. Trembling, Ted stood up from
the wheelchair. Jill lifted her head from the pillow and
unsteadily raised up her arms to him. He held her.

"Oh, darling . . ." he cried softly. "I love you. I love
you."

After a long time, he pulled back and looked at her,
searching her face hungrily. "I thought I had lost you!"

She touched her fingertips to his tears. "The doctor
says I'll be all right." She had luckily been one of the
first people the rescuers found—and it had saved her
life, the doctor said. Another hour out in the cold and
she would have died of exposure. As it was, she was
suffering from severe dehydration, broken bones in both
feet, pulled tendons, torn muscles, and numerous con-
tusions.

A nurse had tied her hair into a bun. Her lips were
cracked and swollen and her skin, in the few places
where it wasn't covered with bruises, looked as white as
the sheets she lay on. Still, Ted couldn't keep his eyes
from roaming over her features, returning again and
again to her blue eyes. Her beautiful blue eyes, empty of
fire.

She tried to smile. "I knew you would do the right thing, darling. I had faith in you."

After a lot of red tape and some help from Meg, Ted got himself transferred to the room next to hers. He spent as much time with her as the nurses would allow, but something kept them from mentioning that night on the Marin headlands until nearly a week later. It was the first day Jill was allowed out of bed, and Ted—much improved himself—took her in a wheelchair up to the solarium on the top floor.

The morning sun was streaming in through the windows and skylights, warming the room. They talked a bit about how good it felt, and then Ted suddenly asked her, "How did you know to tell me to take the crowd and surround the pillar?"

A look of fleeting pain crossed Jill's face.

"I'm sorry," he blurted. "If you don't want to talk about it, darling, I'll—"

"No, Ted. It's okay. The memories are there, whether we talk about them or not. I knew because of the demon in me. I could sense its thoughts—well, they weren't thoughts exactly, but more like emotions. I can't explain. Anyway, I could tell it was afraid of something. There was something very important, something it feared more than anything else, but I didn't know what. I could only feel the fear. But then something happened —I don't remember exactly—and I saw a whole group of people around the pillar and they had crosses in their hands, beautiful, glowing crosses. And then I knew what you had to do." She fell silent, shivering from the memory of what it was like.

"And I almost shot you," Ted whispered. "Satan almost won."

"But you didn't. You threw the gun away, darling. You tipped the balance."

Jill grew better day by day. The color returned to her cheeks and her bruises slowly faded away. And after another two weeks, Ted was able to take her home again.

Nearly a year later, Meg Olson received a letter from them announcing the birth of their first child—a boy, named Simon.

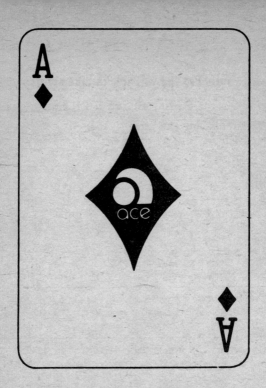

There are a lot more
where this one came from!

78a

Anne Maybury Gothics

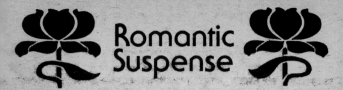

Romantic Suspense

Don't Miss these Ace Romance Bestsellers!

74b